THE RUNAWAY WOMAN

Josephine Cox was born in Blackburn, one of ten children. At the age of sixteen, Josephine met and married her husband Ken, and had two sons. When the boys started school, she decided to go to college and eventually gained a place at Cambridge University. She was unable to take this up as it would have meant living away from home, but she went into teaching – and started to write her first full-length novel. She won the 'Superwoman of Great Britain' Award, for which her family had secretly entered her, at the same time as her novel was accepted for publication. Her ... g, gritty stories are taken from the tapestry of

... ephine says, 'I could never imagine a single day without writing. It's been that way since as far back as I can remember.'

D0544111

Also by Josephine Cox

Josephine
COX

The Runaway Woman

HARPER

This novel is entirely a work of fiction.
The names, characters and incidents portrayed in it are
the work of the author's imagination. Any resemblance to
actual persons, living or dead, events or localities is
entirely coincidental.

Harper
An imprint of HarperCollins*Publishers*
77–85 Fulham Palace Road,
Hammersmith, London W6 8JB

www.harpercollins.co.uk

This paperback edition 2014
1

First published in Great Britain by HarperCollins*Publishers* 2014

Copyright © Josephine Cox 2014

Josephine Cox
asserts the moral right to
be identified as the author of this work

A catalogue record for this book is
available from the British Library

ISBN: 978-0-00-741992-0

Set in ITC New Baskerville Std by
Palimpsest Book Production Limited, Falkirk, Stirlingshire

Printed and bound in Great Britain by
Clays Ltd, St Ives plc

MIX
Paper from
responsible sources
FSC™ C007454

FSC™ is a non-profit international organisation established to promote
the responsible management of the world's forests. Products carrying the
FSC label are independently certified to assure consumers that they come
from forests that are managed to meet the social, economic and
ecological needs of present and future generations,
and other controlled sources.

Find out more about HarperCollins and the environment at
www.harpercollins.co.uk/green

*This story is for every woman
of every age who finds herself
lost, lonely and afraid.*

*Remember — the sun often
shines after the rain has gone.*

For my Ken – as always.

A special message from Jo

Dear Readers,

It's a very strange and exciting feeling to realise that I have written fifty novels, and that my stories have found a place not only in the UK but also in many far-off countries across the world. Many of the millions of people who have taken both me and my stories to heart also take precious time out of their lives to write to me in such heartfelt words; it's almost as though I were a long-lost friend.

With every one of these much-cherished letters I always write back. Because of my many commitments, it may take a little longer than I would like, and it seems there are never enough hours in the day; but I would not want to change my life for anything. Over the years, at signings and events at various venues, I have met many thousands of my readers, who continue to correspond and share their lives with me, as I do with them. We also keep in touch through my magazine, Chatterbox, which HarperCollins sends out with each new book publication, and now through my Facebook page. Every reader knows me so well, and through their letters they feel they can trust me, and that I would never willingly let them down.

Having such a loyal, worldwide following is something I had never envisaged when I sent my first manuscript to the publishers, and now I feel as though I've been accepted into a huge, rambling family. I often think back to my humble beginnings in the backstreets of a northern cotton-mill town. Many of my experiences, good and bad, come into my stories. Characters both angelic and evil people my stories, as they do in life.

At the tender age of four, I would sit on the steps of our house and watch life unfold down the street. I was fascinated by everything around me – especially by the people simply following their daily lives, with all the ups and downs that happen. I took it all into my heart, where it was kept safe, and now those cobbled streets, their mysteries and characters fill my stories – the good and the bad, the darkness and the tears, the joy and the heartache. They're strong stories, hard and real, with dramatic twists we never seem to expect. Not even I do.

In my fiftieth book, The Runaway Woman, *I tell the story of Lucy Lovejoy, a hardworking woman, loyal and true to her family, unaware that her husband, Martin, is cheating on her in the worst possible way. In the wake of her discovery, both her life and the lives of her husband and family are turned upside down, and Lucy knows that this is the moment when she must take a stand. Her incredible strength throughout this turmoil, and in making some unimaginably difficult decisions, surprises everyone. Don't judge Lucy too harshly. She is a woman on the edge, and, for both Lucy and her husband Martin, there is no easy way out. I have already started my new book, a dark story with many twists and turns. The characters have introduced themselves to me; the scene is set and, as always, I am raring to go.*

I have so many stories waiting to be written, and my mind is forever taking me in new and fascinating directions. The truth is, with so much more to come, my fiftieth book seems like just the beginning . . .

With love always, Jo x

PART ONE

No One to Turn to

**Wayburn, Bedfordshire
1962**

CHAPTER ONE

DURING THE DAY, Lucy kept herself busy. That way, she had less time to think about all that was wrong in her life.

At night, though, she would lie awake in her bed, her troubled thoughts wandering back over the years to when she was a fifteen-year-old schoolgirl.

Because of her shy nervous nature, Lucy had always found it hard to make friends. With her plump figure and lack of fashion sense, she believed herself to be unattractive, and unable to fit in with her peers. She was never whistled at, or chatted up by the boys at school, though that didn't really bother her. As was her nature, she accepted the way of things and took it all in her stride.

Martin Lovejoy was a good-looking boy on the verge of leaving school that summer. Outgoing and flirtatious, he was commonly referred to as Jack the Lad, a title he wore like a badge of honour.

Unlike the other boys, Martin had always seen more

to Lucy than her nervous smile and quiet demeanour. He thought her smile was pretty, and her shyness attractive.

Some of the other girls were shameless flirts who would offer themselves to any boy at the merest wink, whereas if Lucy was ever offered a 'bit of fun' down a dark alley, she would probably run a mile. But Martin meant to change all that.

While the other boys regarded Lucy as a shrinking violet who was not worthy of their interest, Martin thought they were missing a trick and, to everyone's surprise, he set his cap at her.

He saw her as a rare challenge, a conquest to be made. A ripe apple, ready to be picked.

On a sweltering hot day during their final week as school children Martin Lovejoy made his move on Lucy; who could hardly believe that one of the most admired boys in the school had made a play for her.

Her younger sister, Paula, and some of the other girls tried to warn her against him, but she was flattered by Martin's attention and chose to ignore their advice.

Later, though, she was devastated on discovering that she had made the biggest mistake of her life. By then it was too late. Life had taken her by the throat and forced her into a situation that she bitterly regretted – and still regretted, some twenty-four years on.

Now, with her fortieth birthday just a couple of weeks away, Lucy felt cheated, and desperately lonely. She'd spent all these years looking after her husband Martin and their children. She also worked, to help make ends meet. Yet she was deeply ashamed of these feelings, believing it was wrong to regret her life, especially when she had been blessed with a family, while many women had not been so fortunate.

Her husband, Martin, was a hard worker who had recently set himself up in business. He professed to love the ground she walked on and, as a dutiful wife, Lucy did her best to keep him happy, but for her, there was something missing from their marriage. Something precious that had been lost . . . way back there, on the long, lonely journey. He never said she looked nice, never noticed what she was wearing, if she looked tired, if she could do with a hand. Never noticed her at all, in fact.

Having suffered yet another sleepless night, Lucy lay very still in the bed, being careful not to wake Martin, who was gently snoring beside her. He was sleeping so peacefully, she was made to wonder if he ever thought about their lives together; about how futile and cold it all seemed.

Yet, for all her regrets and insecurities, Lucy had put her heart and soul into being a good wife, a loving mother and a loyal sister, even though sometimes she resented the manner in which the family took her for granted. They rarely ever asked her how she was, or how her day had been at the factory.

Over the years, she had suggested to her sister, Paula, that it might be nice to spend a pleasant hour or so shopping in Bedford, and maybe enjoying a light lunch before they headed home. Unfortunately there was always a reason why Paula could not go with her. Lucy accepted the situation without question.

She had offered her own daughter, Anne, the same invitation, but she was too busy, or going out with a friend, or just not in the mood. In the end, to avoid embarrassment, Lucy stopped asking.

Every year her birthday was almost a non-event. Even when she put on a little family party, they were either very late to arrive, or they presented an excuse for not arriving at all. She always received a present from Martin and the children, but because of other pressures or simply absent-mindedness, she often had to wait until the next day, when they would rush in with apologies. She never made a fuss, because what would be the point?

They hardly ever made time to sit and chat with her. Anne and Paula's visits would be little more than a cup of tea, then a quick peck on the cheek and they'd be off out the door. More often than not, Martin would then go off down the pub. 'I'll not be long,' he'd promise her. But it would be gone midnight when he got home.

Lucy was daunted by the fact that she would soon be forty years old, especially when she considered she had done nothing with her life. She had never seen much outside Wayburn, and as the years went by, the idea of travelling and doing the exciting things she had once dreamed of seemed increasingly out of her reach. She now feared her life would remain as it was until she became old and unable to make changes.

As with all the other birthdays, she wondered if this landmark birthday would arrive quietly and leave on tiptoe, though if it did she knew she would take it in her stride, as ever, while secretly wondering if her family could ever love her as much as she loved them.

There were even times when she asked herself if she was a useless wife, mother and grandmother. She hoped not, because her family was all she had. In fact, they were her very world. Consequently she felt it was wrong of her to ask more of them than they could give.

There was one bright side to Lucy's life, however. She was immensely grateful for her job at the plastics factory. She took great pride in her work, and enjoyed the company of her lively colleagues. Chatting with them made her feel alive, because to them she was not just someone's wife, mother or grandmother. Instead, she was Lucy, a well-respected and much-valued workmate.

∼

Deep in thought, Lucy was startled to hear the hallway clock strike five. Careful not to wake Martin, she slithered out of bed and into her dressing gown, then she softly slid the eiderdown over the dip in the bed where she had lain.

Gazing down on her sleeping husband, she tortured herself with regrets. So many wasted years, she thought bitterly. So many lost dreams.

Inevitably, her thoughts returned to their two children. Sam was now twenty-one. Like all young men he could be bullish and unpredictable, but beneath all the bravado, he had a sense of purpose.

At twenty-three, Anne was her first-born. She was confident, easily hassled, and occasionally argumentative. She was the mother of Luke, almost one year old.

The thought of her only grandchild brought a measure of joy to Lucy's heart. Full of life, he had a ready smile and laughing eyes that made you want to dance, and he was an absolute delight.

Taking a moment to close her eyes, Lucy cast her mind back to when she was a shy, innocent girl, afraid of everyone and everything; until Martin made friends with her in the school grounds one sunny afternoon.

With his smiling brown eyes and wild shock of thick, dark hair, he stood out from the crowd. Tall and lean, with an attractive, lazy way of walking, he was a magnet to the opposite sex. After that first meeting, Lucy was instantly drawn to him, though never in a million years did she imagine how their lives would intertwine. It would have been impossible to believe that less than two years after their first date she would not only be Martin's wife, but she would also be mother to his child.

Over the years, Lucy had often wondered about that fateful night, when curiosity, excitement and a sense of belonging took away their common sense. The consequence of that had carried them to this point in their lives, and Lucy had come to realise how wrong they had been to get married, especially when they were both so young, with little knowledge of real life and responsibility. The sad truth was, that she had never been truly happy; not on the day they got married, and certainly not now.

For a long time, she had desperately wanted to find a way out of this mundane life, but her strong sense of duty gave her no easy way out.

Now, she often looked down on Martin's sleeping face, and thought that, yes, she did love him; if loving him was to take care of him, to feed him, wash and iron his clothes and do her best to make sure he was content.

She went to gaze out the window. I do love you, Martin, she thought, but I don't know you . . . at least not in the way I should.

She resented the way he had always made the important decisions without consulting her. Also, she resented the cowardly way she had allowed herself to go along with his decisions. When they were still at school and she found herself pregnant, it was Martin who had decided that keeping it a secret was the best thing to do. Also, it was he who'd insisted they should get married as soon as possible so that no one would find out right away. But they had been wrong, Lucy now knew. They should have confided in someone older and wiser, whom they could trust. Someone who might have helped them.

Choking back the anger, she became tearful. I should never have listened to you, she thought. I wanted to tell them the truth, but you wouldn't let me. She recalled vividly how he threatened to say the baby wasn't his.

Though when Mum guessed I was pregnant, you did stand by me. Even so, on my sixteenth birthday, when we were getting married, I was so afraid that you would get scared and run off at the last minute and I would have to face it all on my own.

Her homely features creased in a smile. You didn't run though, did you? She turned, crept back and kissed him softly on the cheek. 'Now though, I can't understand what's happened to us, Martin,' she whispered. 'I'm not happy, and sometimes I believe you feel the same.'

When a tear escaped down her cheek, she angrily wiped it away. It was no good crying. What was done was done, and there seemed no turning back.

She continued to observe him a moment longer, hating herself for being cowardly back then when they were unsure and afraid. How could she ever forget the shame and the trauma when they told their families that she was expecting a child, when she was little more than a child herself?

On the whole, over the years, Martin had been a good man. Right from when their daughter was born, he had proved himself to be a good husband and a fine father – although if she were honest there had been times when she might have preferred him to spend more time at home with her and the baby.

That particular problem still niggled her, especially when he chose to share all his leisure time with his mates, rather than with her. She was at home every evening – at first with the babies, and now alone.

Lucy's insecurities had never really gone away.

What if he had never loved her at all? What if he had only married her because she was having his child? Maybe, unknown to her, he also had regret and doubts about the traumatic decision they had made back then. Yes! Maybe he felt like she did: cheated and alone, in a marriage born out of panic.

As a child, Lucy had always dreamed that her wedding day would be a magical, proud occasion. Instead, on her sixteenth birthday, it was a frantic rush, and all because of one dark and unforgettable night behind the Roxy.

Just two years after their daughter Anne was born, Lucy and Martin were blessed with the arrival of their second child – a boy who they named Samuel. Sam. Martin then decided that two children were enough, and took precautions to make sure their family never grew any larger.

Lucy, over the years, had devoted her life to her family. Martin played his part well, but preferred to be fishing, playing darts down the pub or kicking a ball about on the green with his friends.

After Anne married, and with Sam increasingly leading his own life, Lucy was mostly left on her own.

Inevitably, the distance between her and Martin began to widen. One time he came home so drunk he could hardly stand. 'A mate of a mate was out on his stag do,' he lied, 'so we decided to make a night of it.' Lucy made no comment, but from the whiff of cheap perfume she suspected he may have been enjoying female company.

After the second drunken episode, he gave no explanation, and Lucy asked for none. Consequently, the gulf between them became a chasm, with Lucy feeling increasingly isolated.

She had learned to take the good with the bad, but lately she had grown increasingly restless. One way or another things would have to change. She had no idea how or when, yet change they must, because if they continued as they were now, she would likely spend the rest of her life regretting it. Now, heading towards her fortieth birthday, she assumed that half her life was already gone; did she really want to spend her latter years wishing she had found the courage to put herself first, especially now, with the children grown up?

With that thought burning in her mind, she made her way downstairs. Usually after a bad night there was no spring in her step, but today was different. Never before had she felt so defiant.

If she truly wanted it, she believed that she could make a change. She could rebel. She could do something outrageous – something she had never done before.

But then the doubts crept back. Where would she start? What would the family say if she was to do something out of the ordinary? As Martin had once remarked, 'You could set your clock by our Lucy. Always on time, and everything in its place, that's her.' The idea of timid Lucy Lovejoy actually rebelling was unbelievable.

But then the more Lucy thought about it, the more excited she became. So what if she was coming up to her fortieth birthday – surely it wasn't too late to step out of her routine? To do something so brave and wonderful that she would remember it for ever? What was so wicked about that?

Her imagination ran riot. Twirling round the kitchen, she listed her unlikely ambitions aloud in a singsong way: 'I could go dancing till dawn, or run full pelt along the promenade, in nothing but a tiny swimsuit and flimsy throw-on. Oh, and I might even book myself on to a big cruise ship . . . and sail off to exotic places.'

But then suddenly her mood changed as she sat down at the table. Who am I fooling? she asked herself. I've got no money to speak of, and anyway it's too late now. It's such a pity, though, because there are so many exciting things I've never done. I've never been to London, or a theatre, and though I've always wanted to, I've never learned to roller-skate . . . The sorry list of lost opportunities was endless. She had never worn a short, swingy skirt, or had a ride at a fairground. Never even learned to swim. In fact, she had never done anything exciting or daring. 'You're a hopeless case, Lucy Lovejoy!' she declared.

Instead, she had become a watcher. Watching the children play in the sand. Watching everyone else enjoying themselves while she minded the bags or the pram, or kept the towels dry while they were swimming at the local indoor pool. She had always been a shadow in the background. Hardly noticeable, always in demand to smooth the way for the family. In the end, there was never any time for her.

She never complained, so it didn't cross anyone's mind that she might want to live a little, to join in the fun while someone else watched the bags and the pram.

Lucy cast her mind back. She was sure there must have been times when the family did ask her to join in but, for whatever reason, she never did.

As always, blaming herself was easier than blaming them.

Aware of the clock ticking away on the wall, she began to set the table for breakfast. Silly old fool! she told herself. You're a hopeless daydreamer. Always have been. Put it all out of your mind and get on with the life you have. To have an adventure you need youth on your side, you need money, and you definitely need a plan. You have none of those. At your age a new adventure is just a pipe-dream.

Even so, the idea of a new life lingered.

As she set about cooking breakfast, she couldn't help but wonder what the neighbours would say if they found out that Lucy Lovejoy had done a runner.

She burst out laughing. It might be worth the adventure, just to see the look on their faces!

CHAPTER TWO

THE EGGS AND bacon were all nicely sizzling in the frying pan when Martin rushed into the kitchen. 'For goodness' sake, Lucy, I told you last night I wouldn't have time for any breakfast this morning. What's the matter with you? You even forgot to set the alarm clock for six. Thanks to you, I'm in a rush now.'

'I can't remember you asking me to set the alarm earlier, and anyway, if you were that worried about being late, why didn't you set it yourself?'

'Because you always set the alarm. I thought I could rely on you, but obviously I was wrong!'

'I'm sorry, Martin. I had a lot on my mind.'

Martin glanced at the tasty breakfast. 'Good food wasted!' he grumbled. 'Hard-earned money down the drain, and all because you don't listen!'

'Look!' Lucy hurried to the kitchen cabinet. 'I've got fresh cheese and chutney. I'll make you some sandwiches. It'll only take a minute.'

Throwing on his jacket, Martin was impatient. 'I

15

already told you, I have to get going! I've got three big jobs in progress, and an old biddy nagging me to fit a door at the top of her landing. I can't believe you didn't remember to wake me.'

Lucy knew for sure he had not asked her to wake him, or said that he wouldn't have time for breakfast, but she decided not to argue.

She walked to the door with him. 'It's such a shame, Martin . . .'

'What is?' Pulling on his boots, he quickly laced them up.

'Well, when you set up on your own you promised we'd be able to spend more time together . . . maybe even go out a couple of nights a week, but these past three months we've been out together just once. If you ask me, it's worse than when you were working for the building firm.'

'Is that so? Well, nobody's "asking you", so give it a rest, will you?' He hurried to the door. 'Look! I'm sorry if there was a misunderstanding last night . . . about the alarm clock and that, but I haven't got time to argue. I'll see you after work.' And before she could reply, he was down the path and away, without even a backward glance.

'You've got it wrong, Martin,' she muttered. 'I wasn't arguing. I was just saying, things don't seem to have worked out the way we thought they might.'

When Martin climbed into his old van, she gave a little wave, but he didn't see it. He was already roaring down the street.

Disappointed, Lucy watched him until he disappeared from sight.

After lingering at the door for a moment, she then retreated into the house, and closed the door behind her.

~

Martin drove just a few streets away, then turned into a narrow alleyway. After inching his way along, he carefully parked the van into a deep curve on the bend. He took a moment to satisfy himself that there was no one about, before clambering out and running across the alley and into the back yard of one of the terraced houses.

From the back bedroom window, a woman watched him approach. She smiled. 'Naughty man!' she murmured lovingly.

Finding the back door open, Martin slithered inside, then turned the key in the lock.

Before he could even look round, she was all over him. 'You're late!' she whispered in his ear. 'I've been waiting ages for you.'

She opened her flimsy dressing gown to reveal a slim naked body, and when he reached out for her, she laughed and broke away to run up the stairs.

Martin kicked off his boots and went after her. All thoughts of Lucy had long since vanished from his mind.

~

'Look, he's there again. Disgraceful, that's what it is!'

Mary and Peter Taylor, retired from work these many months, lived in one of the adjoining houses. Having spotted Martin creeping in and out of next door, Mary was now on a mission to keep an eye out for all the unsavoury developments.

Peter, too, peeked out the window. 'Hmm! No wonder her husband cleared off after he caught her in bed with an ex-boyfriend.' Although he would never admit it, Peter was the teeniest bit jealous. 'Some folks never learn. Here she is, at it again with another man, and without an ounce of shame between 'em!'

For weeks now, the old couple had regularly seen Martin hide his car and sneak into Paula's house.

'They should be tarred and feathered!' Mary was up in arms. 'I've a good mind to tell Lucy Lovejoy what's going on right under her nose. How could they?'

'You mustn't get involved, Mary,' Peter quietly warned her. 'It's not our business. I'm sure you would not want to be responsible for breaking up Lucy's marriage, rickety though it might be. Besides, her sister will probably get fed up before long, and move on to some other gullible bloke.'

Reluctantly, Mary had to agree. 'All right then. But Lucy Lovejoy is such a likeable, honest person, and she really doesn't deserve this.'

'I know, but it's not our place to interfere, and if we did, then the two of us would be the baddies, caught up in the middle. But don't you worry, the truth will out. It always does, one way or another.'

~

Glancing at the clock again, Lucy quickly finished her cup of tea and began clearing the table. 'I'll be late for work myself if I'm not careful, and that will never do.' She prided herself on being a good timekeeper at the factory.

She put a flat tin dish over the top of the plate of eggs and bacon, then after turning the grill on low, she slid the plate underneath. That should keep it good and hot. Martin was right: good food should not be wasted, and anyway, Sam would appreciate a hot breakfast before he left.

Lucy glanced at the wall clock. It was high time he was up and ready.

A moment later she was at the foot of the stairs, calling up to her son. When after two calls there was no answer, she raised her voice. 'Sam, are you still in bed? It's gone seven. Hurry up or you'll be late.'

She was about to go up and wake him when his tired, lazy voice called back, 'OK, stop yelling! I'll be down in a minute!'

Satisfied, Lucy resumed her clearing away, but it wasn't long before she was interrupted.

'Mum!' Sam yelled down the stairway. 'I can't find any clean socks!'

'Look in the top drawer of your cupboard!' Lucy

called back. When there came no reply, she was satis-fied that he must have found them. Of course there were clean socks. When had there ever not been? Surely he didn't actually need his clothes laying out ready for him the night before?

A few minutes later, Sam sloped into the kitchen, his shoulders drooping and his eyes still sleepy. 'I don't suppose there's any breakfast, is there?' Dropping his tall, gawky figure into the nearest chair, he glanced at the clock. 'Oh, Mum! You should have called me earlier.'

'Well, you've still got time for some breakfast before you set off.'

Grabbing a tea towel, she covered her hands before collecting the plate of eggs and bacon from under the grill. 'There!' She set it before him. 'Be careful, the plate's hot.'

Sam began tucking in, while Lucy proudly took stock of him.

Sam was just twenty-one years of age – lanky, defiant and often argumentative, like many young men of his age. With his attractive fair hair and light brown eyes, and his outgoing personality, he had enjoyed more than his fair share of girlfriends over the last few years.

'Are you enjoying your new job at the newsagent's?' Lucy asked.

He hunched his shoulders. 'Yeah, I suppose.' Digging the fork into the bacon he remarked sullenly, 'This was Dad's breakfast, wasn't it?'

'Yes, it was, but he was late for work and didn't have time to eat it.'

'I know that.' He gave her a sorry look. 'I heard the two of you arguing.'

'We weren't arguing. It was more of a misunderstanding. The thing is, your father needed to start work early,' Lucy explained, 'and there was a mix-up about the alarm, that's all.'

'Yeah . . . because you forgot to set it, like he asked.' Sam gave a little chuckle. 'I dunno, Mum. You've got a memory like a sieve.'

Pretending not to have heard this remark, Lucy hurriedly set about collecting up the used teacups. 'So, do you think this job might be offered to you on a permanent basis?'

'Dunno.'

'But if you were offered it as permanent, you would take it, wouldn't you? Or perhaps think about going to college, learn a new skill?'

Getting up from the table, Sam made his way to the front door, where he put on his jacket. 'Dunno.' He gave a lolloping shrug. 'You might as well know right now, I don't plan on working in a newsagent's for ever. I suppose it depends on what comes my way. We'll just have to wait and see, won't we?'

Then he was out the door and running down to the bus stop, leaving Lucy wondering why she even bothered to open a conversation.

Beginning to panic, she glanced at the wall clock. She was due at work for eight thirty, which left her just fifteen minutes to be on her way.

Quickly now, she went to the telephone, where she

picked up the receiver and dialled her parents' number. After just two rings, her father answered. 'I were just walking past the phone,' he explained breathlessly. 'It frightened the life outta me. Who is it wants me?'

'It's me, Dad. I meant to call earlier but it's always manic in this house, and now I'm rushing about. How's Mum . . . is she any better?'

'She's not too bad. I must say, that cough seems to be on its way out. She slept much better last night.'

'Oh, that's good. Look, Dad, I'm late for work, so will you just give her my love and tell her I'll be round tomorrow evening?'

'Aw, don't you worry, she'll be fine. But thanks anyway, Lucy. You're a good girl.' And before she could answer, he replaced the receiver.

Lucy smiled. It's a long time since I was a girl, Dad, she thought. Then, reassured about her poorly mother, she replaced the receiver.

~

Having grabbed her bag and put her coat on, Lucy was heading for the door when the telephone rang.

Startled, she grabbed the receiver and pressed it to her ear. 'Hello?'

'Lucy, I need your help.' She recognised her son-in-law's voice. Les sounded anxious. 'Anne's not been well in the night – probably something she ate, or maybe she's got some dreaded lurgy coming on. She hasn't actually been sick, but she was burning up in the night, and now she's feeling a bit rough. I've given her water, but she refuses anything else. She does seem a bit more settled now, but she hasn't had much sleep at all . . . and neither has anyone else. Luke must have sensed she was unwell, because he's cried for most of the night. I nearly called you, but then he fell asleep. Poor little devil's exhausted.'

'Oh, dear me.' Lucy was worried. 'Well, at least she hasn't been sick, and you say she's feeling a little better . . . that's good, but you'll need to keep her warm in bed. Oh, and do keep checking on her. Tell her I'll be round in my dinner hour, just after twelve.'

'The thing is, Lucy—'

Lucy interrupted, 'Les, did you call the doctor?'

'Yes, and he thinks, like me, that she's eaten something that didn't agree. Anyway, he says he'll pop in later, on his rounds.'

'Aw, that's good. You did right to call him.' Glancing at the hall clock, Lucy grew more frantic. 'Now, don't you forget to tell her I'll be there during my lunch break. I must go now, Les. I'm late already.'

'No, you can't! You see, the thing is . . . I've been summoned to a union meeting up North. I should be on my way by now. There's the threat of a strike. The union chap is spitting blood over a change in working hours. Feelings are running high. We have to sort the problem before it becomes a full-blown strike.' He took a quick breath. 'I did ask to be excused this one, but it seems there's no one else qualified to go. As you know, union problems are my department anyway.'

Lucy was devastated. 'You should have rung them and explained the situation.'

'I can't do that. It's more than my job's worth.'

Lucy was torn. 'But you said she's feeling more settled now . . . apart from being tired, I mean. And Luke is OK, is he?'

'Well, yes, but they need you, Lucy.'

'But I'm just off to work myself. You know I'd be round there like a shot out of a gun, but I'm already in the boss's bad books because of time lost when I damaged my foot.'

'I'm sure she'll understand if you explain. Please, Lucy, with my own parents living miles away, and your mother not in the best of health, I've no one else to ask.'

Lucy was panicking now. 'What about Maggie, your neighbour? She's a good sort; she'll be glad to stay with Anne and the baby for an hour or so . . . or at least until I get my lunch break. I'll explain the situation to my boss, and maybe she'll let me leave earlier. Meantime, Maggie's more than capable of keeping an eye on Luke. She's had five children of her own. Anyway, the doctor will be round before you know it. If Anne does get any worse, though, and Maggie's worried, she can ring the office at work. I'll be straight over, whatever the consequences. But from what you say, it seems Anne might well be on the mend. Don't worry, Les. Just ask Maggie to hold the fort and tell her it's only until twelve o'clock, then I'll be on my way.'

'No, Lucy! You don't understand! Anne needs you

right now. With me having been called to sort out an urgent situation, don't you think it's your responsibility as her mother? Anyway,' he explained angrily, 'I've already asked Maggie, and she can't do it. She's been summoned to a meeting with her son's head teacher . . . something to do with him having punched another boy in the school grounds yesterday.' He was growing impatient. 'Look, Lucy, I'm sorry, but you'll have to come over now! I can't leave until you get here.'

He gave an almighty sigh. 'And besides, with due respect, Lucy, I reckon my work might be just that bit more important than yours. At least you and Martin and Sam are all working, while I'm the only one earning in this family.'

Lucy was shocked. 'You don't need to remind me of my responsibilities, Les. Nor my and Martin's financial arrangements. As you well know, my family has always been my first priority. And if Maggie is busy, and there is no one else to help, then of course I'll come over. But, however much you feel the need to rush off, you must stay with her, until I get there. Tell Anne I'll phone the boss now, and explain why I won't be coming in today.'

'Thanks, Lucy. Be quick, though, won't you? I should have been on the road by now.'

As she dialled the factory number, Lucy was decidedly nervous. Luckily, the boss was in a meeting, but her secretary was very reassuring. 'I'm sorry your daughter's ill, but don't worry,' she told Lucy, 'the boss will understand.'

Lucy gave a sigh of relief as she replaced the receiver. In the last few months she had taken a considerable amount of time off from work; mainly because of hospital appointments when she had broken her foot some weeks back. Then there was that time when she looked after little Luke while Les and Anne went away to try to mend their marriage.

Worried about money, Les had started working every hour he could. Anne, however, became restless and uncomfortable about that, and began making life difficult for everyone. There were then arguments, which became so bitter, they were even talking about splitting up.

In the end Lucy had stepped in with some advice, which was something she rarely did. She'd suggested Anne and Les went away by themselves to sort it out, and they had leaped at the chance.

A fortnight later, they were home and more in love than ever. Lucy had been overjoyed to have her little grandson to stay for two weeks. Even so, she had been worried about losing her job, but Martin had reassured her. 'There is no way they'll sack you, girl!' he'd said heartily. 'You work too damned hard for that!'

Luckily, he was right.

~

Although flustered by the morning's events, Lucy lost no time in organising herself. Within minutes of phoning her place of work, she was down the street and climbing onto the bus, almost before it drew to a halt.

'Trying to kill yourself, are you, Lucy Lovejoy?' After working the same route for nigh on twenty years, Johnny, the bus conductor, knew every regular who travelled on his bus. He was a cheery sort, a favourite with the passengers, because of his bright and cheeky smile.

Lucy hurried down the gangway and quickly seated herself. With a great deal playing on her mind, she chose to sit as far away from the door as possible.

A few moments later Johnny came to collect the fare. 'You don't seem your usual cheery self,' he remarked carefully.

'My daughter was ill in the night,' Lucy confided in him. 'Unfortunately, her husband had to leave for the North this morning . . . an emergency to do with his work. So I'm off to keep an eye on Anne and the baby.'

'By, you're a good sort.' Johnny gave an encouraging smile. 'From what I understand, folks are always able to call on you, knowing you'll help if you can.' Lucy often confided in him, whenever the bus was quiet, and this morning there were few other passengers. He recalled how some time back, Lucy had been concerned about the fragile state of her daughter's marriage, but then, with Lucy's help and encouragement, the marriage had been saved.

There was even one occasion when his own spirits were low, and he had asked Lucy's opinion. She had kindly offered some good advice, making him realise that he was working far too many hours, covering for his workmates when they were away, and snatching overtime whenever it was offered.

Lucy candidly pointed out that he appeared to be at work more than he was at home, which did nothing for his health, or his family life.

Johnny had seen the truth of it, because though he and his wife had more money in their pockets, they never seemed to enjoy it. The occasional weekends away had come to a stop, and after work he was too tired to chat with her, so little by little, their conversations and spontaneous laughter had dried up; with their marriage rapidly heading the same way.

Johnny was ever thankful for Lucy's straightforward warning, and he firmly believed that her husband was a fortunate man to have this darling woman, with a heart of gold. From what he knew, she never shirked her many responsibilities, and cared for her family like no woman he had ever known.

Johnny suspected that, with her kind and thoughtful nature, Lucy might allow herself to be walked over. There were times when he sensed that she herself was in need of help and comfort. Sadly, though, it seemed there was no one there to offer it.

As the bus slowed down for the next stop, he excused himself and rushed to welcome the passengers on board.

Deep in thought, Lucy absent-mindedly followed his progress to the door. Then, momentarily closing her eyes, she allowed her thoughts to drift back to when she was a wide-eyed and innocent schoolgirl;

until Martin came along and took her innocence. Although to be fair, she had been a willing partner.

Life was so unpredictable, she mused. It could be kind, or it could be incredibly cruel. From the minute you were born, you found yourself on a fast-moving roller-coaster. However much you wanted to get off or change direction, you were swept along, sometimes unwillingly.

It was a sad truth that you were never in charge of your own destiny, because circumstances constantly changed and spiralled out of your control. Strangers intervened along the way, and people you knew and loved could also change your life for good or bad. Somehow, and without you realising it, strangers and others often led you down a path you might never otherwise have followed. In the end, you could lose sight of your chosen destination and, try as you might, never find your own way back.

'Hey!' Johnny was gently touching her on the shoulder. 'If you want to sleep on my bus, that'll be an extra shilling,' he chuckled.

'I wasn't sleeping,' Lucy promised, her weary spirits lifted. 'I was just thinking.'

'Oh, really? Well, in my experience it's never a good idea to think too much. It could bend your brain, and apart from that, you'll give yourself a headache.' Giving a wink that made Lucy smile, he moved on.

Lucy sat up and casually looked out as the bus route passed her sister's house. She glanced at her watch, thinking it odd that the bedroom curtains were still closed . . .

She was startled when Johnny spoke in her ear. 'Didn't you mention that was where your sister lives? Paula, isn't it?'

'You've got a good memory!' Lucy replied. 'I'm sure she was due to start her new job at the petrol station today . . . early shift, she said. But just now I noticed the bedoom curtains are still closed. She's either had a late night out with her pals, and is still sleeping it off, or she's changed her mind about the job.'

'Or maybe she just forgot to open the curtains,' Johnny suggested.

Lucy nodded. 'I hope you're right. Yes, maybe that's what she's done. She's a good sort, really, and we get on well, but there are times when she's her own worst enemy. Her late nights and devil-may-care attitude have already lost her two jobs. How she is ever going to sort out her life, I don't know.'

She made a mental note to pop in and see her sister soon. She would feel much better once she knew Paula was all right.

~

'Hey, Paula!' Martin was lazing in bed when Paula went across to the window to peek out.

'You'll never guess who I just saw,' Paula teased him, turning with a wicked little smile on her face.

'I don't care who you saw,' he replied, 'because whoever it is, they're spoiling my fun. Come back here, wench. I'm not done with you yet.' His hungry gaze swept her slim, naked body. He loved her firm, toned figure and pert little breasts. When he took her in his arms, nothing else mattered; especially not Lucy who, compared to her sister, seemed old and shapeless before her time.

He did hold a measure of affection for Lucy. After all, the two of them had been together a long time . . . maybe too long, he mused.

Paula laughed as she hurried to the wardrobe. 'Sorry, lover, but your time's up. You've had your fun, and now it's time to go!' She rolled her eyes. 'I should have started work half an hour ago, so now I need to get there. I'll have to drum up some sort of apology and smile nicely at the manager.' Her manner grew serious. 'Honestly, Martin, I really can't afford to lose another job.'

Seeing that his fun was definitely over for today, Martin reluctantly slithered out of bed and began to pull on his trousers. 'OK, you win. But you will make it up to me some other time . . . won't you?'

'Of course.' Keeping her distance, she flirted with him as he dressed. 'You know very well that goes without saying,' she told him softly.

Martin picked up on what she had said earlier. 'So, who did you see just now through the window?'

'I saw your wife . . . my dear sister, Lucy,' she answered mockingly.

'What! You saw Lucy? Oh my God! Was she at the door?' Shocked, he quickly buckled up his trouser-belt and yanked his shirt on. 'Is she downstairs?' His voice shook. 'Quick! Get rid of her!'

Paula enjoyed seeing him panic. 'Calm down,' she giggled. 'She was on the bus. Just as I looked out, she was already turning away. So don't worry, our sordid little secret is still safe.'

Shaken by the possibility that Lucy might discover what he and Paula were up to, Martin slumped onto the bed. 'What the hell is she doing on the bus? She should be at work, not gallivanting about on the damned bus.'

Paula shrugged. 'Don't ask me, because I'm sure I don't know.' She decided to wind him up further. 'I suppose she could be coming to see me even yet. Maybe she's got off at the bottom of the street and she's on her way here right now!'

'For pity's sake, head her off. I'll sneak out the back.'

Paula laughed. 'Relax! Lucy wouldn't be coming round here now – she knows I'm starting a new job today – and even if she did find out we were carrying on behind her back, she'd probably forgive us.'

'Huh! You wish!' Martin was now hurrying to the door. 'She might be soft-hearted, but there is no way she would forgive us. Lucy might not have much going for her but, as you well know, she would be devastated if she found out we'd betrayed her.'

A teeny bit jealous, Paula was suddenly curious. 'If you had to choose between me and her, who would you choose?'

But Martin wasn't listening. 'I don't understand.

Why isn't she at work? You know what a stickler she is for keeping time. So, what's going on? Are you sure it was Lucy on the bus?'

Just then the telephone rang and he almost leaped out of his skin.

'Stay there!' Paula threw on her dressing gown, and ran down the stairs.

Nervously, Martin crept to the door to listen, greatly relieved when he realised that the caller was Paula's new boss, asking why she was not yet at work.

'I'm sorry, sir, but I had a burst pipe in the kitchen. I've managed to get the plumber here, and I've asked a neighbour to come and stay until he's finished. I should be with you in about fifteen minutes.' She put on her sweetest little-girl voice. 'I know I should have called you, but it's been frantic. I've been so worried, I just didn't have time to call and explain.'

There was a pause, while Paula was listening, and then Martin heard her promising, 'Half an hour at the outside, yes, and I'll work the extra time if you want me to. Yes, all right, thank you.'

Before she could replace the receiver, Martin was downstairs and grabbing her. 'Got to go.' He kissed her full on the mouth before reluctantly releasing her. 'You and me . . . we're all right together, aren't we?'

Her answer was to wrap her arms round his neck and draw him in to her. 'Can I ask you something?'

'Ask away.'

'Do you really want me? Would you leave Lucy to be with me?'

'Are you serious?' Martin was nervous. 'I mean . . . after your divorce and all the nastiness, I thought the last thing you might want is to shack up with another man . . . least of all your sister's husband.'

'Well, you were wrong. It might have been that way at first, but I think I've fallen for you, and I want to make it permanent.' She paused, her gaze hardening. 'Or do you just want fun with no strings attached? Is that it?'

'No!' Martin was adamant. 'I never thought of us in that way.'

She visibly relaxed. 'Well, that's OK, because I never thought of us in that way either.'

Martin was delighted and shocked by her serious suggestion that he should leave Lucy. 'I would never willingly hurt you . . . not after what your ex put you through.'

'I took it bad, I know.' She cast her mind back. 'That day when you found me crying . . . when you held me for the very first time, I was in pieces. But I'm well over that now. It didn't take me long to realise that ending the marriage was right for both of us. Never having had children made it easier somehow.'

'Did you want children?'

Paula shrugged. 'I don't suppose I would have minded, but it just never happened. I think Ray was bitterly disappointed about that. As it turned out, though, it's just as well, don't you think?'

'I don't really know but, like you say, I'm sure it

meant that it was easier to end the marriage.'

'To tell the truth, I think I stopped loving him a long time before we decided to break up. In the end it was a relief to see the back of him. He was lazy, quick to temper, and he never showed me any tenderness. You're different, though, Martin. You're exciting and loving, and you know how to make me happy.'

'Really?' He gave her a sly little smile. 'That's nice to know.'

'No! I didn't mean it like that,' she assured him. 'You make me happy in lots of other ways . . . and you care for me like a man should.'

'Well, I'm glad you think like that, but it's like I just said, you and me, we're all right together, and that's good, apart from the fact that I'm a taken man . . . married to your own sister, no less.'

Guilt darkened his face. 'Trouble is, I can't seem to keep away from you, and whatever you might think, I do have a conscience about cheating on Lucy.'

'So, why do you cheat on her, if it feels wrong?'

'Because I love you, that's why.' He tried to explain. 'Remind me again . . . how many years younger than Lucy are you?'

'Three minus a few weeks. I'm thirty-seven and she's just round the corner from her fortieth birthday. But what's that got to do with anything?'

'Well, it's just that here you are, only three years younger than Lucy, and yet I swear anyone could be forgiven for thinking you were *ten* years younger.'

'Thank you!' Paula smiled. 'I'm thrilled that you

should think that, but I don't imagine Lucy would be so pleased.'

'Oh, but it's true, and it's not just your youthful appearance, although that says a lot. Compared to Lucy, you're much younger in your attitude; you are always bright and pretty, and full of life.' Running his hands down her long, brown hair, he smiled into her bright, almond-coloured eyes. 'Hand on heart, Paula, I reckon you could easily pass for a young woman of twenty-one, twenty-two, any day . . . while Lucy could easily be mistaken for an older middle-aged woman.'

'Don't say that.'

'But it's true, and you know it as well as I do. She's old in her ways. She acts and dresses like she's middle-aged. She never fusses over her appearance, or wears make-up. She won't spend money on having her hair done, or her nails painted. She frets if the meals are late. She panics if everything is short of perfect. She's refused so often to come with me to the pub when I'm in a darts match that I stopped asking her a long time back. And to be honest, I can't remember the last time we went out together, or when she actually laughed out loud.'

Paula gently rounded on him. 'Don't be too hard on her, Martin. You know as well as I do, Lucy is a good woman. She loves the family, and she's always there for anyone in trouble. She's a better woman than I will ever be.'

'I do not believe that. You've been through a lot lately. You deserve a bit of fun and love in your life. As for Lucy, I wasn't running her down. I was just stating the facts. I know it's a pity, but she will never change, not now.'

'But she's a decent sort, whereas I'm just a flighty tart. I spend too much time at the mirror, and too much money having my hair styled and cut. I spend a fortune on make-up, and I couldn't cook a dinner for four if I tried my best.'

'Maybe. But you know how to laugh. You can make a man feel good, and you hit life at the run. That's what makes you so exciting. At the end of the day, that's what any man wants in his woman: excitement, laughter, being able to discuss anything and nothing with her, and the occasional fierce rows, and ending up in bed together afterwards.'

Paula grew serious. 'You say that, Martin. But you have a wife who keeps your shirts washed and ironed. She's good with money. She holds down a job and still manages to put a piping-hot meal in front of you when you sit down at the table. She never walks away from trouble, yet she never yells or argues. And she always puts your welfare and the family's welfare before her own. Am I right?'

'I suppose.' Martin reflected on her words. 'Yes . . . Lucy is everything you say, and I love her very much, but not in the way a man should love his wife. And maybe it's my fault, because I was the one who made her pregnant when we were just schoolkids. After that, there was no choice for either of us. So now, we're stuck in a life where there is no closeness, no fire, no tenderness, and nothing to look forward to except more of the same.'

When he seemed to lapse into thought, Paula interrupted, 'So . . . Martin? Have you thought about my question?'

He gave a deep sigh. 'Yes.' His answer was so quiet, she could only just hear it. 'I would leave Lucy, yes . . . without a shadow of doubt.' He craved the idea of making a permanent life with Paula.

But when he reached out to take her, she pushed him away. 'I think it's time you went.'

'What? No kisses, no hugs, just "get off to work". Is that it?'

'Yes . . . for now, anyway. But there'll be time enough to talk again.' Her sister, Lucy, was at the forefront of Paula's mind, and for the slightest moment, she felt small, and deeply ashamed.

As always, though, the moment soon passed.

A short time later, she stood at the kitchen window and watched him hurry away. She was astonished to learn that, like her, Martin wanted them to be together permanently. I never believed you would leave Lucy for me, she thought, and the awful truth is . . . I would not try to stop you, because even though I love Lucy, I love you more.

Determined to push Lucy from her mind, she set about getting herself ready for work.

~

Mary Taylor, Paula's neighbour, called her husband to the window. 'Look at him run!' She pointed at Martin as he scuttled down the alley to his van. 'Like a thief in the night!' she declared angrily. 'They should be ashamed . . . the pair of them! I've got a good mind to tell his wife what they're up to!'

'You'll do no such thing.' Peter was a gentle soul, content with his quiet life. 'It would only do more harm than good, and besides, I've told you before, it's none of our business. Just leave it be. Let them sort it out in their own way. All right?'

When she turned away without giving him an answer, he insisted, 'Mary! Promise me you won't interfere!'

Mary gave a smile and a kind of nod. 'All right, I hear you! Now stop worrying. Finish your breakfast and go for your newspapers. Oh, and you'd best take Rascal with you.' She glanced at the little brown terrier stretched out on the rug. 'He's been waiting patiently. Don't wear him out, though. I might take him to the park later, when you're meeting up with your old cronies.'

'I won't wear him out.'

'Good!' She discreetly looked her husband up and down, noting the droop of his once-broad shoulders and the grey whiskers in his long, curly beard. She glanced at the little terrier and saw the grey whiskers on his chin also; it made her smile to see the resemblance between man and dog. 'Take it easy, you two,' she instructed. 'Neither of you is as young as you used to be.'

'Hey! Enough of that. You know what they say: you're only as old as you feel.'

'Oh, so you feel young and sprightly, do you?'

Edging towards him, she gave a cheeky wink. 'Come on then, let's see what you're made of.'

'Don't be daft, woman. What's wrong with you?' He scrambled out of the chair to grab his coat, and she burst out laughing. 'You're a wicked woman!' he chided her.

'Not as wicked as her down the street!' Mary retorted. 'What woman with any decency would bed her own sister's husband? Not to mention breaking her own marriage by flirting and carrying on with the lodger. Shameful, that's what it is. I'm not surprised her poor husband fled to the hills.'

'Behave yourself!' Peter was never a man to gossip. 'And anyway, you don't know she's "bedding" her sister's husband.'

'Take it from me, Peter,' tapping the side of her nose, she gave a little smile, 'a woman knows these things.'

'Right, well, I'm off. Come on, Rascal!' The little dog was already at the door, chasing backwards and forwards with his tongue hanging out.

When Peter opened the door, the dog set off at a run, clambering at the garden gate, impatient to be away.

Deep in thought, Mary resumed her chores at the sink, one eye on her husband as he went down the garden path. 'Huh! Don't tell me that little slut is not bedding Martin Lovejoy, because I would bet my life on it,' she muttered.

Less than two miles away, Martin drew up at the old barn he was renovating. He yanked on the brake, then switched off the van engine.

He began whistling merrily, happy in the knowledge that Paula wanted the same things he did, but fell silent a moment later when Lucy crept into his mind.

For a few painful minutes he continued to think about Lucy, and how she would react if he ever had the courage to tell her about him and Paula. It's sure to be a messy, hurtful business if I break with Lucy, he thought, leaning back in his seat. Lucy and me, though . . . he slowly shook his head . . . there's just nothing there, and hasn't been for a long time. At least not on my side.

He was truly sorry about Lucy, but he was determined to grab his happiness as soon as he could. It wasn't her fault . . . they had been just kids learning about life. Too young to realise the consequences of what they did.

Looking back, he believed he was more to blame than Lucy. Me . . . the big man in the school ground . . . I had to have her, and I've paid the price ever since. Serves me bloody right! Thumping the dashboard, he softly cursed, thinking back, hating himself, hating Lucy, then loving her. I just can't spend the rest of my life with her . . . not now I know that Paula wants me, he decided.

He tried to visualise what Lucy might say when he told her he and Paula were planning to live together. Lucy would get over it . . . she would! She was a sensible woman. She took things in her stride, always had.

41

Assuring himself that Lucy would cope, he thought of the wonderful times he'd enjoyed with Paula. He and Paula belonged together, and to hell with anyone who didn't like the idea!

He couldn't wait to start a new life with his sister-in-law. But before that could happen, there was much to be done. He thought of his children, Anne and Sam. They too, would be hurt, he knew, but as far as he was concerned there was no alternative.

Taking a deep breath, he blew it back out in a long sigh. His decision was made. *Sorry, Lucy, love, but life is too short for regrets. I can't live with someone I don't love . . . not any more.*

Before he announced his decision, though, he had to be absolutely certain that Paula really meant what she said. They must have another serious conversation.

After he'd spoken with Paula, he would know which way to go.

Settled on his plan of action, Martin scrambled out of the van, grabbed his tools and headed off to work with a determined stride. He had so much to think about, his head was spinning. His troubled thoughts kept coming back to Lucy, that gentle, good woman who had given him two much-loved children. She was one of Nature's mothers: always there when needed.

The truth was that just to be with Paula fired Martin with excitement, while Lucy was just there; like a shadow in the corner, like an ornament you might bring out and polish now and then. She had little to say and even fewer opinions to share. There was no spirit, no naughtiness, or humour of any kind. She was just Lucy, content in her own little world. Happiest when she had family about her.

But though she brought no excitement to his life, she was the mother of his children, and grandmother of his daughter's child.

Other than that, Lucy was simply a sad relic of his wasted youth.

And yet, for all that, he was loath to hurt her.

PART TWO

Revelations

CHAPTER THREE

KATHLEEN RILEY AND Lucy Lovejoy had worked together at the plastics factory for almost two years. It was a busy, happy firm, turning out all manner of plastic goods, including watering cans, children's tea sets, and see-through plastic macs, which were one of the company's best sellers.

Lucy made the belts for the macs, and Kathleen made the collars. Other workers joined all the pieces together and when finished, the macs were attractive, very fashionable and easy to wear.

Sitting at the machines all day was physically demanding work, especially on the legs, which were required to push back and forth with the swing of the metal welder which dropped down rhythmically to seal the pieces together.

At the end of the week, the size of the wage packet depended on how many pieces each worker had produced, which was an incentive for everyone to work hard.

Having started on the same day and followed the training programme together, Lucy and Kathleen had quickly become the best of workmates, though because of Lucy's family commitments, they only very occasionally met up outside of work.

Today Kathleen was worried about Lucy, who had hardly spoken a word since being summoned to the manager's office earlier. In the end Kathleen just had to ask outright.

'Hey, Lucy, is everything OK? Has the ol' dragon had a go at you?'

Short and curvy, with chocolate-coloured eyes, and red curly hair, Kathleen had her hair pinned back so tightly she looked like she'd been in a wind tunnel.

When Lucy seemed not to have heard, Kathleen left her machine to hurry across to her. 'Has she given you a dressing-down because you had the day off yesterday?' Aware of the others watching, she quickly lowered her voice. 'Don't let her get you down. Sometimes her bark is worse than her bite. You're a good worker. She knows you would never be late if there wasn't a problem.'

Lucy was close to tears. 'That's the trouble,' she admitted. 'There's always a problem of one kind or another. When I think everything's going well, and I can rest easy, something happens to mess things up.'

'Ah! But y'see, Lucy, that's sometimes the way of it with families, but it won't always be like that. You're going through a bad patch at the minute, but it's not your fault.' Glancing up to see the foreman on the prowl nearby, she edged away. 'Look, I'd best get on, but we'll talk later. Meantime, don't let the buggers get you down!'

Having quickly returned to her work-bench, Kathleen was head down and working hard, until the shriek of the lunchtime buzzer pierced the air. 'Come on, time for a break, Lucy!' she called out, but Lucy was already on her feet.

'Get your bag, Lucy, and let's get outta here,' Kathleen said. 'Me poor ol' feet have swelled up like two fat puddings, so they have.'

Lucy felt much the same. Sitting at the machines for hours was punishing. With a sense of relief the workers began to filter away in different directions: some to the canteen, some to the alley where they would have a quick cigarette; others headed to the four corners of the factory yard, to flop down wherever they felt comfortable.

Outside in the clean, fresh air, Lucy and Kathleen settled themselves on the wall at the back of the factory, with their legs dangling over the edge and their flasks of tea sitting side by side.

'I've got cheese.' Kathleen opened her lunch bag. 'What have you got?'

'Ham and tomato.' Lucy offered up her box. 'Want to swap?'

'Oh, aren't you the little angel now?' Kathleen did not need asking twice. Holding out her puny sandwich, she made the exchange and licked her lips. 'Go on then, Lucy. Your sandwiches are always better than mine.'

After pouring tea from the flask into a plastic cup, Kathleen was intent again on knowing what had been said in the manager's office earlier. 'She's upset you, hasn't she . . . the old divil?' Kathleen gently pursued the subject. 'You mustn't let her get you down.' Taking a bite of her sandwich, she waited for Lucy's response.

Lucy remained silent for what seemed an age, and then she dug into her overall pocket and handed Kathleen an official-looking envelope. 'Here. Read that.'

Kathleen gingerly opened it and read what it contained.

'Jaysus, will ye look at that! An official, written warning . . . You should inform the union about this!'

'No!' Official aggravation of that kind was the last thing Lucy wanted. 'Considering how many times I've been late, or not turned in at all, it's like she said: I'm unreliable. She has every right to issue a formal warning. She also made it clear that if I can't keep to regular hours from now on, or if I miss one more day without prior notice – unless it's a matter of life and death – then I'll be given my walking papers on the spot!'

She looked at the sandwich she was holding for a moment before sneaking it back into her lunch box. She had not only lost her appetite but, after the grilling she had been through in the office, she felt like a hopeless failure.

Kathleen had seen her reject the sandwich. 'Hey,' she pointed to Lucy's lunch box, 'you can't go without yer food. Sure, that won't solve nothing at all!' She did understand how Lucy must be feeling, though. 'Look, Lucy, I really think you should inform the union. Let me talk to the steward – he's a sensible man. He'll have a quiet word with her. Sure, it doesn't have to go any further than that if you don't want it to.'

Fearful, Lucy told her to leave it be and, being the good friend she was, Kathleen promised she would not say another word, though she was a natural rebel and could not be certain she would keep such a promise.

From previous conversations between herself and Lucy, it was clear to Kathleen that the family did put upon Lucy's good nature, and she felt she had to mention it now. 'As far as I can see, Lucy . . .' she hesitated, before going on, '. . . there is only one solution to this.'

Intrigued, Lucy hitched herself further onto the wall. 'Oh, and what's that, then?'

'Look, don't take offence, but you must stop being a buffer for the family. They're old enough to sort out their own problems. It's not right that they should come running to you at every little hurdle. Y'see, the more you let them lean on you, the less responsible they'll become for their own actions and misfortunes.'

'But they're my family, Kathleen. I can't turn away from them when they come to me for help.'

'Sure, I understand that, and I've helped my own family many a time – show me a parent who hasn't – but we have to draw a line. We have to let them live and learn, allow them to search for their own solutions, otherwise how will they ever cope? I mean, you won't be here for ever, will you, so how will they manage when you're not there to pick up the pieces?'

'I know what you mean. But it's hard not to do what you can, if there's a problem.'

'True, but all I'm saying is, you need to be sure whether it's a problem they could deal with themselves, and if it is, then you should maybe just give advice. That way, it's right for them, and right for you. I've got four grown-up children, as you know, Lucy, and I promise you it took a long time for me to realise I could step back and leave them to deal with their lives themselves . . . much as we had to do when we were their ages.'

She laughed out loud. 'I'll admit we had a few hairy moments with our son Michael. He was the wild card of the family. Even after he got married and had a child, he leaned on us at every turn. But I promise you, we got there in the end, and so will you.'

When one of their colleagues threw a rolled-up newspaper to them, Kathleen caught it and quickly flicked through the pages.

'Look at this!' Holding the pages open, she showed Lucy the photograph of three young men. 'Would you believe, killed in a car smash on the way to a mate's wedding. They were so young . . . the families must have been devastated. But there you are . . . It just goes to show, you never know what's round the corner, do you?'

Realising she and Lucy were the last two left outside,

Kathleen leaped off the wall. 'Hell's bell's, Lucy! Everybody's gone. If we don't get our backsides in there, we'll know well enough what's round the corner! It'll be the length of the ol' dragon's tongue, so it will!'

With thoughts of those three young men in their minds, Lucy and Kathleen made their way back inside the factory.

'I don't know what I'd do if I got my walking orders from here,' Lucy confided to Kathleen as they hurried to their machines. 'If I lost my job, whatever would I tell Martin and the children?'

Kathleen wagged a finger at her. 'There you go again!' she chided. 'More concerned about the family than you are about yourself! Put yourself first for a change, Lucy Lovejoy! Do that, and the chances of you losing your job will be less likely. OK?' She gave Lucy a friendly wink.

Lucy smiled. 'OK.' In truth, she would not even know *how* to start putting herself first.

Eventually the loud screech of the works' siren marked the end of another working day. The machines were switched off and an eerie silence fell across the vast open space of the factory floor.

Very soon, though, the silence was shattered by the march of many feet as the workers made their way out. And then the noise of hurrying feet was quickly overridden by shouts and laughter as everyone relaxed into 'going home' mode.

As always, Kathleen and Lucy merged with the other workers on their way out, but at the outer gates Lucy split away from Kathleen. 'I'm walking home tonight,' she explained.

Kathleen was surprised. 'Even if you cut through the alleys, it's a fair old walk to your street. But why walk when you can catch the bus as usual and be home that much earlier?'

Lucy shrugged. 'No particular reason. I just need to think, that's all.'

'You're not fretting about getting a warning, are you, Lucy? Because I've told you, if need be we can get the union on to it.'

But Lucy was adamant. 'No, Kathleen, I don't want that. Anyway, I won't give her the chance to carpet me again . . . not if I can help it, anyway.'

'All right, Lucy, no union,' Kathleen conceded. 'I'll see you tomorrow. Mind how you go, eh?'

'You too, and thanks, Kathleen.'

'What for?'

'Well . . . for siding with me, and listening to my troubles.'

'You're welcome. Ooh, there's Barney!' Kathleen spied the foreman, a handsome man some ten years older than Kathleen. 'I've been meaning to ask him about my machine. It keeps playing up.' She gave a naughty wink. ''Bye, Lucy . . . see you.'

Lucy had to chuckle. 'Shame on you, Kathleen Riley, you brazen little hussy!'

She set off, leaving the effervescent Kathleen openly flirting with the foreman.

Turning the corner, Lucy crossed the street and

headed for the park. A few quiet minutes there would be just lovely. She reminded herself of how often she used to walk home through that way, but she had not done so for some time, and anyway, the nights were only now drawing out after the harsh winter.

Lately, she seemed never to have the time to linger. Instead, she was forever chasing her tail, with no opportunity to relax.

Now, though, in spite of the teasing breeze, she was determined to follow her instinct. The closer she got to the park gates, the quicker she walked, and the lighter her weary heart felt. There was something magical about the park, with its secret, meandering pathways and majestic trees.

In spring, the park was a surprise and a delight, with its curving swathes of wild flowers, all mixed in with cultivated plants. The riot of colour and profusion could take one's breath away.

Deep in thought, Lucy reflected on that meaningful little talk with Kathleen at lunchtime. It was right what Kathleen had said about never knowing what was round the corner.

Lucy recognised how her own world had become small and restricted. She suddenly recalled her mother's prophetic words of many years ago, when she and Paula were schoolgirls. 'I think Lucy will be the home-maker,' their mother had remarked.

She also made a light-hearted prediction for her younger daughter. 'As for our Paula, it wouldn't surprise me if she turned out to be a home-*breaker*.'

It was no secret that while Lucy was her father's favourite, Paula was close to their mother. However wayward Paula had been when growing up, and however much anguish she had brought her parents, that bond between mother and daughter had not changed over the years.

It was not in Lucy's character to be jealous, for she loved all her family in equal measure. Knowing her sister's penchant for trouble, Lucy was given the responsibility of looking out for Paula. As instructed by both her concerned parents, Lucy would walk her younger sister to and from school.

She was also expected to make sure that Paula actually went into her designated classroom because, being something of a rebel, Paula would not think twice about playing truant, but even though Lucy carried out her given responsibilities with much diligence, the truant officer was forever out and about, searching for Paula.

He once caught Paula playing in the park, and throwing stones at the ducks as they strutted about. Another time he found her playing football in one of the local backstreets with two boys truanting from a different school.

When the truant officer marched all three back to their schools, they giggled and sniggered as though it was all a great adventure.

Shepherded into the headmaster's office, the boys each suffered the slicing heat of a wicker cane on their buttocks. The pain was such that it reduced them to tears, but not so great as to stop them from truanting again.

Paula suffered a severe lecture from her head teacher, who warned her of her wanton ways. She also received two strokes of the best on the palm of each hand, which she endured without even a flinch.

At his wits' end, her father banned her from leaving the house after school for a period of two weeks.

To his younger, more defiant daughter, that was the worst punishment of all.

~

Having taken her little dog for a long walk around the far reaches of the park, Mary Taylor walked him back through the spinney, where she was immensely thankful to sit on a bench and get her breath back.

'You're a demanding little thing!' She tickled Rascal's hairy neck. 'I would never part with you, though, because, hard work or not, I love the bones of you.'

Taking a moment to stretch her aching back, she took a deep, invigorating breath, while chatting to herself as she often did. 'Well, Mary, you've enjoyed the fresh air, you've been dragged round the park by this bag of fur,' she glanced at the dog, 'and you've stretched your legs to breaking point, so now it's time for home.'

When the dog yapped at her as though in disagreement, she told him firmly, 'We've had enough excitement for one day. You might be ready for another round, but I'm well and truly done in!' She wagged a bony finger at him. 'I'm sure I don't know whose bones must ache the most, yours or mine!'

Tightening the scarf round her neck and shoulders, she addressed the little dog as though he understood every word. 'I never meant to stay out this long. What's more, I'm thoroughly ashamed of you, chasing that poor moggy up a tree. I've a good mind to ban you from the park for a week. That should teach you some manners!'

Looking up, she was surprised to see Lucy making her way along the bottom pathway. 'Lucy!' Mary called out to her. 'Lucy Lovejoy!'

Pleased to see her sister's kindly neighbour, Lucy hurried towards her. 'Hello, Mary. How are you?'

'Hmm! You might well ask.' Mary gave a little groan. 'I should have been at home by now, sitting at the fire with a cup of soup to warm my bones. As it is, I'm late getting back, and all because this little devil has a thing for chasing cats up trees.'

She went on to describe the adventure in great detail. 'The poor moggy was terrified, but your lord-ship here,' she pointed to Rascal, 'he thought it was great fun, yapping at her to come down. And when I did manage to persuade the poor thing down it swiped at me with its claws fully drawn before taking off. Like a bat out of hell, it was!'

Lucy wagged a finger at the scowling dog. 'That wasn't very nice, was it, trapping the poor thing up a tree?'

'The cat wasn't altogether innocent,' Mary explained. 'The moggy started it by chasing the birds round and round. When Rascal went after her, she fought back and Rascal got the worst of it. After licking his wounds, he went after the cat again, but she shot up to the highest branch, leaving him in a right frenzy.'

She slumped back on the bench. 'We must have walked ten miles; round and round we went. We came back the longest way, past the gardens and on through the spinney. To tell you the truth, Lucy, I'm about done in!'

Lucy could see how tired Mary was. 'You shouldn't be rushing and chasing about. You'll do yoursef an injury.'

'I know, but I do enjoy it, though I'm not sure whose feet ache the most, his or mine.'

Lucy changed the subject. 'How's Peter? I haven't seen either of you, not since I paid my sister a visit. That must be, what, over a week back.' She tutted. 'Goodness! How time flies.'

'Yes, and yes again. We're both fine, thank you, Lucy.'

Mary was reminded of the bad fall Lucy's mother had suffered at the market some time back. 'How's your mum, by the way, since she tumbled down the market steps?'

'Oh, she's getting there bit by bit. Her wounds are healed, but she's really nervous of going out. Dad coaxed her back to the market the other day, to build her confidence. He walked her gently up and down the stairway where she fell and hurt herself.'

'He did right, but it can't have been easy for your mum,' Mary sympathised.

'That's true. Dad said she was a bag of nerves, that he lost count of how many times she wanted to go home. We're all so worried about her. She frets a lot more than she used to. She's got a habit of pacing up and down all the time. It's as if she can't rest,' Lucy confided. 'And she's got really forgetful of late. It's not like her at all.'

'Give her time, Lucy. She's had a shock to the system, and that can often be worse than a physical injury.'

'She's started forgetting things, like putting food in the cooker and leaving it to burn. Last week she ran a bath and came downstairs, leaving the taps running. It was only when Dad saw the water dripping from the kitchen ceiling that he realised what she'd done. He phoned us, and Martin went round to check for any damage, but thankfully it wasn't too bad once he'd dried it all out.' Lucy went on, 'I'm trying to persuade Mum to see the doctor, but she's being difficult about it.'

'You're a good daughter,' Mary told her, 'and you're right in persuading her to see a doctor. I'm sure it can be all sorted out.'

Lucy hoped so. 'I don't know what's happening, Mary. Just lately, it's one thing after another.'

In that moment, Mary thought of how things were worse than Lucy could possibly imagine, with her two-timing husband and her own sister having a full-blown affair. It was a wicked and shocking betrayal. After what she had witnessed the previous morning, the knowledge that those two were cheating on Lucy had been gnawing at her ever since.

She was on the verge of telling Lucy what was going on behind her back, but then she remembered how Peter had been dead set against either of them getting involved.

Mary, however, did not agree with sweeping it all under the table, and besides, she believed that Lucy deserved to know the truth. One way or another, she must make Lucy aware of what was going on. She had been agonising over it, but how could she tell Lucy without actually getting herself and Peter involved?

While she thought of it now, a sudden, sneaky idea came to her. Yes! The answer was right there all the time.

Lucy's quiet voice jolted Mary out of her thoughts. 'Mary, are you all right?'

Startled, Mary looked up. 'Oh, Lucy, I am sorry.' 'Yes, I'm fine . . . I was just thinking.'

Lucy understood. 'I expect you're tired, what with Rascal's adventure and everything.'

'You're right. I was close to nodding off.'

Mary bitterly regretted having to deceive Lucy, but it was the best way if she and Peter were not to be drawn in. But she had to do it now, in case it was a while before she saw Lucy again. 'Lucy?'

Lucy looked up from stroking the little dog. 'Yes, Mary?' When the older woman hesitated, Lucy sensed her nervousness. 'What is it?'

'Oh, I don't suppose it's anything really, only what with you saying you haven't seen Paula for over a week, I was just wondering . . . is she all right?'

'Well, yes . . . I think so, but what makes you ask?'

'I'm sorry, Lucy, I really shouldn't worry you . . . you've got enough to think about, what with your mother and such . . .'

'Has Paula been a nuisance?' Lucy asked. 'I know how rude she can be if the mood takes her. Come on, Mary, out with it. What's she done to upset you?'

Mary was beginning to regret having started this conversation, but she held her resolve and continued with the deception. 'Oh, no! She hasn't upset me. In fact, we're the best of neighbours at the minute; as long as my cat doesn't get in her back garden and leave his mark.' She went on, 'Look, I don't want to worry you, Lucy. It's just that I had not seen her for a couple of days, but this morning as I passed her house she was talking to the postman and, to be honest, she looked so tired and pale . . . all kind of huddled up . . . not at all like the Paula we know.'

'Oh dear.' Lucy felt guilty. 'She's had a rough time of it lately, but I really thought she was dealing with her marriage break-up. The trouble is, our Paula hardly ever confides in anyone. She likes to think she's invincible.'

Lucy went back over the past few months in her mind. While Paula's husband, Ray, had tried his hardest to keep the marriage together, Paula seemed to be hankering after a life without him and, as ever, she was her own worst enemy.

'Paula was the one at fault in the marriage, but she wouldn't listen,' Lucy admitted. 'She obviously thought that Ray would forgive her, however she behaved. When he walked away from it all, she was shocked to her roots, and it's such a shame, because he idolised her. And deep down I know she truly loved him. But now you've got me worried, Mary. I must find time to go and see her . . . make sure she's all right. The thing is, I planned to check on Mum tonight. You know she's been upset and ill since the fall, and I thought me going over to see them might give Dad a little break. And tonight was ideal, what with Martin working late, and Sam off out with his mates.'

The decision was made. 'I'd best go and see Paula tonight, though. I mean, she's the only one of us who doesn't have anyone at home to talk things through with . . . not since Ray walked out. I can ring Dad from there. I'm sure he'll understand.'

Mary was curious. 'Is Paula's marriage well and truly over then?'

'Well, yes. From what I understand, she's been served with the divorce papers, but she's taking her time to sign them. The trouble is, ever since Ray left, she was certain he would never serve the papers. She was convinced that the two of them would get back together. Receiving the papers knocked her back a bit, though, being Paula, she would never admit it.'

A few minutes later, anxious to make sure her sister was coping, Lucy bade Mary cheerio and set off at a fast pace towards the bus stop, thinking that it wasn't wise for Paula to show a brave face to the world when inside she must be devastated. No one could help her if she didn't let them in. Lucy realised that her younger sister was still reeling from the end of her marriage. It was a huge, painful milestone in her life.

Knowing her sister's unpredictable character, Lucy quickened her steps.

~

Having carefully manoeuvred his van into the narrow alcove, Martin went at the run down the alley, skipped up the two steps into Paula's back garden, and let himself in through the back door.

Having seen his approach through the back window, Paula hid behind the kitchen door and waited to surprise him. She was wearing only a short, slinky slip; and a disappointed frown.

Entering the kitchen, Martin kicked out with his heel to shut the door. He then grabbed Paula and pressed her hard against the wall.

'Ready for me, are you?' His roving hands reached inside her slip.

'Where the hell have you been?' She pushed him away. 'You should have been here ten minutes ago.'

Surprised at the vehemence of her tone, he gathered her to him. 'Hey! It couldn't be helped,' he explained softly. 'I had a last-minute complication with the electrics. It won't happen again, I promise.'

'It had better not, because if you ever keep me waiting again, I'll bolt the door so you can't get in.'

'You wouldn't dare!'

'Huh! Don't bet on it!' Squirming from his grasp, Paula fled up the stairs, laughing and teasing as he chased her into the bedroom.

~

Anxious to speak with her younger sister, Lucy hurried down the street, her heels beating against the pavement as she neared the house. She thought of how Mary Taylor had described Paula as looking sad. Paula had best come and stay with me for a while, Lucy decided as she hurried along. It's a pity she's not full time at the petrol station because now it will give her more time to fret. I can't leave her alone in that house, wittering and worrying, and making herself ill. But who can blame her for feeling miserable? What with the endless rows between her and Ray, then the difficult marriage break-up, and then getting sacked and having to find a new job.

When Lucy took a moment to compare her own life against her sister's, she truly believed that Paula was worse off. While she, Lucy, had a husband and children, and a full-time job, even if it *was* hanging by a thread, Paula had none of these blessings.

She's been through the mill, Lucy acknowledged, but she must know that I will always be here for her.

On arriving at the back door of Paula's house, she stood on the step a moment, wondering what she might say. She reminded herself not to say that Mary had been talking to her. It would only cause trouble.

Bunching her knuckles to knock on the door, she was surprised to find it slightly open. Honestly! she thought. What have I told her about leaving the back door open? Anyone could walk in!

She gently pushed the door open, and was about to shout for Paula, when she heard the sound of voices from upstairs. One of them sounded like that of a man.

A smile crept over her homely face. Maybe Ray had decided to come home after all.

Though nervous about intruding, she made her way to the foot of the stairs, where she was shocked to her roots to recognise the man's voice as belonging to her own husband.

She wondered if Paula had arranged for him to call round because of a problem in the house, but he had not said anything about that at breakfast; she would have remembered.

Think, Lucy! she told herself. Martin doesn't always discuss the details of his work schedule. But if he was working at Paula's house, surely he would have mentioned that?

Confused and a little apprehensive, she sensed that something was not right. Yet still she chided herself for allowing her imagination to run away with her. She told herself that it could not be Martin upstairs – she would have seen his van outside – and the voices were softly intimate, with the occasional childish titter of suggestive laughter. And yet . . .

Ashamed, Lucy tried to blank out the bad thoughts. She told herself that it could not be Martin up in the bedroom; and more shame on her for allowing herself even to think it.

It must be Ray, come home to talk things through, with the hope of repairing the marriage. Lucy's heart lifted at the thought of a reunion between Paula and her estranged husband.

And yet that small, nagging voice in her head was warning her that something was not right here.

Having allowed suspicion to creep into her mind, she wondered whether she ought to make herself known. She was about to call up to them when there came a burst of familiar manly laughter. Lucy's heart stood still.

There was no doubt in her mind now. The voice, the laughter . . . it was Martin, her husband.

For what seemed an age, Lucy stood transfixed, her ears assailed with a burst of intimate groans and excited cries, the kind only lovers might make.

As the stark realisation took hold, she could barely breathe. Although she promised herself that she was wrong, and this was not happening, she knew it was. As the lovers continued to laugh and whisper together, the truth was undeniable. It really was Martin and her sister, upstairs in each other's arms.

Devastated, she turned to leave, wiping away her tears, but then a swell of rage flooded through her and shock turned to anger. No! She had to see them together. She needed each of them to look up and see her standing there. Only then would she be completely certain.

Lucy knew that if she ran away from the truth now, she would live to regret it.

Her mind was set. Whatever shocking images she might discover, and however painful it might prove, she would rather know the truth than be forever wondering.

And so, on nervous legs she continued on up the stairs, and along the landing. The bawdy laughter drowned out the sound of her approach.

In that first, hesitant moment when she entered the bedroom, Lucy was sickened by what she saw.

They lay in the bed, exhausted . . . coupled together. The sheet was crumpled part-way down, their naked bodies entwined. Paula had her hand on the back of Martin's head, her fingers caressing his hair, and Martin was lying over her, his face nuzzling her breasts.

For the longest moment, they remained blissfully unaware that she was in the room, watching them, unable to move forward, or flee from the room. Lucy saw her husband and her sister, as close and together as any man and woman could be, and she realised that as long as she lived, the image would stay with her.

A wave of coldness folded over her, and she began to sob, silently at first; then, as the pain intensified, the sobs became uncontrollable.

Martin looked up, his eyes wide with shock. 'Oh my God . . . Lucy!' Tearing at the sheet, he covered his nakedness and ran across the room towards her. 'Lucy

. . . I'm sorry . . . I'm so sorry!' he screamed after her as she ran down the stairs. 'Lucy . . . please . . . wait!'

Behind him, Paula was nervously giggling; though tears were not far behind.

As Lucy ran out of the front door and down the street, Martin ran back into the bedroom. 'I need to go after her!' he gasped, snatching up his clothes and quickly dressing. A moment later, he was fleeing down the street after Lucy.

Even now, he was arrogant enough to expect her forgiveness.

Lucy, though, was long gone. Bitter tears clouded her vision as she fled, half running, half stumbling, her mind filled with what she had seen. 'How could they?' she kept asking herself. Even though she had seen them together with her own eyes, Lucy found it difficult to believe they could both betray her so cruelly.

~

Having taken a short cut home, Mary Taylor arrived just as Lucy was walking up the alley towards Paula's house. She saw Lucy go in, and now she saw her running away.

She heard Martin calling out, 'Come back . . . please, Lucy . . . we need to talk!'

Lucy gave no answer, nor did she look back. Instead, she ran on blindly, tears streaming from her eyes.

Watching from the window, Mary saw how distressed

Lucy was, and she blamed herself. 'You interfering old woman!' She banged her clenched fist hard on the windowsill. 'Why couldn't you have minded your own business, and left well alone?'

Falling into her armchair, she cried bitterly.

A moment later she felt a comforting hand on her shoulder. 'Don't upset yourself.' The soft, kindly voice soothed her troubled mind as Peter held her to him. 'It was only a matter of time before Lucy found out anyway.'

'Oh, Peter, I feel so ashamed. I should never have interfered. You were right to warn me against it, but I couldn't bear to see how she was being made a fool of.'

Peter's own feelings were much the same. 'I'll admit, when you told me what you'd done, I was angry. But after thinking it through, I believe you did the right and proper thing. Like you, I feel for Lucy, but at least she knows now. You've done what you can, and now we must take a step back. It's up to Lucy as to how she deals with it.'

Greatly relieved, Mary wound her hand into his. 'You're such a blessing to me,' she said softly. 'I do love you so.'

Holding her to him, Peter smiled contentedly. 'I know you do, sweetheart. I also know what a very fortunate man I am.'

CHAPTER FOUR

WANDERING THROUGH THE quiet streets, Lucy made a forlorn figure.

The late April showers had now developed into a heavy downpour, but she didn't even notice. Instead, she pressed silently on, deep in thought, not knowing where she was or how far she had walked.

Try as she might, she could not shut out the image of Martin and Paula, lying together in her bed, the two of them stark naked and unashamed.

She recalled how natural and easy they were together. It must have been going on for a long time, she quickly realised. They were too comfortable with each other, laughing and teasing like long-time lovers; wickedly at ease together.

The more she thought of it, the more she realised the depth of their deceit. Martin's work van had been nowhere to be seen. So had he hidden it? Was the whole thing planned right down to the last detail?

She had so many unanswered questions. How could

Martin do this to her . . . and with her own sister? Martin was her whole life. The man she had loved and trusted all these years, and like an idiot, thought he loved her too.

When the rain spewed down and blinded her so she could hardly see where she was going, Lucy ran along the street and took refuge in a nearby bus shelter.

Completely drenched, she curled up on the wooden seat at the back of the shelter, hoping that there she might be left alone.

Dark was closing in. The street was empty, and the light by the shelter was flickering, creating ghostly shadows to unnerve her.

In that desolate moment, she felt like the loneliest person in the world. She put her hands over her face and sobbed, her heart broken. She had given Martin her whole life – and this was what it had come to.

A short time later, she caught snatches of conversation between two people nearby; seemingly a man and a woman. They were approaching quickly, and then they were running to escape the rain, their rhythmic footsteps clipping over the pavement, every second bringing them closer.

Convinced that they were making for the shelter, Lucy pressed herself closer to the back wall, hiding in the shadows. The last thing she needed right now was for strangers to see her there.

As they approached the shelter, their raised voices became more distinct. Now they were laughing aloud at something the woman had said.

'The place at Littleton is the answer,' the man told her. 'It's absolutely perfect for you.'

Suddenly the woman lost her footing, crying out as she stumbled. 'Dammit! I should never have worn these new, high-heeled shoes. What was I thinking?'

Lucy froze when the woman leaned against the opening of the shelter. 'Stand still!' The man's voice was kindly but firm. 'Hold on to me, Nancy.'

Though they had not yet realised Lucy was there, she could see the two of them clearly. The man was tall and smartly dressed. He held the woman steady while she took off the offending shoe.

'All right, are you?'

'It serves me right,' she replied, 'but I dare say I'll live . . . thanks, Dave.' Gently rubbing her foot, she chuckled. 'Nothing broken,' she reported, 'except for my stupid pride!'

Lucy cowered back, swiftly wiping the tears from her face.

Just then the man glanced up, to see Lucy squashed into the corner of the bench. 'Good Lord, you gave me a fright!'

'What . . . ?' the woman followed his gaze. On seeing Lucy, she quickly slid her foot into the shoe and stood up straight. 'Whatever are you doing here . . . in the dark, on your own?' She glanced about as though expecting to see someone else there.

Realising that these two were not thugs who might attack and rob her, Lucy scrambled off the bench and made her way towards them. 'I got caught out in the rain,' she explained. 'I dived in here to try to dry off. Now that the rain seems to have stopped, I'd best be on my way.'

The man was concerned, and his kind eyes took in her bedraggled appearance and tear-stained face. 'I don't know how long you've been curled up in this damp place, but you must be feeling cold to the bone. Look, we were just popping into the pub across the street. You're very welcome to join us.'

Lucy saw the woman's surprise at her companion inviting a complete stranger to join them, but she said nothing. The woman was indeed taken aback by his generous invitation. Normally, Dave Benson would not be so reckless.

The woman, Nancy, now regarded Lucy, thinking her attractive in a gentle, homely kind of way. Not at all the kind of confident, well-groomed woman Dave might be drawn to. Nancy was both bemused and interested. This quietly spoken, wet and bedraggled woman had clearly stirred compassion in Dave. It was obvious that he was loath to leave her there alone.

Lucy was surprised and moved by the stranger's kind invitation, and touched by his obvious concern for her welfare. Another time, she might have accepted his offer of friendship. Just now, though, she needed solace to try to deal with the painful truth regarding the two people she had loved and trusted.

A multitude of questions reeled through her mind. Was Martin planning to end their marriage? And if he truly wanted that, did she want the same? Could she carry on the sham? Could she even keep quiet about having seen them together?

And what about her sister, Paula – what was she thinking? Was it just a daring fling, a kind of excitement for her? Or did she really want to take Martin away from his wife and children?

Lucy knew that whether or not she lost Martin, she alone would be the biggest loser. So, for the sake of her family, should she pretend, and carry on as usual? The more she thought about it, the more Lucy realised that she alone might be the one either to save, or to break the family. That was the crippling dilemma she now faced. It was painfully obvious that she must decide what to do. One thing was certain: she could never again love Martin; at least not in the same way. Nor could she keep a respectable relationship with her sister.

As for her parents, they would be devastated if they knew but Lucy could never burden them with the shameful truth.

Seeing how distant and troubled Lucy seemed, Dave Benson asked again, 'So, what do you say? Will you join me and Nancy?'

'No, I'm sorry,' Lucy replied. 'I really have to be somewhere else.'

She was in no mood for company. Least of all, the company of strangers, however friendly they might be.

She walked out of the bus shelter and onto the pavement. 'Thank you all the same,' she told the couple. 'The thing is . . . I was already on my way to visit Mum. She's not been very well of late. Then the rain came down and I dodged in here.' She glanced at the brooding skies. 'Thankfully, though, it seems to be clearing now.'

Noticing how Lucy had crossed her arms over her chest and was visibly shivering, Nancy said, 'There's usually a roaring fire going at the pub. Dave is right, you really do need to warm up, and maybe have a bite to eat. With luck, we can grab a table near to the fire.' Like Dave, she sensed that this homely little woman was genuinely distressed and in dire need of a friend. However, they both respected her reluctance to go with them to the pub.

Dave thought they should leave it at that. Albeit reluctantly.

'It's obvious you need to be on your way,' he said. 'Take care now, and I hope your mother's health improves. I'm sure she will be very glad to see you.'

'Thank you, yes, I'm sure she will.' His concern was comforting to Lucy. She liked the way he had somehow managed to ease her trauma, and she liked his easy, gentle smile.

She thought there was something very genuine and caring about the man called Dave. More than that, he had a certain kind of warmth that reached out. She thought he would make a loyal friend.

'Thank you for your kind offer.' She then gave the smallest of smiles and turned away, walking at such a hurried pace that the strangers thought she might break into a run.

Dave and Nancy went on their way, but for some reason Dave glanced back. As he did so, Lucy slowed her pace and turned her head to smile at him. She then waved her hand and hurried away.

Dave walked on, her intimate little smile playing on his mind. In that fleeting moment, he felt incredibly sad.

One thing was certain: he would not forget her in a hurry.

'Hey!' Unaware that he was deep in thought, Nancy linked arms as they strolled along. 'Did you hear what I said?'

'No. What did you say?'

'I asked you, why would anyone curl up all alone in a dark, damp shelter? Very odd, if you ask me.'

For a moment Dave was unresponsive, and when he did speak it was not to supply an answer to her question. 'We didn't even introduce ourselves, did we?'

'Hmm!' Nancy shrugged. 'No, we didn't. But she didn't introduce herself to us either, so that's all right, isn't it?'

'I suppose.'

Dave fell silent, speaking again only as they entered the pub. 'Nance?'

'What?'

'I really feel for that poor woman.'

'Me too. But you need to forget about her. After all, she's gone now. And it was obvious she did not want our help.'

'But did you see how she was?' Dave persisted.

'What do you mean? In what way?'

'Well, she'd clearly been crying.'

'Yes, and we don't really know how long she'd been taking refuge in that damp shelter.'

Something else crossed her mind. 'I'd like to know why she was there, in that draughty, dirty old shelter, anyway. I mean, she obviously didn't dodge in there to escape the rain, because she could have run into the pub, or caught a taxi or something, and she certainly wasn't waiting for a bus.'

'Why do you say that?'

'Well, because it's common knowledge that the bus stop went out of service long ago. Why was she really there, all huddled up in a cold, damp bus shelter? If we hadn't seen her, she probably would have stayed there all night. I think she's in hiding, running away from something. Or someone.'

'Mmm, she has a really sad and lonely look about her.'

Nancy persisted, 'I'm certain she was hiding. Why didn't she make herself known before you saw her huddled up in the corner? And why was she crying – that's what I'd like to know!'

Taking her by the elbow, Dave gently ushered Nancy through to the lounge bar. 'You want to know too much. After all, even if she *was* in trouble of some kind, it's obvious she didn't want to talk about it.'

Nancy chattered on. 'And another thing! Do we really believe that her mother was ill? Or was that another excuse to rush away from us?'

Dave was not about to discuss the matter any further. 'Stop right there!' He gestured to the far corner of the lounge. 'You go and sit down. Usual, is it? Lemonade shandy?'

'Please, and could you bring the bar menu while you're at it? Thank you.'

As she slid into the chair, Nancy's curious gaze was drawn to the window. I don't care what anyone says, she decided, that woman was in some kind of trouble. I just know it!

A few minutes later, on seeing Dave approach, she settled back into the chair. 'OK! Not another word,' she promised. 'Let's just enjoy our meal, shall we? Oh, and you can advise me on this new project of mine. I want you to be brutally honest if you think my ideas are rubbish!'

'Oh, I will, don't worry!'

Dave was thankful when they embarked on the subject of Nancy's new venture into the hotel trade.

Nancy prattled on excitedly. 'With your generous loan, and the promise of financial backing from the bank, I've now put in my bid. It's a little below the asking price, but I've got a good feeling they might well accept it. After all, as you so rightly pointed out, it's difficult to secure finance just now, so there aren't many buyers around.' Leaning over, she gave him a kiss on the cheek. 'I could not even have started on this venture without your help. You pointed me in the right direction, like I knew you would.'

'I believe in you,' he said simply. 'I know my money

will be safe. Honestly, though, Nance, I'm truly happy for you. I realise you were bitterly disappointed when your relationship with Joe broke up. But you came through it, and now here you are, about to embark on a great adventure, doing something you've always wanted to do. I just know your new life will be everything you want it to be.'

Discreetly regarding his older sister, he saw a new, stronger woman, confident and ambitious. 'Well done, Nance. I'm proud of you!'

'Thank you, but I would feel so much happier if you could change your mind and come in as a partner.'

Dave reminded her, 'You do understand why I had to say no, don't you?'

'Yes, I do. It was thoughtless and selfish of me to ask . . . especially after what we've all been through this past year – you more than most.'

When bad feelings now flooded back, Dave leaned forward, his sorry gaze on the table. 'I still find it so hard, Nance. Some days I wonder if I can actually get through it, but then somehow I do. My main worry at the moment is Cassie. I know I have to be strong for her. I can't and won't desert her, even though she's turned her back on me.'

'She *hasn't* turned her back on you – not altogether. When she decided to go to her aunt Ellie's house for a time, she did leave you a note to explain, didn't she?'

'Yes, she did, but I would rather she had discussed it with me first.'

'But she did leave most of her worldy belongings at home, didn't she?'

'Yes.'

'And when you rang Ellie, didn't Cassie come to the phone and talk with you?'

Dave smiled. 'Yes, but like I told you, when we talked it was too polite; too difficult. The thing is, she would not be drawn into talking about her mum, nor would she say when she might be coming home.'

Nancy spelled it out for him. 'Stop punishing yourself, and look on the positive side. Ellie said yes when Cassie asked to live with her for a time. Be glad of that, Dave, because if she had not gone to your sister-in-law, who knows where she might have ended up?'

'She should have come home with me,' Dave reminded her gently. 'That's where she belongs. That's where her mum would want her to be.'

Nancy made no comment. Instead, she continued, 'Remember, when you got home, you found she had left you a note explaining how she felt, and that you should not worry about her. She also left behind a lot of her prized possessions, so that tells you she does mean to come home at some point. It also shows that she does love you.'

'I understand all of that, but she won't let me get close, Nance. She blames me, and she will never forgive me . . . but how can I blame her for that, when I can't even forgive myself?'

When the powerful memories flooded back to cripple him, he leaned forward, running his clenched fists through his thick, dark hair. 'She's my daughter, Nance. With her mother gone, Cassie is everything to me. I need her! And whether she realises it or not, she needs me.'

Nancy laid her hand over his. 'Cassie will eventually accept that the accident was not your fault. The driver was drunk out of his mind. Thankfully, he's in prison now, where he belongs. Don't take Cassie's decision too much to heart. It has been just a year since Molly was killed, and neither you nor Cassie has been able to deal with it completely. I know it's difficult, for both of you . . . for all of us! But you must pick up the pieces and live your lives. It's what Molly would have wanted.'

'I know that.' He looked up, his face worn with grief. 'It's never easy, though. Losing Molly was the hardest, cruellest thing ever. Cassie is just nineteen, and she's been left without her mum. It's like her world has ended.' He added softly, 'Mine too. So, you can imagine, trying to live our lives without her is incredibly difficult.'

'Do you think I don't know that? But Cassie must realise the blame is not on your shoulders. That's too cruel.'

'She doesn't blame me for the accident itself,' Dave explained, 'she blames me for persuading Molly to meet up with my old schoolmates. I hadn't seen them in years and then I had a call from Stuart. He said they were staying overnight in town, before heading off in the morning for Scotland. I was thrilled, but

Molly didn't really want to go out that evening. In the end she got herself ready because she felt guilty.'

He took a moment to compose himself. 'If only I hadn't persuaded Molly to come and meet them, we would never have been on that stretch of road, on that particular night, and Molly would still be here with us.' His voice dropped to a whisper. 'When that madman careered into us, I was in the wrong place at the wrong time.'

'Not your fault, though! Cassie will see that in good time. Give her the space she needs, and I'm sure she'll come round.'

'I'm not sure, Nance.' Dave had lost hope on that score. 'It's been months now. After the funeral, she walked away from me, and turned to Molly's sister, Ellie. Ellie now tells me that Cassie has confided that she can't ever again face living in her own home. I think I should sell up, if that's what she truly wants. But we need to talk about it. I believe we might be able to get through this together.'

'Be patient, Dave.' Nancy squeezed his fist. 'Just keep in contact with Cassie, and respect her wishes. If you can do that, I know it won't be long before you and Cassie are stronger than ever.'

'Nance?'

'Yes?'

'Thank you.'

'What for?'

'For listening.'

'Don't be silly! Isn't that what big sisters are for?'

Changing the subject, she began flicking through the pages of the menu. 'I'm hungry.'

As she bent her head low to peruse the menu, Dave noticed how she narrowed her eyes, struggling to read the small print.

'Nance!'

'What?'

'Let me see.'

Irritated, she thrust the menu across the table. 'Go on then! Read it out, will you? Why on earth they make the print so small I really can't imagine!'

'Hmm! And I can't imagine why you don't bury your pride and see an optician.'

'It's nothing to do with pride,' she argued. 'The reason why I don't go to the optician is because there is absolutely nothing wrong with my eyesight . . . thank you!'

'OK, have it your way.' After he read the menu out, she made her choice and Dave returned to the bar with the order. Glancing back, he couldn't help but smile as Nancy bent her head low to read the 'What's On' sheet that was on the table.

It was a sharp reminder of how Nancy and his wife, Molly, used to play the quiz here on Saturday nights.

In that moment of nostalgia, he remembered with gratitude the wonderful woman he had loved . . . and still loved, even now, though she was not here with him.

While having been blessed in one way, he felt cruelly cheated in another. For twenty wonderful years he had known great love and companionship, and now the love of his life was gone, and Cassie, their only child, was too distressed to come home. He prayed every night for her to return soon. He missed her terribly. But, as Nancy had pointed out, he should remember that he was not the only one to lose someone precious. And so he would try to be patient, and pray that Cassie would eventually come home to him of her own free will. And when that happened he would welcome his darling girl with open arms.

Without Cassie and her mother, the house seemed cold and empty. In the daytime, he had his work, but the loneliness stayed with him. After work, when he got home and closed the door behind him, that was the worst time of all.

Left alone in an empty house that had once been filled with joy and laughter, he felt utterly lost.

'Hey! What took you so long?' Nancy had grown impatient when he had seemed to linger at the bar. 'Chatting to the barman, were you?' she asked.

'Not really. He was too busy serving customers.'

'Good for him! Making money is what it's all about.' She gave a little clap of the hands. 'Oh, Dave! I can't wait to get my hotel up and running.'

While Nancy chatted on excitedly about her new venture on the south coast, he stole a moment to glance out the window, his gaze instinctively drawn to the bus shelter.

He wondered about the woman they had seen hiding there in the shadows. He found it hard to put

CHAPTER FIVE

Lucy's mind was in chaos.

Having trudged through the darkened streets, she was now just half a mile from her parents' house. She was tired, her bones ached from the cold, and the repulsion she felt towards Martin and her sister continued to fester inside her.

Increasingly, she was uncertain as to whether she should continue on to her parents' house, or return home to confront Martin.

But she knew she must put her mother first. Her father had sounded really worried when she'd spoken to him before she went to work that morning.

Her parents' house was still a good twenty minutes' walk away, so when she saw the bus approach, she started running to the nearest stop. The conductor was standing on the platform, having a quiet cigarette. He did not see Lucy approach until she waved her arms and called out 'Stop!'

'By, you cut that a bit fine, didn't you?' Long-faced

and bald as a coot, he looked a peculiar sort. 'Come on then!' He stubbed out his cigarette, squeezed the end of it and shoved it into the top pocket of his jacket. Then he stepped forward to help her onto the platform. 'Where to?'

'Addison Street, please.'

'OK, that'll be one and sixpence.'

Lucy fished the coins out of her purse and handed them to him.

'That's it . . . there y'are, luv!' He rolled the ticket from his machine, and handed it to her. 'I'm pleased to say, you're my last customer, and I'll not be sorry to call it a night.' He coughed like he was on his last legs. 'My back aches, my poor old feet are hot and tired, and I'm starving hungry. But I dare say a pint of the best will do the trick.' He gave a toothy grin. 'I'm hoping to catch the Dog and Duck before they close their doors for the night.'

Lucy feigned interest and duly smiled, when inside she was in pieces. Her thoughts kept going back to Paula and Martin . . . how could they do that to her? She had to face the truth: it was obvious that Martin did not love her. It was equally obvious that Paula cared even less about her. And the more she tried to shut the images from her mind, the more she came to realise that her life as she knew it was over.

But what was she to tell Anne and Samuel, and how would they take it? If all this had come as a mighty shock to her, what would it do to them? The more she thought about it, the more concerned she became.

Thinking of her parents, Lucy faced worry of another kind. According to her dad, it seemed her mother, far from improving in health since suffering that bad fall, was getting worse.

Yet on the occasions when she had gone over to visit her parents, Lucy herself had not noticed any significant deterioration in her mother. But then she was not as familiar with her mother's recovery as her dad was, although she was on the phone every day to check up on her progress.

The trouble was, with her full-time work, the family to take care of, her normal daily chores and the household finances, she was forever trying to balance everything. Sometimes she wondered if her life was her own. There was never enough time to keep a closer eye on her mother, though she did what she could.

Seated at the back of the bus, and with no other passengers on board, Lucy leaned her head back and heaved a big sigh. It makes a change just to sit and do nothing, she thought.

It was not long before her thoughts returned to the couple at the bus stop, and she had to smile. It had been a real jolt when the man saw her there, all curled up at the back of the shelter.

She thought they were a nice couple. The man had surprised her when he asked if she might like to join them in the pub. No stranger had ever invited her anywhere.

Come to think of it, she could not recall anyone,

not even work friends or family, ever asking her to join them for a meal or a drink; except for last Christmas, when Anne cooked the turkey and they all went over to her house for dinner. That had been a rare and enjoyable experience.

Most other times she was at Anne's baby-sitting her grandchild. Other evenings, she might be up to her neck with baking, or doing the laundry, or working overtime to earn a bit of extra money. Or maybe there was a relative in need of some love and comfort. They always turned to Lucy, because they knew she would not let them down. Whatever it took, she was there for them.

When she thought about it now, she realised that when she felt down and worried, she had no one to turn to. Her husband was hardly ever home. Her children had enough problems of their own, and her parents were too old now for Lucy to burden them with her worries.

Basically, however, Lucy was content enough. Or she had been until today, when her world had been completely and utterly turned upside down.

She cast her mind back to the strangers at the bus shelter. She wondered if they were man and wife, or maybe just sweethearts. She thought the woman was attractive, while the man seemed so gentle, and unusually kind. She wondered who he was, and what had prompted him to ask her to join them.

Now though, her thoughts were interrupted when the conductor shouted out, 'Addison Street!'

'Good night, then . . . stay safe.' He lit another cigarette as he saw her off the bus. 'Don't do anything I wouldn't do!' he called after her.

Lucy waved him off. 'Hmm, chance would be a fine thing!' she murmured under her breath.

She turned into Addison Street. Shocked to see an ambulance parked halfway down, she broke into a run. As she got nearer to her parents' house, she was horrified to see the front door wide open and all the lights on.

Bursting into the house, her heart skipped a beat when she saw her father slumped on the stairs, looking older and greyer than she had ever seen him.

'Dad! What's happened?'

Greatly relieved to see her there, he struggled to get up. 'Lucy! Oh, Lucy, thank God you're here!'

When he began sobbing, Lucy ran to hold him. 'Ssh . . . it's all right, Dad.'

'It's your mum!' He clung to her, gabbling so fast she could hardly make out what he was telling her. 'She fell . . . hit her head on the fender. I thought she was dead, Lucy. I really thought she was dead.' He began trembling uncontrollably. 'Go to her, Lucy. She needs you.' Burying his head in his hands, he sobbed uncontrollably.

Just then the ambulance crew emerged from the sitting room, with Lucy's mother secured onto a stretcher. She appeared to be unconscious. Her head was bandaged and there were splashes of blood on the upper part of her clothing.

'Go with them, Lucy!' her father urged her. 'Please! I'll be all right . . . go with your mother.'

Lucy was in a quandary. She hated leaving him behind but, like he said, she had to go with her mother to the hospital. 'You really ought to come with us,' she said, but he shook his head and pushed her away.

Thinking quickly, Lucy ran to the telephone and dialled her home number; she was thankful that it was Sam, not Martin, who answered.

'Hello!'

'It's me, Sam. Grandma's had a bad accident . . . No, there's no time. Just get here and stay with Granddad . . . Hurry! Please hurry!' She slammed the phone down and returned to her father. 'Sam is on his way,' she promised, but all he needed to know was that Lucy was going with her mother.

'Go on!' He ushered her away. 'Your mum needs you more than I do . . . go on! I'll be fine. I'll wait for Sam. He'll get me to the hospital. You go.'

When she hesitated, he yelled, 'Please, Lucy, just go!' He gave her a shove. 'Your mother needs you!'

'All right, Dad, but be sure to watch out for Sam.' She ran down the hallway and onto the street. The ambulance men had already secured her mother and made her as comfortable as was possible.

Quickly, Lucy climbed in. She was concerned when asked to sit a short distance from her mother, as the crewman was tending to her. She understood the urgency and complied with the instruction.

Seated on the tiny bench, Lucy stretched out her arm and took hold of her mother's hand. When her mother grew restless, Lucy squeezed her hand. 'It's Lucy, Mum. I love you so much. I'm here, Mum, and we'll soon be at the hospital. Dad's following on.' Unsure as to whether her mother could hear her, Lucy felt absolutely helpless.

Throughout the seemingly endless journey, however, she continued talking to her mother, reassuring her.

The shock was beginning to take a grip on Lucy, who, like her dad, could not stop trembling, while her anxious gaze was fixed constantly on her mum's bloodied face.

It looked bad to Lucy. The deep gashes and bruises ran from beneath the bandages to her jaw and chin. The wider bandages and dressing over the upper part of her face and head were soaked with blood.

Lucy was relieved when her mother began to breathe more easily, although there was still the occasional shuddering breath that she seemed to hold for ever.

As they rushed through the night with sirens screaming, Lucy's mother grew increasingly agitated. Sliding back the cabin window, the ambulance man yelled to the driver to call ahead with further medical information.

Able to comfort her mother with words of love and a gentle squeeze of the hand, Lucy constantly re-assured her.

When the ambulance turned onto the highway, she caught a passing glimpse of what looked like Martin's van. It was going at speed in the opposite direction, towards her parents' house. 'Thank God!' she murmured, 'They'll take care of Dad now.'

The journey to hospital seemed endless, but soon they were turning in through the gates. 'We're at the hospital, Mum. You'll be all right now,' Lucy told her mother but there was no response.

When they arrived at the emergency department doors, Lucy quickly scrambled out of the ambulance, and the driver and attendant lifted out the stretcher with her mother still unconscious. Keeping her safe between the two of them, they hastened across the tarmac and in through the emergency entrance, where the trauma team was waiting.

Lucy followed. Her voice trembling, she glanced up to the skies and prayed, 'Please, Lord, don't let her die. Don't take her away from us.'

A world without her mother in it would be a bleak prospect indeed.

Inside the hospital, Lucy's mother was rushed away. From the corridor, as the door swung shut behind the stretcher, Lucy caught a glimpse of her mother, white as chalk, the medical staff already closing in around her.

A minute later, the ambulance crew reappeared. One of them paused to reassure Lucy, and when she asked if her mother was going to be all right, his answer was gentle, but evasive. 'I'm sure the doctor will be out to see you as soon as your mother is stabilised. I can assure you, though, she is in the best of hands.' That said, he hurried on his way.

A few minutes later, Lucy was relieved to see a nurse approaching. 'How is she?' She clambered to her feet. 'Please . . . will she be all right?'

The nurse had a gentle manner. 'Your mother is not yet conscious, but she is stabilised,' she said kindly. 'The doctors are now assessing the full extent of her injuries. Meantime, it will help us if you could explain how exactly she sustained those injuries.'

'I'm not altogether sure,' Lucy explained. 'Dad said she stumbled and hit her head on the fender. She hasn't been too steady recently. Only a short time back, she had a nasty fall in the street. It shook her confidence, and left her frail and nervous. She's been unusually quiet of late . . . not at all like her old self.' The tears she had tried so hard to keep back now ran down her face. 'Please, Nurse, she will be all right, won't she?'

'That's not for me to say. She does have serious injuries, but like I say, she is much calmer now.' The nurse was sympathetic, but she had no way of knowing the full extent of the injuries. 'We'll know what to expect after the doctors have concluded their examination. It will be some time yet, before they can talk to you, so I wonder, rather than sitting here worrying, how about I take you for a cup of tea?'

'No!' Lucy was adamant. 'Thank you, but I need to speak with the doctors.'

The nurse was patient. She had been through similar situations many times, and she knew how frantic the relatives could be while they waited for news of their loved ones. 'Please, will you come away for a few minutes? Worrying, won't help your mother. I'll let them know where we'll be, and in any case, we won't be gone too long. Just long enough for you to take a breath and talk to me about your mother.'

She pointed to the door behind Lucy. 'You're badly shaken up, and I do understand why you don't want to move from here. But just a few steps away, through that door, is a little café where we can sit and wait and it's more comfortable than here. The doctors will be a while yet, so how about the two of us go through to the café and find ourselves a pot of tea? Then you can tell me what happened to your mother after she had that first fall. It's important that the doctors know the full history.'

'I'm frightened to leave her,' Lucy murmured, wiping the tears from her face with her hands. 'I need to stay here.'

The nurse laid her hand over Lucy's. 'It's Lucy, isn't it?' She had gathered that information from the ambulance men.

'Yes.'

'Right then. I promise you there is nothing you can do just now. The doctors will be with your mother for some while yet, Lucy. They will also need to take X-rays, and that will add a few more minutes. So, like I say, we have time for a chat and that hot cuppa you look like you desperately need. Just a few minutes, then we'll come back.'

Lucy thought of her mother, hurt and in trouble,

without family near. 'Are you sure they'll know where we are if they need me?'

'You have my word.'

'They will let me see her soon, won't they?'

'That is for the doctors to decide, but I hope it won't be too long now.' The nurse hesitated. She knew how very serious the injuries were but, like Lucy, she had to wait for the doctors to conclude their assessment. Meantime, there was little more she could tell Lucy. 'Look, instead of sitting here in this draughty walkway, let's go to the café. It really is just a few steps away. When we get back, we might know more.'

'My family are on their way. They won't know where to find me!' Lucy began to panic.

'Yes they will. I'll contact the front desk, and let them know.'

Talking constantly, she led Lucy through the door and along the empty corridor. 'The café is open all night,' she informed Lucy. 'The two of us can enjoy a hot cuppa in warmer surroundings, while you tell me all about your mother.'

When Lucy made no response, except to turn and look back towards the door, the nurse drew her attention. 'I know it's difficult,' she said gently, 'but try not to worry, eh?'

Lucy merely nodded.

The corridor was long and curving, with not a soul in sight. All Lucy could see in her mind's eye was her mother, frail and broken.

Now, with the overhead lights turned low, it seemed

gloomy along the corridor, and eerily empty. The only real sound Lucy could hear echoing in her tortured mind was the impact of their heels as they walked along . . . like two soldiers on parade . . . left-right, left-right, left-right. It was a haunting rhythm like no other.

~

Just minutes away from the hospital, Martin grew increasingly anxious. 'We're nearly there.' He glanced at the old man seated beside him. 'Just a few more minutes, Dad, and you'll see her.'

Lucy's dad, though, was not aware of Martin's encouraging words. Lost in thought, he was angrily muttering to himself, 'I should've kept a closer eye on her. After that fall in town, she was really shaken up. She was unsteady on her feet, and sometimes she was lost in a little world of her own. I let her down, Martin. I should have made her go back to the doctor. But she didn't want to, and nothing I said could make her change her mind.'

'She always had a strong mind, Dad,' Martin assured him. 'If she decided not to see the doctor, wild horses would not drag her there.'

'I let her down, and that's an end to it!' the old man continued muttering to himself. 'It's my fault she's in hospital. My fault, and no one else's.'

'Granddad! It's *not* your fault.' Sam leaned forward from the back of the van. 'Nobody could have known

98

she would fall down again. You can't blame yourself, Granddad.'

'All I want is to see your grandma on the mend again,' he said.

'We all want the same.' Sam placed a comforting hand on the old man's shoulder. 'Take it easy. Like Dad says, we're only minutes away now.'

'Hey! Where's Paula?' The old man suddenly real-ised his second daughter was not in the van. 'Has nobody told her that her mother is lying in the hospital? Why isn't she here?'

'She's on her way,' Martin explained. 'I needed to get you to the hospital, so I asked Anne if she would collect Paula. They're following on . . . not far behind us, I shouldn't wonder.'

'How far is it now?' the old man asked for the umpteenth time. 'Are we nearly there?'

'It's not far now. Try not to worry,' Martin constantly reassured him.

In truth, he also was sick with worry, and not just about his parents-in-law. The prospect of Paula and Lucy face to face at the hospital made him increas-ingly nervous. For everyone's sake, and his in partic-ular, he was desperately hoping that common sense and concern about their mother would prevent Lucy and Paula from raising the issue of what had happened back at Paula's house.

He suspected that neither sister would make a scene in the current, sorry circumstances, although he had no doubt that there would be a showdown between himself and the two sisters at some point soon. He had to be sure that Paula meant it when she said she wanted them to be together permanently. He should talk to her about that, and make it a priority. If Paula really meant what she had said about their setting up house together, then he would need to tell Lucy the truth, whatever the consequences.

For now, though, he reassured himself, both Paula and Lucy would be concentrating on the wellbeing of their parents.

Reflecting on Lucy having seen them together, he blamed himself for not locking the back door. But he did not regret being with Paula. His only regret was that Lucy had discovered the truth before he could tell her that he and Paula were hoping to make a life together.

Telling Lucy of his and Paula's long-term plans was not something he looked forward to, although, to give Lucy her due, she was not a spiteful, excitable woman and would probably deal with it in her own sensible, quiet manner.

~

When they arrived at the hospital, the receptionist directed them to Lucy, who was anxiously waiting in a separate room for the doctor to arrive.

While Sam walked with his grandfather along the corridor, Martin went ahead.

Lucy was greatly relieved to see her family arrive, but when Martin stepped forward she quickly side-stepped him and went straight to her father, who looked sad and worn, and older than she could ever have imagined.

'Come and sit down, Dad.' Wrapping her arms round him, she walked him to the seat next to where she had been sitting. Sam followed and sat the other side of his grandfather.

Understanding Lucy's obvious snub, Martin sat opposite. 'What did the doctor say?' he asked Lucy. 'I expect your mum has to stay in for a while, does she? I mean, they'll need to give her a thorough checkup, especially as she's fallen twice now. Try not to worry, though. I'm sure she'll be all right.'

Lucy was shocked that he could be so natural after what she had witnessed between him and Paula. Nevertheless she acknowledged his reassurance with a curt nod of the head, before turning to her father.

'A few minutes before you arrived, the nurse went to have a word with the doctor. Hopefully, it won't be too long before he comes to give us a progress report.'

'So you don't know how she is then?'

'No, Dad. Not yet.'

'Ah, well, they do say as no news is good news . . . so if that's the case, we might be taking her home yet, eh?'

'Well, we won't know until he comes out, so don't get your hopes up. Like Martin said, they should keep her in and check her thoroughly. I mean, she hasn't been at all well lately, has she?'

'No.' The old man's face crumpled in disappointment. 'Lucy! Did you tell them about her fall some weeks back, when she was in town . . . how she's never been the same since then? Did you tell them that she refused to see a doctor?'

'Yes, Dad, I told the nurse everything.'

'And did she say whether or not your mother would have to stay in . . . or can we take her home with us? I'll look after your mother. I'll make her a bed in the sitting room; then she won't have any reason to go up and down the stairs, because I'll take care of everything.'

'No, Dad.' Lucy could see how upset he was becoming. 'From what the nurse was saying, Mum's injuries are very serious. I think they're too concerned about Mum to let her be looked after by you just yet. But, don't you worry, I'll come and stay with you at home while she's in here, then after she comes home I'll stay a while longer, help her to settle in . . . make sure neither of you overdoes it.' She smiled lovingly. 'We don't want you wearing yourself out, do we, eh? Not when you've got me to help you. And don't concern yourself about my work, because they'll understand when I explain to them.'

In the light of her mother's bad fall, and what she had discovered about Paula and Martin, keeping her employers happy was not Lucy's top priority.

Right now, like this darling old fella, she just wanted her mum to be all right.

She glanced around. 'Where's Anne?'

'It's all right, Mum.' Sam could see the strain on his mother's face. 'Anne and Paula are on their way.'

'That's good.' She hoped Paula would have the decency to keep a distance between them.

Five long, anxious minutes passed before the nurse returned. 'The doctor is on his way,' she informed them kindly.

The words had hardly left her lips when the doctor entered the room. 'Doctor . . . oh, thank goodness!' The old man sat up straight. 'How is she? Has she been asking after me? Can I see her?'

The look on the doctor's face set Lucy's hopes plummeting, but his next words broke her heart. 'I'm so sorry.' His voice and manner said it all.

With much compassion he explained quietly to Lucy's father, 'Your wife suffered serious head injuries.' When he paused, they suspected the outcome even before he said it. 'We were not able to save her. I am so very sorry.'

In the wake of the full, devastating truth of his announcement, the silence was palpable; apart from a thin, broken wail of disbelief from the old man. Suddenly, he was shaking uncontrollably, his voice breaking as he called out 'I need to see her!'

Tears of grief flowed down his face as he stared at the doctor in disbelief. His voice fell to a whisper, as though he was trying to reason with himself. 'She was all right. She just fell . . . that's all.' Struggling to stand, he stumbled back into the chair, his voice shaking with anger as he demanded of the doctor, 'Why couldn't you help her? You could have done something. . . . you *should* have done something!'

Sam came over to his grandfather and wrapped his arms round his leathery old neck. 'Oh, Granddad, what will we do now? What will we do without Grandma?' His sobs were terrible to hear.

This was his first experience of grief, and it was too much for him to cope with. Being the only grandson, he had always been close to his devoted grandparents.

Shocked to her roots, Lucy bowed her head and quietly sobbed; a great wave of loneliness consumed her. Her darling mum was gone. How could that be? Her caring, loving mum . . . was gone. It was too hard, too soon, and her tortured mind refused to accept it.

She looked up and saw her father, bent and desolate, and her son, holding the old man, both of them broken by the unbelievable loss. Her father needed her, and Sam, her son. They both needed her, and she must be strong for them. Her own grief would have to wait. She was needed. She must try and be strong for the family. Oh, but how would she cope?

'Why could you not save her?' Martin was asking the doctor.

'I'm afraid her injuries were many,' the doctor explained. 'The broken wrist and collarbone we could of course deal with, but she must have fallen heavily . . . awkwardly. She had suffered severe brain damage. I'm truly sorry . . . we did everything we could. But it was never going to be enough.'

Having just entered the room, Paula and Anne heard everything. Anne ran to Lucy, who held her daughter fast. Paula stood silent at the door, unable to believe what had happened.

Sam held on to his granddad, the two of them drawing comfort from each other.

The old man came from a time when a man might hide his grief, but all he could think of was the impossible: that his beloved wife was gone for ever. And in his unbearable grief he clung to his grandson and sobbed like a child.

Lucy came to sit beside him. 'Dad . . .' her soft, loving tone was greatly soothing, '. . . do you want to see Mum?'

When he looked up, there was a world of pain in his face. 'Lucy?' He choked back a sob. '*You* know, don't you?'

'What do I know?' she asked.

'Your mum – you know she was my life . . . my beautiful girl. The only one I ever loved.'

Like everyone else, Lucy could not hold back the tears. 'I do know that, Dad,' she whispered, 'and I know what you must be feeling right now. Mum was a huge part of all our lives and we will miss her terribly. We will always be there for you, Dad, and I promise to look after you. I'm the elder so it's my place, and Mum would not want you to be on your own. Now, though, is not the time to talk about such matters. For the moment, we need to say our goodbyes.' She held out her hand.

Reaching out, the old man laid his hand over hers and squeezed it tight. 'You're a good girl, Lucy. You and your sister . . . good girls. But just now, I need my Susie. Tell them, Lucy. I have to see her.' His voice broke with emotion. 'Please, Lucy, I want to be with her. I have to tell her how sorry I am, and how very much I love her . . . always have, always will. She needs to know that, Lucy . . .' His voice broke, shivering in a sob. 'I need to see her.'

'Are you sure, Dad?' Lucy was worried that such an ordeal might be too much for him.

The old man was adamant. 'I'm sure.'

Lucy looked up at the doctor. 'Is it all right? Can we see her?'

'Yes, of course, but could you give us a few minutes?' The doctor was used to family reaction after losing a loved one, but the old man's sorrow in particular cut him deep. His training, however, dictated that he must not show his feelings.

'Thank you, Doctor.' Lucy understood. She believed her father might also welcome a few minutes to prepare himself for the ordeal ahead of him.

Her mother had been his constant companion for many years, as dear to him as was his own life. She was his beautiful wife, his sweetheart, his friend and lover. And the caring mother of his two daughters.

Lucy knew how very close they had been, something few people ever encounter in a lifetime; herself included.

Having to say goodbye for ever to this remarkable woman was too cruel. Too final.

At that moment, the doctor turned to the nurse and gave a discreet nod.

'Right away, Doctor.' She fully understood, and hurried away.

~

Paula, Anne and Martin decided they would rather not go in just now, but would pay their respects later.

Sam, though, was undecided, until Lucy assured him, 'You'll have a chance later to say your goodbyes, but if you really want to see your grandma now, I won't try and dissuade you. The thing is, my darling, you've had a huge shock to deal with – we all have. It might be wiser to say your goodbyes later, when we'll all be there alongside you.'

Paula and Anne made no comment, but Martin and Sam's granddad agreed with Lucy. So, having been persuaded, Sam returned to sit beside his father, his sorry gaze fixed on Lucy and Granddad, as they walked out the door and down the corridor behind the nurse.

With a breaking heart, Lucy offered her arm to take the weight of her father. As he leaned against her, he seemed to grow smaller and sadder with every reluctant step.

While they were gone, Martin went outside to smoke a cigarette. When Paula came to join him, he felt greatly comforted.

'Where in God's name does Lucy get her strength from?' he asked.

Paula shook her head. 'I honestly don't know. You can see how devastated she is at losing Mum – as we all are – but whenever there's a need for someone to take the lead and be strong, she's there. She seems to know what has to be done, and she steps forward without hesitation.'

Martin was curious. 'Was she always like that, as a girl, I mean?'

'Yes, always. At least as far back as I can remember.'

There was a short span of silence while they thought of Lucy, and what they had done to her.

'Paula,' Martin glanced back, lowering his voice so as not to be overheard, 'are we wicked, you and me, planning a life together, when this awful business will surely cripple her? I mean, she actually saw us together, yet so far she hasn't said a word about it. It's like it never happened.'

'That's Lucy for you. Like I say, she's strong. She takes the blows, and deals with it in her own way.'

'I never meant to hurt her.'

'Well, it's too late for that, because we *have* hurt her . . . badly.'

For a fleeting moment, Martin felt truly sorry that Lucy had seen them. 'Honestly, Paula, I feel like a right swine. What with her losing your mother and all that, she must be feeling like her whole life is falling apart.'

'So . . . are you finishing with me?' She grew angry. 'Have you changed your mind? Because I haven't.'

'No! I am not "finishing with you".'

'Good! Because losing our mum has knocked me back as well, but I still love you. Lucy or no Lucy, we both know we belong together.'

Just then, Sam wandered out. 'Dad, I think maybe I should have gone in to say my goodbyes to Grandma.'

'No, son,' Martin reassured him, 'your mum was

right. We can all say our goodbyes later, when we're more able to accept what's happened.' He slid his arm round Sam's shoulders. 'It's tough, I know, but I promise we'll get through it.'

He glanced at Paula, and his heart lifted. He knew she was right. However much it might hurt Lucy, and whatever price he was made to pay, it was Paula he really wanted.

The three of them made their way back inside, just as Lucy and her father returned.

Lucy's father looked ashen; his eyes red raw where he had constantly wiped away the tears. He appeared to have shrunk, seeming more like a small child than a grown man. As before, he leaned heavily on Lucy, constantly looking up at her, as though making sure she was still there.

Lucy spoke not a word. She gave the impression that she was coping, but those who knew her well realised that she was holding her grief back, remaining strong for everyone else.

Lost in thoughts of the much-loved lady left behind, Lucy and the family left to embark on their sorry journey home.

Having eased her father safely into the van, Lucy remained a moment to look back at the hospital building. 'Love you, Mum,' she whispered. 'God bless.' When the tears began to burn, she blinked them back. 'All right, are you, Dad?'

'Lucy?'

'Yes, Dad?'

'Will you stay with me tonight? I don't want to be on my own.'

'Of course I will, Dad. Or if you'd rather, you can come and stay with me at my house.'

The old man was adamant. 'No. I need to be at home.'

'That's all right, Dad. I'd best get Martin to pack me a few things, and bring them over.'

As she walked across the car park to speak with Martin, who was comforting Anne, the old man turned to look at her, a loving smile on his face. 'Aw, Lucy girl, you're just like your darling mum,' he murmured. 'It's true, your sister was always the pretty one who drew everyone's eye. Your beauty, though, was always on the inside. Our kind and loving Lucy. Nothing is ever too much trouble for you.'

His sorry gaze wandered back to the building where the love of his life lay. 'My darling Susie,' he whispered, 'why did you have to leave me, just when I need you most?' Closing his eyes, he felt desolate, remembering how it was with her in his life. 'You and me, we still had so much life to live. It was always the two of us, and now it's just me, on my own.'

He caught a glimpse of how lonely he would be from now on. It won't matter how many people gather round me, he thought, because without you, I'll still be on my own. If that's how my life is to be from now on, there will seem no purpose to it.

On seeing Lucy approach, he forced a little smile. Inside, though, his sad old heart was in pieces.

'I'm sorry if it took too long,' Lucy said, 'but I was

worried about Anne. She's been too quiet by far.'

'I know.' He had a soft spot for his granddaughter. 'She never does have much to say, but I expect she's in shock, as we all are.'

'Anne has always been very deep, that's the trouble.' Lucy vowed to keep a wary eye on her daughter. 'She's never been one for sharing her feelings.'

'She's a lot like you in that way.' Lucy's father had always worried about his elder daughter. 'Since you were a little girl, you've always been the quiet one. Always believing you can carry the world on your shoulders, but you can't, sweetheart. Nobody can. Everyone needs someone alongside them through life, like me and your mum. Always looking out for each other. That's why I'm glad you've got your Martin.'

As he continued to praise her husband it was just as well he did not see the sorry look on Lucy's face.

~

Martin drove Lucy and her father back to Addison Street, then he and Sam went on home. Martin promised to return with an overnight bag for Lucy. She set about making her father comfortable in the sitting room. 'I'll make us a hot drink,' she told him. 'Do you need anything else, Dad?'

'No thanks, love.' He felt so empty and desperately sad.

He glanced across at his wedding photo, standing proud on the dresser. 'I remember the day me and your mum got wed,' he reminisced. 'It's like only yester-day. She looked so beautiful. She was my princess, and I was the proudest man on earth. I can't believe that she will never again walk through that door to lighten my life.' In all his considerable years, even with his favourite daughter there beside him, he had never felt so desolate that he could barely breathe. Choking back the sorrow, he covered his face briefly with his hands.

'Never mind the tea,' he suggested, 'you get off. Go to bed, Lucy, love.' He saw how worn she was. 'It's getting late, and you look done in.'

'It's not that late, Dad.' I'll make you a mug of cocoa, and sit with you for a while. Besides, the cocoa might help you sleep.'

'Go on then. And remember to put two spoons of sugar in.'

Lucy chided him, 'Considering the many times I've made your cocoa over the years, how would I forget?'

The old man seemed not to have heard. Without even glancing up, he told Lucy, 'When you've done that, you'd best get to bed, and no argument!'

He was well aware of how hard Lucy pushed herself and, for his part, he needed a quiet time to think; to reflect on what had happened, and to try to make sense of it all. Even now, he still imagined his wife might walk through the door at any minute, and that her terrible accident, the hospital, and the doctor telling them the shocking news would all turn out to be some cruel, twisted nightmare.

'I'm not going to bed until I see you settled.' Lucy

feared going to sleep, because when she woke up, all the bad things would still be there. The nightmare of Martin and her sister, naked in bed. The nightmare of her mother being taken from them. And that dear old man, hurting and bewildered, without his beloved wife.

Her dad said she looked 'done in', yet she did not feel tired. She felt a multitude of emotions, but not tiredness.

She felt drained, until there seemed nothing left of her. She felt strange inside; somehow alienated from normality. More than anything else, she felt lost.

This homely little house where she had grown up had been her life for so many years. Everything was reassuringly familiar. Her mother was here, in every corner, and in the very fabric of those strong, familiar walls.

She wanted her mum to be here now, alive and smiling; and proudly wearing the bright red slippers that Dad bought for her. It didn't matter that they were two sizes too big for her, and made a clapping sound when she walked.

When the wave of grief threatened to swallow her, Lucy hurried to the kitchen and made her father's bedtime drink. As always he was trying to put a brave face on everything, but this time the loss of his wife had taken the strength and purpose right out of him.

Some half-hour later, she and her father had drunk a measure of their cocoa, before they each rejected it.

'It's hard to make it go down,' the old man said. 'I'm sorry, love. I've had enough.'

'Are you ready to go up yet, Dad?'

He shook his head. 'Not really, no.'

'Please, Dad . . . you can't sit down here all night. You need to try to get some sleep.' She stopped short of reminding him what tomorrow would bring. Truth was, she hardly dared think about it herself.

'Not yet, Lucy.' His gaze was constantly drawn to the photo of his and Susie's wedding day.

'I'll stay up with you then.' It was obvious that her father was not in a hurry to climb the stairs; not without his wife alongside him. Instead, he remained slumped in the old armchair, which after too many years of bearing his weight had taken on the shape of its grateful occupant.

So, she sat with him now, each of them thinking of that very special woman who had been a huge presence in both their lives.

When the doorbell rang, Lucy was startled. 'Oh! That must be Martin, bringing my overnight bag.' She clambered out of her chair and hurried to the door.

A moment later, Martin followed her back into the sitting room. 'I've just brought Lucy's stuff,' he explained to the old man.

The truth was, he didn't know what else to say in the circumstances, except to offer the old man the same hospitality that Lucy had offered previously. 'You do know you're very welcome to stay with us . . .' he hesitated, '. . . I mean . . . until after . . .' Growing uncomfortable, he fell silent.

'No, thanks all the same, Martin. I'm grateful, but

I'd rather be here, in my own home, if that's all right with you and Lucy.'

'Of course it is,' Lucy reassured him, 'and like I said before, I'll stay with you for as long as you want me.'

He smiled. 'Thank you . . . both of you.'

He had a request. 'Just now, Martin, I suspect you were about to mention the church . . . and the business of laying my Susie to her rest.' He paused, taking a long, deep breath. 'I wonder, Martin, would you be kind enough to oversee all the arrangements?' Dropping his gaze, he choked back the tears and could not go on.

Martin did not hesitate. 'Of course, Dad. Don't worry, I'll see to it.' He would much rather not have overseen such a sad event, but he hoped it might compensate somehow for what he had done to Lucy.

Just then the mantel-clock struck ten. 'By, it's not that time yet, is it?' the old man was surprised at how quickly time passed.

Feeling uncomfortable in the circumstances, Martin was anxious to leave but he did not blame Lucy. He knew she was deliberately avoiding him. Even so, it would be better that they discussed it like adults as soon as possible at some more suitable moment because, whatever happened, he still wanted to be with Paula, and she with him. And the sooner the better.

'I'd best get back,' he told Lucy and her father. 'I've left Sam with Anne, but she'll be wanting to get home to Les and little Luke. I think Sam might want to go with her. I've decided I won't go in to work tomorrow. Thankfully, it's not that urgent a job. So if either of you need me, I'm only at the end of the phone.'

He gave his father-in-law an awkward, manly hug. 'Take care of yourself, Dad.'

Lucy saw him to the door, but as he stepped onto the pavement, he lingered a moment. 'Lucy, you didn't say anything to your dad . . . did you?'

Lucy was shocked. 'What kind of person do you take me for?' Her voice dropped to a harsh whisper. 'Where's your sense of decency? My mother has just died and you really think I would burden my father with the truth of what you and my sister have been up to?' She could not even bring herself to say Paula's name.

'I'm sorry, I should have realised.'

Afraid her father might wander out to see where she was, Lucy stepped back to close the door. 'Good night,' she said curtly. In return he merely nodded and hurried away.

She heard his foosteps carrying him away from her, and her heart shrank. She had been so content in her marriage, and now it was all ruined.

Something deep inside urged her to forgive him, but then there was this other, darker side, that could not forgive either of them. Not ever!

She felt close to tears, but for her father's sake, she must hide her feelings. She had two options. She could fight to keep Martin. Or she could simply let him go, and start a new life without him.

Neither way appealed to her. But for now she did not have the heart or the stamina even to think about it.

At some point it might be necessary to inform the

children what their father had done. That prospect, though, was too awful to contemplate.

'So, we'll see Anne and Sam tomorrow then, Dad?' Again, she could not even speak her sister's name.

'That's good. But what about Paula? She's coming as well, isn't she?'

'I expect so.'

The old man fell silent for a moment, before his thoughts returned to the dark shadow hanging over them. 'It's good of Martin to take on the business of . . .' his voice tailed off.

Lucy went to him and held him for a moment. There was no need for words.

Safe in his daughter's arms, the old man whispered, 'I would not want anyone else but Martin to see to all of that. After all, he is a son in all but name. I'm thankful I don't have to worry about you, though, Lucy. I know Martin will look after you. You've got a good man there.'

Lucy made no comment. It was true that both her parents were disappointed when they learned of her childhood pregnancy. But they soon forgave that, and learned to accept Martin, and even grow fond of him.

'Yes, Dad.' Lucy acknowledged his comment, while hoping her father would never know of Martin and Paula's shocking indiscretion. There seemed no way it might be overlooked, however, and that would be yet another crippling blow to her loving old dad.

A short time later, after she had returned the cups to the kitchen, Lucy was relieved to see her father was becoming drowsy.

'Come on, Dad, I think it's time you got some sleep.'
When she helped him gently out of the chair, he did
not protest. 'It's time you were up them stairs and in
your bed.'

As she helped him up to his room, he gave no
resistance. But when she went to the drawer to find
his pyjamas, he became agitated.

'I'm quite capable of getting myself into bed, thank
you very much! You get off to your room, and I'll sort
myself out, same as I've done these many years.'

Just now, when Lucy was rummaging in the drawer,
he could see her mother in her. Same caring attitude.
Same warm smile.

'You *will* get into bed, though, won't you, Dad?'
Lucy needed reassurance.

'Course I will. Now leave me be, there's a good
girl.'

'Can I use your telephone, Dad?' She just remembered. 'I need to call Kathleen and see if she can
explain to my boss. Is that all right?' Martin had organised the installation of the big black telephone after
her mother's health started to fail.

'Course it is. You've no need to ask.'

'Thanks, Dad. It'll only take a minute. Try and get
some sleep now.'

'I will . . . once you decide to leave me be!' To leave
him be so he could be with his wife; to talk with her,
and hold her safe in his heart. But as for getting into
bed without her there, he just could not do it.

Lucy kissed him good night. As she left, she recalled

his words just now. Here she was, a woman touching forty, and yet her old dad still called her a 'girl'.

She liked that. It put a kind of sad, whimsical smile on her face.

As she went out the door, she was about to close it when he called out, 'Leave the door open.'

Suspecting he might want to call her in the night, she left the door ajar.

Downstairs in the hallway, she collected her handbag from the peg. Zipping it open, she drew out a small notebook, flicked through the pages and found Kathleen's number.

She dialled, a moment passed, and then, 'Hello? Kathleen Riley here.'

After the worst day imaginable, it was good to hear Kathleen's voice.

'Kathleen! It's me, Lucy.'

'Oh, Lucy! I was just about to get in the bath. You do pick your moments, don't you?' she quipped. 'So, what's wrong?'

Lucy told her everything: about her mother being rushed to hospital, and the dreadful outcome that no one had expected. 'So, I'm staying here with my dad. He's taking it really badly. We're all still in shock.'

'I'm so sorry, Lucy. Me and my big mouth!' She felt ashamed.

'You weren't to know. Honestly, Kathleen, it's so hard to believe.'

Kathleen understood. 'Oh, Lucy, you must be devastated. I knew your mum had been unwell, but I didn't realise. I'm sorry . . . is there anything I can do? If you want me to come over, I'll be there quick as I can, and I'll stay as long as you want me.'

'No, Kathleen, thanks all the same. I appreciate your offer, but I do need a favour.'

'Of course!' Kathleen was keen to make amends. 'Consider it done.'

'Well . . . I just wondered if you might please tell the boss what's happened.'

'I will, yes. That goes without saying.'

Lucy thanked her again. 'Could you please tell her I won't be in tomorrow, and maybe not for a few days yet? I need to keep an eye on Dad. He's being brave for our sakes, but he's broken up. I won't leave him, Kathleen.'

'Nor should you!' Kathleen vehemently assured her. 'I'll explain everything to the boss, so now, you stop worrying. Lord only knows, you've got enough to be dealing with.'

'You're the best friend, Kathleen. I knew I could count on you, and if the boss decides to let me go, then so be it.'

'She won't let you go. She might be difficult, but she's not stupid. She'll understand. And don't forget, I'm here if you need me . . . even if it's the middle of the night.'

'I'll call you tomorrow, Kathleen. For now, though, I have to keep a wary eye on Dad. He's absolutely devastated.'

'Is Martin with you?'

'No, he's at home. Anne's gone home and she's keeping an eye on Sam. I'm worried about Anne, too, Kathleen. She's hardly said a word since it happened.'

'Oh dear, that's not good, but it is to be expected, I suppose. In this kind of situation, people tend to deal with it in different ways.'

'Anne and Sam are coming to be with me and their granddad in the morning. She and Sam are close, so hopefully, she'll talk to him about her feelings.'

'So Martin is on his own tonight, is he?'

'As far as I know. I think he encouraged Sam to stay with Anne for the night.'

'Well, that's not surprising, is it? I mean, a sister will give lots of cuddles, while a father might not. If they need Martin, he's only a few streets away.' She added again, 'And if you need me, I'll be there for you.'

'I know.' Lucy lowered her voice to a whisper. 'Dad asked Martin if he would oversee the business of . . . the church . . . and . . .' her voice broke, '. . . sorry. I can't seem to get it through my head that Mum's gone.'

'Hey! I understand.' Kathleen's warm, loving voice lifted Lucy's spirits.

Lucy could hear Kathleen talking to her, but her mind was drifting back to Paula and Martin. She desperately wanted to confide in Kathleen. But after the enormity of what had happened today, it was all too much to cope with.

'We'll talk tomorrow,' she promised.

'Call me, Lucy, at any time, day or night,' Kathleen reminded her.

Lucy appreciated her offer. In truth, Kathleen was the only real friend she had.

'Goodnight then, Lucy . . . love you lots. And you will call if you need me, won't you?'

'Yes.'

'Do you promise?'

Lucy promised.

With the conversation over, Lucy returned the receiver to its cradle and hurried back along the hallway to the front room, to collect the overnight bag Martin had brought over for her.

Making sure all the curtains were drawn, she then went through to the kitchen and into the bathroom at the back of the house, where she cleaned her teeth and washed herself in lukewarm water. She would have appreciated a hot bath, but was far too tired to bother.

Feeling bone-tired, she went softly up the stairs, skilfully avoiding the creak on that middle step, then made a quick tiptoe along the landing to satisfy herself that her father had got into bed as promised.

He was fast asleep. She bent to place a kiss on his forehead. 'Good night, God bless, Dad.' She drew the blanket over his shoulders, not altogether surprised when she saw he was still wearing his shirt, which was buttoned to the neck.

Very gently, she undid the top four buttons, and after making sure he was well covered and as comfortable as could be expected, she went softly out of the room, again leaving the door ajar.

Standing by the door, she lingered a moment to look

back at him, safe and warm in his bed. She told herself that while he was asleep, his pain was not so crippling.

Now that she was alone in this quiet little house, Lucy realised with a shock that this was the very first time in her entire life that she was here but her mother was not with her.

Even more unsettling, her dear mother would not be with her for the remainder of her life, however long that might be. She would never hear her voice again, nor see her smile. Her mother would never again chastise her, or wink at her like she used to when pleased about some small thing, like when her cake had risen well, or she had managed to replace a light bulb all by herself, by standing on the kitchen chair.

That was all gone, and Lucy knew that life would be bleaker now.

Her dad was still here, though, and Lucy vowed to keep him safe.

Before the grief took a hold of her again, she hurried to her own bedroom, leaving the door slightly ajar, in case her dad might call out in the night.

This pretty little room was reassuringly familiar. Large enough for two single beds, it still contained the old wooden dressing table under the window, with the same heart-shaped scratching that she traced with a nail many years ago. Next to the heart was another scratching, made by Paula. It was the head of a horse, with crossed eyes and a jolly little turban round its ears.

When Lucy now delicately traced the images with her finger, it took her back to a time when she had looked up to her younger sister. She thought she was the luckiest girl in the world to have been blessed with Paula as a sister, so pretty and talented.

Sickened, she turned away to look at the rest of the room.

There was the same wooden wardrobe against the back wall, and the same paper on the walls, but though the wallpaper was exactly the same pink-and-cream striped pattern, this was new paper, pasted on just two years ago, after Mum said the original had to come down before it fell down of its own accord.

This comfortable little room brought back many memories for Lucy, and all of them good.

In this very room she and Paula had shared their dreams and fears. Here they had lived their childhood and, when it was time to fly the nest, each was nervous and unsure; especially Lucy, who because of one weak moment as a schoolgirl, was carrying a child of her own.

Back then, even when Lucy's few friends abandoned her, Paula had stood firm beside her.

Thinking of Paula now, Lucy found it unbelievable that she had sunk so low as to sleep with Martin. But then, Martin was every bit as guilty.

'I'm glad that our mum never got to learn what the two of you have been up to. I swear, hell will freeze over before I forgive either of you!' Lucy vowed.

Deliberately thrusting them out of her mind, she set about unpacking her overnight bag, all the while keeping her ear cocked for the slightest sound from her father's room, just a few steps away. She made herself ready for bed and was grateful to slide between the beautifully white sheets, meticulously washed and starched by her mother's hand. 'You must always keep your house ready for visitors!' she would tell her girls. 'You never know when folks might turn up.'

In spite of feeling incredibly weary, Lucy found it difficult to sleep.

Downstairs the clock struck eleven; then, all too soon, it was midnight and she was still wide awake. Now her father was coughing and muttering, shattering the silence of the small hours.

Lucy grew concerned.

Climbing out of bed, she went on tiptoe to peer through his bedroom door.

Relieved to find that he appeared to be sleeping, she returned to her own bed, all the while listening in case her father woke, but it seemed that he must now be fast asleep.

Still Lucy's troubled mind would not let her sleep.

Her thoughts were alive with memories of her mother and the stark images of her lying, so tiny, in that tall, narrow bed in a white-painted room, lost in the odour of medicines and acrid disinfectant.

Finally, Lucy succumbed to a troubled sleep.

In her haunting dreams, she was still in that room, with her mother, who was smiling at her. 'It's all right, Lucy, my darling . . .' Her gentle, reassuring voice was right there in the bedroom with Lucy.

Then she was no more, and Lucy was left alone, though cradled with such incredible love that she could hardly breathe.

Having woken with a start, she sat up, confused by what she had felt to be so real, but did not understand. Presently, she thrust the dream from her mind, and lay down to sleep again.

While Lucy slept, her father lay awake in his bed, his face turned towards the window. Something had woken him, but he did not know what. His first thought was for his daughter. 'Lucy!' He instinctively called her name.

Quickly now, he scrambled out of bed and, slipping his feet into his frayed old slippers, he shuffled his way to Lucy's bedroom.

'Lucy?' He peered in through the door, but she gave no answer. 'Lucy?' Softly, he went closer and, just then, she turned her head slightly.

Relieved, he nodded his grey head. 'Nightmares!' he muttered. 'Poor girl, she always was prone to having nightmares.'

He made his way downstairs. In the sitting room he stood by his and Susan's wedding photo.

'I can't believe you've left me,' he said tearfully. 'You should never have left me. You and me, we're like day and night . . . we belong together. There are special things that were meant to be together: you and me, black and white, good and bad. Sunshine and rain. Me and my Susie. How can one be, without the other?'

In the whole of his life, he had never felt such pain.

Gently he cradled the picture frame in his hands. Carrying it across the room, he went to his faithful old armchair, where he sat his weary body down.

Gazing down on his wife of so many long years, his

old heart was broken. 'I need you.' He smiled on her face. 'I love you so much . . .' Over and over he professed his undying love for her.

After a while he grew silent. The pain began to ease, and his tears were stilled.

As he closed his eyes to sleep, his grip on the picture frame tightened, as though he would never let it go.

'My lovely Susie . . .' Even in his sleep, he called her name.

~

Upstairs, Lucy woke with a start. 'Dad!' Momentarily disorientated, she scrambled out of bed and across the room, she ran down the landing and into his bedroom. She was shocked to find his bed empty, with no sign of her father. 'Dad!'

No answer.

Thinking he must have gone to the bathroom, she ran down the stairs two steps at a time. 'Dad!' she continued to call, but still there was no answer.

She was making straight for the bathroom when she realised the light was on in the sitting room. And yes, there he was, in his favourite armchair. Taking a huge breath, she calmed herself, while chiding him gently.

'Why didn't you wake me? Honestly, you gave me such a fright.'

Going to the fireplace, she collected the poker from the hearth and prodded the dying embers. 'It needs more coal, but it's not worth putting any on now.' She meant to get him back to bed as soon as possible. 'I'll make us a cup of tea . . . warm you up, eh?'

She went across the hallway to the kitchen, calling to him as she went, 'If you want to make your way back to bed, Dad, I'll fetch your tea up.'

Crossing to the sink, she filled the kettle with fresh water, then she lit the gas hob and placed the kettle to boil. She collected the teapot and two cups from the cupboard, all the while calling back to him, 'If you'd woken me, I would have brought the drink to your room.' She shivered. 'It's freezing cold down here!'

When the kettle began whistling, she scooped the tea into the pot and filled it two-thirds of the way up. Having made the tea, she set the tray and carried it through to the sitting room, where she fleetingly glanced at her father hunched in the chair. 'See! You've got cold now, haven't you? Honestly, Dad, you should have called me.'

Tutting, she set the tray on the side-table. 'I'll go get your dressing gown while the tea settles. I'll only be a minute!'

Noticing the wedding photo clutched in his two hands, she asked him tenderly, 'Dad, would you like me to put the photo back for you?'

Making her way across the room, she told him lovingly, 'Look, Dad, I've made us a hot drink. Let me put the photo back, eh?'

As she reached for the photo frame, it slid out of his hands and slithered to the carpet. 'It's all right,' she assured him, 'it's not broken.' Having collected it from the carpet, she held it up to show him. 'There you are . . . not even a scratch . . .' Her heart lurched. Something was wrong. 'Dad?' Suddenly disturbed, she looked closely at him, and her blood ran cold. 'Dad?'

She began shaking him, gently at first, then harder, and all the while her brain was telling her what she refused to believe. Then her screams echoed through the house. 'No! Oh, dear Lord, no! Please . . . NO!'

Sobbing helplessly, she wound her arms about his neck and drew him to her. She rocked him back and forth, his head against her shoulder and her cries were pitiful to hear. 'Wake up, Dad,' she implored him. 'I can't lose you as well. Dad . . . please, wake up. Wake up! . . . Please, Dad . . .' Then she stopped calling for him to respond and instead, she held him tighter, her face pressed to his still-warm face, and sobbed as though she would never stop.

She whispered of her love for him and her mother, stroking his cheek, and praying that, even now, he might open his eyes and smile at her in that crooked, comical way she knew and loved.

When the finality of losing both her parents hit home, the pain was overwhelming.

Bereft and alone, she whispered to her father over and over, telling him how she would make sure her children never forgot him.

Pressing him to her, she continued to rock him like a child in arms, her tears dampening his cheeks, making them shine. 'You and Mum are together now,' she sobbed. 'I know you'll be watching over us. Oh, but I shall miss you both so very much . . . more than you could ever imagine.'

Since discovering the truth about Martin and her sister, Lucy had fought hard to keep things together. She felt a desperate need to protect the family from learning the truth – Anne and Sam in particular.

Shattered by the deception of her husband and sister, she was now made utterly desolate at the loss of both her parents. There seemed nowhere to turn.

For what seemed an age, she sat quietly holding her father's hand, just as he had held hers as a child.

In the depths of her pain, Lucy decided that somewhere, at sometime in her life, she must have been bad, and these terrible events were her punishment.

As slowly, and ever so gently, the new day peeped shyly into the room, physically and emotionally exhausted, Lucy tenderly eased her father back into the chair.

She gazed on him for a moment, before leaning forward to kiss his wrinkled forehead. Cradling his dear, familiar face, she could imagine his smile and the twinkle in his eye, and she could not hold back her tears.

'Good night, God bless, Dad. I do love you so. I always will.'

One last hug, before she made him safe.

Her father was gone now. Gone to be with his Susie, the love of his life.

CHAPTER SIX

THE CHURCH WAS filled to capacity with both close family and distant family members. There were also many friends, young and old.

April was gone, but a chilly breeze lingered through to early May, but that did not deter the mourners. The neighbours, too, had turned out in their numbers to pay respects to the well-known and kindly regarded couple.

Lucy, being the eldest, had been asked to choose her parents' favourite hymns, which she did with much thought and care.

She had wondered whether she should ask Paula to help choose, but after much agonising she decided it would not be proper in the light of what Paula had done. Once she had chosen what she believed her parents would have wanted, however, she felt obliged to run that final choice past the immediate family, Martin and Paula included. Lucy's choice was well received by all.

Now, after the prayers were said and the hymns sung, the priest offered his blessings and then more prayers followed.

After the service, everyone shuffled out. Some bent their heads in respect; some discreetly dabbed at their faces to wipe away tears, while others left their tears to flow.

Outside in the graveyard, this much-loved couple were laid to rest. Together again.

The priest offered the final prayer, which was followed by a long moment of silence, after which everyone made their way down the path and out through the churchyard gates.

The family, however, lingered to speak with the priest, to thank him for everything.

Lucy told him the service was very beautiful; although she would have given anything for her parents' deaths never to have happened.

Father Patrick assured the family, 'I know how very hard it must be to lose both your parents within such a short time of each other, but in my experience, it is not uncommon for the one left behind to pine for their loved one, and then to quickly follow him or her.'

When Lucy nodded, he smiled on her. 'The hymns you chose were very beautiful, Lucy,' he said. Then he wished the family well, and bade them goodbye.

As Lucy turned and hurried down the path towards the gate, Paula caught up with her.

'Lucy, we need to talk . . . about what you saw . . .'

Lucy quickened her pace. 'I don't think so,' she said

quietly. 'This is not the time or place to be discussing such a thing. Moreover, I do not want to hear anything you have to say. Not today . . . not here. Not ever.'

Quickening her steps, she went through the gate and caught up with her children.

Seeing that Anne was still weeping, she slid her arm about her. 'Do you want to come home with me, Anne?' She had been quietly concerned about her daughter since her grandparents' deaths.

Anne leaned into her mother's open arms. 'No thanks, Mum. Like Les told you when he rang this morning, the neighbour was not available to baby-sit, so he took a few hours off work, and now I expect he needs to get back. Oh, Mum . . . why did they have to leave us?' The tears began to flow. 'Why both of them? I don't understand.'

'It's not for us to "understand", sweetheart.' Lucy, however, knew exactly what she meant, for hadn't she been asking herself the very same questions?

'Les so wanted to come to the service,' Anne went on, 'but only one of us could come, and he thought it best if I was here. He didn't want to bring Luke, and he was right, wasn't he?'

'Yes, I think so. Look, sweetheart, I'll come over and see you later, shall I? We can have a heart to heart.' Lucy was relieved to see that Anne had dried her tears and was now bravely facing the loss of her grandparents. When Anne was slow to answer, she asked again, 'So, what do you think? Shall I come over?'

'Maybe this afternoon. But ring first.'

'Whichever is fine by me, sweetheart.' Lucy had been asked if she might go back to work in the afternoon, but just now that was the last thing on her mind. 'Where's Sam?' Lucy looked about, but she couldn't see him.

'He's over there . . . with Dad.' Anne knew something that Lucy did not, but because Sam had confided in her, Anne believed it was not her place to reveal details of his intentions.

'Oh, that's all right.' Lucy left them to it.

'Mum.' Slowing her pace, Anne touched her mother on the arm. 'Is there anything wrong?'

'What do you mean?'

'Well . . . it's just . . . I mean, is there anything wrong between you and Dad?'

Lucy was taken aback. 'What makes you ask that?'

'Because you hardly glanced at him in church, and when we came out, you seemed to be avoiding him . . . as though you're angry with him, or something.'

'Oh, I expect my mind was elsewhere, that's all.' Which was not a lie.

'So, you haven't had a fight then?'

'Not to speak of, no.'

'Oh, well, that's all right then.'

Sensing that Anne had not believed her, Lucy felt guilty. 'Your dad and Sam seem to be in deep conversation, don't you think?' She had to convince herself that Martin would never reveal the sordid business between himself and Paula.

Anne agreed. 'It's good for them to talk, man to

man, if you see what I mean? Sam has not been his usual chatty self this past week or so. Out of the two of us, he was always closest to Grandma and Granddad. I loved them too, but, unlike Sam, I never seemed to have much spare time to spend with them. I regret that now.'

'We all have regrets, Anne, but it's not good to dwell on them,' Lucy advised. 'Besides, you have a lot to deal with. You're a wife and a mother, with many responsibilities, while Sam is still footloose and fancy-free.'

'And what about you, Mum?'

'What about me?'

'It must be so very hard for you. They were your parents, and out of all of us, this must have hit you the hardest. Paula as well, I suppose, but Grandma once told me that, while you were always popping round every chance you got, Paula hardly ever went round to see them . . . unless she wanted something.'

'You should not say things like that, Anne.'

'Grandma said it, not me!' Anne had never cared much for Aunt Paula, anyway. She always thought her too full of herself. 'I know you'll miss them more than she will.'

Lucy gave a sad little smile. 'Maybe, but we don't really know that.'

'I do, and I'm worried about you, Mum. I know you're hurting, and I don't know what to do.'

'There is nothing anyone *can* do,' she said softly. 'We all have to try to deal with it in our own way.'

Thinking of her parents, Lucy fought back the tears.

'Don't you worry about me, sweetheart. I'll be all right,' she promised shakily.

Anne saw the car approaching. 'Here comes Les.'

She ran to meet him. 'Where is he?' She glanced into the back of the car, expecting to see their baby son.

'I'm sorry, love. He's with the baby-sitter. She turned up twenty minutes ago.' Les was disappointed to have missed the service. 'I hoped I might not be too late. I meant to sneak in at the back and catch the end of the service. I should have been there for you, and to pay my respects.'

'You can still do that,' Anne reassured him. 'We'll go up and you can see all the lovely flowers . . . if you want?'

Les thought that was a good idea.

First, though, having seen how pale and quiet Lucy had become, he asked her, 'If there is anything I can do, just give me a shout, and I'll be there.'

Lucy thanked him. 'If you mean help sort out Mum and Dad's house and such, it's all under control. After all the legal business is attended to, Anne has prom-ised to help me go through their personal stuff.' She gave Anne a warm smile. 'When that's done, the family can decide if they would like any keepsakes. As for everything else – furniture and such – Mum always said that when she "pops her clogs" she would like some pieces to be sent to the local charity shop, to help the needy.'

Les smiled. 'And why does that not surprise me?'

He realised there would be much to do, all of it a

painful business, and that the tasks would mainly fall to Lucy. 'Well, the offer is there if needed, Lucy.'

Lucy thanked him and promised she would call if she needed to.

Anne assured her mother that it had been the right and proper thing not to have a reception after the service. 'Grandma never liked anything like that, and besides, most people, like yourself, have taken time off work and need to get back.'

After saying her goodbyes, Lucy reminded her daughter that she might pop round later, although all she wanted right then was to curl up in a corner and think of what her life might be like now, without her parents.

~

Having waited until Anne and Les started on their way up to the church, Paula made a beeline for her sister. 'Hey! Wait a minute.'

Lucy saw her coming, and tried to make herself scarce. Paula had nothing to say that she needed to hear.

'Lucy!' Paula was none too pleased at being made to chase after her. 'Wait!'

Quickening her steps, Lucy hurried away. Whatever she says won't change what they did. I won't forgive them, she promised herself.

Behind her, Paula cursed under her breath. That's it! Run away, and to hell with you! she thought. But you can't say I didn't try to warn you. Martin and I plan to be together, and there's nothing you can do or say to stop it.

Having seen Lucy hurrying away, Martin and Sam ran to catch up with her.

'Mum!' Sam's voice stopped Lucy in her tracks. 'Mum, wait!'

Lucy glanced about, discreetly checking that Paula had gone.

'Mum, is it all right if I go with Dad?' Sam asked.

'Where to?' With Sam there, Lucy had no choice but to acknowledge her husband.

'We're going fishing for the rest of the day,' Martin explained. 'I thought it might be a good idea . . . in the circumstances.' Looking at Lucy, and seeing how pale and worn she looked, Martin had a stab of conscience.

Then he saw Paula in the distance, and he felt like a man ten foot tall. That beautiful creature was his woman now. Not Lucy.

Not any more . . .

'Dad's given me his spare fishing rod!' Sam had been after that rod for a long time, and he was genuinely excited. 'So, is it all right, Mum? I won't go, though, if you need me.'

'It's all right, love. I've got more than enough to keep me busy just now,' she said. 'You go with your dad and enjoy yourself.' She gave him a quick peck on the cheek. 'It'll do you good . . . take your mind off things.'

'Do you intend going back to work?' Martin asked.

'I'm not sure.'

'See you later then.' Martin gave a curt little nod.

Lucy made no reply.

With heavy heart, she watched them go. When they were out of sight, she looked back at the churchyard and lowered her head in sorrow. 'Love you,' she whispered tearfully. 'Miss you.'

Having already refused a lift from both Les and Martin, Lucy chose to walk back. She had a desperate need to be alone with her thoughts. She wondered where her life was heading. Or if she had a future.

Somehow along the way, she had lost everything, except for her two children and her darling baby grandchild.

She was immensely thankful for having been blessed in that way, but Sam and Anne were old enough to be independent now. They had their own lives to live. Anne was a wife and mother, and very soon Sam would be off to see the wider world; that much she knew for certain. He was increasingly hankering after adventure, and already he had applied to two colleges. The newsagent's job was never going to be big enough for him.

Lucy supposed it would not be long before she was seeing him off, and what would she have then? Both her children having flown the nest; a husband who thought so little of her that he could take another woman into his bed; and a sister who had not only shamed herself and her God-fearing parents, but who had managed to destroy every ounce of love and respect that Lucy had ever had for her.

So now, with her parents gone, Lucy was made to ask herself, what was left for her?

With Anne now happily settled as a wife and mother, and Sam straining at the reins to make his own life away from these parts, and, for all she knew, Martin and Paula maybe planning to build a life together, Lucy's prospects seemed rather bleak. She asked herself, who was she? What purpose did she now serve?

If Martin left her, who would ever want a dowdy, uninteresting, plain-looking woman who had nothing much to talk about? She had no ambitions, no achievements apart from producing two beautiful children. And because she had married at sixteen, heavily pregnant, she had little experience of life outside of raising a family.

With all of that in mind, if Martin did leave her to be with her sister, what kind of life would she have, an abandoned woman, whose children had fled the nest? No parents to look after or lean on whenever she needed someone close.

The more she thought on it, the more she realised that her future looked very bleak indeed.

In truth, right now it felt to Lucy as though her neat little life was falling apart by the minute.

It was as though the water had surged over her bridge, taking her with it. And whichever way she turned, there seemed no way back.

CHAPTER SEVEN

LUCY HAD TOYED with the idea of going back to work for the latter part of the day. Finally, she decided not to go, and rang in to inform the office.

The boss's secretary told her not to worry. 'I know the boss asked if you would try and come back, but to be honest she did not expect you to, and she said as much to me. So, don't give it a second thought, Lucy. We'll see you when we see you.'

Lucy was relieved. Right now she had neither the heart nor the patience to be working that big, noisy machine; especially with everyone keeping a friendly, wary eye on her.

The two-mile walk home would give her time to assess the recent events. She could scrutinise all that was wrong in her life. It would give her time to plan, time to think of herself for a change, because if there was such a thing as a turning-point in life, this was surely hers.

Almost halfway home, she was shocked to realise

that already the day was slipping away, so she pushed on, needing to get home before Martin and Sam returned from fishing. Yet even then, she wondered how she could even sit at the same table as Martin. What had they to say to each other that was not already said?

And how was she supposed to behave naturally when all the while she wanted to rant and rave, and throw him out of the house, with his bag and baggage? In the past few days since her parents died, there had been the funeral to arrange, which had allowed both Lucy and Martin to set aside any confrontation about his betrayal.

Her first priorities now, though, were Sam and his sister. Lucy knew she must keep her dignity, and wait for the right moment to have it out with Martin.

As she passed a red phone box, an idea came to mind, so she turned about. Opening her handbag as she went, she collected the few loose coins in the bottom of her purse, and counted them out. 'That'll do!' She felt pleased with herself.

Inside the phone box, she inserted some coins and dialled the number. After a few rings, Anne's voice said, 'Hello?'

'Anne, love, it's me . . . Mum.' Lucy was relieved to hear her daughter's voice.

'Mum! Where are you? I've been calling the house . . . There's nobody there. Where's Sam and Dad? What's going on?'

'Nothing is "going on", love. Dad and Sam have

gone fishing and probably won't be home till late. I'm walking home. I need to clear my mind. But I've decided to catch a bus to Kathleen's. She'll be back from work by the time I get there. I promised to see her, and now is as good a time as any.'

'But what about your tea? I know for a fact you've hardly eaten anything all day.'

'I'll get something – don't worry, love. It'll do me good to spend a little time with Kathleen. She makes me feel better about myself.'

'What's that supposed to mean?'

'I'm not sure exactly,' Lucy detected a little envy, 'but she does make me smile, and she tells me off when it's needed.'

'Hmm! Well, that won't do any harm, I'm sure. Not when you're always thinking of others above yourself. Yes, Mum, you go and see your friend. If you want, Les can pick you up when you're ready to come home.'

'Thank you, but I'll get the bus. There's no need for Les to disturb his evening, but there is one thing you could do for me if you can . . .?'

'Oh, what's that then?'

'Well, there's no food prepared for your father and Sam, and they're bound to be starving hungry after being in the fresh air.'

Anne put her mother's mind at rest. 'I'll get them fish and chips. The chip shop on Raymond Street is always open.'

'So, how will you let them know? You can't be sure what time they'll get back.'

'Like I said, Mum, stop worrying about everyone else! I've still got your spare key. Les can take a note over and leave it in the kitchen where they're bound to see it. They'll call me, and either they can come to me and have their tea here, or Les will take the food to them. I'll ask Sam to stay over at our house if he wants. See! It's no problem . . . and nothing for you to worry about.'

'Thank you, sweetheart.'

So, in spite of Lucy's worrying, everything seemed to be slotting into place. There you are, Lucy girl, she told herself, it seems you're not altogether indispensable after all. The trouble was, she could not make up her mind as to whether or not that was a good thing.

Ten minutes later, having called Kathleen, she was clambering aboard the bus.

'Where to?' The curly-haired conductress stood back to let her pass.

'Market Street, please.' As Lucy was counting out her change, the bus suddenly moved off, and she quickly grabbed the rail.

'Sit yourself down before you fall down!' The conductress had a voice like a sergeant-major.

It was a ten-minute ride to Market Street, and almost as soon as she sat herself down, Lucy was clambering up again. 'Wait until the bus stops!' the conductress bellowed. 'Watch the step as you get off!'

With three other passengers in front of her, Lucy was impatient to get off the bus and be on her way. As Lucy shuffled along behind the other passengers, the conductress was issuing even more orders. 'Come on . . . come on! We haven't got all day.'

Everyone quickened their steps. 'Miserable bugger!' The fat man in front of Lucy raised his voice in contempt. 'A bit of respect might not come amiss. I was in the army, I'll have you know!'

The conductress ignored him until he was off the bus, when she yelled out, 'In the army, were you?' She was still shouting as the bus pulled away. 'I might tell you, I was a Girl Scout and good at it! So, what do you think to that, eh?' When the man chose not to answer, she raised her voice, 'Oh, dearie me! Cat got your tongue, has it?'

Suppressing a little chuckle, Lucy quickened her steps.

Kathleen's house was just a five-minute walk away.

As she got nearer, Lucy's heart felt a little lighter. Kathleen was always good to be with, and right now, Lucy was really looking forward to spending precious time with her.

On reaching the door, she carefully lifted the brass door knocker, and let it fall gently.

A moment later, the door was opened, and Kathleen flung her arms round her.

'Oh, Lucy, are you all right?' She urged her inside. 'I made us a little cottage pie.' She chatted incessantly as Lucy followed her down the passageway to the kitchen. 'I know it's a favourite of yours, but I'm not as good a cook as you, so you'll have to forgive me if it tastes like rag chopped up.'

Lucy smiled. 'Don't put yourself down, Kathleen,' she said. 'You're as good a cook as anyone, including me.'

Kathleen wasn't sure whether she should mention the day's sad event, but then she decided that might be wiser than pussyfooting around it.

'Did everything go as planned today, Lucy? I mean . . . was it a lovely service? I bet the church was packed, wasn't it?' Kathleen was not quite sure what to say in the circumstances.

'Everything went as it should, I suppose,' Lucy answered quietly.

'Oh, Lucy, I'm sorry I couldn't get the time off to be with you.' Kathleen was desolate. 'I did ask, but the boss seems to be getting stricter by the minute.'

Lucy understood. 'She's under a lot of pressure, I expect, and she did send some really beautiful flowers. Mind you, all the flowers were lovely . . . and the priest was very caring and . . .' When tears threatened, she paused to take a breath and gather herself. 'So many people turned out, Kathleen. It was amazing. I never realised Mum and Dad had so many friends.'

Kathleen was not at all surprised. 'Your mum and dad were a lovely couple. People took to them straight off, so they had a lot of friends. But what about you, Lucy? You look worn out.'

In truth she suspected that Lucy had not enjoyed a good night's sleep for some time – even before she lost her parents. 'Are you coping all right . . . really?' She lowered her voice. 'Please, Lucy, don't try dealing

146

with everything yourself. There are people around you who want to help . . . as I do. You know what they say about a trouble shared.'

Lucy considered herself fortunate to have such a friend. 'I know I would only have to ask and you would be there for me. You always are. I'll admit, though . . . losing Mum and Dad is the hardest thing I've ever had to deal with in my life.' Her thoughts went to Paula and Martin, a burden that she really couldn't share. 'It's difficult . . . but I'm coping . . . just about.' In truth she was not coping at all.

'I'm here for you, Lucy. Please don't forget that.' Kathleen suspected Lucy must be in pieces, but, as always, she was putting on a brave face.

'Don't you worry . . . I'll be fine,' Lucy told her. 'Everyone's been so kind. Anne and Les have been amazing. They can't do enough, but Anne worried me for a time. She was too quiet, hiding herself away.'

'She was just doing her best to deal with it, I expect,' Kathleen sympathised. 'Everyone deals with grief in their own special way. And what about Sam – is he dealing with it?'

'I think so, but it's really hard for him, Kathleen.' Lucy gave a forlorn little smile. 'He was his grand-dad's little mate. The two of them got on so well, always talking about this and that. They had such a lot in common. Of course, Sam adored Mum too. She always treated him as an equal. He was not just her grandson, but also a friend and confidant. But yes, I think he's dealing with it in his own quiet way.

I'm very proud of him, Kathleen. Somehow this whole dreadful business seems to have made him grow up all of a sudden.'

'So, what about his plans for the future? I recall you mentioning that he had a yearning for college?'

'Oh, yes, college is very much on the cards . . . His grandma persuaded him that he should try to do as much as he can before he decides to settle down, and Martin and I have always agreed with that. Like I told Sam, though, if he's really serious about college he must not leave it too late. If he wants to get anywhere in life, he needs to work at it. Thankfully, at long last, he seems to have taken all our advice to heart, because now he is determined to gain a place in college.'

'Well, that's good. And like you say, if he wants it badly enough, I'm sure he'll succeed in making you and Martin proud.'

Lucy agreed. 'He's a fine young man. It's true that some time back he did get kind of lost, but now he seems to have found what he wants out of life, and I'm sure we will always be proud of him.'

'Where is he now?' Kathleen asked.

'Martin's taken him fishing.'

'That was a good idea. It'll take both their minds off things for a while, don't you think?'

When Lucy merely nodded, Kathleen suspected she was keeping something back. 'You do intend staying a while, don't you, Lucy?'

'Yes, of course, and I'm looking forward to a small helping of that cottage pie.' She was not all that hungry, but because Kathleen had gone to a deal of trouble, she would do her best to enjoy the meal.

Kathleen laughed. 'I wouldn't be too keen if I were you. Come on! Off with your coat and on with the kettle! While you do that, I'll dish up the cottage pie.'

While Lucy took off her coat and went to hang it up, Kathleen observed her. Kathleen appreciated how losing her parents had been a huge blow to Lucy – it showed in her sad eyes and the way in which she found it hard to talk about them – but she was convinced that something else was troubling Lucy. Something of a private nature.

Kathleen knew Lucy like she might know her own sister, if she had one, and her every instinct told her that Lucy was in some kind of personal trouble.

Just now and then, she seemed to be miles away, lost so deep in her troubled thoughts that Kathleen was almost afraid to speak.

Kathleen knew that Lucy rarely shared her troubles with anyone. This time, though, Kathleen hoped Lucy might find the strength to confide in her.

Across the kitchen, Lucy had a sneaking feeling that Kathleen was watching her, that she might have guessed how she was nursing another concern, one so crippling that she did not want to talk about it; not even to her one and only friend.

A short time later, the two of them were seated at the kitchen table, enjoying Kathleen's cottage pie.

'Kathleen, this is really tasty.' Lucy had not realised

how hungry she was. 'I'd even go so far as to say it's much better than mine.'

Kathleen laughed. 'You little liar!' she teased. 'Nobody's cottage pie is better than yours.'

They ate and chatted, enjoying being together, but such was the atmosphere, it seemed almost as though a third person was in the room with them.

After a while, Kathleen dared to ask, 'What's wrong, Lucy?'

Taken off guard by Kathleen's direct question, Lucy said the first thing that came to mind. 'That's a strange thing to ask. What's wrong is that I've just lost both my parents.'

'I'm sorry, and I'm well aware of that, Lucy, and I can only imagine how hard it must be to cope with.' Kathleen went on gently, 'Look, Lucy, I've long seen you as the sister I never had, and right now, I might be out of order in saying what's on my mind. And if I am then I hope you'll forgive me. It's just that . . . while I'm aware of the loss of your parents, I'm worried that there's something else troubling you. Something bad . . . of a personal nature, maybe. I just want to help, that's all. Please, Lucy . . . let me help.'

Lucy remained silent, which only fuelled Kathleen's suspicions.

'Lucy, I know you well enough to say what I think, and I feel there is something definitely playing on your mind. Something you obviously don't want to talk about, but you must know, you can talk to me . . . about anything. I want to help. If you're ill, or short of money, or anything at all . . . I want to help you . . . as a friend.'

Lucy remained silent, her gaze fixed on the table. She wanted to confide in her friend, but she was too ashamed, and besides, no one could help. Not even Kathleen.

Kathleen, though, was gently insistent. 'I know you really need to tell me, Lucy, and if you do, I promise, hand on heart, it will never go beyond this room. Talking about it will ease your mind and, who knows, I might even be able to help in some way; whether it's money, or health. And if you're worried about losing your job for whatever reason, I can tell you now, the boss is well aware of how hard you work. She really does value you.'

Lucy glanced up, her heart heavy with the reality of what Martin and Paula had done. 'There is something,' she confessed quietly. 'Like you said, it's a personal matter, and one which I have to somehow resolve myself. It's not that I don't trust you, because I do, and if I wanted to talk about it to anyone I would turn to you. But I can't bring myself to talk about it. Not with you . . . not with anyone!'

Kathleen had never seen her so resolute. Nor had she ever seen those honest brown eyes so very sad. 'All right, Lucy, but will you make me a promise, please? I know you place great value on a promise, and you would never break it. So, will you make a promise . . . for me?'

'If I can, yes.'

'Thank you for that. So, if you do ever get to the point where you feel you need to confide in someone, will you let me help? You have my word, it will go no further, and I'll do my utmost to help you.'

'Yes, yes I will. Thank you, Kathleen. You're a good friend. So now, can we let it go?'

Kathleen reached out and covered Lucy's hand with hers. 'What do you mean?' she smiled knowingly. 'I've no idea what you're talking about!'

For the remainder of Lucy's stay, there was no more talk of Lucy's problem, or the promise she had made. It was as though that particular conversation never even happened.

The unspoken subject, however, continued to weigh heavily on both their minds.

∼

The evening was already creeping in, when Lucy decided to make her way home.

'Martin and Sam are bound to be home by now,' she explained. 'Anne's organised their dinner, but I'd best get back or they'll start to worry.'

At least, Sam might be worried, she thought bitterly.

At the door, Kathleen gave her a big hug. 'Mind how you go, and I'll see you next week at work . . .' she deliberately made no mention of what had been said, '. . . unless you've decided to take a few more days off?'

'No, I don't think so,' Lucy replied. 'I'll be better

off at work – less time to dwell on things – and besides, I don't want to upset the boss.'

'Oh, I'm sure she'll understand in the circumstances.'

'Maybe, but if I'm at home, I'll be on my own, and that's the last thing I need.'

At the top of the street she turned and waved to Kathleen before quickening her steps and heading for the bus stop.

Thankfully, when the bus drew up, she noticed it was a different conductor from the bossy woman of earlier, this one pleasant and round-faced, with a floppy belly that hung over his trouser-belt.

Lucy climbed to the upper deck and sat herself right at the front. When the bus set off, she was mesmerised as the rows of streetlights came on one after the other, creating a kind of landing strip.

With the bus gathering speed, she settled into her seat, thankful to be the only passenger upstairs. The privacy suited her troubled mind, and soothed the ache in her heart.

It was a strange thing, but up here she felt as though she was at the top of the world, safe, hidden away where no one and nothing could hurt her.

Relaxing into the seat, she leaned back and closed her eyes, concentrating on the rhythmic throb of the engine.

She might have fallen asleep if it hadn't been for the fat conductor puffing and panting up the narrow, winding staircase. 'Dearie me!' He paused to catch his

153

breath. 'You've not only made me climb the stairs,' he complained to Lucy, 'but you've parked yourself right up front, mekkin' me travel the length o' the bus!'

Snatching a hankie from his pocket, he wiped the beads of sweat from his pink, chubby face. 'Trying to give me an 'eart attack, are you?'

'I'm sorry. I didn't think,' Lucy said.

'Aw! Don't you lose any sleep over it. Risking life and limb is what I get paid for.'

He took her fare, then huffed and puffed back down the stairs. 'I'll shout when it's your stop,' he called back.

Lucy was worried he might be in the wrong job.

When a few minutes later the bus began to slow down, Lucy heard the conductor calling, and she quickly made her way down the steps.

On reaching the bottom of the steps she grasped hold of the pole to keep herself steady while the bus pulled up.

As the bus slowly approached the stop, she noticed a man – tall, well-built, and wearing a long dark overcoat – emerging from the entrance of a nearby restaurant. She thought she recognised him as the man who had found her hiding in the bus shelter, but because he was facing the other way, obviously waiting for someone, she could not be certain.

Intrigued, she continued to peek at him. Then suddenly he turned and, to Lucy's horror, looked straight at her. She was left in no doubt. It was him. The man from the bus shelter.

Ashamed and embarrassed, she wanted to run, but there was no place to go.

Like a rabbit caught in the headlights, she was momentarily unable to shift her gaze. When he gave a long, slow smile of recognition, she took two steps back on the bus platform, to where she was certain he could not see her.

That night in the bus shelter, she had deliberately remained in the shadows, so how could he have remembered her? And yet, she had recognised him.

Trapped on the bus, she was desperate to get off and make her getaway.

When, a moment later, the bus shuddered to a halt, she feared the man might approach her. Instinctively, she hung back, until the conductor said loudly, 'Hey! Wake up, lady! Are you getting off, or do you want to be locked in the depot all night?'

Apologising, Lucy immediately got off. She did not look in the man's direction. Impatient to get away, she set off at a quick pace, in the opposite direction to where the man was standing.

When a voice called out to her, she knew it was him. 'Wait . . . please! Hey! Hang on a minute . . .'

Lucy broke into a run. Then, dodging down the nearest alley, she flattened herself against the wall, her heart pounding when a long shadow fell across the mouth of the alley. In the flickering light from the streetlamp, she saw him peering down the alley, looking for her. She pressed back in the shadows, hardly daring to breathe.

When he took a stride towards where she was hiding, Lucy was panic-stricken. Why was he after her? What did he want? Her instinct told her he would not hurt her, but the fact that he had caught her crying in the bus shelter was overwhelmingly embarrassing.

She desperately needed to put that particular incident behind her and didn't want to revisit it now, with this stranger.

Suddenly, a woman's voice cut the air. 'Dave!' Then again, 'Dave, what the devil are you doing?'

To Lucy's great relief, the man turned and walked away.

Remaining hidden, Lucy could hear the two voices, the man and the woman, soft and friendly, with the occasional burst of laughter from the woman. And then they were gone, and it was silent again.

Lucy dared to take a nervous little peek round the corner. The two of them were dawdling, arm in arm, along the street, still talking together.

She watched as they climbed the few steps into the entrance of a hotel just along from the restaurant. It was then that she recognised the woman. She was the one Lucy remembered as being with the kindly man on that fateful day.

At the door, the man stepped back, allowing the woman to go first. As he followed, he quickly turned his head and looked down the street, as though searching for Lucy.

Lucy, though, was already fleeing through the darkened streets, eager to get away from there.

A short time later, having put a considerable distance between herself and the couple, she paused to take a breath.

After a while, with a measure of reluctance, she set off again. She did not want to go home. But what real choice did she have? Besides, over these many years she had helped to build the house into a home and, until recently, she had been happy there.

Thinking of home now, though, was painful. Who are you, Lucy? she asked herself. Deeply saddened, she slowed her steps. Where do you belong?

Thoughts of her parents loomed large in her mind. She missed them desperately. It was like the heart had been torn out of her.

When images of Martin and her sister together began to darken her thoughts, she deliberately pushed them to the back of her mind. Even then, the shocking reality of what she had seen continued to haunt her.

How could she live with it? What was she supposed to do?

Could she forgive what they had done, and so keep her marriage and her and Martin's lives together as best she could? Or should she leave the marriage, and turn her back on both of them?

Perhaps the kind and proper thing for her to do would be to let Martin go his own way, if that was what he truly wanted.

CHAPTER EIGHT

SCRAMBLING UP FROM the carpet, Martin took another peek through the lounge window.

'Stop worrying!' Paula tugged at him. 'I expect she's decided to stop over at Kathleen's after all.'

'I hope you're right, but I'm not sure of Lucy's intention.' In a lower voice he added regretfully, 'She hardly talks to me these days.'

'So do you want me to go?'

'You know I don't.' He grabbed her into his arms. 'You little witch! I'm sorry I ever let you in. I should have sent you packing.' Grabbing her to him, he kissed her long and hard. 'Truth is, I can't seem to get enough of you.'

'Is that a bad thing?'

'For us, no. For Lucy, not so good.' Not for the first time, he felt a pang of conscience.

Paula wrapped herself about him. 'Do you want to end it?'

'You know I don't.'

'So . . . do you want us to make a life together?'

'Yes, but it's not easy, is it?'

'Just tell her!'

Martin thought he would find it hard to be that cruel, and evaded her suggestion. Running his two hands over her bare skin, he said, 'Look, I have to be up and away at six tomorrow. Watch out for me later on.'

'I could stay here with you tonight.'

Martin was adamant. 'No, Paula. We have to be careful until it's all out in the open. Think about it: Sam might suddenly decide to come home from Anne's, and for all we know, Lucy could be on her way as we speak. You know what a homing pigeon she is.'

Paula laughed. 'Homing pigeon? OK, tomorrow then.' Getting up off the carpet, she collected her dress from the arm of the chair, slid it over her head and shoulders and wriggled into it. 'Do me up, will you?'

When Martin grabbed her by the waist, she started squealing and laughing, and then they were fooling about, he trying to zip up her dress and she wriggling away.

Having secured the zip, Martin then grabbed his trousers and pulled them on, Paula doing everything she could to stop him from securing his belt. 'Aw, come on . . . we've got time.' She was all over him.

Martin pushed her off. 'Like I said, I'll see you tomorrow.'

'When exactly?'

'I'm not altogether sure. I've got that big roofing job on, and I can't leave it unsafe. It'll probably take me up to midday before I secure it. So, let's say I'll be with you around one o' clock. That'll give us a good hour together before I need to get back.'

'Suits me. But we need to talk, Martin,' Paula reminded him. 'You never did give me an answer about making a life together.'

'OK. Like I said . . . tomorrow. We'll talk then.'

Paula was not ready to leave. 'Are you really throwing me out?' she whined.

'Yes, I am!' he told her, though he was enjoying the attention.

Sensing his weakness, she clung onto him.

'Paula . . . no!' Each time he pushed her away, she came back at him, playfully teasing and laughing, until Martin threw himself into the fun.

Lost in the moment, neither of them heard Lucy let herself in through the front door.

Entering the front room, Lucy was shocked to see them rolling about on the carpet. For one moment she stood in horrified silence. Then filled with an uncontrollable rage, she ran across the room. She grabbed Paula by the arm and yanked her upright, forcing her out of the room and down the hallway to the front door.

She screamed at her, 'Shame on the pair of you . . . carrying on like wild animals – and in my house! You're disgusting!'

'Get your hands off me!' Paula fought like a wildcat. 'It's not my fault if you can't keep hold of him. The truth is you'll never be able to keep him. You're not right for him and never were. If he hadn't been forced into it, he never would have married you!'

Lucy gave as good as she got. 'You're no better than a woman of the streets. No, I take that back . . . because even a woman of the streets would have more decency than to break up her sister's marriage.'

'Huh!' Kicking and struggling, Paula laughed in Lucy's face. 'If your marriage is broken, all I can say is, it couldn't have been very strong in the first place!'

Ignoring her spiteful remarks, Lucy continued, 'I'm ashamed to have you as a sister and, as much as I desperately miss Mum and Dad, I'm thankful they're not here to see what a shameless tramp you are!'

Struggling to break free from Lucy's iron grip, Paula yelled at her, 'At least I've got the guts to go after what I want. You, though . . . you're too timid to strike out. You're too scared and worried . . . and while you're hiding away, life is passing you by. One day soon you'll turn round and you'll be old. Do you hear me? You'll be old before your time!'

She laughed in Lucy's face. 'You think I've stolen your man, do you? Well, trust me, he didn't need stealing. You see, it was him who came after me the first time.'

She yelled out, 'Tell her, Martin! Tell her what you told me – that you've never loved her . . . that you always wanted me. Tell her, Martin!'

Never before had Lucy been in such a rage. Her heart was beating so fast, she could hardly breathe. She felt like a different woman; capable of anything.

161

In a clear, decisive voice she informed Paula, 'From now on, you are not welcome in this house.'

'Huh! That's not what Martin told me.'

'Well, I'm telling you now. What the two of you have been up to is bad enough, but how could you so easily forget that we've only just buried our mum and dad?' She fought to keep back the tears. 'From now on I don't have a sister. Do you hear me? I don't know who you are any more.'

Breaking away, Paula ran off, cursing as she went. Seeing Lucy in such a temper had shaken her. Now, though, she took pleasure in hurting her. 'You're mad! You can't even see what's right in front of you. Martin doesn't love you. He loves me. We love each other. But you wouldn't understand, would you . . . because you're unlovable . . . and cold. Those are Martin's words, by the way, not mine.'

She took great enjoyment in the flush of pain that flitted across Lucy's face. 'Y'see, Lucy, it's like this: Martin needs the kind of partner who sets him on fire. No one would ever blame him for wanting a real flesh-and-blood woman in his arms!'

'Get away from here!' Lucy went after her. 'Don't ever let me catch you round here again . . . do you hear me?'

Paula was already out of reach, her manic screams echoing through the darkened streets. 'Get used to it, Lucy, girl! You've lost him! He doesn't want you any more. He wants us to live together, d'you hear? Martin asked me to move in with him.'

These cruel words brought Lucy to a halt for a moment, her face bleached white with anger. But this was no time for tears. This was a time to stand up for herself, and to hell with the consequences.

With the door firmly closed against Paula, Lucy made her way back along the narrow hallway and into the front room.

Martin was standing by the fireplace, looking pitiful and staring at the carpet, his head bowed low to his chest, and his hands clasped in front of him. He seemed unable – or unwilling – even to look at her.

Lucy stood for what seemed an age, studying this man who had been her life since she was little more than a child. Even now, after everything she had seen, she could not deny that she still loved him. He was her husband, and the father of her two children. That meant something to her; even if it meant nothing to him.

Sadly, there seemed nothing here for her now, especially knowing how Martin felt about her: 'unlovable . . . and cold'. So revealing. And much too cruel.

She waited, hoping he might say something that would show he still loved her, and that Paula was lying for her own ends.

Another agonising moment, and still he did not look up. Nor did he speak.

At last turning away, she told him sadly, 'Do what you like, Martin. I don't care any more. Set up a new life with my sister, if that's what you truly want. I promise I won't get in your way. But whatever happens now, this sham of a marriage is well and truly over.'

When it seemed he was about to protest, she cut in sharply, 'No, Martin! I don't want to hear what you've got to say. I only know what I've seen with my own eyes . . . and I can't forget. I might have forgiven you the first time, but not now. I think it's best if we go our own ways.'

Unwilling to look on him a moment longer, she took a deep breath and walked away.

At the door, she glanced back. 'Just now, the whole world must have heard what Paula said: that you actually wanted you and her to live together.' She gave a sad little smile. 'Don't let me or the children stop you and her from doing whatever you want. The truth is, Martin, the two of you deserve each other.'

For one last, aching moment, against her better judgement, she felt the need to linger.

Martin, though, remained silent.

So, with a heavy heart she left him there, to contemplate his future.

~

Upstairs in the bedroom, she went straight to the wardrobe.

Searching out a small suitcase, she swung it onto the bed and threw open the lid. She paused awhile, the tiniest bitter-sweet smile touching her lips. She remembered where the suitcase had been – a holiday in Blackpool, when the children were just little tots. Then, two years later, it went with them to a caravan in Brighton.

In her deepest, fondest memories, Lucy could picture the babies playing on the sands, while Martin and herself sat by and guarded them.

'They were good days,' she whispered to herself, 'a time to be happy.' Thinking about it now, she could recall only a few such happy times. Each one was incredibly precious to her, and always would be. The question flooded her mind: could there be more good memories made if she stayed with Martin? But if she felt that the marriage was over, and there was no hope of reconciliation, what then would be the consequences? Maybe Anne and Sam would feel that it was her doing if the marriage was ended. They might blame *her* for splitting up the family.

Suppressing the nostalgia, she grabbed a few items out of the wardrobe. She then scoured the room to collect a number of private things – photographs and personal toiletries, as well as her small bag of make-up. Whatever happened in the future, Lucy realised that today was not only changing her life, but *all* their lives.

Lucy had never really mastered the art of making herself look good, but she did like a touch of colour on her lips, and a dash of cover-up for the freckly blemish that sat below the brow of her left eye. She smiled wearily.

Now, as she quickly placed the items into her case, the truth of what she was actually doing hit hard.

'I never dreamed I would walk away from here,' she murmured softly, 'This is my home. It's where my children grew up. If I go, the family may never recover. Is what Martin did bad enough that I should allow it to damage our lives for ever?' Yet she knew that one way or another their lives were already changing.

For the moment she had no idea where she might end up, and so took only the bare necessities: clean underwear, a couple of pretty nightgowns, the old, worn slippers, and a bag of general toiletries.

When the lid of the suitcase was eventually closed, she sat at the dressing table and cried.

After a while she looked up, staring at her image in the mirror. Hmm! You're not much to look at, are you, Lucy? She gave a wistful smile. *Lovejoy*. Well, there's a contradiction in terms for a woman without love or joy.

She stole a moment to study herself in the mirror.

Her mid-brown hair was unkempt as usual, and her brown eyes were heavy with sadness.

Critically observing herself, she gave a wry litle smile. 'Shapeless figure, dressed in shapeless clothes, no sense of style. Hair is too mousy, too wild and too unruly . . . eyes too small, and they aren't even one colour, being neither brown nor grey.' She gave a sorry little laugh. 'Truth be told,' she concluded, 'there's nothing outstanding about you at all! You're a bit of this and a bit of that. You're not exciting, or clever. You have no sense of adventure, and you have no backbone. You should be more assertive, but people walk all over you because you let them.'

In that moment, she loathed herself. 'And now look

what you've done! You've put yourself out of house and home, instead of standing up and fighting for what's yours!'

But then she reminded herself, 'What would be the point, when your cheating husband would rather be with your sister than with you? And who can blame him? She's younger and prettier, and she has a natural excitement about her that you never had, and never will!'

After ranting on, she felt suddenly calm. She collected a few last, private items: her notebook and pen; the wallet carrying photographs of Anne, Sam and her small grandson. There was one of Martin, but she took it out and laid it on the bed.

After checking the money in her purse, and raiding her bag and bedside drawer, she was somewhat relieved. She had enough to keep her going for at least a week.

Now, though, she had a dilemma.

Should she go to see Anne, and tell her the ugly truth? Or should she lie, and make up some excuse as to why she was going away? She agonised as to how she could sensibly deal with the situation. It was an uncomfortable truth that, however she might choose to explain her departure, there would be awkward questions.

After much consideration, she promised herself that she would not tell her children the whole truth, at least not yet. For now, she would explain just enough for the family to know that she would not be around for a while, but that she would be in contact.

Folding her arms onto the dressing table, she leaned

forward and laid her head to rest on them. With her eyes closed and her heart aching, she was suddenly swamped with all manner of doubts.

What on earth are you doing, Lucy? she asked herself. What's going to happen to you? You're not even sure where you might go. And what about your job? You're bound to lose it now. Oh, and what if Martin brings Paula to live in the house? If he did that there would be no way back for you, not even if you wanted it. And what would the children think?

The worries came thick and fast, each one bringing another.

But . . . what if the minute you're gone, he moves out of here, and into Paula's house? What would happen to this house, and where would the children go to visit . . . if they wanted to? The idea of this house standing empty, or being filled with strangers, sent a pang of regret through her.

So now, she began to have doubts about leaving. After all, it was a huge step, and she had never been away from home on her own before . . . except for that one time when her mother was poorly and she stayed over for a few days to help her father cope.

'You stop it right now, Lucy Lovejoy!' She wagged a finger at herself in the mirror. 'Just remember, you're not the one in the wrong. If this house is lost, it won't be your fault!'

Anger surged through her. 'Don't be a coward, Lucy. Do what you need to do, and don't give them a second thought!'

Just then, on hearing the front door close, she scrambled off the stool, and ran to the window. There was Martin, hurrying away, in the direction of Paula's house. Hmm, that said it all!

The grim truth hit hard: He wants her so much, he couldn't even wait until I'd gone? Seeing him run to Paula like that, was Lucy's wake-up call.

Within a matter of minutes, she was ready to leave, though she was not at all easy about it, feeling truly fearful of what might happen to her now.

Deep down, she was afraid of being lonely; and of never again finding a place to call home. Her greatest fear, though, was that she might lose the love of her children.

She suddenly realised that it was the constant love and presence of her children and her beloved parents that had kept her content for these many years.

Their characters were so very different that she and Paula had never really been close, even as children. As for Martin . . . well, he was just there, being Martin; expecting a clean shirt for going out, and a meal when he came home.

Day or night, he went out whenever and wherever he chose, and he came back at whatever time suited him. In between, there were few hugs and gentle words for Lucy, and what there were, were merely part and parcel of having sex. Otherwise, she rarely received a hug or a cuddle from him, except on the few occasions she made the first move.

Outside of the rare snippets of closeness, it seemed

as though she was merely part of the furniture. And sadly, over time, she had come to accept her place.

Martin was outgoing, with a strong circle of friends. Being enthusiastic participants in the darts team, and the football club, they regularly gathered in the pub, to swap stories and enjoy an hour or so together.

In contrast, Lucy hardly ever went out and had no real friends apart from Kathleen. Rarely did she buy herself a pretty dress, and even when she did treat herself to something attractive, she had nowhere to wear it. She did not see the point of spending money on frivolous pretties when it was needed elsewhere.

Consequently, over the years, she gently settled into the mother and housekeeper mantle. Like Martin, she worked long and hard to earn a wage, which went on the house and family.

Work, worry, and family duties. In a nutshell, that was her entire life.

Beginning to feel sorry for herself, she quickly counted her blessings. She had brought two beautiful children into the world, and alongside Martin, she had made a home for their family.

These good, positive things were now sadly overshadowed by the crippling knowledge that her husband preferred to sleep with his sister-in-law, rather than with his own wife.

That shocking discovery had cut so deep that it had

taken away her confidence, her life as she knew it, and whatever small future she might have expected.

There seemed little left for her now.

However hard she tried to be positive, she now felt alone, afraid and abandoned.

CHAPTER NINE

THE EVENING WAS already dark when Lucy closed the door on the house where she had been content for many years.

She glanced nervously down the street, wondering if Martin might come home, having reflected on his position and wanting to talk things through, but there was no sign of him, and in her bruised heart she was glad of that.

She lingered on the step for a sorry moment, remembering the years she had spent in this little house; quiet, uneventful years, where life had gently ticked away without even a noticeable ripple.

Before regrets overwhelmed her, she hurried down the path and onto the street, where she hastened her steps.

Sneaking many a backward glance as she hurried away, she felt a great wrench on realising how very young she had been when she and Martin had moved into that darling little house. It had been her home for more than twenty years, and regardless of recent events, it would always hold a fond place in her heart.

As she hurried along, her mind was alive with all manner of questions. Would Martin miss her? And what about her darling parents – what would they have said about the situation she now found herself in?

Oh, how she missed them both! How desperately she needed just to see their homely faces again, to wrap her arms about their old shoulders and tell them how very much she loved them.

When the searing emotions overwhelmed her, it all became too much. Leaning against an alley wall, she dropped the suitcase to the ground, and holding her hands to her face, she cried like she had never cried before; like her heart was breaking. Like there was nothing left in this whole wide world that could ever make her happy again.

She sobbed until there were no more tears, aware there was no hope, and no one who would understand how lost she felt in that desolate moment.

'What are you doing, Lucy?' she asked herself quietly. 'Where are you going?'

She had no answers; only questions. And a crippling sense of unbearable loneliness.

A short time later, as she continued her way down the street to her daughter's house, Lucy paused to gather her thoughts. She reminded herself not to say anything to Anne or Sam about Martin and Paula. Instead, she would merely say that Kathleen had asked her to stay with her for a few days, and that she had accepted her gracious offer.

Minutes later, she was knocking on her daughter's door.

Anne was pleased but surprised to see her mother standing there. 'Mum! What's wrong?' She noticed the suitcase. 'What are you doing? Have you and Dad had a falling-out?' In the hallway she noticed Lucy's tear-stained face. 'You've been crying! Mum, what's going on?'

'I'm fine,' Lucy assured her. 'Stop worrying. I've just come round to tell you that I'm staying with Kathleen for a day or two . . . just to get out of the house. And you're right, I have been crying. I can't seem to accept that Mum and Dad are gone. It was all too soon, too unexpected. But I'll be fine, sweetheart.' Lucy forced a smile. 'I'm a tough old bird!'

'Come on, Mum.' After standing the suitcase by the wall, Anne led the way into the kitchen. 'I'll put the kettle on.'

When the tea was made and the two of them were sitting in the front room, Anne remarked gently, 'You are not a "tough old bird". You're gentle and kind, and I would have had you here for as long as you want. So, why didn't you come to me?'

'Well, because there was no need. I'm coping all right. In fact, it was not me who asked Kathleen, it was her who asked me,' which was indeed true, as Lucy recalled. 'I told her I needed to be with my family at a time like this, but she said she knew me enough to realise that I was putting on a brave face, after losing your grandma and granddad. She said she understood how hard it was to lose a parent, and that she was fortunate enough to still have her father, while I had lost both of mine.' Lucy gave a sad little chuckle. 'I think she just wanted to mother me, that's all.'

'Well, I agree with her. You do put on a brave face. I mean, even I can't get to grips with losing both my grandparents in such a short time, so Lord only knows how you're dealing with it. Kathleen is right to ask you to stay with her. At the very least, it will give you a nice change of scene for a time.'

Lucy merely nodded, ashamed that she had lied to her own daughter, instead of confessing that she was throwing herself on Kathleen in order to escape from the dreadful situation Martin and Paula had created.

Anne, though, was still chatting. 'I think it's exactly what you need, Mum – to be with a friend, someone to talk to. Especially with Dad working day and night like he does, and when he's not working, he's out with his mates. I'm glad you're getting away for a time. Trust me, Mum, it's just what you need, and Kathleen is such a good friend. But what did Dad have to say?'

Lucy smiled. 'Much like you just said,' she replied wisely, before changing the subject. 'Is Sam here?'

'No, he went out not long ago to meet up with his mates. He might stay over with one of them. Apparently they're hoping to go to college together.'

'Why didn't he give me a call?'

'Oh, but he did, Mum. He rang the house but there was no answer. I expect you were already on your way here. But where was Dad?'

'Oh, he popped round Paula's.' Which was not a lie.

'Hmm!' Anne groaned. 'What's happened now? Her boiler blown up, has it? Honestly, Mum, she always wants something done for nothing. And Dad never complains.'

'Oh, your dad doesn't mind going round there. He's only too glad to help, and besides, who else has she got?' Even now, Lucy found herself offering a way out for Martin and Paula, in order not to make Anne suspicious.

'Well, yeah. I suppose you're right.'

Lucy deliberately avoided the subject, and the two of them chatted about this and that and nothing in particular. Then Lucy said she had best get off. 'There's a bus from the bottom of the street in about ten minutes. If I hurry, I should be in time.'

Anne was concerned. 'I don't like you wandering about in the dark. It's a pity Les isn't back yet. He could have taken you over to Kathleen's.'

'Stop nagging. I'll be absolutely fine! Look, I'll ring you when I get there. How's that?'

'OK . . . but don't forget, will you? I could walk to the bus stop with you, but Luke's asleep upstairs.'

'Is it all right if I peep in at him before I go?'

'Go on then, but try not to wake him. It took me ages to get him off.'

While Anne cleared the cups away, Lucy crept

upstairs and took a peek at her grandson. 'Sleep tight, little fella.' She leaned over to plant a gentle kiss on his forehead. 'Your nanna loves you so very much.'

Taking his tiny hand in her fingertips, she gazed down on him a moment before reluctantly turning away to hurry downstairs.

'Don't forget to call me when you get to Kathleen's,' Anne reminded her as she was leaving.

Anne watched her walk away, and as Lucy turned the corner, she looked back and waved.

'I'll call you. Stop worrying,' Lucy told her.

Another wave, a smile, and in no time at all Lucy was on the bus, heading for Kathleen's street.

She would have chatted to the conductor had it been the lovely Johnny, but it was a sour-faced female, who spoke not a word to Lucy except: 'Make sure you shove that case right under the steps. We don't want folks falling over it, do we?'

Lucy did as she was told, though as there was just the conductress, herself and the driver on the bus, she wondered who the 'folks' were that might be 'falling over it'.

~

Kathleen was just ironing the last garment in the weekly pile when she heard the tapping on the front door.

'Hold on!' Hastily replacing the iron, she switched it off at the wall. 'I'm on my way!'

As she hurried down the hallway, she muttered

177

under her breath, 'Who the devil can this be? I'm not expecting anybody.'

On inching open the door, she was amazed to see Lucy standing there, suitcase in hand.

'Lucy!' She flung the door open wide. 'Come in. Good grief!' She remarked on her suitcase. 'So where are you off to?'

Lucy felt embarrassed. 'I was hoping I could take you up on your offer of help, and stay with you for a couple of days. If not, it doesn't matter. I'm sorry, Kathleen, I didn't mean to impose myself on you.' Now that she was actually here, Lucy felt embarrassed.

'Hey!' Kathleen ushered her in. 'What the devil d'you mean by that? Impose yourself, indeed! We'll have no more of that silly talk, thank you very much! I'm absolutely thrilled that you took me up on the offer.'

She planted a kiss on Lucy's cheek. 'So now, Lucy girl, it's just you and me. I've got a bottle of cheap plonk somewhere, and we can finish it together, while catching up on the latest gossip. What d'you think to that, eh?'

Lucy hugged her. 'Thank you, Kathleen. You really are a friend.'

'You can bet on that, Lucy girl!'

Ignoring Lucy's protests, Kathleen collected the suitcase and shot up the stairs with it. 'Come on then! You can use the posh bedroom. It's been newly painted, oh, and I've made some new stripy curtains . . . not because I wanted to but because the old ones were hanging in rags.'

As always, Lucy felt warm and comfortable in Kathleen's presence. 'Don't make a fuss over me,' she said. But the truth was, she enjoyed being pampered. It was a new experience for her. Normally, it was she doing the pampering, for her children, her husband, even her sister, and her greatest pleasure had been pampering her beloved parents.

'Hey!' Kathleen wagged a finger. 'You're my best friend and my welcome guest. So don't tell me not to "make a fuss"!'

Aside from all the light-hearted joshing, though, Kathleen was concerned.

She could see that Lucy was unhappy . . . that she might even have been crying. Also, judging by the weight of the suitcase, she suspected Lucy's luggage catered for more than just a couple of days. This was all right by her – Lucy was a dear friend, and she was welcome to stay here for as long as she needed.

Lucy loved what Kathleen had done to the spare room. 'It's so pretty!' She ran her hand down the new curtains. 'I didn't realise you could make curtains.'

Kathleen laughed. 'I've never done it before, but I was determined to have a go. I bought the material and stretched it out on the floor, then I laid the old curtains over the top, and cut out the size.' She grimaced. 'The hard bit was the sewing.'

Bringing Lucy's notice to the crooked hem around one of the curtains, she told her, 'That was the first curtain . . . a bit of a mess.' She then pointed to the second curtain, where the hem was tight and straight.

'By the time I got to this side, I had just about got the hang of it.'

Lucy was impressed. 'You've not done so bad, Kathleen. If you hadn't shown me the crooked hem I would never have noticed.'

Kathleen was pleased at the compliment. 'Right then! You unpack, and I'll find that bottle of plonk.' She gestured to the far wardrobe. 'That's yours. The other one is filled with rubbish that I still haven't got round to sorting out.'

Going out the door, she told Lucy with a wink, 'You might find a few manly things dotted about. They belonged to the last boyfriend. He was a real loser, I can tell you! Vain and pretty, he spent all his spare time building his body and looking in the mirror. Muscle-bound with no brains, that was him! He was good in bed, but he couldn't hold a decent conversation. After a couple of weeks he really got on my nerves, so I chucked him out.'

She went away muttering, leaving Lucy trying not to laugh.

A minute later Kathleen was shouting up the stairs, 'Get a move on, Lucy! I've got the wine and glasses at the ready. All I need is a friend to share it with.'

'I won't be long!' Lucy promised.

Throwing open the suitcase, she stole a quiet moment to look at what she had packed. Not much to show for a woman of forty, is it? she thought.

There were two dresses, one black with white spots, and sleeves that were too long, which Lucy always wore rolled up. The other dress was plain blue. Also a dark skirt and a pink blouse.

There were five pairs of knickers, nothing fancy or frilly; just sensible, white, ordinary knickers. They're not likely to set a man's passion on fire, that's for sure! she thought, which brought Paula to mind. I dare say my cheating sister would never be seen dead in anything so plain.

She laid all her garments out on the bed: the dresses, the knickers, and her nightwear: two ankle-length nighties, and a pair of baggy, pink-striped pyjamas.

At this point she sat on the edge of the bed, her gaze fixed on the tired old garments. She tried to see herself through Martin's eyes, and what she saw was a dowdy woman, old before her time. Who could blame him for turning to Paula? Paula was bright, and pretty, and unlike Lucy, not afraid of anything.

Going across to the dressing table, she examined her reflection in the mirror, and what looked back at her was a face that was tired and weary; that told its own sorry story. A face that convinced Lucy that no man would ever look at her twice.

But with that sobering thought came another, slightly more pleasant, one. 'The stranger at the bus shelter noticed me,' she recalled. 'I must have made some kind of impression because the second time he saw me, it was like he could hardly keep his eyes off me.' She smiled at the memory.

Somewhat reassured, she threw off her coat and cast a critical gaze over her figure. She thought it was more the figure of a woman nearing fifty instead of someone of forty. There was no definite waist, no curves to speak of, and nothing to please the eye. Instead, the oblong shape went straight down, from shoulder to buttocks, with barely a curve between.

Feeling dejected, Lucy turned away to sit on the edge of the bed. What happened to you, Lucy girl? she asked herself. Where did that young, bright-eyed girl go? Didn't she capture the best-looking boy, despite her shyness?

She cast her mind back to the day she and Martin got married. Even with a baby-bump starting to show, she did look pretty that day. Everyone said so . . . even Martin.

Thinking back, remembering how it had been, she began to regret so much of her life. 'Paula was right,' she whispered. 'I *am* old before my time! But then I've had to be. At just sixteen, I had a baby and a husband, and family responsibilities.'

'But why did you let yourself go?' she continued to chastise herself. 'Look at yourself in the mirror, Lucy. What you see there is what Martin sees every time he looks at you.'

She drew little comfort from that thought. 'You really are a sorry-looking article. You don't know how to dress, or how to make up your face, your hair is always the same: lank and dull, just like you. It's no wonder your husband turned to Paula! It's no wonder he wants to be rid of you! Can you blame him? What man would willingly be lumbered with a plain old sop like you?'

Raising her hands to her face, she wiped away the inevitable tears. 'Feeling sorry for yourself won't change anything either.'

A wave of anger swept through her. 'It's your own fault! Somewhere along the way, you failed to be a proper wife to Martin, and now you've got what you deserve!'

The shame of losing Martin to her sister was all-consuming.

While she took stock of herself, Lucy had no idea that Kathleen was at the top of the stairs, from where she heard Lucy's every word.

Deeply concerned, Kathleen quietly waited until Lucy busied herself emptying her clothes into the drawer. On softest tiptoe she then made her way down-stairs to the living room.

A few minutes later, she returned to the bottom of the stairs, and yelled up, 'Lucy . . . Come on! What the devil are you doing up there? I hope you haven't gone to bed . . . leaving me to drink all this wine by myself?'

Lucy appeared on the landing. 'Sorry, Kathleen, I was just unpacking, but it's all done now.' She made her way down.

'Good! Come on through.' Kathleen betrayed no signs of having witnessed Lucy's unhappy rantings.

A few minutes later the two of them were seated before the cheery fire, each with a glass of red wine.

'I'm glad you came here tonight,' Kathleen started. 'To tell you the truth, I wasn't really looking forward to my own company, but apart from that, Lucy, I've been really concerned about you, wondering how you might be coping, what with losing your parents so suddenly. I'm always here if you need me . . . you do know that, don't you?'

Lucy thanked her. 'I'm really glad to be here with you,' she confessed. 'I've been so down lately. It's very difficult to cope with having lost Mum and Dad, especially with them going so close to each other I still can't believe it's happened. It's like some kind of nightmare.'

When the emotions rushed in, she paused to take a breath. 'I've been so worried for Anne and young Sam, but thankfully they seem to be handling it . . . probably better than I am.'

Kathleen understood. 'The younger ones do seem more able to handle such things much better than we expect them to. They take it in their stride, probably because, unlike us, they're always looking forward to some new, exciting event, and who can blame them? They have their whole lives in front of them. I suppose it's because they don't see death as ever happening to them. But when you're older, the death of someone you love hits hard. It makes you realise that no one is immortal . . . not even ourselves.'

Lucy agreed. 'You're right; but it doesn't mean that the children don't feel the loss as hard as we do,' she replied.

'Oh, I'm not saying that.' Kathleen felt the need to explain. 'All I'm saying is, thankfully, the younger ones are just beginning to build their lives and so have far more to think about. They spend most of their time looking forward, while the rest of us seem to constantly look back. D'you see what I'm gettng at?'

Collecting the wine bottle from the table, she tipped a good measure into Lucy's glass.

Lucy absent-mindedly took a sip, and then another, before admitting, 'Yes, I do, and you're right. When we're just starting out, we think the future will be rosy and that everything exciting will come our way. We believe the family will always be there.'

Kathleen nodded. 'That's exactly what I mean. In the end, we all come to learn that the ones we love will not be around for ever.' She raised her glass. 'So . . . here's to the loved ones who have gone before!'

Lucy clinked glasses with her. 'To our loved ones . . . wherever they are.'

They each took another healthy sip of wine, and then another, and Lucy remarked sadly, 'Do you know, Kathleen, I was forty not long ago?'

'Well, I thought you might be, but I wasn't altogether certain. And did you know that I am five years older than you?' she groaned.

'No! I thought you might be forty-one . . . or there-abouts. But not forty-five. Well, all I can say is, you look good for your age.'

'Oh, thank you very much . . . and so do you.' Kathleen raised her glass again, and they toasted each other.

'Kathleen? Do you honestly think I look good for my age?' Lucy asked then.

'I said so, didn't I?'

'Yes, but did you mean it?'

'What's the matter with you? Of course I meant it, or I would not have said it.'

'Swear on my life!'

'No! That's tempting providence.'

'So, you were lying, weren't you? You only said it to make me feel better about myself?'

There was a short span of silence, before Kathleen replied, 'Look, Lucy, you really are a good-looking woman, only . . .'

'Only what?'

'Well . . .' Kathleen took another sip of her wine.

'Kathleen! Go on . . . what were you about to say?'

'All right! But if I say what I think, will you promise not to fall out with me, because I couldn't bear that?'

'I promise.'

'Good! But first, we'll drink on it.' Kathleen clinked her glass with Lucy's. 'Here's to us!' And she took a good swig of wine.

'To us!' Lucy also took a generous sip of wine, although she was not at all used to it.

Kathleen wondered how she might tell Lucy what she thought without upsetting her. 'Well, what I was thinking was that I've always thought you could make a lot better of yourself if you tried. I mean . . . your hair, for instance – and I'm not being critical – it's just that you could do so many things with it.'

'Go on, then. What exactly are you saying?'

'Well, it's a nice length and it always has a shine, but

you never change the style. You could curl it, or plait it, or maybe tie it up in a bright ribbon. You could try a loose fringe, or something a little bit different now and then. You asked me what I thought, and I'm just being honest because that's what friends do.'

Lucy understood. She had often thought about changing her hairstyle, which had been the same since her schooldays but with no sense of style, she had no idea what to do.

'You're right, Kathleen, I know you are, but when I've asked Martin if I should try a new hairstyle, he's always told me not to bother. He said it would be a waste of money, because it would only grow back exactly the way it is. I've tried different things before. For instance, I once changed the colour of my lipstick. I'd worn it for years, so I thought it was time for a change, but I soon went back to my old colour. For some stupid reason, it doesn't matter what I try, I always go back to my old ways.'

'Sounds like you're stuck in a rut, Lucy girl!'

Lucy had another question. 'Kathleen . . . do you think I'm fat?'

'No, I do not! After having had two children, you can expect to be a bit out of shape, but you're certainly not fat! All right, if I'm being honest, you might be a bit lumpy here and there, like the rest of us, but that's life. We can't all be perfect, can we?' Kathleen shrugged. 'Besides, it sounds to me as if you're not happy with change, so if that's the case, maybe you should just leave things as they are, like Martin said.'

'Maybe that's really the way he wants me,' Lucy remarked quietly. 'Dull, and always available, to help bring in the wages, to look after the house, do the cooking, iron his shirts and pander to his every need, but when it comes to sex, cuddles and fun, he chooses my sister over me.' She had not meant to say that out loud, but it just tumbled out.

'Your sister? I don't believe it!' Kathleen was visibly shocked.

'It's true. I found them together. Twice.'

'The hussy! Your own sister . . . Unbelievable!'

'Somehow, I've obviously let him down in the bedroom. The way things are, he hardly notices me, except to ask for a clean shirt, or to tell me not to bother waiting up, because he won't be back till late. Then when he does come home, I'm still wide awake wondering where he is and what he's doing. Then, he'll come upstairs, undress and climb into bed without so much as "How are you?" He'll undress quickly, and within minutes he'll be fast asleep with his back to me, snoring his head off. I ask you, Kathleen, is that the actions of a man who truly loves his wife?'

Kathleen was careful in her answer. 'If it was me, I would put that question to him!'

Lucy appeared not to have heard what Kathleen said. Instead she was muttering to herself, 'Sometimes, it's like I'm not even in the same room with him. I've tried talking with him about our marriage and the way he feels about me, but he just makes fun of me, saying I'm being silly, and that I'm imagining things. The trouble is, Kathleen, we were just kids when we got married. I often wonder, if he hadn't got me pregnant, would we have got married? Oh, I'm not fooling myself; Martin has never been a full-on lover. Nor does he say pretty things or compliment me.'

'Some men are like that, Lucy.'

'It's my fault, isn't it?' Lucy was convinced of that. 'I must be doing something wrong, or he would never have cheated on me like he did . . . and with my own sister! What did I do that was so bad he would shame me in that way?'

'Lucy, stop punishing yourself. You've done nothing wrong. You're a fine woman, a good mother, a loyal wife, and you work hard. And if he can't value you for that alone, he doesn't deserve you!'

Lucy's spirits were lifted by her friend's kind words. 'Maybe you're right! If he wants Paula, let him have her. And when he finally discovers what a cruel tease she is, it will serve him right. And he needn't think he can run back to me, because I won't give him the time of day!'

Kathleen was also fired with Lucy's new enthusiasm. 'Attagirl! That's fighting talk.' And when Lucy now held out her glass for more wine, Kathleen topped it up. 'Let's drink to you and me, girl, and to hell with everyone else! We need to be comfortable with who we are. You think you're dull and lumpy, and I fret because I'd like to be taller and prettier, but who cares? Everybody's got faults. You're the way you are, and I'm the way I am. And that's that!'

'You're right, Kathleen!' The wine had put Lucy in a fighting mood. 'What does it matter if I am lumpy, and why should I care if my boobies have shrunk to nothing? I'm the only one who ever sees them anyway. Martin certainly isn't interested. And it's not my fault they've shrunk. It happened after I had the children, and I would not swap them for the world . . .' Roaring with laughter, she fell back in the chair. 'The children, I mean, not the boobies! I'd swap *them* if I had the chance.' She rolled her eyes dreamily. 'I'd like big, pointy ones, with nipples you could hang a hat on!'

Never having heard Lucy talk like that before, Katheen was shocked. 'Lucy Lovejoy, behave yourself! I reckon the wine's gone to your head.'

'Don't be silly!' Lucy's voice was gently slurred. 'I do not . . . drink,' she said haughtily. 'I've never drunk in my life . . . except at Luke's christening. And Anne's wedding. But you know what?'

'What?'

'I should get drunk whenever I like. Drunk as a skunk. Then I could stand up to the lot of 'em!' She suddenly started crying again. 'I can't believe that Martin slept with my sister. But I actually caught them . . . laughing and joking . . . playing about like two teenagers.'

Taking a deep breath, she was silent for a moment, while, in the wake of Lucy's sorrow, Kathleen also began to feel tearful.

'He's never played about with me like that, ever!' Lucy went on. 'They've hurt me, Kathleen, Martin and my sister. They've hurt me badly. And now I'm lost, and I don't know which way to turn. I must have deserved it, though, but what did I do wrong? Why has he stopped loving me?' In her mind she could see the two of them together. 'They were all over each other, and even when she followed him home to our house – after our parents' funeral – he must have wanted her there or he never would have let her in.'

'It was a terrible thing they did.' Kathleen felt like storming round there and giving them a piece of her mind. But it was not for her to interfere.

'It was obvious he didn't want me, so I told him he could have her. Then I packed my case and left. Tell me, Kathleen, what else could I do?'

It seemed like Lucy would burst into tears again. Kathleen wrapped her two chubby arms about her. 'Ssh, you'll be all right, Lucy. It might take a time, but things will sort themselves out, you'll see.' She held on to Lucy but there was nothing she could say that would take away Lucy's pain. All she could do was to hold her, and be there for her, as long as it took.

The two of them clung to each other as Lucy described how she had run away. 'I had a terrible fight with Paula,' she admitted. 'She was in my house, with him. She called me names and she said bad things. Shouting at the top of her voice, she was! I'm sure the neighbours must have heard, and I felt so ashamed, Kathleen. And now they both hate me.'

Kathleen had been shocked to the core by the way

Lucy had been treated. Never in her wildest dreams would she have guessed Martin and Paula were together in that way. The whole disgusting business must have been a horrible experience for gentle-natured Lucy.

'I just don't know what to do,' Lucy confided. 'I couldn't tell Anne the awful truth, so I lied . . . to my own daughter. I told her that you invited me here, and how I needed a few days to gather my thoughts after everything that's happened. Oh, Kathleen, what kind of a mother am I, lying to my daughter like that? I even got Anne to lie to her brother. I was glad he wasn't there when I went round. Thankfully, Sam had gone off somewhere with his friends.'

'Well, at least that's a kind of blessing,' Kathleen assured her. 'And for what it's worth, I would have done exactly what you did, kicking Paula out and keeping the truth from the children. There will be time enough for them to find out the truth. One thing at a time, eh?'

'Yes, I have to deal with it the best way I can. I'm hoping Martin will do the same and keep his sordid affair from the children, at least for now. Meantime, I want to put as much distance between myself and Martin as possible. I need to think it through, and then decide what I should do.'

Even as she said that she felt like a coward for having run away. 'Maybe I should go back now, and talk everything through with Martin. What do you think, Kathleen? Should I go back and have it out with the pair of them, once and for all?'

Kathleen was hesitant to intervene in what could be a broken marriage in the making. 'I can't tell you what to do, Lucy,' she decided. 'All I can do is say what I would do if I was in your shoes.'

'Tell me then. What would you do?'

'Hmm . . . let me see. Firstly, I certainly would not go back with my tail between my legs.'

'So, what would you do?'

'Right! Well, number one, like you said, I might go back and have it out with the pair of them. And even if it resulted in me losing my marriage, then so be it. I mean, it can't have been much of a marriage if the husband feels the need to sleep with another woman, whoever she might be!'

'And the other thing you would do?' Lucy urged.

'You might not like it.'

'It doesn't matter. Tell me all the same.'

'If I still loved him, I might try and win him back.'

Lucy was unsure about that one. 'If he didn't want me before, how could I possibly win him back? I'm still the same woman he rejected. I haven't changed.'

'So why not change then? Take a leaf out of your sister's book. Show him that you can be as attractive and exciting as Paula.'

'That's impossible! All my life I've tried to be more like Paula, but it never happened, and it never will. Me and her, we're like chalk and cheese.'

Kathleen, however, was adamant. 'Listen to me! First of all, throw out most of your old clothes. Then go and buy two new garments. One for bed, and one for going out. You must try them on in the shop, and they must not look anything like the clothes already in your wardrobe. They must be absolutely different from what you've worn in the past. Are you following me, Lucy?'

'I'm not really sure, but go on.'

'You must ask the shop assistant what she honestly thinks, and you must tell her how you're trying to completely change your style, in order to get your man back.' Kathleen smiled knowingly. 'These fashion people often like a bit of a challenge. If you're worried, I'll come with you. I think I have an idea what you should be looking for, but you'll need to try on several outfits. I'll know the right look when I see it.'

Lucy was suddenly excited. 'And after the new clothes, then what?'

'Right! Well, the next stop is the hairdresser's. You want your hair completely restyled . . . sort of sexy, and very pretty.'

'All right . . . and then what?' Lucy urged her on.

'Then . . .' Kathleen had to think hard, 'I would trawl the shops for the most attractive pair of shoes you have ever seen – a daring colour, with heels a little higher than you're used to, but not so high that you can't walk comfortably in them. Oh, and last of all, go into Woolworths, to the cosmetics counter, and ask the girl to show you the kind of make-up you should be wearing. Tell her that you're having a complete make-over and that you're trying to impress your man. Oh! And maybe get some costume jewellery, something like a little butterfly brooch for the shoulder of your new jacket or dress. It will add a bit of class.'

'Wow!' Lucy's head was reeling, and now she could hardly wait to get started.

But then her make-believe world suddenly crashed about her. 'Oh, no! It can't be done, Kathleen!'

'Why not?'

'Because it will cost money, and I haven't got anywhere near enough.'

For a moment, having both got carried away with the idea of transforming Lucy into an eye-catching female, they were suddenly dejected.

Kathleen racked her brains and came up with a possible solution. 'It's all right! I'll lend you the money. I've got a bit put by. Not a fortune, obviously, but enough to get you looking good . . . within limits.'

Kathleen had to admit to herself that Lucy was no raving beauty, though she did have a few admirable assets that a bit of style could enhance. 'Take the money, Lucy. You can pay me back . . . whenever!'

'No, Kathleen! I'm really grateful, but I can't take your money. I have no idea when I can pay you back,' Lucy objected. 'Obviously, I've managed to scrape together a little money, but it's just enough to get me away from home and maybe pay for one night in a boarding house. That's a part of my plan.'

'That's madness! You can't do that. You need to confront Martin. Let him be the one to leave.'

'No, never mind a makeover, I need a breathing space. I need to put a distance between us, and I won't

waste time thinking about Martin. I'll be looking for
work straight away. I don't really care what kind of
work it is – whether it's dirty, or with long hours and
badly paid. It will be a start, and I'll do whatever it
takes to rebuild my life. My parents are gone, and no
doubt my job is lost, along with my marriage. So now,
my two children are my main priority.'

Kathleen was amazed at Lucy's strength. 'You seem
to have it all planned out,' she told her.

'I've had time enough to think about it,' Lucy
answered softly. 'Either I will miss Martin desperately
and try to get him back, or I might discover that he's
just a part of the life I once had, and there is no place
for him in the life I mean to make. Either way, I'll
know soon enough.' From somewhere deep inside,
Lucy realised, she had found a strength she never
knew she had.

She felt suddenly rebellious. 'Come to think of it,
why should I change anyway? This is who I am. What
you see is what you get, and if it isn't enough for
Martin, then let him have his fancy piece, and good
luck to them both.'

'You don't really mean that, do you, Lucy?' Kathleen
was surprised. She thought Lucy would have done
almost anything to get back the man she loved.

'Having a new dress, fancy hairdo and bold
make-up would have been a real experience, and
thank you for suggesting it,' Lucy answered, 'but I
won't do it . . . not for a man who has no need of
me any more.'

'I think the wine's gone to your head,' Kathleen remarked, 'but you're right. Men, eh? Sod the lot of 'em!' She replenished their glasses, and again the two of them toasted their independence.

'So, where might you be off to?' Kathleen was curious.

'I'm not sure. I'm not an experienced traveller. I thought of sticking a pin in the map and heading wherever it pointed, but then I realised that would be plain foolish. So I've decided to just go down to the station and see where the trains are going. I might head for the coast. That way I've got more chance of finding temporary work, if I decide to stay. I just need enough money to carry me through until I find a well-paid regular job.' She sheepishly admitted, 'I hadn't really made any detailed plans. At first, it was just about getting right away from here.'

She sank back into the chair. 'That's me all over,' she went on. 'Full of ideas, but no proper plan. When Paula wants something, she just goes out and does it. Unlike me, the pitiful ditherer.'

'You've got to stop putting yourself down, Lucy. You should give yourself credit.' Rather than reprimand her, Kathleen gently reminded her, 'You've had two crippling blows lately. Just one of them would be enough to floor some people, but not you! You've stood strong throughout. As always, you've been there for the family, and in spite of what Martin and Paula have done to you, you've taken it all on the chin. You haven't buckled under, nor have you given them the satisfaction of knowing how deeply they've hurt you. Instead, you've made the very difficult decision of moving away to rebuild a broken life. Tell me this, Lucy Lovejoy, how many other women – including your sister – would have the strength and resolve to do that?'

Lucy had no answer. But suddenly she felt proud, and with the pride, and too much wine, came the tears. 'Thank you. Somehow you make me feel strong. You really are my bestest friend.'

Kathleen raised her glass in another toast. 'To you, dear Lucy. And I am very proud to be your "bestest" friend.'

The two of them almost leaped out of their skins when the telephone rang. 'Jeeze!' Scrambling out of the chair, Katheen hobbled to the hallway, where she picked up the telephone. 'Who is it?' A pause, then, 'Oh, Anne. Hang on a minute, I'll get her.' She hurried back into the sitting room. 'It's Anne. She's worried that you didn't call her.'

'Oh, crikey!' Getting out of the chair, Lucy instinctively scraped her hands over her hair and nervously patted her clothes down.

When she picked up the telephone, Anne immediately asked, 'Mum! Are you all right? It sounds to me like you've got a cold coming on.'

Lucy pounced on that idea. 'You might be right,' she said, giving another little cough. 'I'll be all right, though. Kathleen's made a kind of toddy for me . . . hot water and red wine . . . it seems to be doing the trick.'

Anne laughed. 'Is it now? Well, just make sure you don't drink too much of it, or you might keel over. You know you're not used to wine.'

'I do know that, and I am being careful.'

Smiling to herself at the other end of the line, Anne changed the subject. 'I'm calling you because you didn't call me, so now I know why, don't I?'

'Do you?'

'Yes, and I'm glad that Kathleen is looking after you . . . even if she is plying you with booze.'

'Hey! Behave yourself. I can look after myself, thank you.'

'I know you can. Anyway, how long do you plan to stay there? I've already said you can come here and stay with me for as long as you like.'

'I know that, sweetheart, and it's a lovely idea, but not just now, eh? I really do need some time away.'

'Dad's missing you. Why didn't you tell him where you were going? He came round here, looking for you. He was worried.'

Lucy had to think quickly. 'Oh! Sorry . . . I thought I told him, sweetheart, but you know what he's like. All he can think of is football, work and darts. Most of the time, he turns a deaf ear.'

'To tell you the truth, I thought he was upset. I reckon you two have had a row, haven't you?'

'No! Well, not exactly a row, but we did have words . . . about something and nothing.'

'What does that mean?'

'Exactly what it says. I can't remember, it was so

trivial. I'm sure you and Les have words and then later, you can't even recall what it was all about.'

'But Dad's really missing you, Mum. He seemed on edge to me.'

'Did you tell him where I was?'

'Yes. You didn't say not to, did you? He was just a bit worried about you. Are you cross with me? Was I supposed to keep it a secret?'

'No! Of course not. Stop fretting. I'll call him.'

'All right, Mum, but if you need to get away from everything, just tell him that. Tell him you need some quiet time to yourself. I'm sure he'll understand. Besides, it'll do him good to look after himself for a few days . . . or however long it takes. I'm more worried about you, though. We all know how devastated you are by losing Grandma and Granddad. But you never show it. You never think about yourself. You're always too busy looking after everybody else. So now, like I say, you need some quiet time. Kathleen is a really good friend – she'll help you come to terms with everything, I know she will. And remember, if you need any one of us, all you have to do is call.'

'Thank you, sweetheart.'

'Love you, Mum.'

'Love you too. Give Luke a big hug for me, and if Sam rings you don't worry him. All he needs to know is that I'm staying with Kathleen for a while, and that everything is fine. Just tell him that, will you?'

'I will.'

Just then the baby started crying. 'Got to go, Mum . . . 'bye.'

After Anne had gone, Lucy stood a moment, absent-mindedly tapping the end of the receiver on her lips. Her head was spinning with all manner of thoughts. Something Anne had said had her wondering. Why had Martin not told Anne about Paula, and what the two of them had been up to? And why had he gone round there in the first place? Looking for her, Anne said. So, did that mean he had decided he'd rather have her back than be with Paula?

Mmm! It's very strange that he should go looking for me; unless he was worried that I had told Anne what he and her aunt Paula had been up to, Lucy thought.

She smiled wickedly. 'I don't suppose he was looking for me at all. In fact, he probably doesn't give a monkey's where I am! He just went round to make sure Anne knew nothing of what was going on. All he cares about is covering his own back. Well, it's too late now, Martin, she decided, carefully replacing the receiver. You made your choice, and now you must live with it. Oh, but I would love to know what's happened. Has she dumped you? Is that it? Yeah . . . Paula's dumped you and now, in your arrogance, you think I'll come running, don't you? Well, you can go to hell. It might surprise you, but I am not in the market for Paula's cast-offs. You've made your bed and you must lie on it!

After a moment of reflection, she returned to the sitting room, trying very hard not to smile.

'Everything all right, is it?' Obviously, Kathleen had caught the gist of Lucy's conversation with her daughter.

'That was Anne, checking up on me.'

'Well, that's good, isn't it?'

'I told her I was staying with you, that I wanted some time away. Anne said she fully understands and that I should take as long as I need.'

'Anne is a very sensible young woman. She obviously has your best interests at heart.'

Lucy explained the phone call. 'She said her dad came round, and that he wanted to know where I was.'

'Hmm!' Kathleen had the same thought as Lucy. 'That was very thoughtful of him!' she quipped sarcastically. 'What's happened there? Paula got fed up with him, has she?' Her comment came straight from the warm wine. 'Sent him packing, has she? Huh! If you ask me, the pair of 'em want a kick up the arse!'

'Hey!' Lucy laughed out loud. 'I've never heard you swear like that before!'

'Well, then, you don't know me as well as I thought you did!' Kathleen laughed. 'When it warrants it, I can curse like the best of 'em. And I reckon them two warrant it now. I just hope they get their comeuppance for hurting you the way they did.'

'Anne told him I was here,' Lucy said.

'Did she now? Well, that's all right, because if he

comes round here, he'll have me to deal with, I can tell you that!'

'Oh, you needn't worry yourself, because Anne will make sure he gives me the time and space I need. Bless her, she thinks I'm here with you because of losing Mum and Dad. Thankfully, she doesn't know the whole truth.'

'Well, now you can relax,' Kathleen suggested. 'Put him out of your mind. What you need is to concentrate on what you might do next. You say you're off to a new life, but how can you manage it? I mean, you won't borrow money from me, and you don't even know where you're going . . . But, look, I've got a little idea. So, d'you want to hear it or not?'

'Yes, go on.' Lucy knew Kathleen would tell her anyway.

'Right!' Kathleen was pleased. 'I've got an old widowed aunt. She's a dear old soul, lives alone in a pretty house not too far from Torquay. She's always asking me to go and stay with her, but it's difficult, what with me working full time. But I've had her to visit here once or twice and she's no trouble.'

Lucy thought she already knew what Kathleen was getting at, but she asked anyway. 'So, are you suggesting I might be able to go and stay with your aunt for a time?'

'Exactly!' Kathleen grew excited, 'Oh, Lucy, you'll love her. She can be cranky at times, but she's got a kind heart, and I know she'll take good care of you. Think about it, Lucy: a house with views you would never believe; the sea air all around you; freedom to do as you please. Oh, and she's a good listener when needed.'

Lucy was not altogether convinced. 'I would be barging in on her without fair warning. And when I get there, she might not even like me. Worse, I might not like her, and it would be an impossible situation. Then where will I be? Right back where I started, only worse, because I'll have used up some of the little money I've scraped together.'

Kathleen took Lucy's worries on board. 'All right, I understand what you're saying. But if it does work out, you really will have landed on your feet. You might even find a job in Torquay itself, and then you would be totally independent.'

'Well, yes, there is that, I suppose. But I'm not altogether sure . . .'

'OK, Lucy. I tell you what, you sleep on it. What do you say?'

Lucy agreed. 'I'll sleep on it.'

PART THREE

Lucy's Brave New World

CHAPTER TEN

IT WAS ALMOST eight o'clock when Lucy woke from a restless sleep, and even now, in the light of day, her mind was in turmoil.

Having walked the floor of her bedroom for more hours than she had slept, she had eventually come to a decision; although she remained unsure as to whether it was the right one or not.

Catching sight of herself in the mirror, she was shocked at her dishevelled appearance. 'Good grief, Lucy! You look a real fright.' Her hair was wild and tousled because of her twisting and turning in her troubled sleep. Her eyes were sore and tired and her whole demeanour looked frantic. 'What's happened to you?' she asked herself angrily. You had best get a grip of yourself, or you'll go under . . . and that's the last thing you want. Pull yoursef together, woman! For once in your life, you need to think of what's best for you. Not for Martin or Paula, not even for the family, but for you – Lucy Lovejoy.

Irritated, she ran the flats of her hands through her tousled hair. You won't get anywhere if you keep looking back, she decided. You need to look forward.

Leaning into the mirror, she studied the tired, worn face and the sorry, red eyes that stared back at her, and she laughed out loud. 'You look like a sorry old drunk the morning after the night before,' she giggled.

Patting her face, she managed to return a flush of colour to her cheeks. Lay off the booze in future . . . you know you're not used to it, she silently admonished herself. Take a good look at yourself, woman. See what it's done to you.

She felt the tiniest bit ashamed, and then she gave a merry chuckle. 'Me and Kathleen . . .' she tutted, '. . . aren't we a pair of bad 'uns, eh?' There was Lucy, looking like something the cat dragged in, and judging by the silence from downstairs, her partner in crime was still fast asleep in bed.

Lucy was both nervous and excited. After examining all the alternatives, she had finally returned to a decision that she instinctively believed must be the right one for her. It felt right. It made her feel good.

Standing here in front of the mirror, she stared at herself for what seemed an age, her frantic mind ticking over, worrying, weighing the possible consequences of the choice she had settled on, although deep down, somewhere in her deepest soul, she was content. For the first time in her life, she had actually made a decision all by herself, without any persuasion from others. Moreover, she now felt strong enough to see it through.

Deep in thought, she walked to the window, drew open the curtains, and looked out. The fateful new day was here. 'A new beginning,' she murmured with a smile. 'A new life for Lucy Lovejoy.'

She felt special. She felt stronger in herself than she had for a very long time. It seemed as though she had actually achieved something.

Excited and unable to contain herself, she opened the window and called out in a strong, loud voice, 'Lucy Lovejoy is off on a real adventure . . . yeah!'

Clenching her fists, she shook them above her head. From now on I need to find out who I really am, and where my place is, she decided. She was afraid. But not enough to change her plans; because this was her time.

When Kathleen's voice called from the bedroom door, Lucy quickly shut the window. 'Lucy, what's going on? Is that you shouting?'

'What?' Lucy was too embarrassed to admit it was her. 'Oh! I thought it was *you*. I thought your radio must be on.'

'No, I don't have a radio in my room. Somebody was yelling, though. It woke me up. Oh, well, never mind. It must have been kids in the street. Are you out of bed, Lucy?'

'I am now, yes.'

'Right, well, I'll get washed and dressed and I'll see you downstairs. You can tell me what you've decided.'

There was a pause before Kathleen asked, 'You have decided, haven't you, Lucy?'

'I have . . . yes.'

~

Some ten minutes later, the two of them were sitting in the small kitchen, sipping tea.

'Right then!' Kathleen urged Lucy. 'So, let's hear your plan . . . what have you decided? Will you be going to stay with my aunt, or not?'

'No. Thank you for the suggestion, but I've decided to go right away . . . somewhere Mum and Dad used to take me and Paula, when we were kids.' She choked back tears. 'I've been missing Mum and Dad so much, I thought it might make me feel closer to them. D'you know what I mean?'

'Oh, Lucy! I think it's a lovely idea. And, yes, I have an idea how you feel. I agree wholeheartedly with your choice, as long as it doesn't make you feel sad.'

'It won't. Oh, but we had such wonderful times there as kids . . . me and Paula. And later, when Samuel and Anne were toddlers, Martin took us there once. The children played for hours on that very same beach where we had played.'

She felt torn. 'I somehow feel that going back might help in some way. Last night when I was in bed, I got to remembering how it used to be. Back then we didn't have too much of anything, really, but there were no complications. Just close family . . . and lots of love and laughter . . . unlike now, when it seems to be one bad thing after another.' She went on, 'For some reason, which I don't fully understand, I feel the need to remind myself of how wonderful it was in that delightful place, when me and Paula were just innocent kids . . .' Her voice tailed off as she recalled the unforgivable liaison between Martin and her younger sister.

Lucy had been left shattered by recent, cruel events, so Kathleen fully understood why she would want to recapture the delightful times she enjoyed as a child, with her sister and parents, and later, with Martin and her babies.

'I think you've made the best decision,' she reassured Lucy. 'I do believe that sometimes, we really need to look back before we can look forward.'

Lucy was greatly relieved. 'So, you're not upset that I didn't choose to stay with your aunt?'

'Of course I'm not upset.' Kathleen was adamant. 'You seem to have made a choice I had not even thought of. But you still haven't told me where it is exactly.'

Joy lit up Lucy's face. 'It's a beautiful little place in Dorset. Somehow, I need to recapture the peace and happiness I felt back then, if that's possible. I remember it so vividly. It's not far from Dorchester. It's a small village off the beaten track, and right on the coast. When we went there, all those years ago, it was little known by holidaymakers.'

'I'll bet it's different now, though,' Kathleen remarked. 'It's been such a long time since you were there, it's bound to have been discovered over the years. Don't you think so, Lucy?'

Lucy thought it would be an awful shame if that lovely place had been spoiled, although it was true that nowhere remained unchanged for all time. 'You could be right,' she answered. 'When we were there with the children some twenty years back, I did notice there were a few more houses dotted about. After all this time, though, as you say, it's not very likely that more people have discovered it.'

'So, if it has changed, will that spoil it for you, Lucy?'

'No. It won't alter my memories.' She was certain of that. 'Besides, the landscape itself is bound to be the same . . . I hope. The high cliffs, the wide, open beach and the waves lapping over the sands . . . oh, and the beautiful views from the pretty, wooden jetty.'

She could see it all so plainly in her mind. 'Oh, Kathleen, I do hope it's still just as I remember.' For a magic moment, she was there, losing herself in the character of that charming little place.

'You know what, Lucy? In a way I envy you, going back there. Revisiting your cherished memories. I can see you in my mind's eye, perched high up on some cliff, legs dangling over the edge while you gaze out over the sea. Oh, Lucy! It's exactly what you need . . . and it's what you deserve.'

She imagined the idyllic seaside village that Lucy had described so vividly. 'It sounds like the kind of quiet, lonely place we all need from time to time, when the big bad world starts crowding in.'

Lucy agreed. 'The first time we went there, with Mum and Dad, I was just ten years old. I've never forgotten it. Then, some years later, after we had both the children, Martin and I took them there. We only went the once, when money was really short. Anne was a toddler, and Sam was a babe in arms.' She paused to remember. 'It was so beautiful, Kathleen. Sadly, though, that was the first and last time for us.'

Kathleen was curious. 'What's the name of this little paradise?'

'If I remember rightly, it was called Limerton or Littleton – something like that – but I'm sure I could find it on the map. The name just popped into my head last night – I can't think why. Oh, and I'll never forget the first time we went, and Dad got lost. We went round and round, up and down, and then the old banger of a car suddenly stopped and wouldn't go. Eventually, we were towed off to a garage, with Dad grumbling and cursing all the way.'

The memory was so real, she could hear her father's voice in her head. 'Roll on the day, when I have enough money to send this useless bag o' bones to the scrapheap where it belongs!' Lucy did a fine imitation of her father's cursing.

Kathleen laughed. 'I don't blame him,' she quipped. 'Driving all that way, only to break down when you get there. I reckon I'd be grumpy an' all.'

'He really loved that old car,' Lucy explained. 'He never did send it to the scrapheap. Instead he kept it for about four years, but it was forever breaking down. In the end he sold it to a neighbour who, as far as I remember, had no trouble whatsoever with it.'

They both laughed at that. 'Maybe the car didn't like your dad cursing it all the time,' Kathleen teased. 'But you were telling me . . . how did you manage to arrive at this little hideaway you loved so much?'

'Oh, yes! The man at the garage couldn't fix the car straight away, so because he had a big old truck, and as we were only four miles from the place we had been looking for, he took us all there in the truck. It was great fun, but needless to say, Dad was not in the best of moods.'

'I'm not surprised.' Kathleen chuckled at the picture in her mind of Lucy's dad ranting and raving.

'He told the man with the truck that the old car had enjoyed its last journey, that it rattled the teeth and shook the bones, and that after that bad experience it would be a week before he could walk properly. He vowed that whenever he managed to get the old rust bucket back home, he would turn it into a henhouse in the back garden!'

Kathleen roared with laughter. 'Your dad sounds like a bit of a devil.'

Lucy smiled at the memory. 'It was one of those days when everything seemed to go wrong, but when we actually got to our destination, it was so beautiful we just forgot all the disappointments. We came off the busy main road, then round a bend, and right there before our eyes was paradise on earth. Tucked away among some high, sloping cliffs, it simply took our breath away.' She smiled. 'It even silenced our dad. One minute we were on the main road, with him swearing and moaning and threatening all manner of punishment for the poor old car, and then we turned a corner into the village, and he didn't even make another peep. At least not until me and Paula scrambled out and ran towards the beach. Then he was yelling, "Be careful, you two!"'

'Careful of what?' Kathleen asked.

'I'm not really sure. Everything, I suppose. "Be careful!" is always what parents say to their kids when they run off.'

'So, did you get onto the beach all right?' Kathleen had this captivating image in her mind of cliffs and a wide beach, and the two young girls running, happy and excited.

'The beach was completely empty,' Lucy recalled, 'with not a soul in sight. I could not believe that we had this great big, beautiful beach all to ourselves.'

The memories came thick and fast. 'I'll never forget it,' she told Kathleen excitedly. 'It was exactly the same when Martin and I took the children there years later. It was still unspoiled, and since that last visit many years ago, I've had a hankering to go back.' Slightly embarrassed, she said softly, 'I know it sounds soppy, but it was the kind of place that somehow gets right into your soul.'

Kathleen smiled. 'Sometimes a place – or a person – can do that to you,' she said knowingly.

She could see the longing and regret in Lucy's eyes. She could hear it in her voice, and she was convinced that Lucy had made the right decision. 'I'm glad you've chosen to go back there,' she said. 'I think it's the right thing to do. It will give you a chance to reflect. The peace and tranquillity, and the comfort of wonderful memories with family . . . it will help to heal you, Lucy, I know it will. And once that begins to happen, you'll find you have a clear idea of what you want to do next.'

Lucy was close to tears. 'Thank you, Kathleen. I don't know what I would have done without you.'

'Don't give it a second thought,' Kathleen chided. 'You would have done the same for me. Just remember, I'm here if you need me.' She gave a long sigh. 'Oh, Lucy! I really do wish I could come with you . . . but I can't.' She had an idea, though. 'After you've sorted yourself out, maybe the two of us can have a week or so in this beautiful place, and you can show me around. What d'you say to that?'

'Oh, that would be lovely!' Lucy got out of her chair and gave her friend a long hug. 'Yes! We'll do that . . . just you and me.' She would not forget.

~

Kathleen called for a taxi to take Lucy to Bedford station.

'He'll be here in ten minutes,' she told Lucy. 'I found his number on a card in a shop window a few weeks back. I thought it might come in handy. Apparently, he's local, and he never overcharges. He also has a reputation for being a safe driver.'

In a surprisingly short time the taxi arrived. Nervous and excited, Lucy said goodbye. 'I can never thank you enough, Kathleen.' She wrapped her arms about this wonderful, caring friend, and held her as though she would never let go.

'Ring me as soon as you get there, will you, Lucy?' Kathleen discreetly brushed away her tears. 'I'll be waiting for your call.'

'I'll ring you the minute I arrive,' Lucy promised, 'and, please, Kathleen, don't forget the story we decided on, in case Anne should come round. I don't like deceiving her, but I think it's a necessary evil. For a multitude of reasons, I do not want the chldren finding out where I've gone, and why.'

'I understand. If she does ask, I will simply tell her that you really needed to get away and be on your own for a while. I'll explain that you've gone to stay with my old aunt, and that she is not on the telephone.'

'Thank you.' Lucy explained, 'I don't want her telling Martin or Paula any different. The less anyone knows where I am, the better . . . for now, anyway.'

'So, do you think you will eventually tell them about Martin and Paula, and that it was the main reason you had to get away?'

'I have no idea how it will all end.' Lucy was deeply ashamed that this was the second time in as many days that she had not been altogether honest with her daughter. But it had to be done because the last thing she needed was Anne, or anyone else, coming after her and upsetting her plans. 'I can't let anyone know where I am, Kathleen, because I know they would chase after me, and just now I must be on my own . . . to think, and plan, and hopefully sort out my life one way or another.'

'Don't fret about it, Lucy,' Kathleen advised.

Lucy appreciated her understanding. 'For your information only, Kathleen, I expect to book into a hotel at the seaside, and I'll call you from there. I'll just have to make up some story about where I'm phoning from if I talk to Anne. Remember, won't you? Any calls I make to you or the family . . . will be from there.'

The tearful goodbyes over, Lucy climbed into the taxi.

'Morning, miss!' The driver was a burly, jolly sort. 'Railway station, is it?'

'Yes, please, but could you make two quick detours first?'

'Don't see why not, my lovely. Especially as you asked so nicely.' He gave her a wide, toothy smile. 'Off on a holiday, are you?'

'Sort of.' Lucy was careful to give nothing away.

'Right then . . . let's be off.' He dropped the engine into low gear and began easing the car away from the pavement. 'So, where are we headed first?'

'To the High Street. I'll tell you where to stop when we get there. Thanks.' She glanced anxiously up and down the street as they drove off.

Thankfully, the street was clear, except for Katheen,

who was still waving from the doorway. 'Stay safe and keep in touch!' she called out.

Lucy wound down the window to remind her, 'I'll call you when I get there!'

She stifled her emotion and turned her eyes to the front. 'I'll only be a minute on the High Street,' she instructed the driver. 'I'll tell you the second detour afterwards . . . if that's all right?'

'Whatever you say, miss. You're the boss.'

'Thank you.' Lucy enjoyed being called 'miss'. It made her feel young again.

Lucy now set her mind to the journey. If all went well at the High Street, she would go straight on to the second destination. From there, it would be the station. But if her first errand did not bear fruit, she would not even be going to the station. Instead, she would probably be heading back to Kathleen's, which, after all the planning and worry while making up her mind, would be a huge disappointment.

Taking a deep breath, she concentrated on what might just be the start of an amazing adventure.

Ten minutes later, the taxi turned into the High Street.

'Now then, let's see if we can park.' The driver knew from experience that it was never easy to find somewhere to park here, what with competition from cyclists and motorists.

Luckily, as he cruised along, he noticed the driver of a grey Hillman Minx signalling that he was waiting to pull out.

'Well, that was lucky! I was just about to drop you off and drive up and down, until you were ready to leave,' he told Lucy.

The moment he was safely parked, Lucy opened the door and got out. 'I shouldn't be too long,' she said. 'About fifteen minutes, or thereabouts.'

'That's all right.' The driver leaned back and stretched his arms. 'It's your time and your money. The sooner you're back, the smaller the bill.'

His gentle warning spurred Lucy on. She could not afford to run up a huge fare because he was having to wait. 'I'll be as quick as I can.' She set off at a run.

At the lower end of the street, she stood outside the chosen shop, gazing in at the window and wondering whether she might regret doing what she had in mind. Come on, Lucy, move yourself! she silently chivvied herself. You heard what the driver said. It's you that's paying for his waiting time!

She glanced at the haphazard display of merchandise in the window. There were numerous collections of what looked like expensive jewellery; a smattering of old leather-bound books; any number of pretty pieces of china and bric-a-brac.

Right at the back of the display, hanging from the back partition, were some small oil paintings, and alongside these, framed photographs of old ships and handsome country houses.

In amongst the particular displays were numerous odd items, a scattering of fascinating curiosities, none of which Lucy could easily identify.

Lucy was concerned to see so many items, most of them obviously valuable, and all no doubt previously owned by someone who had cherished them dearly. It made her wonder about the people who, like her, had found themselves in a situation where they had little choice but to pawn or sell their valuables.

Shifting her sorry gaze away from the window display, she tried to think of another way of raising money, but it was a futile exercise. She suspected Kathleen, had she known, would have moved heaven and earth to help her financially, but Lucy thought her dear friend had done more than enough already, and swiftly dismissed the issue from her mind.

Her thoughts brought her to the taxi waiting down the street. It's make-your-mind-up time! she told herself. The taxi fare is climbing, and you haven't even made a start.

Her attention was then brought to the big sign above her head, which read in large black capitals:

TOM FISHER'S PAWNSHOP
We buy goods, and also lend money on
items of interest

With little choice, Lucy braced herself and pushed open the front door. 'Hello!' The shop appeared empty. 'Is there anyone about?' she called in a firm voice.

She got a fright when a big man suddenly answered from behind her, 'There's no need to raise your voice, woman. I get enough o' that from the missus!'

Lucy swung round to face him. 'I'm sorry . . . only
. . .' At the sight of him she was momentarily struck
dumb. A huge, mountainous blob of a man, he wore
a blue beret that sat in the middle of his head like a
pimple on a haystack, and had a long, thin moustache
sweeping down to a broad chest. His green eyes were
unnervingly piercing.

'What can I do for you?' he demanded impatiently.

Having never been inside a pawnshop before, Lucy
was decidedly nervous.

'Hurry up, woman!' He gave a long sigh. 'State yer
business; we in't got all day!'

Before Lucy could explain her business, he gave an
almighty sneeze, yanked a mucky handkerchief from
his pocket, flicked it in the air, then caught it in his
hammer-fist and wrapped it about his bulbous nose.
That done, he gave another sneeze louder than any
Lucy had ever heard before.

'Got summat to pop, have yer?' he sniffed. 'Let's
'ave a look at it then?' He glanced at her bag. 'In
there, is it?' Impatient and excited, he was almost
jogging on the spot.

Momentarily tongue-tied, Lucy was reminded of a
pantomime character. 'Yes, I have got something I'd
like to pop . . . or pawn . . . if you please?'

'Right, then! 'Ere's the deal. If you've got summat
worth a bob or two, I might buy it off you . . . if you've
a mind to sell, that is. Or I might lend you money
against it, bearing in mind that when you come to get
it back you must return the sum of money that I lent

you in the first place. And on top of that, I shall require another ten per cent over and above the sum of money that you borrowed.' He waggled a fat finger at her. 'We need to get that clear right now, before we go any further.'

'Ten per cent? It seems a lot.'

'Mebbe, but you won't get better terms nowhere else. In fact, you'll more than likely get a top-up of fifteen per cent. I in't that greedy, but I do need to mek a living.'

'Ten per cent really does seem a lot, though.' Lucy was feeling out of her depth.

'Well, if yer want to do business, them's my terms.' He drew in a mighty long breath, then blew it out with such force that it sent the paperwork flying off the counter. 'You either tek the offer or you leave it, meks no difference to me. If you tek it, you pays me back, plus the ten per cent interest, when you comes to collect the item. But this is all on condition that, having seen the goods, I agree to hold them for you. Got all that, 'ave you, woman?'

Lucy gave it more thought. Never before had she met such an obnoxious, rude man, and now she wasn't at all certain that she could trust him with the only valuable things she had in her possession.

'Come on . . . mek up yer mind!' The big man interrupted her thoughts. 'Does them terms agree with you, or does they not? Because if they does not, then I'm not interested in doing business with you. So, what's it to be?'

He gave another almighty sneeze, causing Lucy to jump in fright. This time he pinched his nose with his bare fingers, then swivelled it about a bit before wiping it from side to side with the cuff of his sleeve.

After another loud, drawn-out cough, he was talking to her again.

Lucy found it difficult to concentrate on what he was saying, being both disgusted and fascinated by the long, shivering dewdrop hanging by a thread from the end of his nose.

'Come on then, missus. Like I said, I in't got all day, so does the terms suit you, or does they not?'

'It seems I don't have a choice, so yes. But can you please be quick?' she gabbled. 'I've got a taxi waiting and the bill is getting bigger by the minute.'

'What's that you say?' He gave a raucous chuckle. 'A *taxi*, eh? Well, now, that's a curious thing. There's you in a pawnshop after borowing money, and there's a *taxi* waiting outside, with your name on it. Seems to me you should not be arguing over a ten per cent charge for my help in taking good care of your valuables, when it seems you have money to throw about on taxis! Huh! I should be so lucky.'

Lucy chose not to comment. Instead, she reluctantly produced the little red box from her pocket.

Holding it tenderly in the palm of her hand, she raised the lid. She watched the pawnbroker's eyes grow big and round as they latched onto the items lovingly cradled within the box. 'Bugger me, woman! Where did yer get them?'

When he reached out to take the box, Lucy held it from him. 'These two rings are very precious to me and mine,' she explained softly. 'I would never have come here if I were not in desperate need of money to tide me over.'

When the tears threatened, she took a deep breath to calm herself. Reluctantly, she reached out and placed the box very gently on the counter.

'So, Mr Pawnbroker, how much can you lend me against these? And I assure you that I shall be back for them as soon as I can . . . with the money I borrowed, and your extra ten per cent on top. I know their worth so, please, don't offer me a paltry amount because then I might have to try the pawnshop a few doors down.'

Silently, the big man nervously lifted the two rings into the palm of his hand. After regarding them for the longest moment, he reached into his waistcoat pocket and drew out a small metal eyeglass. He took the eyeglass between finger and thumb and, carefully pressing it to his right eye, he closed his left eye so as to focus on the two rings. Both, he quickly ascertained, were fashioned out of the finest gold.

One ring was deep-shouldered, and bore a small cluster of red rubies. In the centre of the rubies stood a small but attractively cut diamond.

The second ring was indeed handsome, with a complete posy of exquisite, raised hearts, which encircled the entire band like a golden garland.

The big man took great enjoyment in examining

the pair. For a long time he spoke not one word, but occasionally gave a kind of sigh, and twice he threw his head back as though the beauty of the rings had truly dazzled his eyes.

'Hmm! Average, I suppose,' he concluded lazily. 'Interesting designs, but not to my own personal taste . . . much too fancy.'

When he looked up at Lucy, he was red in the face, with drops of sweat crawling over his eyebrows. 'Nice enough, though, but nothing out of the ordinary,' he remarked casually. 'But because you seem to be in dire straits, and I don't like to see a woman in difficulties, I might actually buy them for my wife. Yes! I'll make you an offer, and take them off your hands for a sensible price, which will be agreed on both sides. What d'you say, woman?'

'I say no!' Lucy was emphatic. 'Those rings belonged to my great-grandmother. They were passed down to my grandma and then to my own dear mother. Being the oldest girl, I now have the responsibility of being their guardian. So, they are not mine to sell. They are simply in my keeping. I have nothing else of any value, and if I was not so desperate to raise some money, I would walk out of your shop right now!'

'What if I were to offer you an attractive price – would you sell?'

'Never! Not even if you offered me ten times their worth. All I'm asking is that you lend me a tidy sum against them, in the sure knowledge that I will recover them as soon as possible.'

'Hmm!' The pawnbroker pushed the rings aside. 'So, you won't sell them . . . not even for a handsome price?'

'No! As I've already explained, they are not mine to sell.' Lucy felt threatened. 'They are meant to continue down through the family from mother to daughter, as they have done for these past generations.'

'Look! I can see you're a tough customer – what if I give you twenty pounds for each one, forty pounds in all? A more than generous offer, if I say so myself.'

Lucy's patience was growing thin, and now she was starting to panic. 'I've already told you, I just need to borrow against them. If you are not able, or willing to do that, then I'm in the wrong pawnbroker's. I'm sorry, it seems I've wasted your time, so I'll take the rings and go elsewhere.' She was now in a desperate hurry, being highly conscious of the taxi outside, which was running up a bill she may not be able to pay. 'Thank you for your time.' Lucy instinctively grabbed the box, and scooping up the rings, she hurried towards the door.

From the kitchen doorway, the small dark-haired woman had heard the exchange between Lucy and her husband, and she shook her head in disbelief. When she hurried into the shop, Lucy had already gone out of the door.

'You damned idiot, Tom. What have you done now?' she angrily confronted the big man.

'I don't know what you mean, woman! All I did was to make her a good offer for two handsome rings, but for some sentimental reason she were having none of it. Well, it's her loss, not ours. If she wants to go elsewhere, that's her choice, and good shuts to her!' He was not best pleased at having lost the game.

'So, because you thought to make a quick killing, you've now managed to turn away what might have been a regular customer. Is that what you're telling me?'

When he remained silent, she screeched at him, 'You stupid gormless bugger! When will you ever learn? This is a pawnbroker's shop . . . a place where folks borrow money. If they don't want to sell, they don't need to! Have you got that?'

When he continued to sulk, she asked again, this time in a lower, more menacing tone, 'Tom! Have you got that?'

Mumbling an answer, he slunk off into the back room, desperate to locate the bottle of whisky she kept hidden from him.

Away down the street and heading for the taxi, Lucy was finding it hard to hold back the tears. She was beginning to believe that her plan to get away was already falling apart at the seams.

'Hey, lady!' A shrill voice halted Lucy in her tracks. 'Lady, hang on a minute, please!'

Turning to see a woman running towards her, Lucy was puzzled and somewhat alarmed. 'Now what?' she muttered under her breath. Convinced that she must be in some sort of trouble, Lucy walked back to the little woman. 'I'm sorry, were you calling me?' she asked worriedly.

'Yes . . . I just want to say, I'm very angry about my

husband. I heard him bullying you . . . just now in the pawnbroker's.' She did not give Lucy a chance to talk, being eager to know if Lucy was still of a mind to pawn the rings, and if so, she would be assured that they would loan her the handsome sum of forty pounds against the pair, with a recovery payment of just five per cent, instead of the normal ten.

Lucy was flabbergasted. 'That's what he offered me to sell them,' she recalled, 'but I already told him, I'm not selling them. I don't have the right.'

'No! I'm not talking about you selling. I'm talking about you pawning them, with a view to collecting them at a later date.'

'But why would you do that?' Lucy was immensely relieved, though she had reservations about the pawn-broker himself.

The little woman explained, 'I'm afraid my husband sometimes feels that he can badger customers into selling, even when they don't want to. His bullying treatment of them has caused too many customers to take their business elsewhere, and as my late father started the business, and I am now a partner with my husband, I have made it clear to him that his bad behaviour has to stop!'

Conscious of passing onlookers, she lowered her voice. 'I heard your conversation with him just now, and I got the feeling that you might have been through tough times lately; otherwise you would not be pawning what I believe are family heirlooms. So I suspect that, apart from anything else, it must have been very difficult for you to walk into a pawnbroker's shop in the first place. Am I right?'

'Yes, it was difficult,' Lucy had to admit. 'And now I'm not certain what I should do. I had plans, but now I don't know who I can trust any more.'

'You can trust me,' the woman assured her. 'You can talk to anyone who knows me and they will tell you I am a decent, fair-minded woman, trying to make an honest living, and I would never ask you or anyone else to do anything you did not feel comfortable with.'

The little woman had taken a liking to Lucy. She saw a gentle, kind soul who, for whatever reason, had been brought to her knees. And she genuinely wanted to help. 'If you and I come to an agreement that is fair on both sides, I promise you, hand on heart, that I will personally take the greatest care of your precious belongings. Moreover, you can take your time redeeming them. But when you do come to collect your belongings, as I know you will, then they will be there safe and sound, waiting for you.'

Lucy had a nagging instinct that she might safely put her trust in this woman, but for some reason she was still slightly unsure. 'How will you keep the rings safe?' she had to know.

'Ah, well! You need have no worries about that,' the little woman assured Lucy. 'Many valuable artefacts are left with us for safekeeping, and we have several ways of making them secure. We also have a bank deposit box, which is in my name; and I have the only key. There is also another back-up system, which I would rather not divulge. But, make no mistake, when you return for your goods, I will have them ready for you, be it a month, a year, or even longer. That is the nature of our business,' she smiled. 'Many years back I was taught the business by my late father, and I learned it well.'

She again sincerely apologised for her husband's behaviour. 'My Tom is a bit of a rascal. Once he gets behind that counter he can be loud and arrogant, with few manners, no graces, and sometimes he gets carried away with his own importance. On the whole, though, I promise you, he really is a good and honest man.' She gave a wide smile. 'After your encounter with him, I'm afraid you'll have to trust me on that.'

Lucy glanced anxiously down the street, noting with some surprise that the taxi driver was now out of his cab and sitting on the back bumper, watching her. 'How long will it take?' Lucy was concerned about the taxi fare, rising by the minute. 'I'm in a real rush.'

'So, are you happy to do the deal then?'

'Yes, please. But I need to deal with you, not your husband.'

Lucy was astonished when the woman asked if they might conclude the deal inside the taxi. She also had seen the driver impatiently waiting and watching.

As they walked together down the street, the woman explained. 'Technically speaking it isn't the most desirable thing to do, but having heard my husband give you impossible alternatives, I thought you might feel more comfortable away from the shop . . . and him.

So, in the hope that we might agree, I took the bull by the horns, so to speak, and I've brought the money and the contract with me.'

'I see.' Lucy thought it was very enterprising of her. However, she still felt somewhat nervous. 'I'm sorry, I do want to trust you, but how can I be sure that you really are from the pawnbroker's?'

The little woman smiled. 'If you want to do the deal inside the shop, that will not be a problem for me. Having realised you were in some sort of a hurry, I just thought we might save you some time, that's all. And, besides, it's a two-way thing, don't you know? I might run off with your articles, but you might run off with my forty pounds which, I'm sure I do not need to remind you, is a great deal of money.'

The taxi driver had no objections to them using his taxi as an office. Moreover, he put Lucy's suspicions to rest when he disclosed that the woman from the pawnbroker's shop was his sister-in-law.

'It's a small world,' he told Lucy with a knowing smile. 'Most of the folks round here, are related one way or another.'

The little woman smiled. 'If I was in this lady's shoes, I'd run a mile,' she teased. 'Meeting Tom was enough of a shock, without her knowing she's being driven about by my brother-in-law.'

Concerned that Lucy might not feel altogether comfortable, he offered to get out of the way, while the business was conducted.

'I can take a short walk, if you like?' He gave Lucy a cheeky wink. 'As long as I'm getting paid for my time, I'm happy.'

'Five minutes should do it,' the little woman told him. 'And behave yourself, Harry Parker. Don't you go adding extra time on this good lady's bill, or you'll have me to answer to!'

'Gawd bless us!' he exclaimed. 'Would I ever do a thing like that?' And whistling merrily, he made himself scarce.

Ten minutes later he was back. 'Well, can we get off now?' He was eager to complete his journey.

'All done!' Within minutes the deal had been completed, with enough time to enjoy a little chat.

'I'll see you when you get back from wherever you're off to,' the woman told Lucy. 'Meantime, this precious little box will be kept safe until you come for it. I promise you, I will personally take care of it as though it was in your own keeping.' She tucked it safely away in her inside pocket.

When the woman had gone, rings and all, Lucy felt more confident, especially when the driver told her, 'I don't want to know what kind of deal you two might have concluded, but what I can tell you is that it's a close community round here, and I know that, hand on heart, when Maggie Fisher makes a promise, neither hell nor high water, and certainly not even that gormless husband of hers, would stop her from keeping it.'

After the short time she had spent with the little

woman, Lucy did not doubt his words. Indeed, she was already feeling much easier.

However, she was still nervous as to the decision she had made to go away on her own. It was something she had never done before in the whole of her mundane life.

All manner of unwelcome doubts were beginning to fill her mind, so she was glad of the interruption when the driver called back to her, 'Am I right in thinking you want to go somewhere else, before the station?'

Lucy concentrated her mind. 'Yes! The local church-yard, if you please?'

The driver gave a nod. 'The churchyard it is then.' He was made to wonder about this kindly passenger. From what he could gather, she must be short of money, as she had obviously pawned an item or items that meant a great deal to her. And now, poor soul, she was headed for the churchyard.

Being a man who kept himself to himself, he did not speculate. Nor did he ask uncomfortable questions. But as he headed the car in the opposite direction to the railway station, he glanced at Lucy in the driver's mirror. As a rule he had a good instinct about people, yet this particular passenger intrigued him.

He thought she was not a bad-looking woman. In her forties, maybe; a bit worn and tired, and seeming to lack confidence in herself. Moreover, there was such an air of sadness and loneliness about her that he concluded she might well be putting herself through an ordeal of sorts; possibly to help her escape a deeply unhappy period in her life.

'We'll be there in five minutes,' he promised. 'And then, unless your plans have changed, it's on to the station.'

'That's right,' Lucy confirmed it. 'Thank you.'

In truth, Lucy was so low in spirit, it would not have taken much for her to ask if he would please take her straight home.

~

As they neared the churchyard, Lucy grew increasingly anxious, and when the car was stopped and the driver came to open the door for her, Lucy remained in her seat for a long, uncomfortable moment.

The taxi driver, though, was incredibly patient. He stood silent, his hand on the door, and his thoughts going back to when he had lost his dear wife some ten years ago. He had never got over that, and somehow he knew instinctively that here, in this pretty churchyard, lay someone who at one time or another had been a special part of this unhappy woman's life.

'Well, you're either getting out or staying in, so which is it to be?' he addressed Lucy in a jovial fashion.

'Oh, I'm sorry.' Lucy was lost in poignant memories. 'I won't take too long.'

'You take as long as you like, my dear,' he advised. 'When you're ready to leave I'll be waiting here.' Because of her troubled manner he began to wonder if later he might be taking her to the railway station, as planned, or to somewhere completely different.

Without a look back, Lucy hesitantly made her way to the corner of the churchyard where lay her darling parents.

When she arrived at the gently shaded spot, she thought, as before, how beautiful it was here. Tucked away in this pretty corner, their grave would be blessed by the rising sun in the morning, and cradled by moonlit skies at night. Comfortingly, this little area was constantly sheltered by the wide, strong arms of a handsome cherry tree.

Unable to hold back the tears, Lucy fell to her knees and after tenderly brushing her hand over the two names etched onto the temporary wooden cross among the still-fresh flowers, she whispered of her love and sorrow, telling them that she would never forget them.

'Oh, but I do miss you both . . . so very, very much,' she whispered tearfully. 'There are times when I feel I can't bear it any more, but I don't let the others see me sad, because that would be cruel. I need to be strong for them, because they too are hurting, just as I am.'

She gave a wobbly little smile. 'What are we like, eh? We hide the pain away, and nobody knows the truth of it. What makes us do that, especially when it might be easier to admit how much you're hurting? We should help each other . . . talk about it and not be weak or ashamed.'

Lucy had something important playing on her mind, and now was the time to confess it. 'I don't know if you can see what's happening down here, Mum and Dad, but it's been so very hard lately, and to tell the truth, I'm out of my depth. I can't seem to deal with it.'

Taking a deep breath, she explained gently, 'I don't want to say any more, except to tell you that I've decided to go away and think about things . . . see if I can make any sense of why I'm still here, and you're not. Don't be ashamed of me, but I would change places with you both right here and now.'

Suddenly, the tears broke like a dam giving way inside her and she was helpless to stop them. As the tears rolled down her cheeks, she sobbed bitterly. 'I feel so alone,' she whispered brokenly. 'I don't know who I am. Sometimes I really believe that I don't have a place in this life. I feel as though people look at me, and they don't even see me . . . not the real me! They don't see the guilty child who was forced to marry. Or the frightened child who gave birth before she was even a woman herself. And they never see the girl who went on to spend her adult life with a man who it now seems she hardly knew.'

She glanced about the churchyard, her sorry gaze falling on the many headstones there. 'What is it really all about, Mum and Dad? Is life a gift, or is it a punishment for our sins? Oh, I would give anything to have you here with me, to advise me what I should do.'

Her thoughts drifted back to Martin. From child to adult, he had been a huge part of her life . . . but now he was no part of her life at all. She had to ask herself: throughout those long years together, while living as man and wife and raising two beautiful children, had she ever really known him . . . Martin the schoolboy, Martin the husband, Martin the father?

She gave a wry little smile. 'Martin the cheat. Martin the stranger. Martin the man who does not want or need me any more; and probably never did.'

Saying it out loud cut deep into Lucy's soul. 'It's over now,' she whispered. 'All over.'

She had to ask herself how she could have been so naïve. So blind to the fact that while she was wondering if she had ever loved him, it was now painfully obvious that he must have been having the same doubts about her. Otherwise why would he have turned to her sister? And now, for the first time, she was actually asking: why did Paula not resist him? She felt doubly wounded, wondering if what had happened between those two was somehow her own fault.

All her bitterness poured out in a rush of pain. No! It was not my fault! I've been a good wife, and a good mother. And all the time, there was no room in his heart for me. Maybe it was always Paula, and maybe he was just waiting for her marriage to break down so he could muscle in. I don't know! I don't know the truth of it now, and I don't suppose I ever will.

'I need to be me for a while, Mum and Dad,' she confessed aloud now. 'I don't know who I am any more, or what I've been doing wrong. Why don't my family love me in the same way I love them

– unconditionally, and without measure? What's wrong with me? Am I incapable of being loved? Am I too easy . . . too giving, and while I give, they keep taking? Now I feel like an outcast. In fact, yes, that's exactly what I am: an outcast. And I don't know why. All I keep thinking is that one way or another it must be my own fault.'

Ashamed at her unexpected outburst, she went on softly, 'I'm sorry. I just wanted to come and tell you what I'm doing and why, and to ask you, please don't judge me too harshly.' She smiled. 'There I go again, apologising like I always do. But I don't want you to be sad because of me. I'll be all right, really I will. I'm just tired, and worn, and sometimes I feel so alone. Now, though, I'm going away for a while. I need to do that because if I don't, how will I ever know who I really am? Or where I truly belong?'

She now glanced towards the gate, where the taxi driver was waiting patiently, a pipe in his mouth, and a twirl of smoke rising up to the heavens.

Lucy wiped her face, straightened her hair and took a deep, invigorating breath, before stretching her two arms across the flower-heaped grave. 'Look after each other, you two, and know that I'm always thinking of you. Oh, and don't take any notice of my complaining. I'll be all right, I promise.'

She began to feel that her mum and dad were actually listening, and she felt a lot calmer.

'The children do miss you, though,' she said, 'but they're fine. I'm grateful for Anne's concern over me

– she's a good girl – and as for your grandson, he's doing all right too. He's following his dream and doing what his granddad suggested. He'll be heading for college before long to follow his chosen career. He doesn't say too much to me, but that's all right, because he and Anne are very close and they talk together about their plans. I get to know eventually, though, and that's fair enough, because all I ever want is for them to be content.'

She now had a confession to make, and it made her uncomfortable. 'I've done a bad thing, Mum,' she began softly. 'The thing is, going away costs money, and that is something I don't have much of . . . so . . .' she hesitated, '. . . forgive me, Mum, but I'm here to tell you, I've pawned your beautiful rings. I'm sorry, I really am. But I will get them back. Whatever it takes, I will get them back!'

She felt small and guilty, and yet strangely defiant. 'I had to let you know but, hand on heart, I will get them back as soon as I can. Meantime, I'm going on a kind of holiday, but I'll be back soon, and besides, how could I ever leave you two, for any length of time, eh?'

For long, aching moments, she settled her sorry gaze onto the little cross and the names of her beloved parents written there. 'You must know how much I love you both,' she whispered brokenly. 'It's not the same without you in my life. It's like some great fist has torn the heart out of me, and I don't know what to do any more.'

When the rising emotion threatened to swamp her, she took a deep, calming breath. For a while she just stood there, like a lost soul.

And then she was saying her goodbyes. She stood awhile, lovingly gazing down, admiring the pretty flowers laid across her parents' resting place. 'God bless,' she whispered, then she kissed both hands, before momentarily pressing them over their names on the cross, as though to transfer the kisses to them.

As she walked away, Lucy felt an uplifting sense of calm. In her heart she felt that she had been cut loose, and that from this moment, whatever the consequences, the road she walked would be chosen by her, and no one else. More importantly, she felt stronger in herself than she ever had done before.

This is my time, she thought. Maybe this really is my only chance to stride out into the big bad world, on my own. Without anyone else making decisions for me.

She began to realise the enormity of what she was about to do. Every day of her life since she was a schoolgirl had been planned right down to the last detail, and now here she was, off on a little adventure to find out who she was, and what she wanted out of life. She was actually doing it: she had pawned her mother's rings and was about to buy a ticket to somewhere she had loved long ago, in what now seemed to be in another life altogether.

Suddenly the whole idea was unimaginable. Woa, Lucy Lovejoy! What have you done? she thought.

Giving an odd little skip, she could not deny a bubbling of excitement. 'Lucy, I'll tell you what you've done!' she told herself. 'You have started to take charge of your own life. For the first time, in over twenty years!'

Excited and a little nervous, she hurried back to the taxi, feeling like a naughty child let loose.

CHAPTER ELEVEN

'RIGHT THEN. HERE we are!'
Harry Parker pulled up the handbrake and switched off the engine.

He then climbed out to collect Lucy's suitcase from the boot. 'There you go!' He set the case down beside her. 'Will you be all right carrying that, or would you like me to take it in for you?'

'No, thank you all the same, but I think I've messed you about enough today.' Lucy opened her purse. 'How much do I owe you?'

He clocked up the bill in his head. 'Er . . . what say we call it one pound two shillings?'

Lucy realised that was not enough. 'At first it was just a straightforward, short trip to the pawnbroker,' she promptly reminded him, 'and then a second stop at the churchyard . . . where, by the way, you were made to wait for a long time, for which I can only apologise.'

'Like I say, the fare is one pound two shillings,' he

insisted. 'It's not a charity gesture, nor is it because I suspect you might need the money more than I do, it is my thanks to you because I feel I owe you . . . on two counts.'

'And how's that then?' Lucy was curious.

'First of all, I feel bad because you got a tongue-wagging from Maggie's idiot of a husband, and it seems you didn't deserve that,' Harry said.

'But that wasn't your fault,' Lucy replied.

'And secondly,' he continued, 'while you were in the churchyard, no doubt tending to someone close, who obviously meant a lot to you, I actually took advantage of the time we were there to pay a visit to my own dear wife, who was laid to her rest some long time back. Truth is, I never seem to have enough time to visit, so waiting for you was an unexpected opportunity to make my peace with a very lovely lady who, because of pressure of work, I'm ashamed to say I have sadly neglected of late.'

In the light of his explanation, and because he was adamant that the fare was still one pound two shillings, Lucy paid what he asked and was very glad to do so.

When he kindly offered to carry her case to the platform, Lucy thanked him again, and this time she won the argument. 'I'll be fine with the suitcase,' she said firmly. 'You've been very kind, but I do need to be on my own now. I have to get a ticket, find the platform, locate the train and quickly get on board . . . or I might change my mind and ask you to take me home.'

For the first time since starting out she was beginning to panic, being close to the stage where turning back might seem the easier option.

The taxi driver saw how anxious she was. 'Here, take this. You never know, you might need it.' Dipping into his top pocket he drew out a small white card, which he handed to Lucy. 'My number is written there.' He pointed to it. 'Remember, if you need a taxi, ring me. It won't matter how far away you are, or what time of day or night it might be. I'm used to turning out at all hours. So, like I say, if you're in need of transport, just call me.'

Lucy thanked him; then she grabbed her case and hurried away.

It did not take long for her to locate the ticket office, though she was disappointed to find herself at the end of a queue.

Five minutes passed, and then another five, and then it was fifteen minutes, and though the queue was slowly shrinking, she had to stop herself heading for the street.

'Come on, Lucy!' she whispered. 'If you back out now, you may well regret it.'

Soon enough, the queue diminished and she was next in line. 'Hello, how can I help you?' The thin-faced woman behind the ticket desk looked very serious.

Lucy thought the woman's voice sounded oddly mechanical, and the deep shadows under her eyes told a story of sleepless nights.

Aware of the queue building up behind her, Lucy

quickly asked her questions. 'Could you please tell me if there's a train leaving for Littleton today? And if there is, which platform will it leave from . . . oh, and what time will it be leaving? I need a one-way ticket, because I'm not sure when I might be returning. And how much does a ticket cost, please?'

Because she had no idea when she might be able to locate a job of sorts, Lucy reminded herself that she needed to count her pennies.

'Sorry . . . I forgot to ask, how long is the journey?' Not being a frequent traveller, she had so many questions. 'Are there many stops along the way, or does it go right through?' There! She hoped that was everything.

As quick as a wink, the answers were delivered in a smart, precise manner. 'A single ticket will cost you one pound six shillings, and yes, there is a train scheduled to depart for Littleton today from platform eight at twelve forty-five. The train goes straight through to Littleton, and the journey is one hour and fifty minutes.'

Snatching a discreet breath, the ticket clerk continued, 'If needed, you will find a small refreshment bar on platform two.'

'Thank you.' As quickly as she could, Lucy counted the exact money from her purse and pushed it through the flap on the counter.

Almost immediately a slim, pale hand appeared through the slot in the window and Lucy's ticket was duly passed over. 'Good day . . . have a comfortable journey.'

That said, the woman leaned forward to address the man behind, which no doubt was Lucy's cue to get out of the way.

Glancing at the big round clock high on the wall, she realised that she still had a while to wait and, aware that her ordeal was not yet over, she felt the need for a refreshing cup of tea and maybe a biscuit.

After spotting the stairs, and seeing the sign above that pointed to platforms one to five, she drew a sigh of relief. That's where I need to be, she told herself, but having taken the stairs she wondered where the devil the refreshment bar was.

Beginning to wish she had never embarked on this hazardous adventure, she was rooted to the spot, her mind in chaos and her throat parched for want of a drink. And now she was losing confidence in what the ticket clerk had said.

Did she say it was on platform ten? Lucy continued to glance about. Or was it platform three?

Beginning to fall apart completely, she stared up at the big clock, which told her that time was passing, and if she was ever to locate a drink, she'd better get her skates on. 'Stupid, damned place!'

Close to the end of her tether, she almost leaped out of her skin when a passing porter spoke to her, 'You look lost, madam. Can I help you?'

'Thank you, yes.' Lucy was immensely grateful. 'I'm looking for the refreshment bar.'

'Ah! Platform two . . . that way.' When he gestured to the walkway on her right, she thanked him and scurried away, licking her dry lips in anticipation of a drink at last.

After she had gone up and down twice and still not found the right platform, Lucy was about to give in when the same porter as before came to her aid.

'You must have passed it.' He realised she had got herself in a panic. 'Look! There's the sign!' He apologised. 'It seems our thoughtless management decided to place the newspaper rack in front of it.'

'Well, I must say, that was a silly thing to do.' Lucy shook her head. 'I would have thought the passengers were more important than a rack of newspapers!'

'I agree,' he said, and showed her the way yet again. 'All right now, are you?'

'Yes, thank you for your help.' Lucy felt highly embarrassed and ashamed.

As he went away, the porter chuckled to himself. Poor thing, it was plain to see she was not a regular traveller, which, judging by her useless sense of direction, was just as well!

Having arrived at the correct platform for the bar, Lucy began to relax. At last she had mastered her nerves, and she now allowed herself to feel just a little proud. This was the first time she had ever travelled by train, let alone on her own. She had her ticket safely tucked away in her pocket. She knew how long the journey might take, what time the train was leaving, and from which platform.

She knew also that the train did not stop anywhere along the way, which made her feel a great deal easier, because she feared she might have got off at the wrong station, and that would be a catastrophe!

Astonishingly, she had done all this without trailing like a lost lamb behind the man who, since she'd been a child, had taken charge over her life.

Settling into her new-found freedom, and feeling more confident than she had felt in many years, Lucy bought a cup of tea in the refreshment bar and sat herself on a bench nearby.

A moment or so later, she began to chastise herself. It's a good job that kindly porter helped you, she reminded herself, but if you can't even find your way round the station, what will you do when you're let loose amongst strangers a long way from home?

Even now, with people surging about her, she began to feel the nerves taking a hold again. She gave herself a stern talking to. You're a grown woman, Lucy Lovejoy! Besides, what do you think might happen to you? Do you think somebody might grab you and run off with you? Chance would be a fine thing, I'm sure! The very idea made her smile.

As she sipped the piping-hot tea, her thoughts went back to Martin and Paula, and the shocking manner in which she had caught them. Even now, as she remembered it, she felt sick to her stomach.

Quickly, she thrust them from her mind, and concentrated on where she was going.

Growing nostalgic, she reminded herself of happy childhood days she had enjoyed with her sister and parents. It would be so lovely to see that pretty place again. The thought of sitting on the clifftop and gazing down at the ocean truly calmed her soul.

After finishing her tea, she decided to go to sit on platform eight and wait for her train.

First, though, she really should phone Anne. She recalled passing a telephone box earlier, so she decided to go in search of it . . .

Soon enough, she was inside the telephone booth and counting out her loose coins. That done, she slipped them into the black box one by one, before quickly dialling the number.

When Anne answered the phone, Lucy told her, 'I'm at the railway station, sweetheart. I can't talk for too long, because I need to get on to platform eight and wait there for the train. So, how is everyone? What are your plans for today, and how is Sam?'

'Slow down, Mum!' Anne could hardly get a word in. 'Kathleen told me you've decided to go to her aunt's, and I'm alright with that, Mum, you need a break. I'm not going anywhere special today, but I did promise Dad I would call round later, and do the housework. I might take him fish and chips, as well. Apparently he's got a lot of building work on and could be working late to catch up. I expect he'll be tired out and hungry when he gets home.'

'I see!' Lucy doubted it was work that might tire him out. 'It's more like Paula,' she muttered under her breath, '. . . especially considering their wild appetites for each other.' Anger flooded her thoughts. No doubt Martin was thrilled to have been left to his own devices . . . such as beating a path straight to Paula's door!

'What was that you said?' Anne asked. 'Stop mumbling, I can't hear, what with all that background noise. Anyway, I need to ask you something, and I want you to tell me the truth.'

Lucy's heart almost stopped. Had her daughter found out about her father and Paula? 'What is it, sweetheart?' she asked nervously.

'Are you and Dad all right?'

'What do you mean?' Relief flooded through her. Anne obviously didn't know the truth.

'Well, because just now you asked about me and Sam, but you never asked about Dad . . . not specifically.'

'Oh, I see! But that was the first thing I asked . . . whether you were all OK, and that meant everyone. So are you . . . OK?'

'Yeah, we're fine, thanks, Mum. Sam seems to be getting on with his plans. Luke is fast asleep, which is usual. And, like I said, Dad is up to his neck, working all hours. But he's absolutely fine, though I reckon he's missing you already.'

'Well, that's nice.' Lucy tried not to sound sarcastic.

'Are you missing him?'

'Well . . . yes, I suppose.' Lucy had to think out her answer. 'It's not surprising, though, when you consider that we were childhood sweethearts, and in all those years neither of us has ever been away on our own before; except for that one time your father was away

251

working for six weeks. I don't mind admitting, I was lost without him.' That was the truth . . . back then.

'So you're missing him now, are you?' Anne was persistent.

'Well, if I'm honest, I am finding it kind of . . . strange on my own.' That was not a lie either, although if he turned up at that very moment, she would walk away from him.

'Well, for what it's worth, I reckon you should call him tonight.'

'I will. Meantime, will you tell him that I'm all right, I'm on my way, and that I'm really looking forward to this break?'

'OK, Mum, yes. I'll tell him. But . . .' Anne hesitated.

'But what?' Lucy wondered again if Anne was suspicious.

'Did you and Dad have a falling-out?'

'Whatever makes you say that?' Lucy asked innocently.

'Did you?'

'Why? Has your father said something?'

'Not really. He just said he was worried about you, that's all. What with losing both Grandma and Granddad, and so very quickly. I'm sorry, Mum. Look, we all want you to have a really good, clean break. Take as long as you need, and ring me occasionally, won't you?'

'You know I will, sweetheart. Give Luke a big hug from me, and tell Sam I'm thinking of him.'

'Yes, Mum. And I asked Kathleen if I could have

her aunt's telephone number, just in case I needed to get hold of you, but she said her aunt hasn't got a telephone. So now I'm worried that I won't be able to get in touch with you if I need to.'

Lucy had to think quickly. 'Oh, yes, of course, sweetheart. Well, as far as I know, Kathleen has a friend she talks to occasionally, and she apparently contacts her aunt through her, but I don't have her friend's number, and to be honest, sweetheart, I don't think we should lumber Kathleen like that. She's been so very kind. I hate to ask any more of her.'

'So, what am I to do?' Anne sounded unhappy. 'What if someone in the family falls ill . . . how am I to get a hold of you?'

'That won't be a problem, sweetheart. I'm sure you can send a message via Kathleen. But to be honest, I don't think there's any real need for that, especially as I'll be in touch most nights anyway.'

'Oh, all right then, but don't feel you have to. Just relax, and enjoy yourself. I promise I won't contact Kathleen unless it's absolutely necessary, especially when you're going to be calling us regularly.'

Just then, Lucy could hear the baby crying in the background. 'You go and tend to Luke,' she told Anne. 'I love you, sweetheart. A big hug for baby, and Sam and hubby. And you take care of yourself. Oh, and tell your dad not to work too hard.'

That very difficult throwaway comment was for Anne's benefit, because, in truth, Lucy cared nothing about him.

Anne concluded the conversation. 'Bye for now, Mum. Take care of yourself and, like I say, take as long as you need. And don't worry, I'll look after things at this end.'

After she rang off, Lucy remained in the telephone booth for a moment. So, Martin was out working all hours, was he? She deliberately shut him from her mind.

Checking her remaining coins, she was greatly relieved to have just enough to call Kathleen.

'Hey!' Kathleen was thrilled to hear from her. 'I'm glad you called. I was just thinking about you.'

'I'm still at the station,' Lucy told her, 'but I'm heading for the train in a minute.'

'Oh, Lucy, it's so exciting! I wish I was coming with you.'

'Really? Well, if you get your skates on, you might just make it.'

'It's too late now, but maybe another time, eh?'

'You bet! Just the two of us . . . that would be great.'

'OK then. We'll talk about it when you get back. Now go and get your train, or it'll go without you. Oh, and don't forget to call me when you get where you're going.'

They said their goodbyes, and Lucy reminded her, 'You will clear it for me with the boss, won't you?'

'Of course! I said I would, didn't I? Besides, she knows about both your parents. I believe that under that skin of steel she really does have a kind heart.'

Lucy was grateful. 'Thanks, Kathleen.'

'Aw, don't you worry about a thing,' Kathleen assured her. 'Just take it easy. Try and clear all the bad things out of your mind. Just relax, and get strong in yourself, d'you know what I'm saying?'

'Yes, I do, and thanks.'

'What for?'

'For being the best friend I ever had.'

'Aw, go on with you. You'll have me bawling in a minute. So, go on! Get on that train, and don't look back. Have a lovely time, and call me every now and then; or I might start worrying. OK?'

Lucy's emotions were all over the place. She felt like going back to spend some time with Kathleen; and then she was so angry she wanted to face Martin and Paula and have it out with them once and for all. And yet she desperately needed to get as far away from here as she possibly could.

'Hey, Lucy!' Kathleen's voice broke her dark thoughts. 'Are you OK?'

'Oh, I'm sorry, Kathleen.' On thinking of Martin and the shameful thing he had done, Lucy had actually forgotten that Kathleen was still on the other end of the telephone. 'I'll call you as soon as I can . . . I promise.'

'You'd better! And look after yourself. Don't do anything I wouldn't do.'

Lucy had to laugh. 'That leaves me clear to do whatever I like.'

As always, they laughed together, and then Kathleen told her, 'Go, Lucy, go! Or you'll miss your train.'

Lucy quickly replaced the receiver. The idea of missing the train was unthinkable, so she grabbed her belongings and hurried off to locate platform eight.

Her mind was now firmly set on travelling back in time, to the delights of that small seaside village. It was such a huge step for her, and the more she thought about it, the more excited she became.

There was no turning back.

There were no second thoughts and, so far, no regrets. Except that maybe she should have done it sooner.

When she made her way down the slope to platform eight, Lucy still found it hard to believe that she was actually leaving home to embark on an adventure that might yet turn out to be the worst thing she had ever done in her entire life.

She took a moment to think about what she had achieved in her lifetime, and came to the conclusion that, when compared to many others, she had in fact achieved very little.

So what had spurred her into believing that she could be brave enough to take this gigantic step away from home and family, and everything familiar? She was not a go-getter like Paula; or a madly impulsive soul like Kathleen.

Her suitcase was packed, her ticket was bought, and she was about to climb onto a train that, because of a childhood memory, would shortly deliver her into the unknown.

And what made her think that the delightful place she had loved as a child would still be the same now?

It was crazy that Lucy Lovejoy – a housewife with no ambitions, no adventurous spirit, and no life to speak of apart from being the family keeper – had deliberately planned and executed what could be a dangerous journey into uncharted territory.

Through recent unsettling events she had been forced to review her life. Over the years, she had naturally allowed many responsibilities to fall on her shoulders. She was a daughter, a sister, a wife and a mother. At times, she was also a counsellor, and recently she had been made a grandmother. She was the kingpin that held the family together, so how could she abandon the people who had always relied on her?

After some consideration, she realised it was not family responsibilities that she was escaping from, it was a life that was not her own and never would be if she carried on as before. In all truth, she did not even know who she was any more.

A surprising and dangerous thought entered her head. Once she was gone from here, would she ever want to come back?

For the moment at least, there was no turning back. Especially now, after she realised that she could actually travel alone, without the usual belittling experience of trailing like a little lapdog behind someone who told her what to do and how to do it.

Today, after a few uncomfortable learning curves, Lucy had come to realise that she had somehow

become her own master. It was an amazing achieve-
ment, and it spurred her on to complete her journey.

Moreover, after the shock of recent events she
desperately needed this precious time away to find the
real Lucy Lovejoy; and to mend what was broken inside
her. She had to take stock of her place in the world,
before the person she had lost was never found again.

In that definitive moment the train was actually
pulling into the platform, and very soon she would
clamber aboard and be on her way.

Walking down the platform with her suitcase, she
felt all alone with her thoughts and memories; oddly
isolated in the midst of a thronging crowd. She was
completely and utterly in charge, and for the first time
ever she felt truly proud of herself. After all the heart-
aches of late, she desperately needed to mend, and
grow strong. She had decisions to make, and truths
to be tackled. One thing she did believe, however, was
that everything happened for a reason, and that this
unusual journey was meant to be.

Lucy was determined to leave the pain and heartache behind for now. After all, what was the alternative? She could not bring back her darling parents.
Nor could she mend a marriage that was already in
tatters. Whatever Fate had in store for her now, it
could not be any more painful than what she was
leaving behind.

Above all else, she must cling to that thought.

With her head held high she picked up her suitcase
and boarded the train.

CHAPTER TWELVE

'I RECKON I'VE cut it a bit fine!' Having collected his ticket, Dave Benson was now in a rush. 'You're right, Nancy, I should have left home earlier.' Grabbing her by the shoulders, he looked her in the eye. 'And don't you go worrying, because one way or another, I mean to swing this deal,' he promised.

Nancy believed him. 'Don't let them squeeze more money out of you though.'

Dave smiled. 'I know how to play the game,' he said. 'What I'm offering them is a great deal, and they know it, otherwise they would not even be talking to me.'

On hearing the announcement that his train was about to leave he said goodbye. 'I must go, Nancy. I can't afford to miss this train. There are meetings this afternoon and I can't afford to be late.'

He gave her a swift kiss on the cheek, after which he took off at the run. 'I'll phone you tonight!' he called over his shoulder.

Nancy waved him off along platform eight. 'I know you won't let me down, Dave.' She had every confidence in his business skills.

~

Seated by the carriage window, Lucy saw the man running along the platform, the deep hem of his long, dark coat whipping the air as he quickened his steps. Carrying a large overnight bag and an official-looking briefcase tucked securely under his arm, he looked like a man on a mission. He'll never make it, Lucy thought.

At first she did not recognise him, but when he burst in through the door and turned slightly to wave at someone outside the train, Lucy thought she knew him. On that desolate night when she had hidden in the bus shelter, she had caught just the merest glimpse of the two strangers, but then she recalled when the same man caught sight of her yesterday, and seemed to linger outside the hotel. Yes, it was definitely one and the same man.

For some inexplicable reason, Lucy had kept his face in her mind ever since that first, shadowy meeting. She stole another discreet look at him. The same handsome, kindly face, the impressive build and that thick, dark hair – yes, it was definitely him.

Moreover, as he called out of the window, 'Take care, Nancy. I'll call you tonight!' Lucy recognised his voice. On that miserable night when her whole world seemed to be falling apart, this gentle man had been there, so very kind, and obviously concerned for her.

She had not forgotten the kind stranger, and she never would.

Now, though, as his gaze scoured the carriage for an empty seat, Lucy feared he might recognise her and she began to panic. Realising there was nowhere to hide, she discreetly grabbed a crumpled newspaper that someone had left on the seat beside her. In an effort to deter him from sitting beside her, she quickly laid her handbag on the empty seat.

Opening the newspaper, she thrust it close to her face and pretended to read, desperately hoping he would not look in her direction.

Fortunately for Lucy's peace of mind, he headed towards a vacant seat some four rows ahead of her.

When he sat down and began reading his own news-paper, Lucy was greatly relieved. She thought it would not be difficult to get off the train before he did, especially as she was seated close to the door.

Now that it was too late to turn back, even if she had wanted to, Lucy's thoughts shifted to her destina-tion. She grew curious as to what might greet her on arrival at Littleton. Was she in for a disappointment? Would the seaside village be just a worn shadow of its former self? Or was it every bit as delightful as she remembered?

Oh, and what about the picturesque little jetty – was it still there? Oh, she did so hope it had not been replaced with concrete and steel like so many other beautiful old structures of late.

She felt oddly relaxed; almost as though she was going home to the most wonderful childhood, when she had both her darling parents. Back to a time when her only ambition was to build a sandcastle that might not crumble. Back to a time when she had no worries, no heartache, no regrets of any kind.

And the sun shone, every single day.

As the train ate up the miles, all the guilt fell away from her, and she realised that she had done the right thing in making this journey.

This was for her. It was not for the family, or anyone else. It was her special time. And she could hardly wait to leave the train to begin her adventure.

Now, more than ever, she truly believed that Fate would give a helping hand, and show her the way.

CHAPTER THIRTEEN

Dave benson was not a patient traveller. Once he was on his way, he was keen to arrive and get on with his errand, whatever it might be. The actual travelling was a mere necessity.

When approaching an important business deal, his first priority was to ready himself for the difficulties ahead. In this particular case, he was not the only one who had put a deal on the table, although he was determined to rise above the opposition, and persuade the big boys that they would never get a better deal than he was offering.

He knew it would not be easy, but he had years of negotiating skills, and a healthy appetite for the fight.

Nevertheless, he was in no doubt that he was about to face tough opposition and he must be ready not only to show just how generous his offer was, but for the mighty tussle that would ensue once the business got underway.

He had bought a newspaper at the kiosk before

boarding the train, but his mind was so alive with ideas about how to swing this deal that he found it difficult to concentrate on the items of news. Impatiently, he flipped the pages over, but he was not interested. Instead, all manner of more personal concerns began to creep into his thoughts.

Firstly, there was his daughter, Cassie, who had gone to stay with her aunt Ellie. Up to now, she had shown no signs of returning home, although thankfully, she called him every night. It was a difficult situation; and increasingly hard for Dave to accept. But for all that, he fully understood why she needed to be out of the house. It reminded her too much of her lately departed mother.

He and Cassie had suffered a crippling blow, but while he was fortunate that the cut and thrust of business gave him something of a respite, Cassie was finding it harder to feel her way back. He knew that Cassie's aunt would not let her down, and he was making an extra effort to be patient, and wait for her to come home in her own good time.

The sooner she was back under his roof, the better, however, because then he would know she was beginning to heal.

He folded the newspaper and laid it on the floor by his briefcase. As the train wound through the wild and wonderful countryside, he looked out and saw it all but, his thoughts focused elsewhere, he could not altogether appreciate the beauty of the landscape.

As the train sped nearer to its destination, his

thoughts grew busier, shifting between the imminent business meeting, his family, the wonderful life he had been fortunate enough to experience, and then the cruel manner in which his happiness had been brought to an end.

His personal thoughts centred around Cassie, and the fact that she was now struggling to find a kind of peace in her young life. And his darling sister, Nancy, who kept a close eye on Cassie, constantly comforting and encouraging. Indeed, it was Nancy who supported Ellie's suggestion that Cassie should stay for a while; especially now that Ellie had left home and was feeling somewhat lonely in the small two-bed house she was renting.

The arrangement seemed to be working out fine, especially as they were of similar age, with Ellie in her mid-twenties and Cassie just turned nineteen.

Moreover, Ellie had a funny, warm and kindly nature, and the two of them got on really well. They had the same outlook on life; they shared clothes and ideas, and occasionally, when they could afford it, they went out on the town together.

More importantly, being that bit older, Ellie was mature enough to understand Cassie's deeper needs right now.

Dave thought he could never thank Nancy enough for seeing what he had failed to see . . . that Cassie needed someone nearer her own age just now; someone she could talk to, without feeling guilty. She needed to smile again, to be a part of life again, and most of all, to learn how to forgive.

During the last two conversations with Cassie, Dave had been greatly encouraged. He had noticed a change in her.

She seemed more confident in herself somehow. She even remembered what he had told her about his business trip, and she duly ordered him to stay safe on his travels, and said she was looking forward to seeing him when he came home.

Just now, with good thoughts lifting his spirits, and with the train chugging out a musical rhythm, he felt he could close his eyes and snatch a few winks.

Unfortunately, he had copious notes to make, and a few ideas to set out. He leaned down to dig into his briefcase, and as he glanced up, he noticed the woman who was seated by the door. For some reason, she caught his attention.

He had a feeling that he knew her from somewhere – the naturally unkempt, brown hair in particular seemed familiar to him – but she was reading a newspaper so he could not see the whole of her face. If only she would just look up, he might remember.

Turning his attention to the documents in his briefcase, he decided he must be wrong about knowing the woman; he must just have simply caught a fleeting glimpse of her on the platform.

He was soon deep in figures and calculations, although he could not resist stealing another glance at the woman before finally concentrating wholly on his work.

For the umpteenth time he scrutinised the terms

he had outlined in the offer. To his mind, both the offer and the terms were fair, especially considering the amount of money that was needed to rescue the dilapidated building.

Having considered all that, he reminded himself that he must not be too rigid in his terms. A good businessman should always leave room to wheel and deal if necessary. He did not want to leave that meeting without having secured Nancy's long-held dream of owning her own hotel on the coast; even if it meant spending money and long hours bringing a derelict building back to life.

Nancy had considered three other possible buildings, but the first time she and Dave had visited this once grand place, she instantly fell in love with it.

'This is the one,' she had declared, and nothing and no one could change her mind.

~

For the two-hour journey, Lucy decided to remain in her seat.

She noticed with interest that the stranger also remained seated; although on the two occasions when she stretched her neck to look at him, he appeared to be busy working.

Lucy was intrigued as to what his business might be. Something about his demeanour and constant attendance to his briefcase made her curious as to whether he might have his own business. Certainly he had the air of an ambitious and capable man.

As she shifted in her seat, she groaned at the twinge in her lower back. She so wanted to get up and walk about, but her every instinct warned her not to draw the man's attention to herself. So in order to relieve her aching bones she found a semblance of comfort in slipping off her shoes and wiggling her feet.

When the train slowed and finally swept into the station, Lucy gave a huge sigh of relief. She knew she had arrived at the correct place when she noticed the big sign outside: 'LITTLETON'.

'You've done it, Lucy girl!' she whispered excitedly. 'You've actually done it!' And her glad heart gave the tiniest little lurch. She felt quite emotional.

A curt announcement over the tannoy reminded passengers that they had arrived at their destination, and requested that they disembark with care and remember to collect their luggage and belongings on leaving.

Determined to get off the train before the stranger might catch sight of her, Lucy was quickly at the door and in front of the queue as the train drew to a halt.

She deliberately kept her back to where the stranger had been sitting, even though she suspected he might be getting off at the door further up.

When the train stopped safely, Lucy quickly clambered off.

Hiding herself in the centre of the surging throng of bodies all sweeping forward in the same direction, she noticed the stranger some distance in front. He was slightly taller than those around him, and easily recognised by his thick, dark hair and the straight, broad cut of his shoulders.

Lucy kept her distance, being immensely thankful that so far he had not seen her.

A moment later, the stranger was through the turnstile and instantly approached by a man in a dark suit. From the friendly greeting, Lucy deduced that they knew each other. She was glad that they fell into what appeared to be a very deep conversation, because now she was able to go forward with less fear of being spotted.

Taking her chance, she quickened her footsteps and forced her way through. She kept on the far side of the crowd, away from the stranger, who remained huddled in conversation with the other man, who was holding out a document.

Lucy twice caught the stranger's gaze drifting around as though he was wishing the other man might leave.

Having grown confident that she had successfully avoided what could have been an awkward encounter with him, Lucy was horrified when, curious, she dared to glance up, only to see the stranger looking directly at her, astonishment on his face as he appeared to recognise her. She quickly turned away, panicking as she hurried forward to force herself through the crowd.

A minute or so later, having successfully got through the turnstiles, where she hurried through to the exit as best she could with her luggage. Outside, she headed for the taxi rank. 'Taxi!' She waved her arms to attract attention. 'Taxi!'

The first taxi driver cruised towards her and wound down his window. 'Climb in, lady.' He was a skinny, bony man, with a long face. As she walked towards him, carrying her suitcase, he poked his head out of the window and impatiently raised his voice. 'Hey, lady! Just so's you know, I'm still waiting on you, and the clock's already ticking.'

'Just a minute!' Lucy frantically searched her handbag for the name and address of the hotel.

She was so flustered that she dropped the piece of paper on the ground. Grabbing it up, she quickly glanced over it. 'Er . . . let me see . . . Littleton village,' she told him breathlessly. 'Hotel . . . what was it? Oh, here we are, Hotel Lorriet.' She gave a sigh of relief.

'OK. I know the one!' He smiled, and his entire face disappeared behind a mouthful of big, yellow teeth. 'Are you all right with your case?'

Whether she was 'all right' or not, he made no effort to get out and help. Impatient, he revved the engine.

Having secured her case on the floor of the cab, Lucy was frantically trying to swing the door shut when she saw the stranger heading straight for the taxi rank, his neck craned as he focused on the row of cabs, seemingly looking for someone.

Lucy wondered if he was looking for her. And now

she was convinced that he really had recognised her
back there.

Fearing he might see her, Lucy slammed the door
and urged the driver, 'Please! Can we go?'

'Absolutely.' He absent-mindedly ran the flat of his
hand down his long, thin hair. 'Oh . . . sorry, the hotel
. . . the Lorriet, wasn't it?'

'Yes, that's it. Can we please go now?'

But Lucy then became increasingly concerned that
she might have got the name of the hotel wrong.
'Wait a minute . . . I'm not sure now.' She grabbed
her handbag and searched again for the paper on
which she had written the address. She frantically
delved through the thousand and one items rammed
into her bag. Inevitably the bag toppled over and out
spewed the entire paraphernalia, rolling away in all
directions on the floor.

'Dammit!' She glanced up. 'Sorry. Just a minute.'
For just the smallest moment, she began to regret
ever setting out on this trip.

The driver was none too pleased. 'The clock is still
ticking, miss! So, is it the Lorriet, or not?'

'I'm not altogether sure now.' Lucy was completely
flummoxed. 'Please, you're making me panic. Could
you just drive out of the station? I've got the hotel
written down here . . . somewhere.'

'So, are you saying it's not the Lorriet after all?'

'No! I'm not saying that. I'm just saying I want to
make sure . . . if you'll just take us out of the station,
please? And I do know the clock is ticking, but I would

really appreciate it if you would try to be patient. The thing is, I'm not really used to travelling.'

'Yes, I can see that.' In fact he thought she should never have been let out in the first place, wasting his precious time.

And another thing! How could he be sure that she even had enough money to pay for his fare?

He informed her that if he was being made to run up unnecessary mileage because she had given him the wrong address, she would have to pay the bill, because it would be her fault and not his.

His caution fell on deaf ears. 'I've got it!' she cried, holding out the piece of paper. 'Yes! That's it, the Lorriet.' She thrust the paper under his nose. 'See! The Lorriet Hotel on Balmont Street.'

Seeing the many articles strewn all over the cab floor, he grinned wickedly. 'My! My! You really are in a panic, aren't you?' he chuckled. 'And why's that, I wonder, eh?' He fancied himself to be a bit of a joker. 'For all I know, you could be an armed prisoner on the run . . . or you might have just done a robbery and there's a wad of money hidden about your person. Is that it? Or maybe you're planning to kidnap me, hoping to get a ransom.'

He then launched into a string of childish, bawdy innuendoes, which did not impress Lucy at all, though he seemed enormously amused with himself, chuckling and then roaring with laughter. Lucy couldn't decide whether to make him stop the car and let her out, or smack him one round the ear.

Either way, she did not enjoy his company, or his lousy jokes. She just wanted to reach her destination sooner rather than later. 'How long will it take us to get there?' she asked.

'Dunno, lady. How long is a piece of string?'

Unimpressed by his gormless wit, Lucy decided to ignore him.

~

Having perused the documents from his architect on the train, and learned some very useful information regarding his business venture from them, Dave Benson made his way out of the station.

As he came through the outer doors, he was saddened at the sight of Lucy being driven away in the cab. 'Hopefully our paths may well cross again,' he murmured, and went on his way.

He knew now without a doubt that this was the same woman he and Nancy had found hiding in the bus shelter on that cold, rainy night. She had seemed terribly sad and alone, and he knew just how that felt. He hadn't been able to rid his mind of this odd connection between them – first at the bus shelter, then the night he had seen her on the bus, and now here she was in Littleton!

He flagged down the next taxi. 'Meridian Hotel, on Viaduct Street, please.'

Without waiting for the driver to acknowledge, he climbed into the cab.

As they moved on, Dave asked the driver, 'Did you happen to see the woman who got into the cab in front of you?'

The driver thought a moment. 'Let me see . . . oh yes! Mid-thirties . . . early forties . . . not what you might call a beauty, at least not that I could see. But she did have a fine shock of chestnut-brown hair . . . and a tasty set of pins. Is that the one you mean?'

Dave smiled. 'Yes, that's the one.' Although he had not noticed her 'pins', tasty or otherwise. 'You wouldn't happen to have heard where she's headed, would you?'

'Nope, 'fraid not. Why? Know 'er, d'you?'

'Well, no, not really . . . I mean, I have met her before.'

'And you'd like to meet her again, is that it?' The driver gave a sly little wink. 'Can't say I blame you. Her figure's not bad, and she does have an attractive face.'

'I don't suppose you know the driver of that cab?' Dave asked.

'Sorry again, but no. Most of us are freelancers . . . we rarely have time to chat.'

'So, you wouldn't know of any way I might get in touch with him, then?'

'Sorry, mate. I'd help you if I could, but . . .' He shrugged, and Dave got the message.

'I see. Well, it's no matter, but thanks anyway.' Dave was curiously disappointed to think that this gentle and intriguing woman was actually here, and he had lost his chance to renew their acquaintance.

Also, most interestingly, she appeared to be all alone, as she had been the first time they met, and when he'd seen her in the street. That made him wonder. Was she divorced . . . widowed, or maybe she'd got family responsibilities and she had never married?

More questions, he thought. And no answers.

'I'm not really sure if I can help,' the taxi driver interrupted Dave's thoughts, 'but if I do manage to discover the driver's name, I'll drop a note off at the Meridian, if I'm in the area.'

In fact he had no intention of digging about for information. He was simply angling for a bigger tip when he dropped this seemingly love-struck passenger at his destination.

'Thanks. I would appreciate that.' Dave was onto the driver's little scam. No doubt at the end of this journey, he would be holding his fist out for a more generous tip than normal. But he might be disappointed.

Dave's thoughts returned to the mystery woman, and the night he and Nancy had met her.

Back then, he thought she might be in some kind of trouble, or she would surely never have been hiding inside the shelter, especially on such a miserable night. Nancy had pointed out at the time that the buses were not scheduled to run from that particular shelter any more, which meant she was not waiting for a bus. So what was she doing there, and why did she run away so quickly after they turned up?

Since that night, he had not been able to shut her from his mind. There was something about her . . .

something so innocent and fragile. He just felt a need to scoop her up and hold her safe.

And how odd for her to be on the same train as himself.

Realising he had thought of her as 'his woman', he called her image to mind. She was very special, though it was difficult to say quite why, and the thought of not seeing her again, now he knew she was here in this little seaside village, made him sad.

He did not believe it was a sexual attraction, and, besides, she did not come across as being sexy or – dare he say it – not even what you might call 'delicate'. Or even 'beautiful', as the taxi driver had noted.

So, what was it that had attracted him to her?

He made an effort to analyse the reason he was so drawn to her. Maybe it was because that night at the bus shelter, she had seemed such a sad and pitiful soul that he felt the need to wrap his two arms about her, and make everything all right. In a kind of ridiculous way, he had likened her to a shy little rabbit he once had as a small boy.

He had loved that little rabbit so very much, and because he was shy himself, and not very good at mixing with other boys, the little grey rabbit became his best friend. When, at just a year old, the rabbit had died, he had been utterly devastated.

Now he gave a wry smile for likening that dear little rabbit to the lonely woman. Feeling somewhat foolish, he shook the ridiculous idea firmly from his mind.

So why was he attracted to this shy, lonely woman? Maybe because he knew what it felt like to be both shy and lonely . . . so that in this woman he saw himself. Was that what had drawn him to her?

No! He also quickly dismissed that idea, because he and the woman were not the same. She seemed too painfully shy, and appeared to like her own company. Also, whatever troubles he had – and over the years there had been plenty – he would never hide away in a bus shelter. He would fight to do something that might change the situation – get out there and face the demons, as he had had to do many times.

But then again, how was he to know whether or not she was already facing her demons? Was that why she was in the shelter? To work it out . . . to think of a way to deal with her dilemmas?

The taxi driver was right when he said that this woman was no beauty, and yet, in another way, he was totally and utterly wrong, because she *did* have beauty of a kind. Maybe it was not evident to all, but he himself could see it.

He had seen it today. In the softness of her person, and the gentle sadness in her eyes. In the manner in which she probably cared little about herself, and yet she would be kind and sympathetic to those who needed a friend.

He suddenly realised that the essence of her sadness was who she was, and therein lay the beauty. A beauty more precious than perfect skin, or made-up eyes, or a fashionable hairstyle. She did not flaunt herself.

Indeed, he imagined that this woman probably did not even know how very beautiful she truly was.

Somehow or another, in ways he could not understand, she had managed to get inside him, without even trying. Would she laugh in his face if she knew how intrigued he was with her? He did not believe so.

Suddenly his drifting thoughts were drawn back to the work in hand. What would Nancy say if she knew he was asking about a woman he had seen on the train – someone he did not even know?

With Nancy in mind, and now that his thoughts were beginning to focus, he remembered that he had much work to do. He should focus on what he was here for, and fate would determine if he met the mystery woman again before it was time to go home.

CHAPTER FOURTEEN

STEPPING OUT OF the taxi, Lucy was amazed to realise that the hotel was much the same as she remembered, although it appeared to have been recently renovated.

She was pleased to note that the chosen architect had retained some of the period character and that the new was in keeping with the old.

With her heart beating faster, and the warmest of memories in her mind, she stood on the pavement taking in the scene, her senses heightened by the salty sea air and her glad heart beating fifteen to the dozen because she was really here . . . in Littleton . . . her childhood joy, and fantasy playground.

For one poignant, fleeting moment, she was that little girl again, standing outside this very hotel together with her mum and dad, and her baby sister.

The magical nostalgic moment was threatened as she thought of Paula. Even now, she found it difficult to believe what she had seen with her own eyes: Martin and her sister, fornicating, so lost in each other that it took a while for them to realise she was even there.

Forcing the hurtful memories to the back of her mind, she took stock of the hotel again.

Surprisingly, she felt the same excitement looking at it now as she had when she first came here as a child.

The Edwardian windows were tastefuly retained, with the brick surround having been renovated to reveal the characteristic zigzag pattern on the bricks. The glass in the windows had been replaced, but with the same attention to detail as elsewhere. Noticeably, the panels at the top of each pane were in keeping with the period.

The narrow, wooden front door that Lucy recalled from her childhood was now replaced with a welcoming wide glass façade, which was respectfully flanked by two long patterned glass panels. Far from spoiling the surrounding period detail, the new additions served to enhance the stalwart character of the original.

Now Lucy's attention strayed towards the tiny harbour, where the colourful fishing boats and pleasure craft merrily bobbed on the shifting water.

Contented, her sorry heart was uplifted, and when she smiled it was as though she had let the sunshine in.

Here, in this quiet place, she felt at home. She felt her parents' gentle presence and her tears came almost without her realising. They brought a soothing sense of peace to her troubled soul.

She recalled how her mother would go over and over their first visit to this haven 'when you and Paula were just a twinkle in your daddy's eye'.

Lucy heard the same story many times from her mother – never her father, who would grow embarrassed and escape to the pub.

On that first visit here, they had been so young and in love, Lucy recalled.

With the sound of seagulls in her ears and the cloudless, blue skies above, she stole a few quiet moments just to look and listen, and fill her senses with the peace and beauty around her.

She was soon brought back from her daydreams by the taxi driver's impatience. 'Hey, lady! While you're off daydreaming, I hope you won't forget the clock is still ticking away here!' In truth, he did not care one jot . . . so long as he got his money.

'Oh!' Lucy had momentarily forgotten him, and now she was panicking again. 'Oh . . . I'm sorry.' She opened her handbag and drew out a stream of bits and pieces: handkerchief, lipstick, a box of hairclips and two mouldy sweets that she had overlooked, but no purse.

Ramming the things back into the bag, she dipped her hand into her coat pocket and, thankfully, withdrew her purse. 'How much is it, please?'

When he advised of the cost of her daydreams, she gulped hard, but said nothing.

Instead, she quickly paid the fare with a smile and a bright 'Thank you', while reminding herself that she must be careful not to squander the meagre amount of money she had managed to acquire. The prospect of not being able to recover the precious articles from the pawnshop made her feel physically ill.

With that grim thought firmly in mind, she gingerly counted out an extra coin or two, which she tipped into the driver's outstretched hand.

'Huh!' He was obviously not pleased. 'You're very generous, I must say.' He went away cursing and grumbling, 'Some folks are tight as a duck's backside and no mistake!'

A moment later, she was standing at the hotel reception desk, while a fresh-faced young porter guarded her case.

'Good day. Booking in, are you?' The receptionist was a narrow-faced woman with a soft, friendly smile.

'Yes, please.' Lucy thought it all very formal.

'Could I have your name, please?'

'Lucy Lovejoy.'

'Miss or Mrs?'

Lucy wondered what difference it might make to her booking, 'It's just "Lucy",' she replied quietly, 'Lucy . . . Lovejoy.'

There followed a split second of silence when the kindly woman looked up at her. 'I shall take that as being a *Miss* Lovejoy, is that all right?' she asked with a smile.

Lucy nodded, her tortured mind wandering back to what she was running away from. Martin and Paula. Her many responsibilities. Two children, a beloved grandchild, and a good job that she was now in danger of losing . . . along with the wages it paid.

As ever, she thought of her parents, gone to their peace, leaving her behind; just as life itself had left her behind.

Only now, signing into the hotel as 'Miss Lovejoy', did she truly realise the enormity of what she had done. It made her feel somehow uplifted, but also terrified; out of her depth.

The thought of being a real wife again to Martin sickened her to the stomach. Yet the repercussions of breaking up with him frightened her. If she did let him go, what would happen to her? For most of her life, Martin had been her mainstay. How would she discover where she belonged if Martin was not in her life?

The insistent, disturbing questions continued to trouble her.

What about the children? How would they deal with the family being torn apart? Because that was exactly what it would be − a family broken; beyond repair.

And, who would she turn to now that her beloved parents were gone? Her one and only confidante now was Kathleen, and she was too good a friend for her to lean on and burden with troubles not of her own making.

Lucy gave a whimsical smile at the idea of not being at the heart of her beloved family. The very prospect of such a thing was unthinkable. And yet, because of what Paula and Martin had done, she believed that putting a good distance between herself and them was probably the only way forward, if she was ever to discover where she might belong.

At this moment, though, she had no idea where she belonged. But she did know that whatever the result of her fleeing to the seaside of her childhood, and whichever way she turned, her life would never be the same.

Thankfully, here in this place where she had once been so happy, Lucy felt a sense of hope brush through her heart, and she was determined not to let painful images taint her thoughts.

She must put all that behind her and find the time to discover where her future lay. Right now she felt as though she belonged nowhere.

Her attention was now drawn to the receptionist, who was scribbling in her ledger. Lucy could not help but notice the woman's hand trembling as she wrote, and now, when she took a sneaky glance at the woman's downturned, pretty features, Lucy noticed the angry, red blush on her cheeks, and the rings of dark shadows beneath her eyes.

Lucy concluded that this was a very unhappy woman; much like herself. Possibly, Lucy suspected, the woman might even be ill.

But then she noticed the half-empty wineglass on the woman's side of the desk. Partially hidden behind a folded newspaper, and sadly, it told its own story.

In that sorry moment, Lucy reflected, and not for the first time, that there were many people in this world who were fighting their demons and that, rightly or wrongly, they might find solace in different ways.

She cautioned herself. She might be wrong – she might be doing this kindly woman a huge disservice – but glancing again at the woman's face with its tell-tale signs of a troubled soul, Lucy knew the truth.

However, it was not for her to make judgements. When the formalities were done she thanked the woman graciously and smiled warmly, and when the woman unexpectedly smiled back in an easier manner, Lucy was oddly comforted.

As she walked away, following the porter and her suitcase, the receptionist called after her, 'Lucy Lovejoy?'

Lucy turned round. 'Yes?'

'Please . . . do enjoy your stay!'

For a long moment, Lucy choked back a tear. 'I will,' she answered softly. 'Thank you.'

As Lucy walked away out of sight, the receptionist leaned back in her seat and momentarily closed her eyes.

When she opened them they held the softest gleam. 'My troubles seem small, compared to hers,' she mused. If I'm right, that lady has been through hell and back, she thought.

She looked about nervously, before reaching behind the newspaper and drawing out the partly filled wine-glass, which she then stealthily lifted to her lips to enjoy a crafty little swig. She gave the merest smile as she glanced after Lucy. 'It must be true what they say,' she murmured. 'It really does take one to know one.'

285

She believed that she had met a soul mate in Lucy Lovejoy.

Acutely aware of her position here, regrettably she had to put aside any thoughts of making a friend, to whom she might offload details of her acrimonious divorce and recent money troubles. She could not afford to lose this well-paid job.

~

On the third floor, Lucy followed the porter out of the lift.

'Here we are, miss.' The smart, young man led Lucy to her room, where he opened the door and guided her inside.

After advising her of the usual facilities, he told her, 'If you need anything, just call the desk. I'm never far away.'

When he lingered at the door, Lucy realised what he was after and dug into her purse once more.

'Thank you, you're . . . most kind.' He went away whistling, leaving Lucy suspecting that she must have counted out too many coins to send him away with such a wide smile on his face. You do well to whistle now, she thought, but it might have to be a smaller tip on the way out.

With a little chuckle, she went to the window and looked out across the harbour. But as she looked out, her smile fell away and her heart was sore.

She had noticed a middle-aged couple walking arm

in arm alongside the harbour. It made her think: that could have been me and you, Martin. With the children grown up, we should have grown closer . . . able to go away occasionally . . . enjoy each other's company.

Her mind was now alive with memories. 'What happened, Martin?' she murmured softly. 'Was I so unattractive that you preferred my younger sister? Or maybe you never loved me at all. When we were all children at school together, maybe you always had a hankering for Paula, but she was too young and you were afraid to pursue her. Is that what happened, Martin? Did you only go for me, because you could not have my sister?'

The very idea shocked her, and then she felt a rush of shame for even thinking such a terrible thing. Clenching her fists, she wanted to punch something, someone, anyone. She hated Martin. She hated Paula. And then she hated herself.

'Was it something I did to make you both turn against me?' she asked herself. 'Am I such a failure as a wife and a sister that neither of you needs or wants me? That's it, isn't it? I'm a failure, and a fool.'

Drained of emotion, she leaned against the wall, her fists clenched tight as she rhythmically knocked her knuckles on the wall, over and over again. And when the tears broke free, she could no longer hold back the painful emotions. 'I never even suspected anything . . . not even for a minute! What kind of an idiot am I?' she wondered out loud. 'Was I too giving . . . too loving? Too accommodating . . . too easy to fool?'

Then suddenly she was fighting back. 'No! Why should I take the blame for their cheating?' She paced the floor, angrily ranting, 'You . . . my own sister . . . and you, Martin – I really don't know either of you, do I ? You used me . . . ignored me, like I was nothing – like I didn't matter – and for that I can never forgive you. Either of you! You are without conscience. You don't give a damn for the children, or how this would affect them if they knew. But you know what? We don't need either of you. So, yes, if you want each other, then go ahead, because I for one don't care any more.'

But even while she was ranting, Lucy knew that was not true, because when she gave her love it was unconditional and for ever. She regretted being that way now, but she could not change her nature.

She could not stop caring, but any semblance of loyalty and respect she had for her husband and sister were now gone.

'I can't be near you any more,' she whispered. 'How could I ever again look either of you in the eye?'

Taking the stool from the dressing table, she carried it to the window, where she sat down, and deliberately focused her mind on the scene below.

She was delighted that she had been given a room with a sea view. The hotel overlooked the pretty harbour. Lucy had not forgotten it, and from what she could see now, it was still exactly the same as she remembered: the narrow walkway alongside the harbour, and the little stone wall that ran the entire length of the walkway.

Oh, and there was the doughnut stall, and the ice-cream stall, and the bric-a-brac stalls either side. And beyond them was the restaurant with the same, wide decking she remembered, the tables set beneath parasols, and beneath the decking, the massive, wooden pillars.

Lucy recalled the manager himself explaining to her parents how the whole ensemble was skilfully brought together, with the giant wooden pillars driven into the sea bed in order to take the considerable weight of the decking.

Drawing the stool nearer to the window, Lucy began to notice many other landmarks, and the more she discovered, the quieter of heart she became. After the anguish and turmoil of the past few days, she was finding such a great sense of peace here, in this precious, hidden gem, away from the hassle and rush, and the bad things that she had no control over.

High above, the sun was shining in the bluest of skies. In the harbour the little boats were being got ready to go out, and as they swung about to enter the narrow causeway to the open sea, the water made wide, mesmerising patterns as it swirled beneath the chugging engines.

The cliffs around the bay and the endless blanket of shifting blue sea completed the picture. So quaint, and magnificent.

It was as though a tiny piece of heaven had some-time fallen from the skies and settled here.

Lucy's attention was drawn to a small child playing

on the beach, her parents ever watchful as she began to wander. Lucy saw herself in that small child, and tears once more threatened as all the earlier, precious memories of this idyllic little seaside hideaway came back with a rush of love and appreciation. 'Are you here, Mum and Dad?' she murmured brokenly. 'Are you watching over me?'

A moment later, Lucy's inquisitive gaze followed the couple, who had stopped at the ice-cream stall before, strolling along arm in arm again. They were so easy with each other, she assumed they must be man and wife; or maybe old sweethearts. Or both!

Lucy continued to watch their progress, as they turned off the walkway, obviously still enjoying their ice creams. Then they skirted around the path, as though heading for the jetty.

In her troubled mind, Lucy saw her mum and dad walking the same path, also eating ice cream. And she turned away. It was too much too soon. She could look no longer.

She stood and turned her back to the window, eyes closed, thinking of how it used to be.

Gently shifting the memories to the back of her mind, Lucy reminded herself there were loved ones at home waiting for her to call.

~

Kathleen wanted to be home when Lucy called, so today she had swapped her afternoon shift with a colleague.

With no word from Lucy, she was now concerned. So when the telephone rang, she grabbed up the receiver. 'Hello?'

'Kathleen, it's me!' Lucy was relieved to find her at home. 'I'm calling to say I got here all right. I thought you might be worried.'

'Yes! I was worried! Sure, I've been worried all morning. So, where are you now?'

'I'm at the hotel, and oh, Kathleen, it's wonderful. It's the same hotel we stayed in when I was a child, but it's been renovated, and it's just lovely. Everything here is the same – the harbour, the ice-cream stalls – and, oh, Kathleen, it's like being a child again.'

'Well, that's good, isn't it?'

'Yes, but the trouble is, I can't stop thinking about what Martin and Paula did. And I do miss my parents. Looking out at the harbour just now, I saw this middle-aged couple, and for some reason, they reminded me of Mum and Dad . . . and—'

'Whoa!' Kathleen smiled. 'You're talking so fast, I can't take it all in. So, you've seen a couple who reminded you of Mum and Dad. Well, that's kinda nice, but don't go looking for your parents in every couple you see. It will only make you tearful.'

'I realise that, Kathleen, but it isn't easy.'

'You need to remember why you're there. You, Lucy Lovejoy, are there to think about your future, and what you want to do next. So, please, don't torment yourself with painful memories. Focus on the real reason why you're there. Walk a lot. Laugh a lot. Go dancing. Flirt with every man that looks at you, and go a little bit mad if you feel like it. Let your hair down. If your cheating sister can do it, so can you.'

Lucy actually laughed out loud. 'Kathleen Riley! You're a terror! If I took notice of you, I'd get locked up.'

'Yes, you probably would. But then it would be a new experience for you, don't you think?'

'I suppose so . . . yes.' Lucy thought herself very fortunate to have such a crazy friend. 'Only, I haven't come here to get locked up, or to flirt with every man I see. I'm not you, Kathleen, though sometimes I wish I was. But Lucy Lovejoy is not and never will be wild and wanton, more's the pity!' She quickly changed the conversation. 'It was a straightforward journey here, thank goodness.'

'Aha!' Kathleen clicked her tongue. 'What's been going on then? Come on, out with it!'

'I don't know what you mean.'

'Yes, you do, Lucy, girl, so . . . what have you got to tell me?'

Lucy groaned. 'All right . . . and don't read anything into it, but . . .'

'Come on.' Kathleen grew excited. 'I'm waiting.'

'It's nothing really, but there was this man at the station. I've seen him before, but I don't know who he is. But when I got off at the station here, he saw me . . . and I rushed away from him.'

Intrigued, Kathleen was now like a dog with a bone. 'Out with it, Lucy girl. What are you not telling me?'

'He recognised me.'

'So, there's more? Go on, get on with it!'

Begrudgingly, Lucy related the incident at the bus stop soon after she'd learned of her husband's affair with her sister. She then described the events at the station today.

'What makes me curious is why two complete strangers would offer to take you for a drink?' Kathleen replied. 'I reckon you did right to run off.'

'I had wondered the very same but, he was so kind and caring – good-looking, too – and he seemed honest and genuine. And then, like I said, today I got on the train and a few minutes later, he got on. I think he must be a businessman because he seemed to be looking at official kinds of papers. I kept my head down. I was so afraid he might see me.'

'And did he?'

'Yes! When I got off the train he looked straight at me, and I ran away again. I jumped into a taxi and came here, to the hotel.'

'Don't tell me he was waiting at the hotel . . . was he?'

'Crikey, no! But, honestly, though, it's spooky to see him twice in as many days. It was all a bit worrying.'

Kathleen thought about everything Lucy had told her, and she now had a question for Lucy: 'Do you want to know what I would have done?' she asked.

'No, tell me.' As if she couldn't already guess.

'I would have encouraged him,' Kathleen admitted. 'I would have smiled and enticed him, and got him to take me out to dinner, and spend lots of money on me. And then, I would flirt outrageously, and dance really close to him, so he could feel the thrust of my boobs against his chest. Then, afterwards, when he was all worked up, I'd let him take me to bed, and I would ravish him like he's never been ravished before. After that, when I was ready for off, I'd make sure I left him gagging for more.'

Lucy laughed at that, 'Kathleen Riley!' she chided. 'What are you like? You're a shameless, teasing harlot, that's what you are!'

The two of them giggled before chatting some more. Kathleen remembered speaking to Anne. 'She called me less than an hour since. She was in a bit of a state, because she had not heard from you. When I had to admit that I hadn't heard from you either, she was even more frantic.'

Lucy blamed herself. 'It's my fault. I should have called her the minute I got here.'

'Well, Lucy girl, as soon as I put the phone down, you'd best call her and put her out of her misery. And if you ever see this particular fella again, don't be frightened. Enjoy what he's got to offer. You need to let loose, and show him what you're made of.'

Lucy sighed regretfully. 'I wish I was more like you, Kathleen. But there you go. I'm not and that's the end of it!'

'If I give you some good advice, would you take it?'

'I won't promise, but give it to me, anyway.'

'Right then! And it's nothing terrible, or shameful

either. I just want you to get out and about, Lucy. I know it will be hard, but try not to dwell on what you've lost. Think about what you could gain by taking this precious time for yourself. Try exciting things. Take your mind off your worries. Do something completely different from anything you've ever done before.'

'Oh, so now we're going back to the man on the train, are we?'

'Well, that would not be a bad idea, but I was not about to say that. Though, while we're talking, don't you think it's strange that you met him in the bus shelter, and then he turns up on the very same train that you were on? I reckon Fate was taking a hand there, Lucy girl!'

Lucy agreed but she now assured Kathleen, 'I'm sure it was just coincidence and it has nothing to do with Fate.'

'If you think so. But, look, sweetheart, all I really want is for you to take things easy.'

'What else would I do anyway, except take things easy? This is a very quiet little village, with lovely scenery, delightul walks, and a pretty harbour, with cafes and little shops. To be honest, that's enough for now.'

'I'm glad to hear it. And you're right. You do best to just walk in the sunshine. Feel the sea breeze against your face. And please, Lucy girl . . . do not come back until you feel you're ready to deal with everything. And if you do find yourself short of money, just give me a shout.' She gave a naughty chuckle. 'Unless, of course, your sugar daddy turns up again, pouring money at your feet, in exchange for a favour or two . . . know what I mean, Lucy girl?'

'Oh, yes! I know what you mean all right.' As always, Lucy felt easier when chatting with Kathleen. 'I have sufficient money for my needs,' she confessed, although she did not go into detail. 'I'll be alright, honest.'

'Well, the offer is there if needed,' Kathleen assured her. 'Call me again tomorrow, but for now, don't forget to talk with Anne. Call her right now!'

'I will,' Lucy promised.

When she had rung off Lucy couldn't help but reflect on what Kathleen had suggested. The very idea of allowing a stranger to take advantage of her just to get her own back on her husband was unthinkable.

Partly indignant and partly amused, Lucy promised herself that she would not even think about the man from the train any more. Hopefully their paths would not cross again. Ever! The very thought of allowing a stranger to get close to her in the way Kathleen had joked about made her shiver!

Somewhere in the back of her mind, though, she could not help but wonder if he might actually be attracted to her in that particular way.

Banning the thought from her mind, Lucy picked up the telephone receiver again. She dialled the prefix number for outside, and then her daughter's number.

I hope she's in, Lucy thought. I know she often takes the baby across the park to feed the ducks.

Anne was just securing the baby into the pram, ready for their walk, when the telephone rang. Taking the pram with her, she hurried to the telephone and snatched up the receiver.

'Hello?'

'It's me, love.' It was good to hear her daughter's voice.

'Oh, Mum! I've been worried about you, waiting to know if you got to Kathleen's aunt's all right.'

Lucy had been so preoccupied, she'd forgotten that Anne believed she was taking her break with Kathleen's old aunt. 'Yes, I had a good train journey and then I got a taxi, and now I'm just settling in.'

She was careful not to reveal her true whereabouts. The last thing she needed was for Martin or Paula to find out where she really was.

The baby was making sounds down the telephone. 'He can hear you, Mum,' Anne told her. 'He's reaching out to touch the phone. Go on, Mum. Talk to him.'

For a few precious moments, Lucy listened down the line, while her grandson made familiar noises close to the receiver.

She laughed. 'He really does know who I am, doesn't he?' She was thrilled. 'He'll be holding proper conversations before you know it,' she told Anne. Then it was back to chatting with her little grandson. 'Love you, big boy. I'll be home soon, and then Nanna will take you out to feed the ducks, or walk across the park, through the trees and up to the top of the hill. You'll enjoy that.' The thought of her darling grandson brought the slightest gleam of a tear to her eye. She was glad that she had managed to move the conversation away from where she actually was without lying to her daughter. 'I'll call again tomorrow, and you are not to worry about me. I mean to rest a lot and think things through, and hopefully, come home a stronger person.'

Anne was greatly relieved. She knew her mother was capable enough to achieve what she had set out to do. Although she was also aware of the grief and pain her mother was being made to deal with just now.

'Please, Mum, don't rush home. We're all OK here. This is your time. Use it well, eh?'

'I will, yes, and you're not to worry. Oh, and as it's not easy for you to get hold of me, you can always ring Kathleen. But, I will try to ring you as often as I can.'

'Oh, Mum! Don't be worrying about calling us. Unless, of course, you might feel the need to talk. OK?'

'Yes. Oh, and give my love to Sam and everyone.'

Just as she thought the conversation was coming to an end, Lucy was taken aback when Anne asked, 'Does that "everyone" include Dad?'

'Well . . . of course!'

'And have you spoken to him yet?'

'No. But I will.' In truth she had no intention of calling him.

Anne reminded her, 'He's still working every hour God sends. I expect he misses you, but he's being well looked after.'

'Oh, thank you, Anne. It's good of you to keep an eye on him, but your father is quite capable of making his own tea. You've got enough to do without taking his meals round and running after him.' Realising that she was being a little too harsh, Lucy quickly tempered her tone. 'And besides, knowing how busy you are with the baby and everything, I'm sure your father would not want you to run yourself ragged on his behalf.'

'Oh, no, it's all right, Mum!' Anne assured her. 'Dad's being well taken care of, but it's Paula who's keeping an eye on him. I went round there this morning to make sure he had his breakfast before he went to work, but Paula was already there. I didn't realise you had asked her to keep an eye on him. Anyway, they were both enjoying bacon and eggs. Then I helped her clear up and we left the kitchen sparkling.'

'Really?' Lucy felt physically sick. 'Paula is taking care of him. Well, that's good of her.'

'Yes, and she may be popping round tonight . . . to keep him company. Apparently there's some programme they both want to watch on television, so Dad suggested they watch it together. Paula told me not to fret about Dad, because she doesn't mind keeping an eye on him while you're away. Paula is a good sister, isn't she, Mum?' she finished kindly.

Lucy was truly shaken. 'Well, she does seem to have everything in hand, doesn't she?' she replied eventually.

'Yes, and she promised me, that it was no trouble

at all. So, there you are, Mum. That must be a load off your mind, eh?'

Lucy was thoroughly shocked and disgusted at what Anne had just told her, yet she must pretend that she was grateful to Paula.

'Yes, of course, and it's good that you don't need to keep running round, cleaning the house and cooking his meals. If Paula wants to do it, let her get on with it. Now that she's on her own and not working full time at the minute, she has little else to do.'

She was desperate to assure Anne that she need not go round every day. Her greatest fear was that Anne might find Paula and Martin together, just as she herself found them in Paula's bedroom.

To that end, she told Anne, 'Paula has obviously decided to take the weight off your shoulders, so she might feel hurt if you do interfere. I should leave her be. Since Ray left, Paula seems to have lost her way, and taking care of Dad will give her a focus. Just leave her to it, love.'

'You're right, Mum. Anyway, Dad's always on the telephone, and sometimes he pops in on his way home from work, so it's not as though we don't see him, is it? I think he's making a big effort because Sam's decided to stay here for the time being.'

'That's fine then.' Lucy was somewhat relieved.

'We all love you so much, Mum . . . and we want you to feel strong again. Without you, Mum . . . whatever would we do, eh?' Anne finished emotionally.

Lucy was still reeling, but she made a valiant effort to sound her usual self. 'Oh, sweetheart, that's a lovely thing to say . . . thank you.'

'Take care then, Mum. I'll tell Dad you called, shall I?'

'If you like, sweetheart.'

'Mum . . . before you go . . .?'

'Yes?' Lucy was anxious that Anne had not detected anything to make her suspicious about her father and Paula.

'Well, it's you and Dad really. *Have* you had a falling-out or something?'

'Goodness!' Lucy was partially relieved. 'Whatever makes you think we've fallen out?'

'Nothing really . . . only Dad said you hadn't called and he seemed worried. You said you haven't spoken to him yet, and to be honest, Mum, I really thought you would call him first.'

'Goodness! Don't you think I tried?'

'Oh, I see . . . I'm sorry, Mum. I did think you might have been trying. I said that to Dad.'

'Oh, you know what your father's like – in and out of the house like a Jack-in-the-box. It's never easy to pin him down. I'll catch him later. Besides, from what you've told me, it seems he's being looked after very well.'

'So you haven't had a row then?'

'Like I said . . . he's not the easiest man in the world to track down. Just tell him I'm OK. Will you do that for me?'

'Yes, Mum, and I'm sorry I got the wrong end of the stick.'

'Aw, that's all right, love. Stay safe. Say hello to Les for me, and tell Samuel not to get into any bother, but to keep his head down and get on with what he's supposed to be doing.'

Anne laughed out loud. 'If I gave him a list of instructions like that, he'd tell me where to go, but I will send him your love.'

'You're right, he wouldn't appreciate a list of do's and don'ts. Oh, and give my little grandson a great big kiss from his nanna, will you?'

'I will. 'Bye, Mum. Love you.'

''Bye for now, sweetheart. Love you too.'

While Anne put the receiver down, Lucy was still reeling from what she had learned.

For the moment, it was all too much to take in.

Replacing the receiver, she fell back onto the bed.

'So! It seems Paula is now the Angel of Mercy, eh? Round there all hours, making his tea, curled up to watch television together, and no doubt climbing the stairs to my bed!' Her voice trembled with anger.

The memory of finding them together in Paula's bed was still vivid, like a moving picture in her mind. She wondered if she would never be rid of it.

Right now, though, her first instinct was to check out of the hotel and go back home, where she would tackle them head on, once and for all, regardless of the consequences. Greatly agitated, she began pacing the floor, muttering to herself. 'In my house! Making herself at home, is she? In the bedroom as well, I shouldn't wonder! Martin and her . . . together . . . *in my bed*!'

She wanted to scream to the heavens, but instead she wept bitter tears.

After a time, when rage had mellowed to sorrow, she felt the need to get outside, to walk in the fresh air and rid the bad ideas from her thoughts.

Too uncomfortable to settle, she paced the floor, up and down, backwards and forwards, sometimes pausing with her hand on the telephone. She was burning to relay what she had just heard to someone who might understand what she was going through . . . someone who would advise her as to whether she should go back and face it full on. One thing was for sure: it was painfully obvious that Martin was not missing her. Not while he had her sister close at hand. Lucy was sorely tempted to stay here, until her mind and heart were quieter.

She needed to talk things through. But who would she call? Kathleen? No! Kathleen must not be drawn into this particular problem. And besides, Lucy thought Kathleen had done more than enough for her. She could not burden the children with it. Who then? Who would care one way or another about her predicament?

Inevitably, her parents came to mind, and as always, the tears were not far away.

The truth was plain enough. Apart from her dear friend, Kathleen, there was no one in the whole wide world she could call.

Going into the bathroom, she splashed a handful of cold water over her face, then dabbed it dry with the flannel.

Collecting her handbag, she made her way out of the room, and to the lift, which thankfully was already waiting.

She had no idea where she might go. All she knew was that she had to get out of there. She had to get as far away as she could, and find some quiet, lonely corner, where she might think of what to do next.

When the lift stopped at the ground floor, Lucy got out.

Rather than hand the key in at the desk, where the receptionist might notice that she was upset, Lucy slid it into her handbag. Then, careful not even to glance in the direction of the desk, she took a wide sweep, and headed for the main doors.

In her haste to get away, she was almost running. And when at that moment she dropped her handbag in a panic, she was more flustered when the clip on the bag sprang open and her purse fell out, spilling its contents over the carpet.

Quickly, she grabbed them up and went through the main doors at speed.

Lucy had no idea that her rushed exit had been seen by those at the desk. 'My word! She's in some haste, isn't she?' That was the receptionist, who was grateful for the momentary respite from the awkward conversation she was having with her new guest, a businessman with a lovely smile. 'Wonder where she's off to, in such a dash?' she remarked.

Dave Benson had also seen Lucy's hurried exit and had recognised her instantly. 'She does seem a little flustered, doesn't she?' He was surprised to see Lucy again, and asked, 'Is she one of your guests?'

Like the receptionist, he was eager to bring the conversation to a close. 'I think we're almost finished here,' he said. 'I have only one complaint to speak of: that I was not informed earlier that I was being transferred here, to the Meridian's sister hotel. It was not the best welcome I have ever experienced – to be walking into what looked like a bomb site, only to be told that the hotel was undergoing a complete refurbishment, and that I, along with others, was being transferred to various sister hotels. I have no problem with that, but I would have expected a prior warning.'

'I do understand that, Mr Benson, and I thank you for being most patient. I can assure you that notices were sent out, and I'm sorry you seem to have been overlooked, probably because, as you say, it was a last-minute booking.'

With his mind on Lucy, he gave no answer, until she went on, 'I really am sorry. But we do have a very nice room ready for you with a harbour view, and as compensation we've arranged free breakfasts throughout your stay with us.'

Dave was past being interested in what she had to say, but he thanked her all the same. 'That's very kind. So we'll let the matter rest there, shall we?'

'Yes, thank you. I'll call a porter to take your luggage up.'

But Dave was now in a hurry. 'Is it possible I could leave my bag behind the desk? I need to go out just now. I'll collect my belongings on the way back.'

'Of course!'

Dave opened his overnight bag, slid the briefcase inside, snapped the lock shut and swung the bag onto the desk. 'Thank you.'

Then he gave the receptionist a smile to remember, before hurrying towards the main doors, his eyes peeled for a sight of the woman from the bus shelter. He did not want to let her out of his sight a second time.

Behind him, the receptionist reached under the desk for a small bottle. She drew it out and was about to take a sip when another guest arrived. 'Oh! Good afternoon, Mrs Armitage. What can I do for you?' With sleight of hand, she discreetly returned the bottle to its hiding place.

~

Outside, Dave Benson went in search of Lucy, his heart beating rapidly.

He glanced along the jetty . . . no signs of her. He scoured the walkway and the far harbour-side, but while there were people milling about and children playing, there was no sign of his woman.

He was just minutes behind her, so where could she have gone, so quickly?

He crossed the street and walked along by the row of little shops. He peeped into each one, and still there was no sign of her.

Disappointed, he turned to walk back, and there she was, seated on a bench alongside the beach. Even though she had her back to him, he knew he was not mistaken. The wild, thick brown hair gave her away.

As he drew closer, she appeared to be so lost in her own little world that he was made to wonder if it was right to impose himself on her.

Disheartened, he actually turned and started to walk away, but the compulsion to speak with her was too powerful. Swinging back, he quickened his feet in case he might be tempted to change his mind.

The skirt of shingle across the walkway made a crunching sound beneath his feet as he went on towards the sandy beach. His heart was warmed by the knowledge that at long last he was about to make contact with her again. Since their first hurried meeting, he had kept her in his mind; hoping and wishing that he might see her again. He had no idea why he had been so drawn to her on that cold, dark night, but the experience had left its impact.

Maybe it was because he recognised a kindred spirit in her. Certainly, there was an air of loneliness about her . . . a certain vulnerability.

He knew only too well how easily the cruelty of life could bring a person down.

But there was something else about her. Something strong yet needy. Something immensely beautiful in her deeper nature, that allowed her to creep into his mind and heart.

The nearer he got to her, the more nervous he felt.

Twice he paused, and twice he started off again. What's wrong with you, man? he chastised himself.

He could not reasonably understand why he felt he must talk with her again. Unfinished business, that's what it is, he thought. Once I know she's all right, I'll be able to get her out of my mind.

CHAPTER FIFTEEN

UNAWARE THAT DAVE was approaching, Lucy was in a world of her own. A warm, kindly world, of light and sunshine, with children's innocent laughter carried to her on the wind.

Sitting here, in this lovely place, miles from home, it was a little easier for her to shut out all her sorrow and fears, and feel somehow at peace with the world.

Her gaze was drawn to the seagulls soaring on the breeze. She smiled, thinking if she could only be as free as that . . . no responsibilities or regrets . . . just to open your wings and let the warm breeze take you where it would.

In this delightful, familiar place she was beginning to feel settled and more positive. Yet still she could not decide what to do.

There were so many questions running round in her head. Was her marriage over? Was it her fault in some way? Did Martin truly want to spend the rest of his life with Paula? And did Paula want that? Or was she just toying with him, as was her nature?

No! Martin was a grown man, capable of making his own decisions. Like Paula, he was in the wrong. Both he and Paula should be made to answer for what they had done.

With all that in mind, Lucy asked herself how she might now deal with the embarrassing and awkward position she had been put in. Whichever way she turned, she found herself in the most impossible situation. At least for now she was the only one who knew the sordid truth – apart from Kathleen, who would never reveal a confidence.

Unaware of Lucy's torment, Dave Benson was moving ever closer, still agonising as to whether he was doing the right thing in making contact with her. After all, she had refused his invitation that night they first met, so what made him believe she might want to talk with him now?

He deliberately gave a little cough, so as not to alarm her.

Lucy spun round, astonished to see him there. When he smiled at her, she was concerned that he was actually making a beeline for her.

'Please . . . don't leave on my account.' He realised she was making a move to get up from the bench. 'I saw you in the hotel and I thought I might come and find you. I'm sorry if that sounds a bit forward and intrusive, but it's not meant to be.'

He was now standing before her. 'Please, may I sit

down here, next to you?' His smile was warm and friendly. 'Only I've got a kind of corn on my little toe, and it's begnning to aggravate me.' He gave a little-boy smile. 'It really hurts,' he lied lamely.

Lucy knew it was a ploy, but she had to smile. 'Well, in that case, you'd best sit down.'

As he sat down next to her, he realised that Lucy was making another move to leave. 'No, don't go, please stay . . . just for a while.' He held out his hand in friendship. 'I'm Dave Benson, and I'm glad I found you again, especially after that night at the bus shelter. I know, it was rude and thoughtless of me to ask you if you would like to join myself and Nancy at the pub. I promise you, I do not make a habit of asking strangers to join me for a drink.'

'So, why did you ask me, Mr Benson?'

'Well, first, the name is Dave, and the thing is, I could see that you'd been crying, and I really did want to make sure you were all right. Also, you might have caught pneumonia in that damp bus shelter.'

Lucy shook her head. 'I had no intention of staying there for too long, and besides, I was wearing a warm coat.'

He put his arms out in despair. 'I am sorry . . . really I am. And I do realise now that I was too forward, for which I sincerely apologise. You obviously needed time to yourself, and I do regret intruding.' He dared to lean forward. 'So . . . am I forgiven?' He again put on that little-boy-lost face. 'Please?'

Lucy thought he was so very charming that it would

be churlish of her to walk away now. After all, what harm could he do her, out here, in the open?

Also, she had not forgotten how kind and concerned he had been on that particular unhappy night.

Dave was careful to maintain a fair distance between them. He did not want to scare her off now that he was making headway. At least they were talking and, more importantly, she was not running away this time.

Settling back into the seat, Lucy accepted his apology, and thinking he might leave now, she continued to look out to sea.

Her quiet gaze followed the colourful speedboats as they shot across the water. There were so many boats out there. She could see any number of speedboats; also a smattering of colourful fishing boats, and even a man in a racing boat towing a skier behind him.

Reaching her gaze right out to the horizon, she noticed a big, white cruise ship travelling along slowly, large and lazy against the blue skies.

'It's very impressive, don't you think?' Dave had been watching her; how lost in everything she appeared to be . . . like a child, overwhelmed when seeing the big, wide world for the first time ever.

'Oh, yes.' Lucy was surprised to realise he must be watching her, but somehow it didn't seem to matter. 'I know it must sound ridiculous,' she confessed, 'but I've never seen a cruise-ship before, at least not as close as this.' In truth, she felt as though she could reach out and touch it. 'They really are huge, aren't they?'

'In comparison to some, that one is of medium size.'

Dave felt he had broken the ice with her. 'Some of them can carry over a thousand passengers and, on board, the corridors are so long it can take you twenty minutes or more to get from one end to the other.'

'Really?' Lucy was amazed. 'I bet they're beautiful inside, though?'

'Oh, yes! And there is so much going on, you can be entertained from morning to night.'

'Goodness!' Lucy was amazed. 'I had no idea.'

'I don't know about the smaller ones,' he admitted. 'The larger cruise liners contain any number of swimming pools, amusement arcades, restaurants and bars, and there are extravagant musical shows in full-size theatres . . . even shopping arcades. Oh, and much more!'

'I never realised,' Lucy gasped. 'It's a wonder they don't sink, with all that weight.'

'Oh, but they can, and do. You must have heard of the *Titanic*, one of the biggest shipping disasters ever?'

'Oh, yes, of course!' In truth, Lucy tended not to dwell on disasters of any kind. 'You're right, of course.' Somehow, she had not identified the *Titanic* with the beautful white cruise liner, now gently crossing the horizon.

'The *Titanic* was the forerunner of these magnificent monsters.' Dave gestured to the white ship. 'That one there is far more intricate a vessel, more sophisticated, and fitted with every device known to man, in order to be sure that such a disaster as happened to the *Titanic* might never occur again.'

Lucy understood. He seemed so knowledgeable, it made her curious. 'Have you ever travelled on one?'

'Yes . . . only the once, though,' he explained. 'About two years back I travelled to New York on such a cruise liner as you see out there. It was quite an experience, but I will confess I'm not the happiest sailor in the world. I tend to get seasick. Sounds petty, doesn't it? But I can assure you, it's no small thing . . . not to me, anyway, because I hardly went outside my cabin, I was that ill.'

'Aw, that's such a shame.'

'Yes, I suppose it was, but fortunately the entire journey did not cost me one single penny. You see, at the time, I worked for a firm of international lawyers and, thank goodness, my boss paid the bill, right down to the sickness pills.' He smiled at the memory. 'Lucky for me that he did, because financially I was not in his league and never will be.'

Lucy was curious. 'Do you mind me asking, are you a lawyer?'

'No. I was a kind of high-class courier then, toing and froing and bringing all the tag ends together. When the British arm of the company moved to America, I was offered redundancy, and I took it.'

'And did you miss the travelling?' Lucy asked.

'No. Not in the slightest. In fact, it all turned out to be a lucky break for me. With the redundancy payout I was able to start up my own business, as a consultant and a deal-maker. I had a lot of experience, and I used it to my advantage. I love the work, so, in a modest way, I am a happy man.'

For a while, Lucy digested all that information, and her mind went back to the night she first met this charming, interesting man.

'Can I just say something?' she asked thoughfully.

'Of course. Ask away.'

'Well, that night at the bus shelter, you must have thought I was ungrateful when I refused your offer of joining you and your wife at the pub.'

'Oh, no! As Nancy pointed out later, it was a wrong thing for me to do. Looking back, I realise she was right, I should not have put you in that situation, so I apologise.'

'Apology accepted.'

'Thank you. And secondly, Nancy is not my wife. She's my sister.'

'Oh! I just kind of assumed . . .' Embarrassed, Lucy apologised. 'That's just like me, to get it wrong.'

'You weren't to know,' Dave replied. 'My trip here is to try and clinch a deal for her.'

'Oh, I see,' Lucy answered confidently, even though she didn't 'see' at all.

'I'm sure Nancy won't mind me telling you. Some time back, she acquired a tidy sum of money when her marriage collapsed – all very amicable, I might add. And now, after years of being one half of a whole – that was how Nancy saw it – she's itching to find some kind of independence by setting up her own business.'

'Good for her!' Lucy admired her for having the

ambition and courage to strike out on her own. She had often craved that kind of belief in herself, but sadly, she did not possess any kind of business acumen.

Dave went on, 'She's been searching for the right property, and just recently she learned of a large, dilapidated building not too far from here. She wants me to check it over. If I'm happy with it, then I am given *carte blanche* to bring about a purchase deal through my agency.'

He outlined the plan. 'The property is located in a perfect setting some two miles from here. I've seen it, and I can also see the potential. Presently, sad and forlorn, it sits just a few hundred yards from the beach. It's situated high up, with an amazing view from the cliffs.'

Lucy was impressed. 'It sounds idyllic.'

'Oh, it is. So far, all the costings are done, and planning permission is being discussed at this very moment. It looks promising. So the last hurdle is getting the seller to lower the price, which, because other investors are interested, is bound to be tricky. But I'm convinced we'll get there in the end, even if I have to put up some of the money myself. If that turns out to be the case, I will, of course, get all my money back eventually. I'm ready to do whatever it takes to secure the property for her.'

He gave a little wink. 'Nancy firmly believes I can swing the deal for her. And with that sort of faith in me, how can I not come away with a successful outcome?'

'Oh, you must get it for her!' Lucy was adamant. 'You cannot let her down.'

'Whoa!' Dave laughed. 'Don't you gang up on me as well!'

Lucy was drawn to the idea of his sister having been through a divorce but, instead of bemoaning her loss, she was now striking out on her own.

'If you do manage to secure the property for her, what will she do with it?'

'Ah! That's the easy bit. Because of its wonderful location, she means to renovate and create a hotel. Or at least that's her idea at the moment. Knowing Nancy, she could yet change her mind.' He gave that boyish little smile again. 'Somehow, though, I don't think so. I've never known her so excited, so I do sincerely believe she will stick with her original plan.'

Lucy could sense his respect and admiration for his sister and before she could stop herself, she was asking, 'You love her very much, don't you?'

'I do, yes, and for many reasons. Nancy is the best sister ever!' He went on softly, 'Just over a year ago, I lost my wife in a car accident. I was driving . . .'

He paused, slowly shaking his head. 'There was nothing I could do. The speeding vehicle careered out of a side road and rammed straight into us. My wife took the full impact.' The memories flooded back. 'Nancy was truly amazing. She was there for me and my daughter, Cassie. And she's been there for us ever since. I owe her . . . big time!'

He gave a crooked grin. 'I'm not saying she's an

angel, because I know better than anyone how bossy she can be if she puts her mind to it. She's kept me well on my toes over this property, I can tell you.'

'She sounds like a very strong person,' Lucy remarked admiringly. 'It can't be easy to come through a divorce and go straight into the idea of owning your own business.'

She thought of Martin, and was convinced that she also might end up losing her marriage. But the difference was that if she and Martin did part company, there was no way she could build her own business; even if she did have the money, because sadly, she had neither the confidence nor the ambition to do so.

'Your sister must have the heart of a lion,' she remarked.

'Yes. That's Nancy all right. She goes in head first without giving it too much thought. She can be a little overwhelming at times, I can tell you.'

His tender smile said it all. 'She also has a way of always saying and doing the right thing, especially where I and my daugher are concerned. For instance, she keeps reminding me that over a year has gone by since the accident, and both Cassie and I should now be thinking about moving on – especially Cassie, who was greatly traumatised by what happened to her mother.'

Lucy asked gently, 'And are you both "moving on" with your lives?'

'Yes, I believe we are . . . absolutely. I've decided to sell the house and Cassie is to help me choose our new home. Now, though, I'm tied up and busy with my own business, and Cassie is growing up fast. She has lots of friends and she enjoys life, though now and again, the trauma all comes flooding back, and she takes off . . . to Nancy's, usually. Or she moves in with her aunt, Ellie.'

'It's good that she's got friends.' Lucy thought of Kathleen, and how much she had relied on her.

Dave went on, 'Cassie is a lovely, caring girl, but she has a mind of her own. Little by little she's coming to terms with what happened, and yes, she's all right. She's coming through it, thank goodness.'

Dave was pleasantly surprised at how easy it was to talk to this lovely woman. 'She's presently staying with her aunt Ellie, who is young enough to be her cousin. They're good together. They like the same things. Just now, Cassie is excited about her freedom. She's even planning her own future.' He groaned. 'It wouldn't surprise me to find her teaming up with Nancy . . . especially if I secure this deal. Oh, yes! Cassie would love to spend her time swanning about the beach and such.'

He went on, 'I could be wrong. I mean, she has mentioned college a number of times lately. And if that does happen, judging by the clothes crammed into her wardrobe, she'll probably want to be a fashion designer. Nancy reckons she's got a talent for it; especially as Cassie has altered every item in her wardrobe.'

'She does sound capable,' Lucy replied. 'And I'm glad you have both been able to move on. Life can be very cruel, and sometimes you have to stand up and face the bad things full on. It's the only way. You can't

319

hide from them because they follow you around, and haunt you. Try as you might, you can't easily forget what happened and you can't turn back the clock.'

She thought of her own recent troubles. 'It seems that moving forward and being thankful for what you still have is the right thing to do. Although often, for some of us, it can be a hard road.'

Realising she had said too much, she fell silent.

After Lucy's outburst, Dave was made to wonder what kind of 'bad' things' were haunting her.

For a while, the two of them sat quietly looking out to sea, and reflecting on what had been said.

Eventually Dave asked her, 'I hope I'm not intruding again, but am I right in thinking that you have recently suffered a sadness?' He paused before asking gently, 'Is that why you were crying . . . that night, when we first met?'

With the tears threatening, Lucy nodded but said not a word.

Dave understood, and he did not push it. 'Look . . . I think – *hope* – that I've found a friend in you. So would it be too bold of me if I suggested the two of us might walk along the beach? It is a lovely day, after all. Such a shame to waste it, don't you think?'

'Yes.' Taking a long, deep breath, Lucy composed herself. 'I believe I would like that very much,' she answered shyly.

The two of them set off at a leisurely pace, at first merely skating the rim of the beach, before somehow they began to meander towards the water's edge.

'You're right,' Lucy said, kicking her toe at the sand. 'It is a lovely day. And I'm so glad that you came and sat on my bench.'

Dave laughed at that. 'Oh! So it's *your* bench, is it?'

'Well . . . no, I didn't mean that.' Lucy felt so natural in his company, it seemed as though she could tell him anything. 'I saw you today,' she confessed. 'I was behind you on the train, and when I got off I ran away.'

'Why did you do that?' he asked kindly. 'I saw you hurrying away from the station, and I even asked a taxi driver how I might find out where you'd gone, but he couldn't help me.' He looked Lucy in the eye. 'I did so want to talk with you.'

'I'm sorry. I just felt so ashamed at the way I was when we first met. I needed to put it behind me.'

'Tell me, on that particular night, would you have run away if you'd known that Nancy was my sister?'

Lucy blushed bright pink. 'I don't know.'

Just then, the heel of her shoe went into a dip of sand where children had been making sand castles, and she nearly fell over. 'Whoops!'

Reaching out, Dave caught her. 'Careful! I don't know if I'd be strong enough to carry you back if you injured yourself,' he teased.

Lucy laughed at that. 'You cheeky devil. D'you think I weigh a ton, or what?'

'Well, I can't answer that, can I?' he finished cheekily. 'Never having held you in my arms.'

For some strange reason, this man's natural friendliness brought out the devil in Lucy. Kicking off her shoes, she set out at the run. 'Catch me if you can!' she taunted. 'I bet you can't!' Her idea was to put a distance between them because, surprisingly, she was enjoying his company much too much.

'Hey! I never turn down a challenge. Here I come!' Kicking off his own shoes, he went after her.

Within a few minutes he was on her, sweeping her into his arms and swinging her round. 'One thing I can do, is run!' he admitted. 'So, come on, then. An apology, if you please!'

'Give over. Put me down!' Lucy was a little angry at being manhandled, then she was flattered, and now she couldn't stop laughing. 'You're a crazy man!' she shouted. 'Absolutely crazy!'

He did not put her down as she asked. Instead, he swung her over his shoulder, and ran back to collect his shoes, Lucy screaming for him to stop.

As he ran along the beach with her, the holidaymakers laughed at their antics, and one even called out, 'Go on! Throw 'er in the ocean. That's why I brought my missus 'ere! Only I'd need a winch to lift 'er!'

The big woman beside him, bursting out of her swimsuit, did not appreciate his joke. 'Shut it, birdbrain!' she roared. 'Or you'll be the one thrown in the ocean!'

When someone else joined in, a slanging match broke out, and Dave suggested, 'We'd best run for the hills, before his missus comes after us . . . what d'you think?'

Carrying their shoes, the two of them went at a

run, stumbling and laughing, towards the harbour café.

Once on the wooden walkway, they poured the sand out of their shoes and put them back on their feet. 'I've haven't had so much fun for ages,' Dave confessed breathlessly. He felt like a teenager again; albeit a bit foolish.

As she hurried alongside him, Lucy, also, was invigorated and happy. 'If someone had told me that I'd be carried along the beach over some stranger's shoulder – with people pointing and laughing, and calling out – I never would have believed it,' she smiled.

Dave was surprised at his own behaviour. 'Like you, I never intended making a fool of myself, and if my business associates had seen me, they'd have thought I'd lost my senses. But you know what, it was such great fun I could do it again. Right now.'

'You can forget that!' Lucy chided him. 'As you've discovered I'm no lightweight, and anyway I haven't got my breath back yet. Also, I'm ready for a cold drink.' She shook her head in disbelief. 'I don't know what came over us!' she giggled, 'but you're absolutely right. It must be this place. It seems to have brought out the child in each of us.'

'It's not this place,' Dave said softly. 'It's you. To be honest, I really don't know how you managed it, but you made me want to run wild . . . without a care for what anyone thought.'

'I'm glad.' Lucy smiled up at him. 'It seems we

helped each other forget our troubles . . . just for a few crazy moments. And that's good . . . isn't it?'

He was silent for a moment, smiling into her shining, brown eyes, and noting how curls of that rich chestnut-brown hair were blown every which way by the playful breeze. Instinctively, he took hold of her hand. 'You're right,' he agreed. 'A sunny May day with you and me together on the beach. That's what you might call a rare bit of magic.'

Suddenly conscious of her hand in his, Lucy withdrew it. She felt the need to create a little space between herself and this stranger; this warm-hearted stranger who had made her laugh out loud. Made her squeal with delight, and completely lose her inhibitions.

More worryingly, she now felt a certain intimate affinity with him, and that made her truly nervous.

~

The café reminded Lucy of a picture postcard, its setting was so perfect. The café itself was an ancient stone building. It possessed the most amazing views of the towering cliffs, and the beaches stretching away.

Outside, the wicker tables and chairs made a very welcoming sight.

'Where shall we sit . . .?' Dave paused, looking at Lucy in disbelief. 'Well, I never! I've just run across the beach with a beautiful woman over my shoulder . . . and I don't even know your name!'

With the widest, warmest smile, he looked down on

her face, held out his hand and said softly, 'Let's start again, shall we? I'm Dave . . . Dave Benson.'

'Ah! Well, hello, Dave Benson. I'm very pleased to meet you.' Lucy held out her hand and introduced herself in a jovial manner. 'And I am Lucy Lovejoy.'

Dave gave a cheeky wink. 'Lovejoy, eh? Well, that's very apt, I must say. Yes . . . I like that. How do you do, Lucy Lovejoy?' He shook her hand again. 'And, may I say, I am very pleased to meet you as well.'

Just then, Lucy noticed that the people at a nearby table were watching them with interest.

She blushed bright pink. 'Let's sit down,' she told Dave quietly. 'We're causing a scene.'

Dave now noticed the couple, and when he smiled at them they got up and left. 'See! That's the way to get rid of nosy parkers.'

Lucy laughed, but fearing the couple might over-hear her laughter and mistake it for rudeness, she covered her mouth with the flat of her hand, although tears of laughter sparkled brightly in her eyes.

Dave leaned closer to her. 'Now then, Lucy Lovejoy, let's concentrate on the menu, shall we?'

He handed it to her, while putting on a stiff, though pleasant manner. 'May I ask, what would you like from the menu, madam? I can heartily recommend the chocolate ice cream topped with nuts and choc flakes. Or if you prefer, how about a dish of fruit topped with strawberry ice cream? But if you're really hungry, we do a wonderful cheese and bacon on toast.'

Trying hard not to giggle, and feeling just a bit

embarrassed, Lucy played along. 'Oh, now let me see . . . oh, yes. I think I would like a portion of . . . mmm . . . yes! The chocolate ice cream, please, with choc flakes and nuts on top. Oh! And could I also have a wafer, please?'

'Of course, madam. Thank you.'

Smiling broadly, Dave spoke in a soft, suitably officious manner. 'One chocolate ice cream, topped with nuts and choc flakes, and a wafer on the side. And would madam like a drink of sorts?'

'Yes, please, I would love a ginger beer . . . if you don't mind. Thank you.'

Lucy played the game until Dave gave a very waiter-like bow from the waist. 'Ooh!' He made a pained face. 'Sorry, madam . . . only I just felt the most uncomfortabe twinge. Anyone would think I'd been carrying a very heavy weight over my shoulder.'

'Hey! Are you saying it's my fault if you've got a twinge? I didn't ask you to throw me over your shoulder like a caveman. That was your idea.'

Dave looked shocked as he told her stiffly, 'Maybe it was, madam. But I must say . . . you certainly seemed to enjoy the experience!'

He then departed in a mock-huff, taking the order, written on a piece of scrap paper that he found in his trouser pocket.

Behind him, Lucy again had to put her hand over her mouth to smother her giggles.

What am I doing here? she asked herself. I've been carried off by a madman!

Even so, she had not felt so free and happy in a very long time.

For a fleeting moment she gazed up at the skies. Then she looked along the beach, and in her mind's eye she saw her parents, right there.

One minute they were strolling hand in hand along the beach, and the next they had spread big, white towels on the sand. Then they sat down together and lovingly watched, as she and Paula made wobbly sand castles by their feet. In the unfolding memories, her parents seemed impossibly young, and so very much in love – laughing together and holding hands, just as she had seen them many times as a child.

Since losing them, she had often closed her eyes and thought of them, and inevitably she had shed tears. Now though, as they invaded her senses, so wonderfully happy together, she could not feel sad. Instead, she felt blessed. And so very grateful to have known and loved them; those two, very special, unforgettable people.

In that precious moment, as she was thinking of them, she knew that somehow, they too were thinking of her. Suddenly, something inside her had changed. 'They really are here,' she murmured. 'They want to show me how they are now together, for always.'

For some wondrous, inexplicable reason, Lucy believed it was true, as sure as day followed night, and she felt calmer, and very much stronger in herself. In that uplifting moment of acceptance, it was as though part of the weight and sadness was lifted from her. It was a disturbing, yet oddly reassuring experience.

Even so, she was still frighteningly uncertain as to where life might take her from here.

On returning, Dave noticed that she was in a quieter mood. 'I haven't upset you, have I?' he asked. 'I hope I haven't embarrassed you.'

'No!' Lucy assured him emphatically. 'You haven't done anything wrong. To tell you the truth, I haven't had such fun in ages.' She wagged a finger at him. 'You really are a bad influence, Mr Dave Benson!'

He smiled graciously, and a moment later, having placed the ice creams on the table, he gently leaned down and kissed her on the forehead. 'Thank you for making me feel special again,' he whispered.

Lucy blushed, and thought it best not to say anything, though she felt a warm glow of acceptance. And when he held her gaze for too long a moment, her heart gave the merriest little skip.

They ate their ice creams and chatted about things in general, such as the pleasantness of the hotel, and Lucy said it was lovely being so close to the harbour and the beach. And Dave agreed, and then he bought them each another drink, and Lucy said it was so peaceful here, she wished she could stay for ever.

What they did not discuss was how they were drawn to each other, and how one seemed to bring out the best and craziest in the other. Yet Lucy dared not dwell on her deeper feelings for this stranger – such dark feelings, strictly forbidden – and rightly so.

When Lucy fell silent, Dave quietly studied her face. He thought she was the loveliest person, inside and out. 'Penny for your thoughts,' he asked softly.

Lucy looked up. 'Oh, I'm sorry. I was miles away.'

'Yes, I could see that.'

'I was just thinking . . . about things in general.'

'Lucy?'

'Yes?'

'I hope you didn't mind me confiding in you . . . about the car accident and everything?'

'No! Not at all. After what you've been through, you must need someone to listen.'

'You're very kind, but it won't happen again, I can assure you. Like Nancy said, there comes a time to move on and leave the sadness behind. No good can ever come from dwelling in the past.'

Lucy suddenly felt very lonely. 'Dave?'

'Yes, Lucy?' He gave a cheeky smile. 'Am I about to be chastised?'

'No! I need to get back and wash off the sand. It's got between my toes. It would be nice, though, to walk back along the beach?'

'Sure! On the way I need to dip my toes into the sea.'

'Can I ask why?'

'Because I haven't dipped my toe in the sea, not since I was a little boy.'

'OK! Fine by me.'

Some few minutes later, after Dave had insisted on settling the bill, the two of them set off, clutching their shoes.

As agreed, they walked along the beach, and very soon Dave led Lucy right down to the water's edge.

He was the first to venture into the water. 'Brr!' He gave a little shiver. Having rolled up his trouser legs, he walked right out, with the water lapping at his ankles. 'It's not as warm as I thought. Come on, Lucy Lovejoy. It's invigorating. Be brave.'

Tiptoeing across the crunchy sand, Lucy nervously dipped one of her feet into the playful waves. 'Whoo!' She jumped back. 'You lied! It's freezing.' Even so, she was eventually standing beside him, with both feet in the water. 'You're right,' she acknowledged, 'it *is* "invigorating".'

The two of them were like children, swishing their toes and running along the water's edge, until they were opposite the hotel where, oddly silent, they set about wiping their feet with two handkerchiefs found in the bottom of Lucy's bag.

When they were virtually dry and feeling more comfortable, they put on their shoes, also in silence.

In stark contrast to when Dave had Lucy over his shoulder, and they had laughed and screeched as they ran down the beach, they now strolled along the stone walkway, deep in thought, although, much to Lucy's surprise, Dave very tenderly took hold of her hand as they crossed the road.

She made no protest because what was there to protest about?

At the hotel entrance, Dave brought her to a halt.

'Can we see each other again later?' he asked softly.

'That would be lovely,' Lucy told him shyly.

'Good.' His smile was unusually intimate; a smile that set Lucy's heart racing.

'The problem is, I need to wash and change, and then it's quickly off to my first meeting. I suspect that could run on a bit. Then it's straight on to the next and most important meeting of the day.'

Lucy was disappointed. 'Don't worry if you're too busy,' she said regretfully. 'Your work must come first.'

'Oh, no! I definitely mean to see you tonight – if that's all right with you? But I don't think I'll surface until quite late. So, I was wondering, how about I take you to dinner this evening?'

Lucy was thrilled. She had never in her whole life been formally invited to 'dinner'. 'Oh, that sounds wonderful!' she said. 'But only if it doesn't put you out, because you're bound to be tired after your heavy day.'

Dave shook his head. 'I would never be too tired to take you out.'

Blushing once more, Lucy said she would look forward to it, and then she wished him well. 'I hope you can swing the deal – for Nancy's sake,' she said with genuine feeling.

'Thank you, Lucy,' Dave replied. 'It won't be easy, but you can bet I'll do my damnedest! There is still a way to go, though, before we get right down to the nitty-gritty. These people are good. They know what they want and they don't easily back down.'

'They might be good, but not as good as you, I'll bet!' Lucy assured him.

He laughed softly. 'Well, thank you, and I'll tell you something else.'

'What's that, then?'

'I think that beneath Lucy Lovejoy's soft and lovely exterior, there's a feisty, ambitious woman waiting to get out. Am I right?'

'Of course! And don't you forget it!' she warned with a cheeky smile.

It occurred to her that the more confidence he instilled in her, the more she believed she could tackle anything.

In the hotel foyer, Lucy apologised for having to hurry away, but, 'I really do need a hot bath.'

'Need any help?' he asked with a cheeky grin.

Softly blushing, she gave a genuine tut-tut. 'I thought you were a gentleman!'

'Shame on me!' he teased. 'Don't forget we're meeting up for dinner.'

'Oh, I won't forget.' She was so excited at the idea of a gentleman taking her to dinner, she could hardly breathe. 'I'm really looking forward to it . . . as long as you don't want to run across the beach with me on your shoulder.'

'I wouldn't mind,' he quipped. 'Somehow, though, I reckon I've done my Tarzan thing for today. Unless you'd prefer to find a fancy restaurant somewhere close, we could have dinner here. I understand the menu offers much more than ice cream with nuts and choc flakes. So, Lucy . . . what do you say?'

'Well, if it's all right with you, I'd rather stay in the

hotel. I'm not used to fancy restaurants.' In truth, she had never even set foot in one.

'That's settled then!' Lucy's decision pleased him. 'I took a quick peek into the restaurant earlier while I was waiting for the receptionist to deal with another guest, and I thought it looked very pleasant. Moreover, we won't even have to get our feet wet.'

His casual comment made Lucy think back over the past few hours, and her heart was warmed by the memory. 'So, what time shall we meet,' she asked 'and where?' She was starting to feel nervous.

'There is just one thing, Lucy. I'm really worried about tonight.'

'Why?'

'Because the lady I am taking to dinner has a bad habit of running away, just when you think you're getting to know her.'

'Oh, no! I won't do that . . . I promise.'

'That's good enough for me, then. So, I'll book a table for what . . . nine thirty? That'll give me time to get back, have a quick bath and change, then make my way down to meet you at . . . say nine-fifteen. All right?'

'OK, yes. I'll be here waiting . . . and I'm not planning on running anywhere.'

'Good!' He touched her gently on the hand. 'We could be up till the early hours. Does that worry you?'

'Why should it worry me?'

He lowered his voice. 'Well, now, let me see . . .' He took a long look at her, and when she looked up with those nutmeg-brown eyes, he was taken aback, and for a moment he lost his train of thought.

Amused, Lucy jogged his memory. 'Excuse me, you were about to tell me why we might be up until the early hours?'

'Oh, yes! First, I think we have so much more we need to say to each other, and secondly, I was half hoping I might be able to lure you to take a stroll under the stars.'

Placing his hands on her shoulders, he held her there. 'For now, I'd best make tracks, or they'll have a head start on me, and that would not be good for my purpose.'

'You forgot to say where we should meet?' Lucy reminded him.

'Ah, yes! Down here in the lobby. I'll book the table now.'

'I'll be ready,' Lucy promised.

Suddenly, almost without her meaning to, she went up on her tiptoes and kissed him very swiftly on the cheek. 'Thank you.' The last time she had enjoyed herself so much was when the children were small.

Before he could recover from the tender and much appreciated surprise, Lucy was gone, pink-faced and embarrassed, leaving him tenderly stroking his face where she had kissed it.

For the longest moment, he stood there, his gaze resting on the place from where she had got into the lift. 'Lucy Lovejoy . . .' He thought back on the wonderful time they had just spent together. 'You're like a welcome breath of fresh air,' he murmured.

As he walked towards the reception, he took another lingering glance towards the lift.

To his great surprise, he was already missing her.

CHAPTER SIXTEEN

PAULA WAS CLEARING away the ironing board when she heard the back door creak open.

'It's only me!' Martin's voice rang through her house.

Rushing through the kitchen, Martin grabbed hold of her and swung her round. 'Hello, beautiful! Oh, I thought I would never get that damned job finished. I fixed the water problem, then I found the plaster crumbling from behind the wall. The whole lot needs stripping out. On top of that, the new boiler wouldn't start up. I had to take the useless thing back, and oh, I tell you, it's been one setback after another.'

'Oh, that's a shame.' Folding the ironing board into the cupboard, Paula half turned to give him a fleeting kiss. 'I wondered where you were. But never mind, you're here now. I don't expect you've had time to eat, so why don't I make you a sandwich or something?'

Martin shook his head. 'Thanks, but I'm not hungry. I'm just that pleased the work is finished! I've been itching to get it over with, so I could come and see you.' Turning back the collar of her blouse, he drew her close and ran the tip of his tongue along her neck. 'I really hate it when I'm not with you.'

When she opened her mouth to speak, he silenced her by gently squeezing her face between his two hands. 'Oh! And while I remember, I've told you before about leaving that back door open,' he complained. 'Anybody could let themselves in. You could be upstairs in the nuddy, and they'd have you before you even realised.'

'Aw, stop fussing!' Paula was not in the mood for a lecture.

'It's not a case of me "fussing",' he said. 'It's for your own good. I've told you time and again . . . there are bad people out there, my darling. Why won't you ever listen to me?' Tugging her forward, he grabbed her round the back of the neck. 'I don't want anyone putting their grubby paws on you.'

Paula drew away. 'Get off! You're hurting me.' She stroked her fingers over her neck where he had held her tight. 'I've told you before, Martin, I don't like you telling me what to do.'

'Hey!' He followed her to the kitchen sink, where she appeared to keep her distance. 'I would never hurt you . . . I'd lop off my own arm before I would ever hurt you, and you know that.'

She smiled up at him. 'I know, but you keep on about that damned back door, and it just gets me

down, that's all. I don't like being locked in all the
time.'

'Aw . . .' He gently hugged her to him. 'It's just that
I'm concerned about the way you never lock the door
at either your house or mine. It's dangerous, sweetheart . . . I've lost count of the many times I've found
it unlocked . . . just now, I could have been a thieving
tramp, or anybody looking for easy pickings. I've told
you time and again, and still you don't listen.' He
kissed her on the mouth. 'I've upset you, haven't I?
Please, don't be angry with me.'

Paula looked at him with puppy eyes. 'Then don't
nag at me, Martin,' she said. 'You know I'm not used
to being told what to do.'

Martin had to remind himself that he was not
dealing with Lucy now. Paula was a very different kettle
of fish altogether; she was feisty, and passionate. She
was also attractive enough to make a man jealous. And
as he had already discovered to his delight, she was
wild and exciting in bed.

'I'm sorry, sweetheart,' he mumbled, tenderly
sliding his hands around her slim waist. 'It's just that
I worry . . .'

'All right.' She kissed him full on the mouth. 'I'll
forgive you this time. But you have to stop nagging.
It aggravates me.'

'It's a deal.' He would promise her anything.

After making certain that the doors were securely
locked, the two of them went up the stairs together.

'I'll have to get back soon, though,' Martin informed

her. 'Anne's coming round later. I expect she's had another call from her mother, and wants to run it by me . . . not that I care one way or the other.'

'Aw, that's not a nice thing to say,' Paula declared with sarcasm. 'Poor, dear Lucy!'

'I don't mean to be spiteful, but I can't lie, and I can't help the way I feel.' Martin spoke with conviction. 'Especially now, when I've decided who I want to spend the rest of my life with.' He smacked her bottom, and when she ran into the bedroom squealing and laughing, he was right on her heels.

When Martin shut the door behind him, she laughed aloud. 'Frightened some bogeyman might come up and get me, are you?'

'No, because *I'm* the bogeyman today.' He growled like a wild animal, sending Paula into fits of laughter.

Martin, however, recalled briefly how, because of the open door, Lucy had found them together in this very bed.

Undeterred, he ran at the bed and grabbed hold of the now naked Paula. 'I've been waiting for this all day,' he cooed wickedly.

And, for the moment, it seemed that peace had prevailed.

∼

'They're at it again!' Mary Taylor had seen Martin go in through the back door. She had heard the raucous laughter, and then the revealing silence. 'It's disgraceful!'

She angrily thumped her fist on the table. 'There's poor Lucy, gone off for a well-earned break since losing her parents, and here's her sister . . . blatantly flaunting her affair with Lucy's husband. I'm sorely tempted to go round there and give them a piece of my mind, the pair of them!'

'You'll do no such thing, Mary!' Peter came up behind her. 'I agree with you, it *is* disgraceful, and I, too, would like to give them a piece of my mind, but I won't and neither will you! It would not make the slightest difference because people like that don't give a damn about anything or anyone. They would simply laugh in your face, and just carry on with what they're doing. And what we must also remember, Mary, is that what they do in the privacy of their own homes is none of our business.'

Mary did not agree, but she was wise enough to heed her husband's advice.

Reluctantly, she returned to her armchair, and resumed her crossword puzzle.

When she continued to mumble, Peter grumbled, 'Are you still worrying about that pair next door?'

'Yes, I am,' she admitted. 'But don't concern yourself, Peter. I promise, I shall mind my own business, as you say. But I'll tell you this – and trust my word – before too long there'll be murder done.'

'Hmm!' Her husband said nothing more, but he, too, thought the goings-on next door were a recipe for absolute disaster.

~

Unaware that they were the subject of conversation between their watchful neighbours, Martin and Paula now lay on top of the bed, talking, making plans, and generally winding down from their wild activities.

'I'd best get ready for home,' Martin said lazily. 'Anne might even be there now, waiting for me.'

Paula was nervous about that. 'Lucy didn't say anything to Anne, did she? About finding us together.'

'No, not as far as I can tell. You know Lucy as well as I do, and we both know that she would rather die than hurt her children. So, I think we can rest assured that she's said nothing to them . . . or anyone else. She'll keep what she saw to herself, for Anne and Samuel's sakes. Whether or not she'll tackle me, I don't know. Maybe that's why she took off – to decide what to do next – but like I say, she won't want the children to know what she saw. Never in a million years!'

Paula had no conscience about Lucy learning the truth. 'She's too soft, and forgiving, the silly cow! She's always been a bit of a softie, even when we were kids.' She gave a twisted little smile. 'I mean, she let herself get pregnant by you, didn't she? Huh! You would never find me being so vulnerable.'

'Hey!' Martin stopped her right there. 'We're not talking about Lucy and you. And we're not talking about what took place over twenty years ago. I'm just saying that if Samuel and Anne knew about you and me, they would be up in arms. That's why even though I'm impatient for us to be together, we still need to be careful and keep it low-key until your divorce is through.

Maybe then we'll be in a better position to make plans . . . even move away, if need be. I'm self-employed with good references, so I can find work wherever I choose.'

Paula nodded in agreement. 'I thought you were in a hurry to get home?' she reminded him.

'Oh, I see!' He was instantly suspicious. 'Now that you've had your wicked way with me, you can't get rid of me quickly enough, is that it?'

'Don't talk silly, Martin. You just said you needed to go home because Anne might be there for you. And what if she is, and she gets so impatient that she makes her way over here to see if I know where you are? She's done that before. So, don't think I'm trying to get rid of you, because I'm not! I'm just a bit worried, that's all.'

'Yes, you're probably right.'

Scrambling off the bed, he quickly got dressed. Then he had a sudden thought. 'By the way, the divorce papers . . . have you signed them, like I asked?'

'Not yet.' She got out of the other side of the bed. 'I haven't had time. I've been busy. Like you, I haven't stopped all day, but I'll sign them tonight, and get them back. Then we can both breathe easy. At least that part of the plan will be dealt with, won't it?'

'Yes, but I did remind you last night and you said you would have them signed and posted by midday today. You can do it now and I'll drop it in the post box on my way home.'

'No! I'll take them into town myself. It will be much quicker that way, and I can have a word with the solicitor while I'm at it; ask him to get it done as quickly as possible.'

'Good thinking. We'll both rest easy when you're no longer married to that gormless lump of a husband! We'll have a good wedding, my sweet, and you can name your own destination for the honeymoon. I'll make sure that money will not be an object even if I have to work my fingers to the bone. Although, come to think of it, you should get a nice little settlement with the divorce.'

'What makes you say that?'

'Well, Ray beat you black and blue . . . or so you told me.'

'He did!' Paula asserted angrily. 'What . . . you think I was making it up, do you?'

'Of course I don't. But it does mean that he'll be made to pay through the nose, and serves him right. I hope he gets all he deserves.'

Martin tidied himself, brushed his hair into place, and made his way downstairs, with Paula just behind him.

At the door, she kissed him cheerio and made sure there was no sign of lipstick on him. 'Go on . . . you look decent enough.'

Suddenly he turned back. 'Where are the divorce papers?'

'Why?'

'Because I need to watch you sign them, and then I know it's done.'

'So you think I'm not capable of signing the papers all by myself, do you?'

'I never said that, but you didn't sign them last night, did you? And you promised you would.' He grew irritated. 'Get them now and sign them in front of me.'

'I thought I asked you not to tell me what to do?' Paula argued.

'That was before. This is different. Please, Paula, get the papers, will you?'

When Paula hesitated, he asked her outright, 'Do you love me?'

'You know I do!'

'And you want to be rid of your big oaf of a husband – is that the truth or not?'

'Yes, it's our part of the plan. You know that!'

'Then, please, sign the papers in front of me.'

'OK. If you don't trust me, I suppose I'll have to.'

'It's not that I don't trust you, I just don't trust your memory. So, go on, do it now, then we can both relax.'

Realising he would not leave until she signed them, Paula went to the hallway drawer, where she drew out the papers and signed them quickly. 'There!' She showed him the signature. 'Happy now, are you?'

'And you will take them to the solicitor first thing, won't you?'

'I've said, haven't I?'

'Don't forget!'

'I won't. I promise, I'll put them into my handbag right now . . . look!' She collected her handbag from the lounge and placed the papers inside. 'I have to go into town first thing, and I need to take my handbag with me, so I can't possibly forget, so stop your fretting!'

She kissed him goodbye, and he climbed into the van and drove off, waving out the window as he went.

~

Ten minutes later, as he turned into his own street, he was not altogether surprised to see Anne, who was walking towards his house, with his grandson in the pushchair.

As he neared the house, Anne caught sight of him, and started to hurry. Breathless, she drew up at the door, just as her father pulled up. 'Hiya, Dad!' When Martin got out of the car, she gave him a big hug. Martin was pleased to see her too, and he was also thankful that he had not lingered too long at Paula's, because Anne might well have gone there looking for him.

'You're late tonight, aren't you, Dad?' Anne chatted while Martin unlocked the front door.

'I had a ton of work on today,' he said. 'It was one of those plumbing jobs that you dare not leave unfinished . . . damned nuisance.'

Anne took the baby out of the pushchair. 'I've been round here once, but there was no sign of you. I thought you might be round Paula's. I know sometimes you pop in for a few minutes . . . especially now Mum's away.'

'I don't go round that often.' Her comment put him on his guard. 'I'm just a bit concerned about her, what with all that nasty business going on with the

345

divorce. That great bruiser of a husband seems to be making it as difficult as he can for her!'

'Hmm! I never did like him. He always was a bit of a brute.'

'That's right. So, as your mother isn't here to listen to her sister's troubles, I do try to find a spare minute to slip round . . . just so she doesn't feel abandoned . . . if you know what I mean?'

As he turned the door key and ushered Anne and the baby inside, he had a disturbing thought. 'Does your mother ask about Paula?'

'Sort of, yes.'

'What's that supposed to mean?'

'When she rang the last time, I told her what you said . . . that Paula's ex is hassling her to speed up the divorce.'

'And what did your mum say to that?'

Anne shrugged. 'Not much really. She didn't make any comment. I expect, with her still grieving for Nan and Granddad, she's trying to keep her mind clear of Paula's problems, and in a way I don't blame her. Mum is always thinking of other people, and it's high time she started to think of herself. Mind you, she seems to be enjoying her stay with Kathleen's aunt.'

'Really?' Martin could not relate Lucy with the word 'enjoying'. 'And is that what she actually said – that she was "enjoying" herself?'

'That's what she said, and it was lovely to hear her so calm and content. I had been really worried about her. She was so down the weeks before she left, I really thought she might have a breakdown.'

'You never said anything to me.' He was made to wonder if that was after Lucy had caught him and Paula in her bedroom. And his greatest fear was that she would tell the children.

'I expect deep down, as well as grieving for her parents, she must be worried about Paula. I mean, she is her sister, after all, and you know what Mum's like about family.'

'Yes, I know what she's like, but as you say, she's got to put herself first now and then, and not be too involved in other people's problems.' He was thinking that once Paula was divorced, and Lucy would have to deal with her own marriage break-up, she would need to toughen up in order to get through it all.

Anne was still thinking of Paula, and she now had a suggestion. 'D'you think Paula might like to come and stay with me for a while, just until Mum gets back?'

Martin was shocked. 'No, I don't think that's such a good idea. It's a very kind thought, though, but when I popped in just now, she was having one hell of a battle with her husband on the telephone . . . all to do with divorce papers and all the other stuff that goes with a divorce. And besides, you've got enough on your plate, with keeping an eye on my grandson, and taking care of your house and husband. You've said before now that you never seem to have enough hours in the day, and the little one is getting some new teeth coming through, and you've not had a good night in ages.'

'Yes, that's true enough. And then there's Samuel, worrying about Mum. I told him she was absolutely fine, and that she would likely be home at any minute. First, though, she needed to get her head straight, what with all that's happened lately.'

'And what did he say?'

'He wanted a number where he could call her, and I explained that she was staying with her friend's aunt, who is quite old, and we were not to intrude on the old dear. I told him that Mum was ringing me regularly, to keep us up with everything.'

'And what did he say to that?'

'He said that was good enough; as long as she was all right, that was all he needed to know.'

'You're a good girl, Anne. A good daughter, and a good sister to our Samuel.'

It flashed through Martin's mind that sooner rather than later, if he had his way, he would be obliged to break the news to his children that he and their mother were breaking up. It would be a huge blow to them; especially so soon after losing their grandparents; but they were young enough to get over it. Besides, he and Lucy had gone far enough with this sham of a marriage. Things happen, and sometimes it's best to move on.

'Dad!' Anne's voice invaded his thoughts. 'Have you suddenly gone deaf or what?'

'Oh, sorry, I was miles away.' He glanced at the push-chair. 'Ah, look there, the little man's nodded off.'

'He's been crawling all over the place today,' she told

him proudly. 'He's worn himself out. Y'know, Dad, I reckon he'll stand up and try to walk, any day now.'

Martin proudly pointed out, 'You and your brother were both up on your feet at a year. So this little fella-me-lad here should be running amok any time now.'

'Hmm!' Anne chuckled. 'I expect I'll have to lock up my china when that happens.'

Martin, too, laughed. 'That might be a good idea.'

Anne asked him if he was hungry. 'I'll cook you something if you like?'

'No, it's all right, sweetie, there's nothing in the cupboards to cook. I haven't been shopping yet . . . you know what it's like.'

'That's just what I thought!' She went into the kitchen and checked the cupboards. 'I'll do you a big shop tomorrow,' she said, returning to the lounge. 'Give me three or four pounds . . . that should easily cover it. But, if you're hungry now, Dad, it won't take me long to pop down the street for fish and chips.'

With Paula at the forefront of his mind, Martin wanted to be on his own for a while. 'Thanks all the same, sweetie, but I had a pie from the café at lunch-time . . . and I had cornflakes this morning before I set off, so you see, I haven't gone hungry.'

'OK, Dad, but give me a ring if you need anything. Oh! And like we agreed, I'll be round tomorrow to hoover through and change the bed. OK?'

'OK, yes, and thanks for that. Oh, and you'd best take that spare key from the hallway cupboard.'

Anne glanced up at the mantelpiece chimer. 'Oh, my goodness, it's gone eight o'clock! I didn't realise it was that time. Les said he was hoping to make it home tonight.' She gave him a brief cuddle, ''Bye, Dad, see you tomorrow.'

''Bye, love, and give my regards to Les.' He bent to place a kiss on the sleeping child's forehead. 'G'night, little man.'

~

With Paula on his mind, Martin grew increasingly restless.

Turning on the television, he absently-mindedly watched the news. A little envious, he watched the report on how Lieutenant Scott Carpenter was launched in a spacecraft. The craft made three revolutions round the earth, before the capsule was recovered from the Atlantic. 'Whatever next, eh?' It'll be Mars, soon, I shouldn't wonder.' Martin commented.

Leaning forward in the chair, he turned the television off. You wouldn't catch me going up there . . . not for a gold clock or a million pounds . . . no way! he thought.

Even now, when he needed to think of the next job on his work list, he found himself growing angry again by the thought of those divorce papers not having been sent off before, when Paula promised faithfully she would do it.

It's hard, he thought, but, like she said, I have to

learn to trust her, or she could very likely scupper our plans for getting together. And I can't have that . . . not when we're so close to being together for good and all. The thought of going to bed every night with Paula gave him a warm and satisfactory feeling.

The house was locked up, he was alone, and he did not much like it. 'Maybe I'd best go back and persuade her to let me go with her to the solicitor. That way, I'd know she means what she says,' he muttered.

One minute he was sorely tempted to go to see Paula, and the next, he thought better of it. She won't thank me for keeping on about that damned letter. He was just a tiny bit afraid. 'No . . . best not go crashing in on her just now. Leave her be until tomorrow, then we'll see . . .'

After a few anxious minutes he managed to get her out of his head, and then, the worries crept back again as his thoughts ran over Paula's lack of urgency regarding the papers. All the same, if it hasn't been delivered by tomorrow morning, I'll have to put my foot down and take it in myself . . . whether she likes it or not! he decided.

Now he switched his attention from Paula to Lucy.

'I don't think Lucy is all that bothered about our marriage. If she was, she never would have gone away like this, and why is it she calls Anne instead of me? All right, I work all hours, but why doesn't she call late in the evening, when she just might get hold of me?'

But, reminding himself of what Lucy had burst in on, with him and Paula, he realised that Lucy had

351

every right to bypass him. He gave a shrug and made a mental note that it might be best if Lucy didn't ring, because he would probably be round Paula's anyway.

He thought ahead: like Paula, I do feel a bit sorry for Lucy. I mean, she's had a lot to deal with lately . . . including what she saw with me and Paula. But she must now realise that our marriage is over. But there you are! We've had a good run, and nobody can say that I didn't do the right thing in marrying her . . . right thing for her, and the family, maybe. But not for me. There's never been any love on my part, and I'm sorry to say there never will be.

A wide smile enveloped his features. 'As long as I get my Paula, that's all I'm bothered about, and to hell and buggery with the lot of 'em!'

His mood lightened and he began to relax. In the morning, she'll take the letter in, and things will run their course from there, he thought. 'When Lucy comes back, she'll have to know that Paula and I intend to marry. She will have to let me go then, and the sooner the better.

Actually having to tell Lucy that he wanted a divorce as soon as possible so he could marry her sister was not something he was looking forward to.

Now that he was beginning to look ahead, he felt good, and much calmer, in himself. 'Paula promised she would take the letter in, and she will,' he said confidently. So, there's nothing to worry about.

Leaning back in the chair, he laid his head down, closed his eyes and relaxed. He thought of himself and Paula together . . . like it should have been right from the start.

As far back as when they were at school, it was Paula he fancied. Going with Lucy was just a ploy to make Paula jealous. Then, when it was discovered that Lucy was pregnant, his chance was gone.

My time with Lucy is done, he told himself now. The debt is paid, and now my place is with the one I wanted all along. It's taken a long time, but we're almost there.

CHAPTER SEVENTEEN

Lucy had never felt so very special as she did right now.

'Did you know, Lucy Lovejoy, that when you walked into the room, all eyes were turned on you?' Dave Benson thought himself a very fortunate man to be sitting opposite the most beautiful woman in the room.

Not used to compliments, Lucy blushed. 'Well, thank you. That's a kind and lovely thing to say,' she replied softly, 'but I'm sure that's not so.'

'Oh, really?' For the umpteenth time, Dave Benson discreetly roved his eyes over Lucy, and what he saw was a woman of mature years, but with the air and presence of a young girl. Her wild brown hair was swirled into a coil in the nape of her neck, and held together with a pink ribbon.

In the soft glow of the candlelight, her beautiful, nutmeg-brown eyes were softly shining, and her light make-up gently highlighted the high cheekbones, and the delicate, oval shape of her face.

The dark, slimming skirt accentuated her height, and the pink top with the discreet, V-shaped neckline flattered her flawless skin.

Dave reached out and covered her hand with his. 'You are truly a lovely woman, Lucy,' he murmured, 'and I really am so very proud to be here with you tonight.'

This time, Lucy remained silent, amazed that a man like Dave Benson could ever consider her to be 'lovely' or even be proud to be with her. No one, including Martin, had ever said anything remotely like that, and now she felt embarrassed and lost for words.

Impulsively, shyly, she reached out and held his hand, and for what seemed like the longest moment of Lucy's life they might well have been the only two people in the room while all those about them who chatted and laughed, and drank their wine and generally enjoyed the evening, faded into the background.

While she sat quietly with her hand cradling in his, Lucy thought she would keep this very special moment safe in her mind and heart for the rest of her life.

Just then the mood was shattered when the waiter arrived at their table. 'Are you ready to order wine, sir?' He waited for Dave to check the wine menu, and when Dave asked Lucy if there was any particular wine that she might prefer, she shook her head.

'I'll leave it to you,' she told him with a wide and lovely smile. She felt happy, even beautiful, though she was wearing nothing more glamorous than a simple skirt and an ordinary pink top that had been in the back of the wardrobe since Noah's ark set sail!

She could have told Dave that both the top and the skirt were bought in a sale at the market some years back, but after the wonderful compliments he had given, she thought it best to keep that information to herself.

~

Two hours later, having thoroughly enjoyed their evening meal together, Dave and Lucy were now seated in the hotel bar.

Dave had a glass of wine in front of him, while Lucy had opted for the tiniest measure. 'I'm not used to too much wine,' she admitted. 'It makes me laugh too much, and feel giddy.' She had learned that much at Anne's wedding, when she had fallen over and made a fool of herself in front of everyone.

So now, when the barman came across to ask, 'Is there anything else I can get you?' Dave shook his head and asked that the evening's expenses be added to his overall bill.

'I've had the most wonderful evening,' Lucy told him when the waiter had gone, 'so, thank you, Dave.' She still felt guilty somehow, in using his first name. 'You really are a knight in shining armour, and I'll tell you something else.' Suddenly, she felt shy and awkward, but she had to finish what she wanted to say. 'Since I met you, I've had the most exciting and wonderful time of my entire life.' And that was the truth.

'So have I.' Dave did not want it to end. 'But now you're making me worry.'

'But why?'

'Because it's almost as though you're saying goodbye.' He leaned forward and lowered his voice to the smallest whisper. 'Lucy, please tell me, you're not leaving me . . . are you?'

Lucy did not know what to say, and so she simply said, 'Did you know it's eleven thirty . . . way past my bedtime?' She did not want to leave him, but being so close to Dave Benson felt wrong somehow, especially as he was making her heart leap, and more especially as she was a married woman. The fact that Martin had cheated on her was not an excuse for her to cheat.

Dave could see how nervous she was, and so he smiled and said he had an early start in the morning, so it was probably best if they called it a night. 'Shame, though, don't you think, Lucy?'

Lucy changed the subject. 'I'm glad you did well today . . . with the deal, I mean.'

'Ah, but it's not altogether clinched yet. Although, like I said earlier, I have managed to get them on the back foot. Maybe tomorrow I'll move in for the kill.'

Lucy shivered. 'It all sounds a little brutish to me, but I know you'll swing it for Nancy,' she said stoutly.

He smiled at her. 'I wish everyone had the same belief in me that you do.' He leaned forward and looked her straight in the eye. 'You are a lovely soul,

Lucy Lovejoy,' he told her tenderly. 'And I am so very glad I met you.'

'Me too.' She was saddened at the idea of never seeing him again. 'I've had a wonderful time, but now I'm begnning to think I should make my way home.' It truly pained her to say that.

'I understand,' he said regretfully, 'but I will miss you . . . terribly.'

'And I will miss you, the sharp-dealing Dave Benson. I wonder what your business associates would say if they knew how absolutely crazy you are.'

She stood up to say softly, 'Good night, Dave . . . and thank you for everything.'

The silence was heavy as he walked her to the door, until Dave asked quietly, 'Please, Lucy, at least let me see you to your room?'

'Not necessary, Dave. Stay and finish your drink. I'll be absolutely fine. Really I will.'

'Trust me, you never know what oddball is roaming the corridors.'

Lucy grew nervous. 'Now, you've got me worried.' She had never stayed alone in a big hotel before, with its long, winding corridors and so many doors in and out, and lifts that might break down, for all she knew, and the thought of being stranded in a lift – possibly with a stranger – was a nightmare.

'So, will you let me escort you to your room?'

Lucy did not now need to think twice. 'Yes, please.'

A few moments later the two of them were getting into the lift.

'I never asked which floor you were on,' Dave said.

Lucy had a moment of panic before she realised it was on her key-tag, which she now took from her purse. She took a quick look. 'Third floor. I'm in room twenty-two.' And now she could relax, especially with Dave alongside her.

'Well, I never!' Dave said. 'I'm only four doors down from you, in room twenty-six.'

As Lucy's room was further from the lift than his, Dave walked her down to room twenty-two, where he said good night.

'You are the loveliest woman,' he whispered intimately. 'I can't bear the thought of never seeing you again.'

Regretfully, Lucy felt obliged to close the conversation. 'I'm sorry, but I think it's time I went back and faced up to my obligations.'

He nodded. 'Yes . . . I understand. I'm sorry.'

Impulsively, she reached up to kiss him ever so gently on the cheek. 'Good night . . . and thank you . . . so very much for a wonderful time.'

He merely nodded, then walked back to his own room.

When he got there, he turned round, but Lucy was already gone.

Saddened, he bowed his head and let himself into the room where he sat on the edge of the bed, thinking of Lucy. And feeling so incredibly lonely.

~

In her room, after the excitement of the day, Lucy felt guilty.

Guilty because she had given herself over to a stranger, a man who knew how to laugh and have fun. A man who thought she was beautiful and said so. A man who had such kindness and warmth in his eyes when he had gazed on her tonight, saying not a word, yet his eyes were saying so many things it made her dizzy. It was almost as though he was gathering her up and keeping her to himself.

Deliberately thrusting him from her mind, she undressed, then went into the bathroom, where she cleaned off her make-up.

She then ran a bath and climbed into it. She lost all sense of time lazing there, thinking of her family; especially Martin and Paula and the shameless things they had done.

Then her thoughts drifted to Dave Benson, this wonderful man who had shown her a side to life she had long forgotten. He had reminded her how to laugh out loud, how to smile, and to feel it in her deepest heart.

Lying there with the warm water lapping over her, she could hear his voice, soft and vibrant, saying things to turn her heart over. She smiled.

'He held my hand,' she whispered. 'He told me I was beautiful.' Tears welled up in her brown eyes. 'No one in my whole life has ever told me that . . . not even my own husband.'

Throughout the short time she had been in Dave's

company, she had felt so very special. He made her come alive like never before in her entire life. And now she was leaving him, and her heart was heavy at the thought. Remember what your mum once said to you, Lucy, she thought. When she warned you that she would not get better and you said she mustn't talk like that, she told you that sometimes you have to face up to things that you can't change. 'Nothing is for ever,' that's what she told you.

Tears clouded her eyes. Her mum was right, and tonight, Lucy Lovejoy, she told herself, you must see that what happened between you and Dave Benson was just a fleeting moment in time. It can never happen again.

A short time later, she climbed out of the bath and slipped on her nightgown. She got into bed and lay there thinking, regretting. Wishing that her life might have been different. If I hadn't been bad and got pregnant, my life would have been so very different, she thought, but then realised she could never regret the way her life had gone. If Martin had not singled me out at school, I would never have had Anne, or Samuel . . . and my beautiful grandson would never have been born to us.

When she thought of it like that, she felt guilty at wishing she had never met Martin. Never got pregnant. Never seen him and Paula together. 'Your life is a mess, Lucy,' she told herself aloud. 'You're married to a man who doesn't love you. You have no money. No prospects. Nowhere to go.' She gave a wry little smile. 'Truth is, there is no way you could change your life now . . . even if you wanted to.'

For a long time, she lay on top of the bed, allowing herself the luxury of just being there . . . arms akimbo, staring at the ceiling and marvelling at the swirls of plaster that made a unique pattern above her head.

Her gaze was drawn by the tiniest spider; she watched it, balancing and dancing across the ceiling, and now it was hanging upside down, like an act in a circus.

After what seemed an age, she shifted a little and, picking up her watch from the bedside cabinet, she glanced at the time. 'Crikey! It's gone midnight!' she exclaimed in surprise.

Replacing the watch, she allowed herself another few lazy moments to think of her family and her parents, and her dear friend, Kathleen, whom she must not forget to call first thing in the morning. Oh! And, she'd best let Anne know that she was on her way back.

Just then, thinking of her friend made her wonder . . . 'I wish I could be adventurous and devil-may-care, like you, Kathleen,' she murmured. 'I bet you would never leave if you found a man like Dave Benson. I bet you would do whatever your heart tells you to. But then, you're impetuous, while I'm not . . . more's the pity.'

She lay very still, thinking for a while longer, then she got into bed and drew the clothes over, her busy mind assailed by any number of naughty thoughts.

Should I? she asked herself mischievously. Or should I not?

The more she tried to push the idea away, the more confused she felt.

If she denied what her heart was coaxing her to do, she would probably never forgive herself. Yet, if she surrendered to her heart and instincts, would she bitterly regret it afterwards?

By now, she was so worked up and undecided, she was way past sleep. Think, Lucy! she told herself angrily. If Kathleen was here, in this situation, what would she do?

The answer glared her in the face.

Within moments she was out of bed and throwing on her dressing gown. Sliding her feet into her slippers, and without a second thought, she collected the key from the dressing table and quietly let herself out.

Softly closing the door behind her, she had never felt so excited, so afraid, and so absolutely wicked, in all of her life.

~

Dave was lying awake when the knock on the door startled him.

Curious, and not too pleased at being disturbed, he scrambled out of bed and put on his dressing gown. Going to the door he gingerly opened it, and almost fell over with shock when he saw Lucy standing there in her dressing gown, her wild brown hair looking tousled and damp, and her face clean and pretty as a child's.

'Lucy! What's wrong? What's happened?'

'I couldn't sleep,' Lucy said innocently. 'I've come to see you . . . is that all right?'

'Well, yes . . . come in. Come in.' His heart was thumping, but he could not understand why she was here. He wondered, but dared not let himself believe it.

Lucy sat on the bed, and after closing the door, he sat beside her. 'Was it that small glass of wine you drank?' he asked. 'Is that why you can't sleep? It's my fault . . . I'm sorry, Lucy. You did say you don't really drink alcohol, and I should not have persuaded you to have the tiniest one . . . only I did want us to toast the wonderful memories we made together. I really am sorry. I should have known better—' When Lucy got up as though to leave, he stopped halfway through the sentence. 'Please, Lucy, don't go.'

Lucy had no intention of leaving. Instead she walked round the bed, and climbed in. Then to his astonishment, she stretched out her bare arm and patted the space beside her.

'I've been thinking,' she said, 'and I've decided that we should listen to my friend's advice.' She looked up at him with big eyes, and a knowing smile that told him everything. 'What do you think, Mr Benson? Should we listen to my friend's advice?'

Dave was almost afraid to ask. 'She's the friend who thought you should "ravish" me. Am I right?'

Lucy nodded. 'Yes! So tell me, Dave Benson . . . do you think we should listen to my crazy friend's advice?' She felt wonderfully shameless and so bold and excited, it frightened her. But she was past caring. If she had learned anything these past few days, it was that life was for living. And why should she let it pass her by?

She looked across at Dave, who was gazing on her, and slowly shaking his head as though not able to believe that Lucy was actually lying in his bed . . . inviting him in.

Lucy smiled up at him. 'Well?' That one word was enough.

Dave stripped off his dressing gown and, stark-naked, he climbed into bed beside her.

'Lucy Lovejoy . . . oh, my beautiful . . . wonderful woman.' The warmth of her smooth skin against his, felt amazing.

Tenderly now, he ran his fingers along her neck, and down, towards her thighs. Wrapping his two arms about her, he drew her into him, surprised and thrilled when Lucy made no protest.

Instead, without a word, she carefully drew her nightgown over her head and sent it slithering to the floor.

CHAPTER EIGHTEEN

A<small>FTER FALLING INTO</small> a deep sleep in the armchair, Martin woke with a start.

Momentarily disoriented, he sat up straight and glanced around, woolly-headed, not yet fully awake.

Paula! The first thought that came into his head was the divorce papers, and whether or not she would remember to take them in to the solicitors in the morning. Paula might know how to please a man, he thought, but there were times when a man might be forgiven for wringing her neck.

Getting out of the chair, he began to walk up and down, slowly at first, and then in a panic. She'll forget, he decided, I know she will . . . absent-minded, fluffy-headed, wonderful woman . . . that's what she is.

He paced the floor a while longer, unsure whether to take matters into his own hands if the letter was ever going to reach the solicitor. He could see he'd have to keep on at her, make her realise that the sooner she got the divorce papers lodged, the sooner they could get things moving towards their new life together.

He spread his hands over his face in despair. What to do? What to do? He didn't want to risk losing her.

Calm down, man! he warned himself. You'll go crazy if you keep on like this. Paula said she would take the papers in tomorrow, and she will. And why would she not? She wants rid of that useless waster, as much as you do. If not more.

He began to feel calmer, more able to think straight, now that he was wide awake. Yes, she'll take them in, he told himself, and the sooner Lucy gets back, the sooner she'll know what I'm planning. There is nothing she can do about it. Me and Paula are made for each other, and I won't rest until the road is clear for us to be married.

The thought of putting a ring on Paula's finger and spending the rest of his life with her was too exciting for words.

I don't care how long it takes, or who gets hurt in the process, Martin decided. It's what me and Paula want, and if her ex thinks he can drag his feet and put barriers up I'll make damned sure he rues the day!

Far from calming himself down, he was now wound up and ready for anything, so he made his way into the kitchen and put the kettle on for a calming brew.

By the time he had got out the tea-caddy and sugar, the kettle had boiled, but instead of making himself a cup of tea, he hurried down the hallway and put on his cap and coat. Growing increasingly agitated, he found his house keys and let himself out of the house.

He started up the van, rammed it into gear, then drove at some speed down the street and onto the main road in the direction of Paula's house.

Once he had eased the van into the alley, Martin was not surprised to see that Paula's house was in complete darkness, except for the light over the back door.

He was now disgruntled. Huh! She was the one who forgot to send the divorce papers, and he was the only one losing sleep . . . typical!

Then his mood changed from irritated to thinking that maybe he would get to spend the night with Paula. With Lucy gadding off like that, there was no one to worry where he might be.

Carefully, he parked his van in the bend as always, switched off the headlights, then made his way up to the house, trying to avoid the wide beam from the streetlight that lit up part of the alley.

Arriving at Paula's back gate, he had no idea he was being watched.

~

'There! I was right . . . I said it was Martin's van.'

During her nightly ritual, when she would look out of the bedroom window to make sure there were no prowlers lurking in the alley, Mary Taylor had seen Martin arrive.

'He's heading for the house. Peter, come and see!'

Peter came to see, but only to pacify her so the two of them could get back to their bed.

Just then, when Martin seemed to glance up, they quickly stepped back a little.

'He's looking for trouble,' Mary decided. 'Why else would he come visiting at this time of night? It's poor Lucy I feel sorry for – married to a cheating monster like that!'

Her husband, Peter, was bone-tired. 'Mary! I have no idea why he's visiting his wife's sister . . . nor do I think we should be monitoring the neighbours when we could be getting a good night's sleep.'

Reaching over her, he closed the curtains, before gently taking her by the arm and leading her back to bed. 'All right, so he's visiting Lucy's sister, but we already knew he was having an affair. Besides, as I've told you before, many times, it is none of our business. For pity's sake, Mary, if he really is looking for trouble, and he finds out that you're spying on his every move-ment, he could just as well take his anger out on us.'

'You're right, of course you are.' Mary settled back into bed. 'Only . . . well, I've got such a bad feeling about all this business. Think of it, Peter. There's Lucy away, Martin is creeping round Paula's house at all hours of the day and night, and Paula seems to be enjoying it all. It's a bad situation and as far as I'm concerned, it'll make for trouble. You mark my words.'

Peter smiled to himself. 'Right, my dear, it's all duly "marked", as you say. So now, can we please get some sleep?'

'Yes, of course.'

She closed her eyes, but was too restless to sleep. Her thoughts went to Lucy, that dear woman who had never put a foot wrong, and would always do a good turn for a friend or neighbour.

~

Completely unaware that his every movement had been monitored by the watchful neighbour, Martin approached the back door. He raised his fist, and was about to knock when, on an instinct, he decided to try the door first.

Gently he turned the door knob and gave it the slightest push. When the door opened he was both thrilled and furious. Stupid woman! Why was it she could never remember to lock the back door?

So as not to alarm her, he leaned inside and softly called out, 'Paula?' When there was no answer, he wondered if she was off out somewhere, but it was gone midnight, so where the hell could she be? And why hadn't she mentioned anything earlier?

He checked the kitchen and the lounge, and now he was on his way upstairs, careful to be quiet in case she was fast asleep. He did not want to alarm her.

As always, the landing light was on, but that did not concern him; at least not as much as did the back door always being open. She'll get the length of my tongue for not locking the house up, he thought angrily as he neared the bedroom. I'd best fix it somehow, so she can't possibly leave it open. Only, just now he was not quite sure how he might do that.

He tapped on the bedroom door. He thought it best to let her know he was here, otherwise she could get a fright to see him creeping into her bedroom. 'Paula, it's me, Martin. You left the back door open again.' When there was no answer, he raised his voice slightly, and called again, 'Paula! It's me, Martin. Are you in there?'

Sounding sleepy, Paula's voice gentled over to him. 'Martin! What are you doing here? You say I left the back door open . . . oh, I forgot again. Go down, Martin . . . put the kettle on. I'll only be a minute. OK?'

'I'd rather come in.' The idea of spending the night with her was very appealing. He opened the door and peeped in, to see her sitting on the edge of the bed, looking drowsy.

'Martin, for once will you do as I ask?' she yelled. 'Go down and put the kettle on! Please . . . I need the bathroom right now. Go on!'

Having woken her into a bad mood, his desire to get into bed with her had quickly faded. 'Right!' He backed off. 'I'll have the kettle boiled and the tea made by the time you get down. Don't be too long. There's something I'd like to discuss with you.'

On the way there he'd had an idea that he was itching to run by her. He was hoping to persuade her that all in good time, after everything was settled, it might be sensible to sell up and move away from these parts. New life, new start, that's what he fancied; away from anything and everyone.

After boiling the kettle, he got out the milk, sugar and two cups and set them out on the kitchen table.

Going quickly down the hallway, he took a long look at the back door lock, trying to see how it could be made safer, or to somehow fix it, so that it might lock automatically. What Paula needed was simply a great big notice pinned to it, and maybe another one hung at the bottom of the stairs, so when she closed the door and when she went to bed she would see the reminders.

He gave the mechanism one last inspection, and having now convinced himself that he would be spending the night in Paula's bed, he began merrily whistling, delighted when he heard foosteps on the stairway.

He swung round smiling, only to be confronted with a heavy fist in his face, the force of which sent him hurtling to the wall.

'So you thought you'd steal in while me and my wife were in bed, did you?'

'Bloody hell!' Hurt and bleeding, Martin struggled to get up, but he was knocked back down again. Realising that he was no match for Paula's husband, Ray, he stayed where he was. 'What the hell are you doing here?' He was more furious than afraid.

'Well, now, before you came barging in – where you were neither invited nor wanted – my lovely wife and myself were having such fun renewing our marriage vows . . .' the big man grinned slyly, '. . . if you know what I mean? And then you spoiled it by butting in and would you believe, I had to climb out of my wife's warm bed, and hide like a criminal in the bathroom.' He tutted. 'In my own house, with my own wife. It doesn't seem right somehow, does it?'

Shocked and inflamed by the big man's taunting words, Martin scrambled up, and threw himself at Ray. 'She won't be your wife for very much longer! The papers have already gone to the solicitors. She wants me, not you!' He looked up at Paula, who had appeared in the doorway. 'Go on, Paula, tell him!'

Paula smiled. 'I don't know what you mean,' she said sweetly. 'I tore the divorce papers up last night.' She glanced up at her husband. 'Ray turned up unexpectedly the night before last. He managed to talk me out of the divorce. Oh! Sorry, Martin, I really should have told you,' she taunted.

Paula's husband laughed out loud. 'I would have thought you might have learned by now what a real cow she is. But, you see, she's my sort of cow. We belong together, me and her.'

'You're lying . . . Paula, sweetheart.' Martin pleaded, 'Has he threatened you, is that it?'

Suddenly Martin was yanked off his feet when the big man grabbed him by the scruff of the neck. 'You heard what she said, now get out of here . . . and don't come back. I'm here now, and I'm here for good. D'you understand what I'm saying?' He shook Martin like a rag doll, then he swung him across the floor and sent him hurtling into the back door. 'Now get out while you're still in one piece!'

Scrabbling to get up, Martin urged Paula, 'Tell him, sweetheart, tell him it's me you want . . . that we were planning to get married as soon as the divorce came through. Tell him, Paula!'

Paula smiled and slowly shook her head. 'I was using you, Martin, to make Ray jealous. It worked and now we're back together. So you served your purpose and I don't need you any more.'

'No!' Martin was broken. 'Please, Paula, don't say that. How can you let him back into your life, after the way he's treated you? You know I love—' Suddenly, he was lifted off his feet and thrown out of the back door, landing with an almighty bump on the concrete pathway.

The big man laughed, a loud, raucous rumbling sound that frightened the cats and woke the neighbourhood. 'Sorry, Martin, but you're the loser! So get lost. And don't let me catch you round here again . . . or I can't promise you'll walk away on your own two legs.'

Behind him, Paula was taunting, 'Poor Martin! I can't imagine why you thought I would ever trade my Ray for a weak man like you.'

Paula's jibe cut Martin deep. He adored this woman and now she was goading him, shamelessly admitting that all along, she intended getting back with her husband. He realised what a fool he'd been, and he went crazy.

'Bastard!' In a fit of rage, he launched himself at Ray.

The fight was bitter, with no holds barred. Soon, all the lights were on in the neighbouring houses. Mary Taylor looked out of her bedroom window. 'Peter! Quick, they're killing each other!'

Peter hurried to the window and was sickened to see the two men at each other's throats.

Fearing someone was about to be killed, Paula forced herself between them, but there was no stopping them. Fists were flying and Paula was taking the fallout as Martin tried desperately to shield her from Ray. And now the big man had got a long bar of sorts in his fist and he was thrashing Martin. Paula was screaming, 'Stop! You're killing him!'

The two men were at each other's throats, with Paula screaming and hanging on to Ray's mighty arm, until suddenly she was thrown to the ground. Then Ray swung the bar down again, as hard as he could in all directions. There followed a series of piercing cries from Paula and scuffling noises, and then silence.

Absolute, eerie silence.

'Quick, Mary, call the police,' Peter screamed at her. 'Hurry, love . . . hurry!'

While Mary rushed away to do as she was asked, the silence thickened. She was right, he murmured sadly, nodding his head. 'My Mary was right all along.'

CHAPTER NINETEEN

WITH A NEW day dawning, Lucy opened her eyes, and saw that it was four o'clock. She was shocked to find herself in Dave Benson's room . . . in his bed, and lying in his strong, protective arms. Everything rushed back into her mind. The way she had knocked on his bedroom door, almost naked, and virtually asked him to take her to bed, made her feel ashamed.

Being careful not to wake him, she slid out from under the bedclothes, and for a long, precious moment she looked down on his sleeping face. She realized then without a shadow of doubt that she truly loved this man . . . this stranger.

She hoped he did not think less of her for being so easily taken.

But, for all that, she did not feel guilty. Instead, she felt unbelievably exhilarated and alive like never before. And to her shame, she wanted more of him. But sadly, for a multitude of reasons, it could not be.

So, very softly, she drew the covers over his chest. Then, going to the desk, she wrote him a heartfelt note.

My dearest Dave,
   Regrettably, I now have to return to my family. But I so want you to know that although we will probably never see each other again, I will forever cherish the memories of our time together. Thank you, for your understanding, and for the wonderful experiences we've shared, in this beautiful place.
   I won't forget you, Stay safe.
                    God bless.
              Lucy Lovejoy

Placing the note beside his pillow, she quietly made her way out of the room, carefully closing the door behind her, so as not to wake him.

In the privacy of her own room, Lucy shed bitter tears. 'Why do I need to go back?' she asked herself aloud. Then she answered her own question. 'You are not a free spirit. You're a married woman, Lucy Lovejoy. You have responsibilities . . . children . . . a grandson . . . a family waiting at home for you. Your place is with them. And the sooner you accept again the responsibility resting on you, the better!'

Feeling kind of lost, she picked up the telephone receiver and dialled '0' for reception.

When the night receptionist answered, Lucy asked, 'Do you have a train timetable at all?'

'We do, yes. Would you like me to send it up to you?'

'No, thank you. I'm on my way down. I just need to get to the station and catch the first available train home.'

'So, will you be wanting a car to take you to the station?'

Lucy was embarrassed to ask, but it was necessary. 'Can I ask how much that will cost?'

She had put money aside for her stay here, and she had a few pounds left over for the train home, and for small emergencies, but a car . . . well, that may be too expensive.

'Oh, no, Miss Lovejoy!' the receptionist informed her. 'The hotel runs two courtesy cars. Just tell me when you would like to leave, and I'll arrange a car for you.'

Lucy's mind went back to Dave – could she just run out on him like that? Or should she stay and explain further . . . face to face? No, I can't see him, or I may change my mind! she decided.

'Sorry,' the receptionist said. 'I'm sorry, Miss Lovejoy, I did not quite catch what you said.'

Lucy told her, 'I would like you to please book the car for me. I'm almost ready.'

'No problem, Miss Lovejoy. And would you like me to send a porter for your suitcase?'

'No, thank you. It's only a small case. I can manage that all right. I'll be down shortly, and if I could have a peep at your train timetable, that would help me.'

'Of course, I'll have it ready for you.'

Half an hour later, after rushing about before Dave might wake up, Lucy was downstairs in reception.

As good as her word, the receptionist had everything ready: the bill; the train timetable; and the courtesy car was already waiting outside for her.

Lucy was delighted to see that the first train out, at six thirty, was en route for Bedford.

Desperate to be gone, she paid her bill. She then left a modest tip, and climbing into the courtesy car, she was whisked away in good time.

~

Not long after she'd departed, the telephone rang at reception.

Picking up the receiver, the receptionist put on her greeting voice: 'Lorriet Hotel. Good morning, can I help you?'

She listened patiently to the person on the other end, and then found the need to apologise. 'Oh, no, I'm very sorry, but Miss Lucy Lovejoy has already left . . . about twenty minutes ago.'

She listened again. 'Oh, I see . . . No, there is no way I can get in touch with her unless I send someone to the station, but that would probably be too late. I understand she's catching an early train. Yes. It leaves in about twenty minutes. Yes, thank you, and I'm sorry I could not be of more help.'

With the short conversation over, she replaced the receiver and set about checking her tasks for the day.

~

Kathleen replaced her receiver with huge relief but not before wishing her 'aged aunt' a tender goodbye, saying, 'Thank you, aunt, take care of yourself.'

'What did your aunt say?' Pacing up and down, Anne was growing increasingly anxious.

Crossing her fingers behind her back, Kathleen explained, 'Your mother is already on her way back. Apparently, for whatever reason, she seemed anxious to get home. No doubt she's been missing all of you.'

Anne continued pacing the floor. 'Mum isn't used to staying with strangers. No offence to your aunt, but Mum's a real home bird and, like a mother hen, she worries about us all.' Looking up with a tear-stained face she went on, 'Poor Mum. She doesn't know what she's coming home to, does she?'

'No, she doesn't, and it's just as well. When she learns the bad news, she'll be shaken to the roots.'

'How long will it take for her to get here?'

'It is not a short journey, as you know,' Kathleen cautioned her. 'I don't suppose she'll be here for a few hours yet.'

'Is there a way we can contact her?'

'What would be the point in upsetting her when she can't change anything?'

Anne shook her head, 'Kathleen, I really need my mum,' she said tearfully. 'I need to hold her.'

Kathleen hugged her. 'I know you need her, but she'll be here soon enough.'

Just then, the baby woke up in his buggy and started crying. 'I'd best get home and feed him,' Anne said.

'Okay, but you're always welcome to come back here to be with me. It's fine, and I want to help.'

Anne thanked her. 'I know you do, and I'm so thankful Mum has such a good friend in you. She's going to need you, Kathleen.'

Kathleen smiled. 'I know that, and I'll be here for her . . . like she's always been there for me.'

Anne said her goodbyes. 'You will ring me if you hear anything, won't you, Kathleen?' she called back from the street.

'Of course I will, but try not to worry. Now . . . you get off and feed that baby.' Remembering something, she ran after Anne. 'I forgot to tell you, the boss phoned when she heard the reason for your Mum's absence. Anyway, she asked me to tell your mum that her job is waiting for her, when she's ready.'

'Aw, that's good news.' Anne knew her mum would be relieved. 'I know Mum's been worried about her job, what with having so much time off, and everything.'

Kathleen assured her, 'Don't think the old battleaxe wants your mum out of the goodness of her heart; it's because she's a damned good worker.'

Anne smiled. 'Why does that not surprise me?'

~

Some hours later, Kathleen opened the door to see Lucy standing there.

'Oh, Lucy . . . come in. Come in, love.' She hugged her as though she would never let her go. 'It's so good to have you back, you little darlin'.' She wondered if it was her place to tell Lucy the news, or should she call Anne, but then Lucy told her that she had been round to Anne's but there was no one there.

'Fancy a nice hot cuppa?' Kathleen was trying hard to delay telling her the truth.

'Yes, go on then.' She followed Kathleen into the kitchen. 'Martin wasn't home either. I dare say he's out working, but where's Anne? She's never out at this time of day.'

'Shall I give her a ring . . . see if she's back yet?' Kathleen asked.

'Yes, please, Kathleen. Maybe she was out the back. I never thought to look.'

There was a knock on the door, and when Kathleen opened it she was surprised to see Anne standing there.

'Sorry, Kathleen, could I stay with you for a while? I've just been round to Mum's and she's still not home. I'm getting really worried.'

Lucy heard the conversation from the kitchen. 'There's no need to worry,' she said cheekily, and Anne ran down the hallway to hug her.

'Oh, Mum! I'm so glad you're back. Something terrible has happened, and I don't know what to do.'

'Hey!' Lucy took hold of her and walked her to the living room, while Kathleen kindly took care of the baby. 'I think you had best tell me what's happened that you find so terrible!'

Anne started crying – from relief that her mum was back, and also the realisation of how very much she had missed her. 'Mum, I have to tell you . . . there was a terrible fight . . . between Dad and Paula's husband. Paula tried to get between them and she was badly hurt. She wants to see you, Mum. She's sorry . . . and so am I, because I never knew what was going on . . .' Now all the pent-up emotions broke loose and she sobbed in her mother's arms. 'I didn't know, Mum . . . I hate Dad for what he's done to you . . . cheating on you with your sister . . . sleeping with her! Oh, Mum . . . how could he do that to you?'

Lucy gave no answer, because she did not have one. Instead she held on to her daughter, comforting her while she sobbed bitterly.

After a time, when Anne was calmer, Lucy asked her solemnly, 'How bad is Paula? I must go and see her.' Even after everything Paula had done, Lucy could find no hatred in her heart for her, or, indeed, for Martin. And besides, she herself had learned how easy it was to do something out of character.

'She's really poorly, Mum.'

'Look, you two, I'll mind the baby if you want to go and see Paula,' Kathleen offered.

It was agreed, and with Kathleen insisting on paying for a taxi from the High Street, Lucy and Anne hurried away.

~

At the hospital Lucy was shocked to see her sister all trussed up, her arm and shoulder in plaster and her face black and blue, with a cluster of deep bruises and a multitude of bloodied stitches reaching from her eyebrow down to her chin, which was also encased in plaster.

'Oh, my God, what's happened to her?' Lucy was in tears, anxious to see the doctor and impatient when told he was in surgery just now, but he would be along shortly to speak with her.

The ward sister came to explain Paula's injuries to her. 'She's broken her nose, arm, shoulder and both legs, and three fingers. And her chin is fractured in two places. She is being kept sedated until we can see how she's responding to treatment.'

Lucy grew anxious. 'So, are you saying she's not responding to treatment?'

'No, I am not saying that, but she's in a good deal of pain. Right now she's sleeping, which is helpful for her recovery.'

Anne had an idea. 'Mum, you look absolutely shattered. You need a hot drink and to get your thoughts together. The sister says Paula is being kept sedated, so why don't we go down to the canteen – just for a minute or so – give you time to catch your breath?' Her voice broke. 'Please, Mum. I'm worried about Aunt Paula, but I'm worried about you as well.'

'Aw, sweetheart . . .' Lucy laid her hand over Anne's. 'I should have been here. I might have been able to stop what happened, though even now, I'm not altogether sure what that was. Yes, I'll ask the doctor, and if he says it's all right we'll take ten minutes out, then I'll come back and sit with Paula while you get off home and get some rest. Is that a deal?'

Anne told her that yes, it was a deal.

The doctor arrived just then. 'It was touch and go when she was brought in, but I believe she is now settled and stable, although, of course, she'll be with us for some time yet,' he explained to Lucy. 'There are several injuries that will take a time to heal.'

When he was called away, Lucy leaned over her sister. 'Paula, it's Lucy. I don't know if you can hear me, but all I want to say is, I'm not angry about you and Martin. I realise you didn't do it to hurt me. We can none of us help who we fall in love with. If you can hear me, Paula, don't worry about a thing. You are my sister, and I love you. I always have, and I always will.'

Leaning forward, she tenderly whispered in Paula's ear, 'Please, Paula, be strong. You're going to be just fine. Make sure you keep that at the front of your mind.'

Paula's eyes flickered for a moment.

'She heard you.' Anne grew emotional. 'Mum! Aunt Paula heard you.'

Lucy bent to kiss Paula on the forehead. 'You're going to be fine,' she promised. 'You're a tough little thing . . . I know you would never give in, and besides, you have so much to live for.'

~

Later, in the canteen, Anne got them a cup of tea and a biscuit each, but neither of them felt like eating.

'She heard you, Mum,' Anne assured Lucy. 'I know she did.'

Lucy nodded. 'It's out of our hands now, sweetheart,' she reminded her. 'But I think she heard me, and I hope that what I said will make Paula realise, I bear her no malice.' Her thoughts wandered back to Dave Benson. 'These things happen, sweetheart,' she said. 'Life is short, and whether it's right or wrong, we do what we do, and often we seem to forget about the consequences.

'But what exactly happened? Who was it that hurt Paula like that?' She could never believe that it was Martin, but then again, who knows what anyone would do, if in the wrong circumstances? Never in her wildest dreams would she have thought that she, Lucy Lovejoy, would willingly go to a stranger's bedroom, dressed only in her nightgown, and offer herself to him, but she had done just that, and she was still shocked at her actions.

'It was Paula's husband,' Anne replied. 'From what I can get out of Dad, he went round there to see Paula, and her husband had come back. Apparently, he was in the bedroom with her when Dad arrived. There was a big fight, and Paula's husband went for Dad with a crow bar, or some such thing. Apparently, Paula got between them, and she took the full force of the blows . . . or so Dad says.'

THE RUNAWAY WOMAN

She shook her head. 'I still can't believe what they did to you, Mum – sleeping together and cheating on you. Dad told me everything. I hate him for what he did to you, Mum, I really do!'

'Oh, no! Don't be filled with hate,' Lucy told her. 'It won't change anything. All it will do is make you bitter and miserable . . . and rob your son of his Granddad.'

'Well, if that happens it won't be my fault, will it?'

Lucy warned her, 'You know as well as I do, that darling boy idolises his grandfather. So, think carefully before you let your son pay the price for any resentment you might be feeling. Apart from that, I hope you won't let yourself be affected too harshly by what's happened between your father and Paula, because if you do, it will eat you away inside.'

'But what they've done to you is shocking!' Anne had tried so hard not to show her deeper feelings, but she could not deny the disgust she felt at the manner in which those two had hurt her mother.

'Shocking it may be,' Lucy conceded, 'but we all make mistakes, and we should not allow them to affect our children or grandchildren. Love is a wonderful thing, while hatred is dark and destructive.' She gently stroked Anne's face. 'I know you're disgusted and upset, sweetheart, and I don't blame you, but it would mean a lot to me if you could promise that you will try to forgive them.'

Instead of answering, Anne had a question. 'Can *you* ever forgive them?'

'Like I say, the alternative is unacceptable, and besides, your father and I have had a fair run. He's been a good father and a good husband. I think in life we are all entitled to make one mistake, don't you?'

Anne looked at her mother's face, at the shining light in her pretty brown eyes, and she saw a good and kind woman; a woman who took the bad with the good, and dealt with whatever life threw at her.

Then she had another question. 'Mum?'

'Yes, sweetheart?'

'Would you ever take Dad back as your husband? You know what I'm saying, don't you?'

Lucy understood and, after some soul-searching, she gave her answer. 'I've already forgiven him and Paula for what they did. But as for taking your father back – as a husband in the full meaning of the word – the answer would have to be no. Our marriage is over now anyway. And if Paula and your father want each other, I would never stand in their way. It would serve no purpose for me to do such a selfish thing.'

Anne had got the answer she knew she would get, and, for some reason that she did not understand, she began to feel less angry about the whole thing.

'I hope Paula gets well, Mum.'

'So do I, sweetheart.' Taking hold of her daughter's hand, Lucy gave it a long squeeze. 'And now I'd like to go back in and sit with Paula for a while.'

'Mum, Les should be home by now. Do you mind if I call and ask him to pick me up? It's been a long day. And anyway, Dad said he was coming back within the hour, so you'll have him to talk to, I suppose.'

Lucy understood. 'Look, you make your call, and by the time Les gets here, Dad should be here to sit with Paula, and I could cadge a lift with you. Like you say, it's been a long day. But I intend to be back here first thing in the morning.'

With so many worrying matters on her mind, Lucy was not yet ready to talk with Martin. And anyway, there was time enough to sort out what needed sorting out.

It would not be easy, for there were so many factors to be taken into account, not least the practical matters such as finances and other unpleasant things that had to be dealt with, one way or another.

Whichever way it all turned out, Lucy hoped it might be for the best, to give herself and Martin every chance of moving on with their lives.

But in that moment, Lucy was certain of only one thing: nothing would ever again be the same.

So for now, and with so much still unsaid, she could not bring herself to think beyond the day.

PART FOUR

Painful Decisions

CHAPTER TWENTY

AFTER SPENDING A month in hospital, Paula was allowed to come home.

Lucy and Martin spent that evening discussing whether or not Paula would be able to manage on her own.

Lucy was emphatic. 'That's impossible! Her wounds may be well on the road to healing,' she argued, 'but she still has a long way to go, and emotionally she's in a mess. We can't let her go home on her own. She would never cope. She's far too vulnerable. We can't risk her having to go back to hospital.'

Martin knew Lucy was right but he could not see a solution. 'So what are you suggesting, Lucy? Are you asking if you can bring her here . . . after what we did to you? No, I will not let you do that!' Deeply agitated, he began walking the floor. 'I don't know any other woman who would even suggest that. Already you've taken all of this on the chin, and you've never once complained. I know you've been hurt by what me and Paula have done, but I'll be honest with you, Lucy. It's true I do love her. I think I always have, but I love you as well. To be honest I sometimes think I must be going out of my mind. I don't know which way to turn. I need to be with her. I'm sorry . . . I really am.' His voice broke with emotion. 'Tell me, Lucy, what should I do?'

He went to sit in his chair, leaning forward, his head in his hands and sobbing like a child. 'I've never felt so lost in all my life. I honestly never wanted to hurt you, Lucy. I'm so sorry . . . so very sorry.'

Lucy quietened him. 'First of all, there is nothing to be gained from looking back at what's happened. As we're being honest, I can tell you there were times when I could have walked out the door and never come back, but that would have solved nothing. So now we need to look forward, to be thankful on three counts. First, Paula's lawyer has managed to secure a quickie divorce from that madman of a husband. And secondly, he's been charged and found guilty of GBH, and now he's rotting in prison, where he belongs!'

When she seemed to have spoken her piece, Martin asked cautiously, 'And what's the third count?'

'Well, it's kind of a third and fourth count, I suppose,' Lucy answered. 'You and me,' she looked him in the eye, 'and you and Paula.'

'Go on.'

'Well, when you think about it, the solution is quite clear. I think we both agree that our marriage is well and truly over, which is just as well, because you want to be with Paula. You said that yourself, just now.' When he went to speak, Lucy put her hand up to signal that she was not yet finished. 'I've been giving the sorry situation a great deal of thought these past weeks, and I think – hope – that I've found the answer.'

'What d'you mean exactly?'

'Well, if you remember, Paula told us that her solicitor has got together an agreement that will allow Paula to buy the house from Ray at the market price. There's no way she ever wants to get back with Ray.'

'But how can she buy the house? She has no money to speak of,' Martin commented. 'And she's been told she cannot return to work for weeks . . . maybe months. So, if she can't be working, how will she ever be able to pay a mortgage?'

'Well, she won't, will she?'

'Lucy! You're talking in riddles.'

'No, I'm not. You see, I realise that Paula will not be able to pay the mortgage. But *you* can!'

'What? I think you'd best explain yourself.' He was lost as to where she might be going with this.

'Like I said, it's simple when you think about it. Paula needs help, and you want to be with her, so why don't you just move in with her? Help her to buy the house.'

'But how can I do that?' Now, he was more confused than before. 'Have you forgotten that I'm still paying the mortgage on this house . . . and at my last reckoning we've got another six years before it's paid off.'

With a secret little smile on her face, Lucy looked him in the eye. 'Sell it!' she told him. 'Sell it, and you'll have money enough to start a new life with Paula.'

'What!' He could not believe his ears. 'Lucy! Have you lost your mind? And what about you? I'm not having you lodging with anyone, not even with our daughter. And don't forget, you've paid every bit as much into this house as I have, and I would never dream of taking away your home. So, you can forget that idea altogether!'

Lucy was insistent. 'I would not be lodging with our daughter, and I'm well aware that I've paid into this house as well, and yes, I would need to have an amount back if it was sold.'

He was baffled. 'Let me get this idea of yours straight in my mind.' He gave it a moment's thought, and then he reiterated her thinking. 'OK. So Paula has got rid of her ex, and is shortly coming home. Ray wants the house, but he's residing in prison at the moment and he's willing to sell it to her. And you have an idea that I should sell our house, then move in with Paula and help her to buy the house from her ex. And in order for me to help Paula, you say I should sell our home. But if I do that you say you won't have to lodge with our daughter. So, have I got it right so far?'

'Absolutely!'

'I don't understand, Lucy.' He shook his head. 'Are you going crazy, or am I?'

'Trust me, Martin. I know what I'm doing.'

At that moment, there came a knock on the door.

'I'd best see who that is.' Lucy hurried to the door, already knowing who was there.

A moment later she returned with her friend, Kathleen, in tow. 'I think you'll understand after you've heard Kathleen's news,' she informed Martin. 'Don't say a word until she's done, OK?'

Thinking ahead, Martin was on his feet. 'No, Lucy! What do you take me for? I know I cheated on you, but do you honestly think I would sell the roof from over your head and let you move in with a friend, while I go about saving Paula's house? No! The answer is no!'

Lucy smiled. 'Listen to me, Martin,' she urged. 'Lately, I've come to believe that some things are made to be. Sometimes, good things really can come out of bad,' she said softly. 'Look! I really want you to listen to what Kathleen has to say. Meantime, I'll go and make us all a cuppa. Is that all right, Martin? Will you listen to her . . . for my sake?'

'All right! I'll listen to Kathleen . . . so long as you understand that I will never sell this house and see you lodging in someone else's home.'

Lucy thanked him. 'I'll leave you to it then.' She went quickly out of the room.

'I have no idea what's going on here and, to be honest, I really don't want to hear what you have to say,' Martin informed Kathleen. 'Lucy was wrong to discuss our business with you, but, like I say, I've let her down once, and I don't mean to let her down again. I will never sell this house while Lucy needs a home, and I will never allow her to become a lodger in someone else's house – not even yours. And that's an end to it!'

Kathleen handed him an envelope. 'Please, Martin, before you say any more, just read this. It should explain everything.'

In the kitchen, Lucy realised that Martin must be reading the letter, and she was made increasingly anxious. A moment later, having made the tea, she brought the tray into the sitting room and placed it on the table.

Martin was still perusing the letter.

Lucy remained by the table, waiting. Hoping he would understand and go along with her plan.

Suddenly, Martin looked up, his gaze falling on Lucy. 'Well, I never!' He smiled. 'You crafty little bugger, and you never said a word.'

'It was not my place to tell you,' Lucy replied. 'It was for Kathleen to explain. And, like you, my mind was on Paula. There was so much going on, I needed to put it on the back burner.'

Martin understood. 'And now?'

'Well, if you agree, I'd like to spread my wings at last. That's why I thought we could sell the house. That way, you could help Paula, and I could have a sum of money from the sale of the house and include myself in Kathleen's plans. Maybe even work my way up to being a businesswoman. I'm ready, Martin. The children are grown up, and what's happened to us recently has taught me that life is very short, and events often creep up on us, and make us realise how very vulnerable we all are. It's time, Martin. I need to get out there and be a part of it, and, thanks to Kathleen, I now have that chance. So . . . what do you say? Will you sell the house, help Paula to buy hers, and let me go to find my place, at this new point in my life?'

Martin was silent. The words he wanted to say were stuck in his throat, though his respect and love for Lucy were never greater than now.

When at last he spoke, there was a tremble in his voice, and tears of gratitude in his eyes. 'My dear Lucy, I promise I will move heaven and earth to help make you happy.'

~

Over the next hour, Kathleen and Lucy outlined their plans.

'With the money my great-aunt has left me, I intend moving away – to the coast, preferably,' Kathleen told Martin.

Lucy explained excitedly, 'Kathleen has asked me to go with her, and be a partner in the business she buys – maybe a little tea-room, or a small boarding house for holidaymakers. So, if you are able to give me a sum of money when the house is sold, that will go towards me buying into Kathleen's business, what-ever business she might choose.'

Kathleen stopped her right there. 'Not what busi-ness *I* choose!' she reminded Lucy. 'When we see the right opportunity, you will have as much say as me in what we go for.'

So, now that the air was cleared, and the tea had gone stone cold, Lucy went away to make another pot of tea.

'You will look after her, won't you?' Martin asked Kathleen.

'We'll look after each other,' Kathleen replied softly. 'And, who knows, each of us might just find a new man to light up our lives.'

'So where exactly are you thinking of going to?' Martin was curious.

'I'm not altogether sure yet. I do have a little place in mind, though. It's a place I believe Lucy will like. Yes, I'm sure that when she sees it, she will be pleasantly surprised.'

A sense of mischief made her look away and smile.

PART FIVE

Sometimes Dreams
do Come True

CHAPTER TWENTY-ONE

O N A WARM afternoon in July, Lucy and Kathleen switched off their machines at the plastics factory, and the entire eighteen-strong workforce raised their voices and sang a merry song to send their friends on their way.

While their workmates sang, the two friends stood side by side smiling, but feeling a little sad to be leaving.

When the song was done, everyone cheered, and the boss came forward to address them all. 'Seeing as these two have given me more grey hairs than anyone, I really should be delighted to see them go.'

There was a roar of approval and a volley of cheeky calls: 'Fling 'em out!'; 'Make them work another fortnight with no pay! The buggers have had more holidays than the rest of us put together!'

When the cheering raised the roof, Lucy and Kathleen had tears in their eyes. When the boss presented them each with a bouquet of flowers, their

403

tears began to fall. 'We love you all!' Kathleen told them, and Lucy was too filled with emotion to speak, so she simply put up her hand and waved a thank you.

When the blower screamed out, telling everyone that the day was over, one by one the workers came to say their goodbyes to Kathleen and Lucy, and when they were all gone, the boss led the two of them to the office, where she gave them their last pay packets, and wished them well.

'I hope your business venture works out for you both,' she said, and gave them each a hug. 'Keep in touch. Don't forget us.'

Kathleen and Lucy thanked her and bade her goodbye. 'I don't know how you ever put up with us . . . me in particular,' Lucy told her.

'I put up with you because you are two of the best workers I've got,' the boss assured Lucy. 'And I know what difficulties you have had to deal with.'

A few moments later, the two went away to start their new lives.

~

They walked together as far as the corner, then Lucy went one way and Kathleen the other. 'I'll be round later to help you pack up the last of your stuff,' Lucy promised.

Kathleen told her not to worry too much. 'You have your own packing to do,' she said, 'and you still have to tie up all the loose ends with Martin.'

'When did you say you hand the house key in?' Lucy asked.

'Tomorrow morning. I have to finalise everything with the solicitor. He's already tied up all the loose ends with the buyers, and managed to get me a few days' grace into the bargain. So now it's just a matter of dotting the i's and crossing the t's.' Clapping her hands, she laughed out loud. 'And then, Lucy girl, we are on our merry way! Off with the old and on with the new. See you later.'

She went away down the street, whistling like a drunken navvy.

Lucy chuckled to herself, 'Kathleen Riley, what am I going to do with you, eh?'

Her heart was so light, she might have whistled, but she didn't know how, so instead she sang softly in gratitude for the way things had turned out. 'A new life, eh, Lucy girl?' She shook her head as though in disbelief. 'Well, it's about time, an' all!'

Martin had been watching for her, and opened the door to let her in.

'Paula wants to show you something,' he said excitedly, leading her down to the sitting room.

When Lucy entered the room, she saw Paula seated in her chair the way she had been for these past weeks. 'Hi, Sis! Martin says you've got something to show me?'

'Yes, I have,' Paula said. 'So, do you want to see?'

'Of course I do.'

Lucy watched in awe as Paula grabbed hold of the

wheelchair handles and very, very carefully pulled herself up to a standing position, which she held for a minute before falling back into the chair.

'See!' Paula was thrilled. 'I stood up all by myself!'

Lucy took her into her arms. 'Oh, Paula! I'm so very proud of you, but you must be careful. You fell back hard. You could have hurt yourself.' She choked back the tears. 'You said you would stand up before I left and you kept your word. Oh, Paula, you must be so thrilled. But have you spoken with the doctor about it?'

'Yes. Martin took me to see him, and he said I could try, but I must not stand for more than a minute – not yet, anyway.'

Martin went to the cupboard and took out three glasses and a bottle of wine. 'I've been saving it,' he said. 'And now I think it's time, what with Paula standing on her own two feet, me with a new works contract in the bag, and you and Kathleen off to find a new life. I'm proud of us all, especially you two.' He glanced from one to the other. 'My girls.'

The three of them toasted all their recent achievements, and then Martin asked Lucy for the umpteenth time, 'Are you absolutely sure you don't mind me and Paula selling her house, instead of selling this one?'

Lucy assured him yet again. 'I said at the time you first mentioned it that it would be wise to get Paula away from the house where she was so viciously attacked. And the way she's been coming on since we moved her here is just remarkable. It's all done and dusted now. I have the money to invest in the business, and you and Paula have a house that has no bad memories for her. And besides, both Samuel and Anne agreed with the decision to bring Paula here. So, if you love the house as we did, it will love you back.'

She gave Paula another hug. 'And you, my darling, take it one step at a time. Don't overdo it.'

Paula promised, hand on heart, that she would be careful. She was reconciled with Martin now, and he had shown her a lot of love and tenderness as she slowly recovered.

~

Soon, the goodbyes were said, and Lucy promised to call them.

'Well, that's it, Lucy girl!' Kathleen said as she and Lucy climbed into the back of a cab. 'Time to go.'

Lucy could hardly tear herself away from the little group who had come along to see her off.

'Go on, Mum, you go for it!' That was Samuel. 'We'll all be coming to see you as soon as we can. Love you lots!'

They each kissed Lucy goodbye. From the pavement, Martin, Paula in her wheelchair, and the children waved them off.

As they set off, Lucy wound down the window and waved until they were out of sight, and then she fell silent.

'Hey! You're not about to cry all over my shoes, are

you?' Kathleen moaned. 'I've only had them a couple of days.'

'I was not crying!' Lucy was adamant.

'Huh! We'll both be crying if we miss the train, just because I had to buy a new pair of shoes!'

The taxi driver chuckled, and Lucy laughed out loud. 'Don't be so dramatic!'

Back at the house, Martin opened the sealed envelope, addressed to him, which he found lying on the bed when he went up later that day. It contained a ticket, and a note in Lucy's handwriting.

Dearest Martin,

I had to borrow against Mother's jewellery, and since I've been back so much has gone on that I have not yet been able to retrieve the jewellery. Here inside is the money you will need, and I would very much like Anne to take responsibility for keeping her grandmother's jewellery safe. After all, it now belongs to her.

With my dearest love, and blessing. Take care of each other. I do love you all so very much.

Lucy xxx

Taking a moment to himself, Martin sat on the edge of the bed. Suddenly tearful, he looked back at all that had happened.

'You've been a good 'un, Lucy,' he murmured, 'and I'm sorry that I hurt you.' Feeling a little sad and somewhat guilty, he murmured softly, 'I tried so hard not to hurt you, but Paula was always the one for me.'

He smiled knowingly. Strange, isn't it? he thought, how, after all these years, everything seems to have found its rightful place.

~

Seated comfortably on the train, Kathleen and Lucy sat in total silence, until Kathleen asked, 'Lucy?'

'Yes?'

'Are you content?'

'Yes, I think so. And are you . . . content?'

'Absolutely. More than I've ever been in my entire life. And why wouldn't I be content, eh? I've got my best friend with me. We've got money enough to buy a business, and we're on our way to the best week's holiday we'll ever have, because once we're business-women, we won't have time for holidays and gallivanting about all over the place.' She chuckled, 'Hey, Lucy?'

'What now?' Lucy had never met such a chatterbox.

'Tell me the truth, Lucy. Did you ever dream this would happen to us?'

'No! Never in a million years!'

'Me neither. First, though, before we get cracking on the business, we need to thoroughly enjoy our week in Littleton. Are you absolutely sure you don't mind going back there . . . to the same place . . . the same hotel?'

Lucy smiled. 'No. Like I already told you when you first asked, I had the most wonderful time there. Going back will only make me remember how beautiful it all was.' She lowered her voice as though talking to herself. 'My time in Littleton, and what happened there . . . I will cherish it for ever.'

'Are you sure, Lucy? Because if not, we can always go elsewhere. It's still not too late.'

'I already told you, I'm perfectly happy with everything. In fact, if I had been making the choice, I probably would have chosen the very same.'

'Aw, you're not just saying that, though, are you?'

'No! So now, will you stop worrying? Everything is perfect.'

'Good!' Kathleen congratulated herself on her 'perfect' arrangements, and sat back in her seat and relaxed.

Lucy, however, was so excited she could not rest. 'You're right about what you said before, Kathleen!' she commented. 'You and me . . . we're about to set the world on fire! We're free as birds. You got your husband out of your life years ago, and now I also am a free woman. We're off to enjoy a holiday in the sunshine, and we have money enough to buy a little business, and so, Kathleen girl,' she mimicked Kathleen's raucous voice, 'what's not to like, eh?'

Kathleen laughed. 'That's right, so now, behave yourself. Read a paper, get a nap. Relax! Because once we get started our feet won't touch the ground!'

CHAPTER TWENTY-TWO

A COUPLE OF long hours after Lucy and Kathleen got on the train, it drew into Littleton station, where the women collected up their luggage and went to find a taxi, which took only a few minutes because the line of taxis went on for ever.

Climbing in, Kathleen relaxed into the seat. 'My bum's gone to sleep,' she told Lucy. 'How far is the hotel from here?'

'I can't recall, but the driver will know. Four miles, maybe a bit less.'

Just now, when she was walking through the station, she recalled hiding from Dave as he went ahead of her. She had thought it might be upsetting to re-member him, but it wasn't, and so now she let herself completely relax.

'Your hotel is about five miles along the coast,' the taxi driver informed Kathleen as he packed their cases into the boot. 'I'll have you there in no time at all.'

As they drove along, Lucy recognised all the

landmarks: the little shop on the corner as they turned out of the station, the lifeguard tower, and the flower-seller. It was all exactly the same as she remembered, and far from upsettng her, it made her feel alive. And whenever Dave came into her mind, she saw his hand-some smile, and it made her heart give a little bump.

The taxi driver was a chatty sort. 'On holiday, are you?'

'Yes, but only for a week, and then we're looking to buy a business,' Kathleen told hm.

'What kind o' business?'

'We're not sure really, but maybe a ladies' clothes shop, or a knick-knack shop, where holidaymakers can browse and spend their money.'

While she chatted, she smiled, because she had already made enquiries concerning small businesses on the coast, and there was one in particular that had struck her as interesting. Later, she would discuss it with Lucy, but she wanted them both to enjoy this holiday before even thinking of work.

On arriving at the hotel, Kathleen went into raptures about it. 'Blimey Nora!' She looked at the classy entrance, and the beautiful well-tended gardens either side, and even the porter at the door. 'No wonder it cost an arm and a leg!' she remarked a little too loudly, which made the taxi driver smile, and Lucy chuckle.

As he collected the two suitcases, the porter gave Kathleen a little wink. 'I reckon he fancies me!' she told Lucy as they went to the reception desk.

Turning round to see the porter shamelessly eyeing Kathleen, even Lucy had to agree.

The receptionist remembered Lucy. 'Oh, how nice to see you back again,' she said genuinely. 'I recognised the name and, I'm sorry but we're so busy I couldn't put you in the same room as last time. You're on the other side of the hotel . . . on the floor below, is that all right?'

Lucy nodded. In a way, she was pleased about that.

'You are right next door,' the receptionist informed Kathleen. Kathleen was pleased.

'I'm afraid the café bar won't be open for another hour or so yet,' the receptionist informed them, 'but if you like, I'll have tea or coffee sent up to your rooms.'

Kathleen thanked her, but, 'I thought we would unpack and take our time having a look round. What say you, Lucy? Do you fancy a walk along the front?'

'Yes, that would be nice.' In truth, she was about to suggest the very same herself.

So, after collecting their room keys, they followed the porter to the lift. And when he insisted on taking them right to their doors, Kathleen gave Lucy a wink, and rolled her eyes in astonishment.

At the door, she was about to tip him, when he smiled and shook his head. 'That's all right,' he said softly. 'Maybe later.' And his meaning was very clear, both to Kathleen and to Lucy.

'I told you, didn't I?' Kathleen did a little jig in the corridor. 'I said he was after me . . . and who am I to refuse the man his tip!'

Lucy went into her room, in fits of laughter.

'We'll meet up in ten minutes,' Kathleen called out, and Lucy replied that she would be downstairs waiting, because, 'I know you won't be ready in ten minutes. More like half an hour.' She knew Kathleen only too well.

Exactly half an hour later, Lucy got up from the chair in the foyer. Kathleen was dressed up as though she was off to a party. She had on a pretty green dress with swirly skirt, short sleeves and a revealing neckline. Her legs were bare and she wore white sandals.

'Oh, Kathleen, you look really nice.'

'You look nice as well.' Kathleen saw that Lucy had chosen to wear a blue, short-sleeved top, with a straight skirt and blue sandals. Her hair was brushed to a shine, and her eyes were especially sparkling.

'Come on, Lucy girl!' Kathleen led the way. 'Let's go frighten the locals!'

They went along the beach, and with every step, Lucy recalled how she and Dave had run along here, with her on his shoulders, and the two of them making fools of themselves. But it was too wonderful to regret, and so she remembered it with joy.

As they entered the café, Kathleen told her, 'I'm hot . . . how about we get an ice cream or something? What d'you say, Lucy girl?'

'Yeah! Let's go for it!'

And they did.

They noticed one empty table in the far corner, and they made straight for it.

Sitting down, Kathleen stretched out her legs. 'Is this the place you told me about?' she asked Lucy.

'Yes.' Lucy was torn in so many ways. 'This is it. Don't you think it's pretty . . . set in the cliffs like this?'

'I do, yes! I think it's very pretty, right on the beach and nestling into the cliffs. What else could anyone ask for?'

A moment later the waitress arrived. 'Yes?' She opened her notepad.

'Right, Lucy girl!' Kathleen quickly glanced at the menu. 'What takes your fancy?'

Lucy wasn't quite sure. 'You get yours, and by the time they bring it, I'll have decided.'

So, Kathleen ordered a banana split and a cup of tea.

Lucy continued to look through the menu as the waitress went to fetch Kathleen's order. 'I think I'll have a banana split as well,' she told Kathleen.

The girl arrived with Kathleen's order, but before Lucy could say anything, a voice behind her asked, 'Would the lady like an ice cream, topped with nuts and choc flakes?'

Lucy's heart almost stopped, and when his hand touched hers she knew. 'Dave!' She looked up and there he was – the man who had stolen her common sense, along with her heart.

'Hello, you,' he said, bending to kiss her. 'I've missed you . . . so much.'

Lost for words, Lucy felt like crying, she was so taken aback and so very happy to see him again. When he sat down beside her she thought she might be dreaming.

Kathleen, however, was beaming. 'After you came home and told me about this "wonderful" man you met, I thought you two should get to know each other better,' she confessed. 'So I rang the hotel and asked if they would forward a letter to this man called David, who had been in the room four doors away from my friend Lucy Lovejoy. I sent my letter and here we are. Am I a miracle worker or what?'

Lucy dared not say a word, because if she did, she would surely break down and cry. And when Dave's arm slid about her shoulders, she leaned into it, and it was like all her dreams had come true at once.

And then he was whispering in her ear, 'I've got an idea. Why don't you and me run along the beach, like we did before, and give the natives something to talk about?'

Lucy shook her head, laughing too much to answer.

Kathleen diplomatically left for a walk along the cliffs, leaving Lucy to bond with Dave all over again.

'If I behave myself, will you walk along the beach with me?' he asked her. And how could she refuse?

From the clifftop, Kathleen looked down and smiled. 'You two belong together,' she whispered.

Then she walked along a little further. She was enchanted by this place and she wondered, if she offered the owner enough money, whether he or she would consider selling that picturesque café to her and Lucy.

Once the idea had taken root in her mind, there was no turning back. So, without delay, she made her way back down.

~

Much later that evening, the three of them turned out in their best party wear to spend the evening in the open-air where a gala of music and dancing was about to start.

'They couldn't have a more beautiful setting,' Lucy told Dave as he led her onto the makeshift dance floor.

'And I could not have had a more beautiful dance partner than you,' he whispered in her ear. 'You look wonderful.'

Lucy smiled at that. 'Do you know, you are the first man ever to call me beautiful?'

His answer was a soft and loving kiss, and the whispered comment, 'All I can say is, they must all be blind.'

He gestured to where Kathleen and Billy the porter were dancing some way to the other side of them.

'Kathleen said he fancied her,' Lucy said, 'and she was right.'

Later, they sat in the hotel bar, and chatted with Kathleen and Billy, who had the evening off work.

'I've got some news, Lucy girl!' Kathleen announced.

'What? Is it good or bad?'

'Both.'

'Go on then.'

'Well, I kind of took a fancy to that picturesque little

café, and I wanted to talk to you about it, but you were too tied up with this handsome man who wouldn't let you go. So . . .' she took a deep breath, '. . . I bought it for us!'

After the initial shock, everyone congratulated her. Lucy was thrilled. 'So now, we'll need to start looking for a house. We can't stay at the hotel for ever.'

While Katheen thought about Lucy's reminder, Dave slid his arm round Lucy's shoulders. 'You won't need to find a house . . . not if you marry me,' he told her.

Lucy looked at him, astonished, and then she said, 'But I can't. I'm still waiting for my divorce to go through.' She reminded him, shyly.

'I don't mind how long I wait,' he answered, 'as long as the answer is yes.'

'Then, yes.' She laughed out loud. 'I'll marry you!'

Everyone burst out laughing, and Kathleen turned to Billy, 'Seems like everybody wants to get married, so, what about you and me?'

'Are you free?' he asked cheekily.

'I am . . . yes.'

'Then I'll certainly bear that in mind.' He laughed.

The evening ended in happiness and great excitement.

~

A year later, the double marriage was arranged.

It was well attended, by Dave's daughter and relatives, alongside Lucy's children, and Martin and Paula.

Paula was now fully recovered, and both she and Martin were wonderfully happy.

Kathleen's uncle and a nephew came from Ireland to see her get married, along with Billy's entire family of sixteen people, young and old.

Kathleen was shocked. 'Blimey! I can tell you right now, we ain't having an army o' kids to look after. No way!'

~

Four years later, the same people attended the double christening of Kathleen and Billy's third child, alongside Lucy and Dave's first son – named David.

In quiet moments, when Lucy managed to hide away for a few minutes, she sat thinking of all the heartache and pain over the years.

But that was all in the past, and she could not possibly be happier than she was at that moment.

At last, she was content in herself.

And life was good.